"STUNNING!"

"Fascinating . . . a stunning job."

—Ernest K. Gann, author of *The Aviator*

"A fascinating, compelling tale . . . of the skeletal remains of a missing child."

—Wendell Rawls, Jr., *The New York Times* Southern Correspondent

"STUNNING!"

"A stunning debut by a wonderful new and original American writer. Stuart Woods has written a classic!"

—Pat Conroy, author of *The Lords of Discipline* and *The Great Santini*

"A riveting story of the Deep South that mixes murder mystery with political intrigue . . . the plot has bestseller written all over it."

—*Publishers Weekly*

"STUNNING!"

"A gripping saga of race, politics and chilling mystery in small-town America. The stunning debut of a fine new novelist."

—Larry L. King, author of *The Best Little Whorehouse in Texas*

CHIEFS
Stuart Woods

CHIEFS

By STUART WOODS

BANTAM BOOKS
TORONTO · NEW YORK · LONDON · SYDNEY

CHIEFS

*A Bantam Book / published by arrangement with
W. W. Norton & Co., Inc.*

PRINTING HISTORY
Norton edition published May 1981
A Selection of American Circle (Bertelsmann) Book Club,
September 1981
Serialized in Crime Digest, *January/February 1982 issue*
Bantam edition / March 1982

ISBN 0-553-20560-9

Published simultaneously in the United States and Canada

PRINTED IN THE UNITED STATES OF AMERICA

0 9 8 7 6 5 4 3 2 1

This book is for Judy Tabb

CONTENTS

PROLOGUE

THE BOY ran for his life.

He poured forth an effort born of fear and a wild sense of freedom regained. At first he ran entirely unconscious of his injuries, then, tearing recklessly through the dark woods, he struck a tree and went down. He lay stunned for a time he could not account for, and when he was finally able to struggle to his feet, the full force of the pain and the winter air swept over him and made him stagger.

He heard the dog and the man crashing through the brush, and he ran again, wildly, blindly, the undergrowth tearing at his naked body. Abruptly, he broke through onto a road, hesitated, decided against it, and threw himself across the open area into the brush on the other side. He was momentarily in thick, thorny blackberry bushes, then found himself on a narrow path.

He was failing now, sucking in air with a loud, rasping noise, his muscles aching, legs wobbling. He heard the man fighting through the blackberry bushes, cursing, and he flung himself forward with his remaining strength. He knew he would rather run until he died than go back to that house. He willed his heart to burst, God to take him, but his exhausted body still carried him unsteadily forward.

The path turned sharply to the right, but he lunged ahead into thick brush again, hoping for safety. Then he saw stars ahead through the bushes and thought he might break through into a field, while his tormentor followed the path. He gathered his last strength and *plunged forward and down, hoping to lie on the ground undetected.*

There was no ground; the earth fell away beneath him. He believed himself to be falling into a ditch, but his ditch had no bottom. He fell, twisting in the air, trying desperately to get his feet under him, while the hard earth waited far below him.

BOOK ONE

Will Henry Lee

1 HUGH HOLMES, president of the Bank of Delano and chairman of the Delano City Council, was a man who, more than most, thought about the present in terms of the future. It was one of his great strengths, both as a banker and as a politician, but on a cold morning in December of 1919, this faculty failed him. It would be many years before he would have some grasp of how that morning changed his future, changed everything.

Holmes prided himself on being able to look at a man as he entered the bank and predict what the man would want. On this morning he watched through the sliding window in the wall between his office and the main room of the bank as Will Henry Lee entered, and Holmes indulged himself in a bit of his usual prognostication. Will Henry Lee was a cotton farmer; his standing mortgage was due the first of the year, and he would want it renewed. It took Holmes only seconds to review the circumstances: Will Henry's debt amounted to about thirty-five percent of the value of his farm, in reasonably good times. That was a lower level of debt than was borne by most farmers, and Will Henry had paid his interest on time and made two payments against principal. But Holmes knew, the boll weevil situation being what it was, that Will Henry might fail with his next crop. Still, he respected the man, liked him, even; he decided to renew. He leaned forward at his desk and pretended to read a letter, confident that he had anticipated the content of their approaching discussion and had worked out an appropriate response. Will Henry knocked at the open door, sat down, exchanged pleasantries, and asked Holmes for the job of chief of police.

Holmes was stupefied, partly by the completely unexpected request, and partly by the total collapse of his early-warning system. His mind was not accustomed to such surprises, and it lurched about through a long moment of silence as it struggled to assimilate this outrageous input and get it into an orderly framework of thought. The effort was a failure. To give himself more time, he clambered onto familiar ground. "Well, now, Will Henry, you're not overextended on your farm. We could probably see you through another crop, even with things the way they are with cotton." To his credit, Holmes maintained his banker's face throughout the exchange.

"Hugh, if I extended I'd have to have more capital, which means getting deeper in debt to the bank. If I did that for another crop things wouldn't get any better; they'd just get worse. Better farmers than me are going under. I think you'd be doing the best thing for the bank if you took the farm now and sold it. I might get something after the note was paid. To tell you the truth, Hoss Spence offered me nearly about exactly what I owe for the place just last week, but I think I'd rather let the bank take it than let a man buy me out for a third of what the place is worth. Hoss's peaches and cattle are going to be on a lot of land where cotton used to grow, and I'd just as soon my land didn't get included in that." He stopped talking, looked at Holmes, and waited.

Holmes's brain was beginning to thrash through the gears now. Item one: Will Henry was right about the bank's position; taking the farm now would give a better chance of coming through the transaction profitably; things could truly be a whole lot worse next year. Item two: Delano had long been big enough for a chief, but the town wasn't big enough to attract an experienced officer from another force. Holmes, as chairman of the city council, had been looking hard for months for a suitable man. The chief at La Grange had put it to him bluntly. "Mr. Holmes, I'll tell you the truth; right now Delano couldn't even attract a decent patrolman from a larger town, let alone a sergeant. My advice to you would be to find a local man that people respect, and give him the job. In a town like Delano, he can do about ninety-nine percent of what he's got to do with just plain old respect.''

Holmes looked across the desk at Will Henry. He respected the man, and he was a harsher judge than most. Will Henry was well known in the community, even though he and his father before him had been country men. Maybe his always having lived in the country would mix a little distance with familiarity and give respect a sharper edge. Holmes resisted an urge to pump Will Henry's hand and pin a badge on him right on the spot. He had to preserve a reputation for caution, and, anyway, he couldn't make the decision entirely on his own.

"Well, I'll have to bring this up at the next council meeting." He paused. "Have you talked to Carrie about this, Will Henry?"

"No, I wanted to talk to you first. Carrie's all ready to worry us through another crop, but I think it'd be a kind of relief to her to have done with the farm. We'd have to find a house in town, and I think she'd like fixing that up. She's really always been a town girl at heart, I think. What's your opinion of my chances for this job, Hugh?"

Holmes cleared his throat. "Well, I guess you could say it's within the realm of possibility. I'll see that the council gives the proposal serious consideration." The two men rose and shook hands. "I might be able to help you with finding a house in town, too." He already had something in mind. The banker's brain was in high gear now.

But Holmes's morning was just beginning. When he opened his office door to show out Will Henry, he found someone else waiting to see him. Francis Funderburke, better known in Delano and Meriwether County as Foxy, because of an uncommon resemblance to that animal, stood waiting at a not-too-loose parade rest. The stubby, wiry little man, dressed in stiffly starched and tightly tailored khaki, with trousers tucked into lumberjack boot tops and a flat-brimmed, pointy-peaked army campaign hat raked at a regimental angle over his bright, close-set eyes, looked for all the world like a demented forest ranger or an ancient Boy Scout. "Foxy, how you doing?" asked Will Henry.

Foxy directed a narrow glance at the farmer. "Lee." He turned back to the banker. "Holmes, like to speak to you." Foxy addressed all men by their unadorned surnames and usually in the manner of a high-ranking officer speaking to a recruit. To females he offered a grudging "Miz" before the name, regardless of age or marital status. At meetings with Foxy, Holmes always felt as if he had been summoned rather than sought out, and for some infraction of an unnamed set of rules. He invited Funderburke into his office, with the distinct premonition that his morning was again about to come unglued. He was not wrong.

Before either man had reached a chair, Foxy said, "Holmes, I want that job."

"What job is that, Foxy?" Holmes asked, with a sickly foreknowledge of exactly what job Foxy meant.

"Chief of police, of course," said Foxy, his tone implying that Holmes had been attempting to withhold information from him. "I know you've been looking hard for an experienced man, and you can't find one. Well, that means you're going to have to hire a civilian. With my military experience and knowledge of firearms I'm the man for the job." Foxy had served briefly in France as a second lieutenant in the supply corps. He had been sent home when a wagon had overturned, landing on his foot. The injury had got him a medical discharge. In Foxy's mind, and in his telling, the injury was a combat wound.

Holmes began to marshal his faculties once more. "I don't see the connection."

"I've been trained. I know how to lead men."

"Well, now, Foxy, a Delano chief of police isn't going to have any men to lead. He's going to be a one-man department."

"It'll grow. Besides, this town is going to need discipline."

"Discipline," Holmes repeated tonelessly.

"People have got to respect the chief."

There was that word again: respect. Holmes admitted to himself that Foxy did command respect of a kind in the community. His father had left him a small block of early Coca-Cola stock that Holmes estimated must be worth a considerable sum, judging from the size of the dividend checks Foxy deposited in his bank account. Wealth brought a kind of respect. Foxy had served his country in a war, and people respected him for that, although they were hazy about the details. And Foxy was a super-American. In a burst of patriotic fervor he had built a log cabin with his own hands, and he lived in it. True, the improvements added by a series of builders had since made it arguably the most expensive log cabin in American history, but Foxy could still, with some justification, say he had built it with his own hands.

So people respected Foxy. But they also thought he was crazy.

Foxy was certainly an eccentric, but there was considerable tolerance for eccentricity among the people of small towns like Delano, Georgia. Discipline? Foxy was congenitally incapable of requesting anything. Holmes had a brief vision of people driving their automobiles on the sidewalks and shooting each other just to spite Foxy.

"You know, Foxy, I'm not authorized to hire anybody. I've only been conducting a search on behalf of the council. I'd suggest you make application in writing to the council, and I'll see that it gets the council's full attention." Holmes would certainly do that.

This clearly seemed an orderly and efficient procedure to Foxy. "You'll have my application today, Holmes," he barked, and with a curt farewell Foxy Funderburke marched out of the office and the bank.

Holmes took off his glasses and massaged the bridge of his nose. And people wondered why he was almost entirely gray at forty-five.

One of the tellers stuck his head in and said, "A man wants to open an account." At the thought of a familiar request Holmes revived. He greeted the new customer warmly. He could, in fact, have kissed him.

2   THE REGULAR weekly meeting of the City Council of
Delano was duly convened at 4:00 P.M. on December 31,
1919. Present were Hugh Holmes, banker; J. P. Johnson,
Coca-Cola bottler; Frank Mudter, Doctor of Medicine; Ben Birdsong, druggist; Willis Greer, city manager and honorary member; Lamar Maddox, undertaker (or funeral director, as he
preferred to be called); and Idus Bray, peach farmer, landlord,
money lender, and co-proprietor of the Delano Telephone Company.

The minutes of the last meeting were read and approved, the
treasurer's report (Ben Birdsong's), showing an estimated end-
of-year surplus of $6,300, was read and approved, and a motion
for an extension of the sewerage system to Lower Fourth Street
was made, seconded, and approved by all but Idus Bray, who
changed his vote when it was pointed out to him that new sewerage extensions meant new houses, which would require new
telephones. Hugh Holmes, as acting chairman, asked for further
business. There was none. Holmes cleared his throat and assumed a look which the others had come to learn meant there
was serious business afoot which would likely be settled to
Holmes's satisfaction before the meeting was done.

"The council has two applications for the position of chief of
police." There was a loud sigh from Idus Bray. Several chairs

creaked as their occupants assumed new positions to indicate their willingness to settle down and resolve a matter which has been hanging over the council for nearly a year.

Idus Bray said wearily, "You going to start that again, Hugh? This county has a sheriff. A good sheriff."

J. P. Johnson cut in. "Skeeter Willis lives in Greenville. That's twenty-two miles up the road, and you know as well as I do that Skeeter won't get out of bed for anything less than a shooting."

Holmes cut the discussion short. "Gentlemen, this council passed a resolution eight months ago that a chief of police would be procured for Delano. Unless somebody wants to introduce a motion repealing that resolution, this discussion is out of order. The matter now before the council is who the man will be. As I said before, the council has two applications."

"Experienced men?" asked Ben Birdsong.

Holmes's reply had an air of finality about it. "During the past eight months I have talked either in person or on the telephone with twenty-one chiefs all over the state and in Alabama, asking for recommendations. A total of fourteen men were mentioned. Six of them were interested enough to come and talk with me about it. None of the six wanted the job. I have come to the conclusion that it is not possible to attract an experienced police officer of good character to Delano without paying approximately fifty percent more money than we can afford. The best advice I had was from the chief at La Grange. In his opinion, the kinds of problems a chief would face in Delano could be handled by a local man of good standing, with the support of the council and the help of the sheriff and state patrol when needed. I concur in that opinion."

Frank Mudter spoke up. "Our problems here are traffic and petty crimes, with a little peacekeeping thrown in down in Braytown. Anybody with a good head on his shoulders and a fairly strong arm ought to be able to handle the job." There were murmurs of agreement from Birdsong and Maddox.

"Who are your applicants?" asked Idus Bray.

Holmes took a deep breath. "The first application I'd like for the council to consider is that of Francis Funderburke." There was a moment of silence, followed by a shout of laughter. Holmes kept a straight face. "Foxy feels that his military experience and his proficiency with firearms qualify him for the job."

Ben Birdsong smiled. "Well, if we want anybody shot, I guess

Foxy's our man."

"More likely, somebody'd shoot him," said Idus Bray.

Holmes persisted. "I told Foxy I'd see that the council would give his application serious consideration."

"Consider it considered," said Ben Birdsong. There was a chorus of agreement.

"I move that the application of Francis Funderburke for the position of chief of police be put to a vote," said Holmes.

"Seconded," said Dr. Mudter.

"All those in favor of acceptance of this application, signify by saying, 'Aye.' " Silence. "All those opposed to the acceptance of this application, say, "Nay.' " There was a volley of nays. "I also vote nay, so the decision of the council is unanimous in rejecting the application of Francis Funderburke." Holmes set aside Foxy's letter and picked up another sheet of paper. "The next applicant for the position of chief of police is William Henry Lee." There was a thoughtful silence.

"Will Henry?"

"Weevil get him?"

"Yes."

"Well, he's as honest as the day is long, like his daddy."

"He's a good persuader. At deacons' meetings he seems to be able to put a point without getting folks mad at him."

"Can he take care of himself?"

"I went to country school with him. I never saw him start a fight, but I never saw him let anybody push him around, either."

"Will he do it for the money?"

"Yes," said Holmes. "But if he works out, I think we ought to consider giving him more after a while. He's got a family."

"Is he all right with guns?"

"He won't use a shotgun, but I've seen him shoot squirrel with a .22."

"He's a good man in the church. I reckon he's about as respected as any man around here his age."

"How old is Will Henry, anyway?"

"About thirty. He was two years behind me in school."

There was silence again. Holmes had not spoken except to answer questions. Now he said his piece. "Will Henry's a responsible man. He's not stupid, and I don't think he'd ever use the job to push anybody around, the way Foxy might. He pays his bills, and he's from an old family in Meriwether County. He's never been a very successful farmer, but he's had the gumption to stick to it until the weevil came along. When that happened he had the good sense to get out before he was over his head in debt. He's well known as a man of character and a Christian. He's never done anything but farm, but I think if he took the job he'd feel obligated to give it his best, and I think that could be pretty good. I think we should hire him."

"So moved," said Frank Mudter without hesitation.

"Seconded," said Ben Birdsong.

"All in favor, say, 'Aye.' "

There was a collective aye from everybody but Idus Bray. "Well, I guess if you're bent on having a chief, Will Henry'd do about as little damage as anybody. Aye."

"The council unanimously approves the application of William Henry Lee as chief of police," said Holmes. There was a stir and a scraping of chairs. "There's one more thing. This is the first time the city has ever hired a man to do what might be a dangerous job. We're asking this man to carry a gun and protect us, and there's always the possibility that he could get killed doing it. I think we ought to do something about some insurance for his family if he should be killed or disabled in the line of duty."

Idus Bray spoke up. "I don't think the city ought to go buying insurance policies for its employees. Sets a bad precedent."

"Why don't we give him another ten dollars a month, with the provision that he spend it on insurance?" replied Ben Birdsong.

"So moved," said Frank Mudter.

"Seconded," said Lamar Maddox.

"All in Favor?"

"Aye," said four men.

"All opposed?"

"Nay," said Idus Bray. "It's a bad precedent."

"The motion is passed," said Holmes. "Any further business?"

"Move we adjourn."

"Seconded."

"All in favor?"

"Aye!"

"Happy New Year, Gentlemen."

3 WILL HENRY LEE stepped from his front porch with the fear and resolve of a man who has finally decided to jump from a great height into unknown waters. His historical perspective was sufficient for him to know that his descent of the five steps to the front yard was changing not just his own life, but the future of his line. Somewhere in one of the boxes stacked on the flatbed wagon was a Bible that recorded his forebears back to the year 1798, and now, at noon on this last day of 1919, he was to be the first man of that succession to leave the land, except to go to war.

He joined the small group of people who stood shivering near the idling car. Two of the black people made a farewell and separated themselves from the group, trudging over the frozen ground to one of the small, unpainted houses a few yards away. The other two remained to say a few parting words. The black woman dabbed at her eyes as he approached.

"Now, Flossie, don't you do that," Will Henry said. "You know you're going to be back with us real soon."

"That's right, Flossie," said Will Henry's wife, Carrie, dabbing at her own eyes. "You know we can't get along without you and Robert."

"Yes'm," Flossie replied. She turned to the children in an effort to distract herself. The little girl, the smaller of the two, was carefully holding a box tied with string. "You children make that lemon cheese cake last you awhile, now. It's gon' be a little while 'til I can make you another one. And Eloise, don't you let Billy eat it all up, hear?"

"Don't you worry about that, Flossie," replied the child firmly.

Will Henry called Flossie's husband, Robert, aside. "Don't say anything to Flossie yet, but I think I might be able to get things fixed up in a week or ten days. I've got to talk to Mr. Holmes at the bank one more time, and we'll have to find you a house in town. Mr. Holmes wants Jesse and Nellie to stay on at the farm and keep it up until the bank can find a buyer." Jesse and Nellie Cole were the only other remaining employees on the farm. Nellie was Flossie's sister.

"Tha's jes' fine, Mr. Will Henry, jes' fine. An' I'll git the rest of yo' things into town jes' as fast as that mule will move."

The two men shook hands, the first time they had ever done so. Robert held on to Will Henry's hand for a moment. "Mist' Will Henry, you a good farmer, a good farmer."

Will Henry smiled gratefully, though he knew this was not true.

"Couldn't nobody do no better," Robert said. "Couldn't nobody beat the weevil 'cept a rich man, a mighty rich man."

As they climbed into the Ford, Will Henry took in the yard and the house with a final glance. Everything looked as cold and hard as the weather. It would be pretty in the spring, if there were anybody here to see to it. He forced himself not to think of anything that had happened to him here, of his father and grandfather. He would think of that later, alone with himself. He drove the car out of the yard, picking his way carefully through the red winter mud, toward the main Delano road. In the bouncing mirror he caught a glimpse of Flossie and Robert standing in the yard, looking after them. He quickly looked away.

In the car Billy hung over the front seat. "Mama, why can't I have my own room in town? I don't want Eloise to have half my room." Will Henry heard Billy catch himself, knowing he was sounding selfish. "I can't sleep with Eloise in the room," he continued, trying another tack. "She snores."

Carrie disposed of this transparency with a reproachful glance. "Billy, you know we have to have a guest room."

"But we hardly ever have any company; it'll just be emp—"

"Billy."

The boy sank into the back seat, glaring sullenly at the back of his mother's neck. Eloise stuck her tongue out at him.

Will Henry glanced at Carrie. He knew she was both looking forward to life in Delano and frightened. She would enjoy having friends within walking distance, but she would feel insecure at first without the farm. He had given her no clear definition of his job. He would be, he had said, "working for the city," and he was vague about what the work entailed. She had accepted that, at least for the moment. He was not looking forward to telling her the whole of it.

Will Henry retreated into himself as he drove. He tapped out a rhythm on the steering wheel and sang absently to himself. "Bringing in the Sheaves, Bringing in the Sheaves. We shall come, rejoicing, Bringing in the Sheaves. . . ."

He felt the way some men feel when they leave the army; the way some men feel when they have paid their debts; the way any man feels when he is free.

"We shall come, rejoicing, Bringing in the Sheaves!"

4 HUGH HOLMES had anticipated the outcome of the city-council meeting, even to the method of arranging the insurance policy. He had expected Idus Bray to object, but he was prepared to suggest the extra money as a compromise. Nevertheless, he was pleased that somebody else had suggested it.

He had anticipated the results to the extent that, on the day after Christmas, he had given Will Henry Lee a year's lease on a house recently repossessed by the bank when its owner had simply disappeared, on the occasion of the failure of his grain and feed business. Holmes sent his own housekeeper to clean the place before the Lee family arrived. He knew Carrie would be exhausted enough from the packing and unpacking without the additional chore of making habitable a house which had been disused for some months. Before the lease was signed Holmes raised the insurance question.

"Will Henry, have you thought about the possibility of your getting killed if you take this job?"

"Well, I guess I'm going to have to carry a gun. That's part of the job. But I figure I'm about as likely to get kicked to death by somebody's mule while I'm directing traffic on Main Street on a Saturday afternoon as I am to get shot."

"I expect you're probably right, but I'll tell you the truth, I think that just by carrying a gun—and you have got to carry one, folks will expect it—you'll increase your chances of somebody taking a shot at you. You know, the English policemen, the bobbies, they're called, don't wear guns. They figure if criminals know they're not going to get shot at by the police, they're less likely to carry guns themselves, and I think they're probably right, at least for England. But we Americans, especially we southerners, don't see it that way. We're not very far from a time in this country when a man was more likely to get shot at if he didn't carry a gun, and we can't seem to forget it. So I think you ought to keep the possibility of getting shot at in mind. That's why I want you to make me a promise, and I won't recommend you for the job unless you do."

"What's that, Hugh?"

"I want you to agree to take out a ten-thousand-dollar insurance policy. I'll make the arrangements for you." Holmes already had arrangements in mind.

"Ten thousand dollars!"

"I know that sounds like a lot, Will Henry, but it's not. Your children are still young—what are they?"

"Billy's eight, and Eloise is six."

"Yes, young, and if anything happens to you Carrie's going to need fifteen hundred or two thousand dollars a year to raise and educate them. In fact, her expenses would be just about as high as they are with you around. You don't eat all that much. Even with ten thousand dollars in the bank she'd have to go to work to make that last until they're finished school, don't you see that? If she didn't go to work she'd have finished spending that money just about the time Billy would be ready to go to college. You want him to go to college, don't you? He's going to need that kind of education to make something of himself in this country."

"Carrie and I have talked about it. We'd like him to go; Eloise, too, if we can manage it."

"Well, if you save your money, you can. But Carrie could never manage it by herself. Not unless she has some capital to see her through. Now, I'm not going to have a widow and two children on my conscience or on the city's conscience if something happens to you. Will you promise me to take out that insurance policy?"

"Well, all right, Hugh. I guess you're right. How much is it going to cost me?"

"Several dollars a month, but the council is going to add enough to your salary to take care of it."

"I appreciate that, Hugh."

"There are going to be a lot of expenses connected with a chief of police that the council hasn't even thought about yet. We're going to have to have a jail. When you start arresting people, we've got to have a place to put them. You're going to need a car—I figure you can use your own and take gas out of the city pump until I can get that through. They've already approved a firehouse, and I reckon a couple of extra rooms onto that will do for a jail. Why don't you think about what you might need? After you're appointed, you might go up to Greenville and talk to Skeeter Willis and see what he's got up there. Then you and I'll get up a budget, and I'll spoon-feed it to Idus Bray and the rest of them, and one of these days before long we'll have us a proper police station. I'll tell Idus the station will have to have a telephone. That'll do it for him."

While the council was meeting to approve Will Henry's appointment, the Lee family moved into the house on Lower Third Street. Delano was situated at a point where Pine Mountain began its rise from the valley. Broad Street cut across the town at the place where the hillside started to be steep, and streets numbered two, three, and four ran vertically up the hill, at right angles to Broad Street. The upper ends of the streets attracted more expensive homes, since the sites afforded a view of the town. The lower ends of the streets contained neat frame and brick houses occupied by small merchants and the better-paid railroad people. Upper Third Street was the prettiest and most desirable in town. Lower Third Street, therefore, had a slight edge on Lower Second and Fourth streets.

Carrie was delighted with their location. It made it, in her mind, all the more necessary to have a guest room, and Billy was quartered with Eloise in spite of increasingly loud protests and, eventually, hot tears. Eloise maintained a smug silence, but permitted herself an occasional triumphant glance in his direction. Carrie banished Will Henry and Billy to the yard, where they discovered a swing blade and a rusty lawn mower in the back shed. They set about taming the overgrown lawn and pulling weeds from the skimpy flower beds. By late afternoon the two of them were thoroughly muddy. They enjoyed their first bath in their running-water tub, and when they sat down to a fried chicken supper, Will Henry experienced the odd sensation of having lived in the house for a long time. He felt they would like it here. Carrie was certain of it.

Will Henry and Carrie Lee were town people now, after having spent all their lives on middle Georgia farmland, half that period in hard times. Both, at thirty, were handsome people. Will Henry stood just under six feet tall and was of a muscular build, the product of sturdy ancestors and hard, physical work. If his ears were a bit large, his nose a bit blunt, and his jaw square and aggressive, his eyes softened the total effect considerably. Large and brown, they conveyed intelligence and sensitivity, and the soft tenor of his voice and his manner of speaking reinforced the impression immediately. He had a temper, which he took pride in not showing, and this restraint enhanced the aura of strength, both physical and psychic, which he exuded. He was shy, but not withdrawn.

Carrie was tall and trim of figure and very nearly beautiful. An Irish grandmother had willed her black hair and green eyes and a sense of humor. She had none of her husband's shyness and little of his restraint; pragmatism and often bluntness ruled her existence, but a natural charm and lack of desire to wound made her views seem refreshing rather than offensive to others.

They both came of families that preceded their republic, the Lees claiming a connection with those of Virginia, and the Callaways, Carrie's family, going back to seventeenth-century Kentucky and a connection with Boone. Given an opportunity, Carrie would refer to Fenimore Cooper's description of Boone's daring rescue of the Callaway girls from the Indians.

Neither of their families had had anything but land since what was locally referred to as the War Between the States. Still, they had inherited intelligence and gentility and a love of music and books. In their home they entertained themselves and had done so even before the children came. They both sang, and Carrie played serviceable Mozart and Bach. They had read Twain and Hawthorne and Dickens, among others. They had both had some higher education, though neither had earned a degree. While Will Henry had been in his third year at Gordon Military College at Barnesville, his father had died suddenly, and the farm had demanded his presence. Will Henry, after an adolescence of waiting, had proposed to Carrie; and she had come home from Bessie Tift College at Forsyth and unhesitatingly become his wife, as she had known for a long time she would.

Will Henry had had ambitions for the law, but the land had been in the family for a long time, though much had been sold during Reconstruction, and he felt a responsibility toward the ten families who lived upon it. At the beginning of their marriage, the farm had offered security and familiarity and even promise, so they had not felt thwarted—not, at least, in a way they could admit to each other.

And now they had left the farm, something Will Henry had begun to think he would never do. He had grown up there, and when it became his, it waited for him each day, demanding to be sown, reaped, milked, repaired, fertilized, and made profitable. He had hacked away diligently, but he had worked without fervor and without much talent, and the land had yielded a profit only so long as the soil and the times had been easy enough to require neither fervor nor talent. When the boll weevil had come, Will Henry had at first seen it as simply another demand upon his efforts. But when the pestilence had shown signs of hanging on, when even the best of farmers was struggling for existence, then the weevil began to look like something Will Henry had begun to despair of ever finding: an honorable way out.

After supper Carrie read to them from *Great Expectations*, because, she said, that was what they all had of their new life, then the children were put to bed. Will Henry and Carrie tidied up about the house until nearly midnight, then woke the children. At the stroke of twelve, somebody blew the siren at the firehouse, and they all sang "Auld Lang Syne" and kissed. Carrie read a passage from the Bible, Will Henry said a prayer of hope for the new year, and they all went to bed. Will Henry and Carrie were alone for the first time in their new existence. A weight had been lifted from them, and they enjoyed their love more than they had in months. They fell asleep exhausted and happy.

5 IT WAS his first morning on the new job, and Will Henry and Carrie sat in the car in front of the city hall. The car had no heater, and lap robes were pulled tightly around them. As they talked, the windows of the car misted over. Will Henry was glad, for he did not know what her reaction would be when he told her about the job as chief, and he did not want passers-by to see her upset. When he told her, her expression changed only slightly, and she was silent, her eyes remaining on his face. He could not look away from her, for fear of seeming even more guilty than he felt.

Soon he could bear the silence no longer. "It's not a dangerous job, not really." She still said nothing. "Not in Delano. Nothing ever happens here that's dangerous. I'll be spending more time fooling with the traffic on Main Street and watching out for speeders on the Atlanta highway than anything else." She turned and stared at the foggy windshield. "It's just a city job," he said, almost pleading.

"All right," she said finally.

The members of the city council gathered in the back room office of the city manager. They removed their coats and gathered around the wood stove but did not sit down. They were taking time away from their work and did not wish to prolong the occasion. John B. ("Skeeter") Willis, sheriff of Meriwether County, had driven down from Greenville to be on hand. When they were all present, Hugh Holmes called the meeting to order.

"Gentlemen, I suppose this is a kind of an historic occasion. We're here this morning to appoint our first law-enforcement officer. I guess it's a credit to our citizens that we've been able to get along so far without one, but we've got more than a thousand people in Delano now, at least that's my estimate, and I think the census this year will bear me out, and a police department is something every town must have. We've chosen a local man for this job, not because he is an experienced policeman, but because we know him and respect him and believe we can trust him to preserve the peace and protect life and property."

"Amen," said Idus Bray.

"Idus, was that amen for life or for property?"

Everybody laughed.

"I suppose any councilman can swear in our new chief, but if nobody has any objections I'd like the honor." There was a murmur of assent, and Holmes produced a battered Bible. "Will Henry, place your left hand on the Bible, and raise your right hand. Do you, William Henry Lee, swear by Almighty God to uphold and enforce the laws of Delano, the state of Georgia, and the United States of America and to do so impartially, without fear or favor?"

"I do."

"Well, I guess that makes you chief of police of Delano, Will Henry."

Holmes had given some considerable thought to the content of the oath he had just administered. He had considered including a phrase along the lines of "carry out such instructions as the city council shall give from time to time," and as he watched his fellow councilmen offering hurried congratulations, then scrambling into their coats and returning to their interrupted work, he felt glad that he had not. Too much city business, he believed, was conducted hurriedly and without proper consideration. He was forced to use this impatience at times to push something he considered vital through the council, and he did not like doing so. He felt that the responsibility for major acts should be carried by a consensus rather than by one councilman who had railroaded something through purely by the force of his personality or the weight of his standing. But he had found that if he did not do this, then the councilmen's impatience, coupled with their native caution, caused important business to be neglected, while time was taken up with pork-barrel trivia. Because of the indifference of his fellow councilmen, he was becoming, against his better judgment and considerably before his time, a Town Father.

As the meeting broke up, Dr. Frank Mudter reached into an overcoat pocket and pulled out an enormous pistol. "Will Henry, I don't know if you own a gun, but this was my daddy's. It's a little rusty, but I expect it'll still shoot all right." Will Henry and the others had a good laugh over the pistol. "It's an old Colt .45 Buntline, with a twelve-inch barrel. Wild Bill Hickock wore one, they say."

Will Henry laughed. "Well, Dr. Frank, I hope you don't think you've got yourself a Wild Bill Hickock." He weighed the pistol in his hand. "I don't know if I'm strong enough to carry it for very long, but I guess if the rust is scraped off it'll weigh a pound or two less. Thank you, Dr. Frank. I'll keep it until I get a pistol of my own. I guess I need some sort of badge of authority."

Skeeter Willis spoke up. "I reckon I can help out there." He took a small star-shaped badge from his pocket. "You can wear this until you get yourself a Delano badge. I've got a catalogue that's got a lot of police stuff in it. You'll need a lot of things out of that pretty soon. I'll go over it with you, and we'll make a list. They've got a salesman comes through Greenville every now and then. I'll send him down to see you. He'll be glad to get his hands on a new boy."

Will Henry pinned the badge onto his coat and polished it with his sleeve. "Well, now, Skeeter, I feel real official."

"I'll talk to Hugh about getting you a budget for some equipment," said Willis, and he moved off toward Holmes.

Will Henry and the doctor left the city hall together, the long pistol cradled in Will Henry's right hand. He had almost forgotten about it. As they walked down the short flight of steps to the sidewalk, a car backfired twice around the corner in the square. They reached the curb and stood next to the doctor's car. Will Henry raised the hand holding the gun and pointed toward the corner. "You know, Frank, it's occurred to me that we could use one of those automatic traffic signals at that corner. The traffic is pretty heavy off the Atlanta highway there, and it seems to me to be a better use of the city's money to have a light there than to have me down there waving my arms. One light could—"

As he spoke there was a roar and a clatter of a car's engine, and around the corner, literally on two wheels, came a large Packard touring car. The car straightened, lurched back onto all four wheels, and roared unsteadily down the street toward them. Will Henry stopped talking, but his arm remained up, pointing toward the intersection and the car. Across the street a Model A roadster began to back out of a parking place. The Packard slammed on brakes and veered away from the backing car, pointing itself directly toward the doctor and the new chief of police, who stood, openmouthed, staring at the huge car which seemed about to run them down. Less than a dozen feet from where they stood, as they were about to jump out of the way, the car screeched to a halt and both doors on the curb side were thrown open. As Will Henry stared at the car, a double barreled shotgun flew out the door, followed closely by a pistol. Two very large, very blonde young men stumbled out of the car, their hands in the air, terror written across their faces. They stood there in the cold sunlight, staring wide-eyed at the man pointing a huge pistol in their direction. Into the sudden silence came the sound of silver striking cement. A large bag of half dollars was spilling slowly from the front seat into the street.

Frank Mudter recovered first. "Will Henry," he said in a hoarse whisper, "I think you've made your first arrest." Will Henry snapped to. He lowered the gun to waist level and slipped his finger into the trigger guard.

"Just stand right there. Don't move." Skeeter Willis was coming through the door of the city hall with Hugh Holmes. Holmes had been explaining that he thought it was a little soon to go asking the council for more police money. They stopped and stared at Will Henry and his prisoners.

"Jesus Christ," Skeeter Willis said.

The following few minutes were a jerky montage for Will Henry. There was Skeeter snapping handcuffs on the two young men; Holmes leading the party around to the bank, where two large holes were discovered in the front window; the staff still lying on the cold marble floor, two of them (one a man) weeping; and Holmes, while the two young men were being securely cuffed to a water pipe in the next room, conducting an impromptu city-council meeting during which motions were swiftly adopted authorizing an addition to the new firehouse for police headquarters and an expenditure of a $350 for firearms, handcuffs, uniforms, and other essential police equipment.

Before Will Henry had fully come to terms with this situation, he was faced with another: that of explaining to Carrie all that had happened. He did not relish the thought.

6 "THEY WERE BROTHERS. Their name was O'Brien." Will Henry looked carefully at Carrie, who was seated across the kitchen table, staring out the window. She had been just as quiet when he had told his story as she had been earlier, in the car. "They'd got liquored up on New Year's Eve over at Thomaston, that's where they're from, and they stole the Packard from in front of the country club. As a joke, seemed to me. They ran around all night with some girls, and when they sobered up they were afraid to take the car back. They got drunk again, spent all their money with a bootlegger in Yatesville, and they were between here and Woodbury when they had a flat tire. When they got the trunk open to get the jack out, they found the shotgun and two pistols, and they decided to stick up somebody and just keep going. They look like redneck farmboys to me, and I guess they were tired of it."

"What happened to the girls?" It was the first time she had spoken, and he took the show of interest as a recovery from some kind of shock.

"They took them home before daylight." He paused to wait for a reaction. She nodded as if she were satisfied that the girls hadn't been involved. He continued, "The shotgun wasn't even loaded. I doubt if they even bothered to look. When they got to Delano, first place they saw was the bank, it being on the corner.

They just walked right in and told everybody to stick 'em up. The oldest one, Jimmy—he had the shotgun—he climbed over the teller's bars and emptied the cash drawers into a sack, a money-bag from an Atlanta bank. They took two other bags that were already full and walked out. Never even looked at the vault, which was wide open and had about forty thousand dollars in it. As they walked out the door, Danny, the young one, turned around and fired two shots through the front window into the ceiling, and everybody inside hit the floor pretty quick. Then they drove around the corner, and there we were. I was showing Frank Mudter something, pointing with the gun, I guess, and they thought I was pointing it at them. Well, anyway, we got them, and everybody in town except Frank Mudter thinks I'm a hero. I don't like that much, but Frank's right, the alternative is for everybody in town to think I'm a helpless fool who got lucky, which isn't too far wrong, I guess. But if I'm to go on being chief I'm going to have to live with being the fearless hero." He laughed. "Even Skeeter was impressed, although he didn't let it get in his way when it came time to question the boys. I'm glad he was there, though, or I guess they'd still be handcuffed to that pipe. Hugh Holmes got a motion passed real quick to build a jailhouse onto the fire station."

He stopped abruptly, realizing that he was talking very fast. Carrie got up and went to the big wood stove and stirred something. "I suppose you're the chief now," she said. "I think I had hoped to talk you out of it, to find something else for you to do, but after this I'd have the whole town against me." She stirred slowly for a moment. "I'll try and get used to it, Will Henry. But I want you to make me a promise."

"All right."

"I want you to promise me that you'll always be real, real careful, that every time you see something coming on that could be dangerous even a little, that you'll think about Billy and Eloise and me, and that you'll do everything you can to be careful. Will you promise me that?"

"Yes, I promise. I'm not fool enough to want to get hurt, Carrie. I'm not William S. Hart against the badmen, and I hope you believe that I'll always think about you and the children."

She smiled for the first time that day. He went to her and kissed her on the cheek. She smiled. "Now get out of here and let me set the table for your dinner."

Will Henry stepped out the back door, aware now that Billy and Eloise had been playing in the back yard while he and Carrie had talked in the kitchen. He looked up to see Eloise, her hands up and her back against a tree. Perhaps six feet from her stood Billy, the Buntline revolver in his two small hands, pointing at Eloise's head. "The only good Indian is a dead Indian," he was saying. He had a thumb around the hammer and was cocking the pistol. Will Henry's first reaction was to scream as loudly as he could at Billy, but in a small part of a second he realized that Billy might jerk the trigger and that Carrie, in the kitchen, would hear him and come to see what was the matter. Instead, he spread his hands and clapped them together once, as loudly as he could. Billy's head jerked around. He dropped the pistol as if it had suddenly become hot and stood, wide-eyed, looking at his father. The Buntline lay on the ground, still cocked, still pointing in Eloise's direction. Will Henry strode down the steps and across the yard and picked up the pistol. Billy seemed to be trying to speak, but nothing came out. Will Henry eased the hammer down, opened the retaining piece and turned the cylinder slowly as Billy watched. There were cartridges in all six chambers.

He shook the cartridges out into his hand and put them into his pocket. Then he stuck the pistol into his belt, grabbed Billy by an upper arm, and spun him around, hitting him across the buttocks hard, once, with his open hand. He spun the boy around again. Tears were streaming down his face, and he was trembling violently. Angry as he was, Will Henry could not bring himself to chastise the boy further. After all, he himself had left the pistol, fully loaded and in plain view, on a straight-back chair in the living room, on top of his coat. "Take your sister around to the front of the house," he said in a loud whisper. "Wash your face under the spigot and wait out front until you're called to your dinner. Don't you say a word about this to your mother, and don't you be crying when you come in." He forced himself to relax a little, to look less angry, to let the child know that it was all right now. "Go on," he said.

As the children scurried around to the front yard, Will Henry walked quickly to the tool shed at the back of the lot. Inside he found a rusty pair of pliers. He twisted the lead from all six cartridges and emptied the powder charge onto the dirt floor. He rummaged around until he found a chisel and a ball peen hammer. He placed the pistol in the bench vise and locked it. Then he chipped at the firing spur on the hammer until it broke off, rendering the weapon useless. He put the pistol back into his belt, gathered the empty shell casings and the lead, took them around back of the shed, and mixed them with the contents of the garbage can. Then he leaned against the back of the shed and vomited.

Later, as they ate their midday meal, each quiet with his own thoughts, Will Henry said, "That pistol Frank Mudter gave me is too old-fashioned to be any good to anybody, so I broke off the firing part of the hammer to make it harmless. Billy, why don't you clean the rust off it, and we'll keep it as a souvenir."

He smiled at the boy, and the boy smiled back.

7 WILL HENRY left the house after his midday meal and walked up the hill to Broad Street. He turned left and started toward the corner where Broad met Main Street, where the bank was. He had to pass a number of stores on the way, and he was nervous about it. He knew that word of the arrest that morning would surely have got around by this time; he began to wish the incident had never happened.

As he approached the hardware store, he saw Ralph McKibbon, the owner, standing out front talking to a man. "Hey, Chief!" Will Henry winced. McKibbon came over and punched him playfully in the ribs. "I hear you really took care of those bank robbers this morning! Whole town's talking about it! Why, you've only been chief a couple of hours, and everybody feels safer already!" Will Henry mumbled something, smiled as best he could, and continued on toward the corner, receiving greetings and congratulations from three more people on the way. He stopped outside the bank and looked at the window. A man was nailing boards over the broken glass. He walked inside.

"Why, Mr. Lee! Or I guess I should say, Chief Lee." Miss Bessie Simmons, the teller, was smiling broadly from her cage. "I sure do want to thank you for catching those awful men this morning."

"Well, Miss Bessie, I just wish we could have done something to stop them before they scared you so bad."

Harold Bowen, the clerk, came over. "Just get me a pistol, that's what I told Mr. Holmes. Just get me a pistol, and we won't have that kind of trouble no more. I could have shot both of them dead this morning." Will Henry remembered that Harold had been lying on the floor weeping, when he had come into the bank after the robbery.

"Harold, I don't think those boys would have shot anybody even accidentally. They were drunk, but they weren't killers. They just shot those holes in the window to scare you. They were so scared themselves when we caught them that they seemed almost relieved. I think this thing this morning was just a kind of fluke. But if it ever happens again, you do just what you did this morning. It's no use getting killed for a few hundred dollars of somebody else's money."

"Well, it's our duty to protect folks' money here. They put it in the bank and they expect it to be safe. We need a pistol or two around here, that's what we need."

"What did you do with those two boys, Chief Lee?" Miss Bessie asked.

"Skeeter Willis took them up to the county jail. The council has voted to build us a jail onto the new firehouse here, so we'll be able to handle it if something like this happens again. Matter of fact, I'm due over there in a minute to talk to Mr. Holmes and Skeeter about it. Just wanted to see if everything was all right here."

He excused himself and crossed the street toward where the new firehouse was being built behind the city hall. There was a sound of hammering and sawing as he approached. He walked through a half-completed doorway and looked at what was being built. There was a large garage for the engine and three rooms and a bathroom with a shower in the back. It seemed adequate, even comfortable, for the one full-time fireman, Jimmy Riley, and his group of volunteers. The plan was to have a siren on top of a pole outside the firehouse. When a fire was reported, Jimmy would switch on the siren, and the volunteers, all of whom lived or worked less than two blocks away, would come running. Will Henry wondered what he would do if he ever needed help. It was something else to discuss with Holmes. He heard a car pull up outside. Holmes and Skeeter Willis came in together. Holmes called the building foreman over, and they walked around to the side of the building.

He indicated the piece of ground between the firehouse and the back door of city hall. "I thought this would be a good place to build. The city owns a few feet more frontage on this side than on the other. Will Henry, have you given any thought to what you're going to need here?"

"I've got one or two ideas, but I think we ought to ask Skeeter what he thinks about it. He's the only man I know with his own jail."

Skeeter grinned. "You got a real smart chief here, Hugh; knows when to ask the advice of his sheriff. That won't last long, though. He'll know it all before long."

"Well, Skeeter," said Will Henry, "I guess we better get our money's worth out of you while we can. You'll be back up in Greenville tomorrow, sleeping next to that potbellied stove, and we won't see you in Delano again until next election."

"That's exactly what I'm going to do, boy, after I give you the benefit of my experience. I'm going to let you take care of the trash down here." He pointed to the rear of the new building. "Hugh, I'd make the jail just as deep as the firehouse, but maybe not as wide. Will Henry don't have to get a fire engine in it. I'd put four cells back there at the back, about eight by eight apiece. That may sound like a lot, but the first rowdy Saturday night you have you'll wish you had more. Now, you want a flush toilet and a sink in every one of them, for two reasons. First of all, you don't want to put your brand new chief to work carrying slop jars right off, and second, if you get anybody mean in there, and you will 'ventually, you don't want to have to open the cell door any more than you have to. That's basic security. Once you got 'em in there, keep 'em in there. Now, some of these things might sound like they're extravagant, Hugh, but they're not. Once you build this jailhouse, nobody is going to want to hear about doing anything to it until it falls down all by itself. If you do it right the first time, it'll last you a long time. You do it wrong, and you'll have people busting out of it, and you'll have some ladies' group or other down on you for conditions. Believe me, I know what I'm talking about."

Holmes nodded. "I see your point, Skeeter. What else?"

"Well you're going to need a window in every cell, 'cause in about a month after it's built this jailhouse is going to smell just exactly like every other jailhouse in the United States, and it's going to need air. Remember, your officers spend just about as much time here as your prisoners. You're going to need a drain in every cell, so washing down the floors will be easy, and I'd put two double-decker bunks in every cell."

"You'd put four men in an eight-by-eight cell, Skeeter?" Will Henry was surprised.

"I'm talking about the minimum, Will Henry. If you want to, you can make 'em bigger. Two of 'em anyway. Your prisoners are only going to be short-timers, fellows waiting to be tried or sent to Greenville or the county camp. You don't have to pamper 'em. Something else, though. I'd partition one of the cells off from the others, because sooner or later you're going to get a woman or two in here, and you'll even get a white woman now and then. If you want to keep the place quiet, you have to be able to keep 'em separate from the men." He moved to the front of the lot. "Now you'll need a kind of office, and you better make it pretty big, 'cause you'll have to work and keep records in there. I'd make it as wide as the building, except for room for a corridor back to the cells. Then you'll need a waiting room up front that's as wide as the building. Somebody is always waiting in a jail-house, and you don't want 'em in your working area, where you've got files and records and weapons around. You need some benches in there, but don't make it too comfortable. You don't want folks waiting around too long."

"That's roughly what I thought would do, Skeeter," said Will Henry, "but bigger. I think you're right, though. I'd like to have a sort of window with a counter between the office and the waiting room."

"Good idea. I've found it's better to have something, a desk or a counter or something, between you and the public. Makes things a little more official. Might be a good idea to have a little window in the wall between you and the firehouse, too. You're both going to be shorthanded, and you can cover each other's phones that way. Make sure, too, Hugh, that you have separate numbers for the two things. Nothing worse for folks than having a busy telephone when they want to get through to you."

"I think that window would be good for the city," said Holmes. "And Idus Bray will like the idea of two phones. I think we can get this general plan approved on the wave of enthusiasm over our chief's first day in office."

"Another thing, Hugh," said Skeeter. "You ought to pass

some sort of motion giving Will Henry the authority to deputize. He's by himself here, and he's going to need help from time to time." He turned to the new chief. "Will Henry, I'm going to deputize you as a deputy sheriff, the way I have the other chiefs at Warm Springs and Manchester and the rest. That way you won't have to get me out of bed if you want to chase somebody past the city limits. But be careful how you use the authority. Keep it within the limits of official investigations of crimes committed inside the city limits. Otherwise you're crossing onto my territory. Raise your right hand. Do you promise to uphold the laws of Meriwether County and the State of Georgia and to do your duty and to wash your face and hands every day and behind your ears where you're still wet and to be a good boy in general?" Will Henry started to speak. "Good. You're a deputy. Holmes is a witness."

"Has your wife made the speech yet?" Will Henry and Skeeter were alone at the jail site. Holmes had returned to the bank.

"What speech?"

"The one about being careful and not getting killed."

"Oh, well, yes."

"She's right, Will Henry. You can get killed real easy in your job, and you can get hurt bad even easier." Skeeter squinted off into the distance. "I've been sheriff of Meriwether County for eight years, and I've had one deputy killed and one nearly 'bout killed, beat up so bad he'll never do a man's work again. But nobody's ever laid a hand on me, personally. You want to know why?"

Will Henry nodded. Skeeter was standing with his considerable weight on his left foot, the one nearest Will Henry, his hands on his hips. Will Henry was standing with his legs apart and his hands shoved into his hip pockets. Skeeter pivoted on his left foot and drove his right forearm hard into the upper part of Will Henry's abdomen. Will Henry emitted a loud grunt and sat down, hard, on the grass. He sat there, dazed, gasping for breath. Skeeter squatted in front of him and peered into his face concernedly. "That hurt, didn't it?" Will Henry nodded, still trying for breath. "Now, right now, at this particular moment, you don't feel like getting up and doing that to me, do you?" Will Henry shook his head. "In a minute or two you will, but right now all you want to do is hold your belly and get your breath." Will Henry weighed 180 pounds, but Skeeter reached under his arms and lifted him to his feet like a child.

"I'm sorry I had to do that, Will Henry, but I could explain that to you for a week, and you wouldn't get it. There's two things: first, you've got to always be ready for somebody to try to do that to you, or worse, and somebody will try, believe me. Let's say you stop a fellow for speeding. He might be the nicest, friendliest fellow you ever saw when you walk up to him, but you don't know what he's got in that car. He might have a trunk full of white lightning or a back seat full of some bank's money. If you don't know him, watch him. If you expect a fellow to hit you or shoot you, chances are he won't get to. Second point is, don't ever take no crap from anybody, and if you have to hit a man, hit him hard enough so you only have to do it once. Don't you ever, ever let yourself get in a fight with a man. Your job is to stop fights, not get in 'em. The way to stop a man fighting is to fix him so he can't fight. After you've stopped one or two fights that way you'll be able to stop a lot of 'em just by speaking to 'em. If you're going to get in that position you have to keep an edge all the time." He reached behind him and pulled out a small blackjack. "This is an edge. It's got lead inside and leather on the outside, and you can hit a man on the head with it almost anywhere except the temples, hit him hard and not do him any permanent damage. And for a minute or two you can put the cuffs on him or get him in a car or a cell without any problem."

Skeeter set Will Henry, who was still having trouble breathing, on a nail keg and pulled one up for himself. "I know it seems unfair to hit a man with a blackjack when he isn't holding anything himself, but you've got to get a new idea of what being fair is. I've got a reputation in this county for being tough and fair. It gets me reelected every four years, and believe me, if I wasn't tough I'd never get a chance to be fair. Do you understand me, Will Henry?"

"Yes," said Will Henry, finally drawing enough breath to speak.

"Another thing. Don't ever threaten anybody. Don't ever say to a man, 'You come with me, or I'll hit you with this blackjack.' If he's a problem, hit him, and he'll come with you. If you're always ready to hit a man first, then you'll almost never have to draw a pistol, let alone use it. Now, I've heard some peace officers say that you shouldn't draw your gun unless you're going to use it. Well, that sounds tough, but it's stupid. You can threaten a man with a gun, that's common sense. You pull it out and you point it at his head and you cock it, and he'll do pretty much what you tell him. Something else about the blackjack; it's official. If you pick up a two-by-four and hit a nigger with it, he'll hold a grudge and be a problem to you forever. But if you hit him with a blackjack—when he deserves it—well, that's official to a nigger; he figures you're just doing a job."

Skeeter paused for a moment. "Now, about guns. I've pulled my gun a dozen or fifteen times in eight years, and I've fired it at a man twice. Killed 'em both. One of 'em was about to try to kill me with a pistol, and I didn't bat an eye; I just shot him. The other one was running from me, and I told him to halt, and he wouldn't, and I shot him. I didn't mean to kill the second one, just bring him down. I was aiming at the seat of his pants, but I hit him in the small of his back and cut his spine." He looked away. "I didn't lose any sleep over the first one; it was me or him. The second one hadn't done much, though, just stole some tires from a filling station, but he was trying to escape and would have if I hadn't shot him. I guess I didn't feel too good about either one of them. I can't give you much advice about when to shoot at a man, Will Henry, unless he's trying to kill you. You'll have to work that out by yourself. But I'll tell you this, you'd better work it out in your mind right now, 'cause when the time comes you won't have time to think about it."

Will Henry's breath was coming more easily now; he stood up and filled his lungs. "Well, thanks for the advice, Skeeter. If I ever recover my health enough to use it, it ought to come in real handy."

"I'm just giving you the little lecture I give when I get a new deputy. You'd be surprised the way some of 'em act as soon as they get a badge on. I have to pick 'em real careful." Skeeter traced some obscure pattern in the dirt with a toe. "I wouldn't have picked you, Will Henry. If Holmes had asked my advice I'd of told him to find somebody else."

Will Henry was stung. "You think I'd push people around?"

"Oh, no, no, no. That's not why I wouldn't of picked you. Just the reverse. I don't know if you've got it in you to be hard enough. I think you're likely to hesitate when the time comes. That'll breed disrespect, and word'll get around. You won't be able to keep things straight. And when that happens, Carrie's going to have good reason to worry. Somebody'll kill you, Will

Henry, as sure as you're standing there."

They were both silent for a moment. It occurred to Will Henry that this must be one of the most solemn moments of his life. Skeeter Willis, with patent sincerity, was giving him the most earnest possible advice, based on knowledge and experience. The man was trying the very best he knew how to help him survive the work he had chosen to do. Will Henry was moved.

"Skeeter, I understand you, and I'll try to remember what you've told me. I reckon if I don't die in bed it won't be your fault. Thank you."

Skeeter heaved a deep sigh and nodded. He patted Will Henry's shoulder heavily a couple of times, gave him a small smile, and walked away toward his car.

Will Henry stopped in front of the house and looked at it. Although chilled from the walk home, he felt compelled to pause and reflect. The night was clear and very cold, even though it was not much past six. The rising moon gave the white frame house a luminous quality. It looked secure and inviting. He still felt somewhat disoriented. Only the day before he had left the house he was born in, left a country life, changed irrevocably his existence. The farm was receding into the past at an astonishing rate; it surprised him to feel, standing in front of this strange house, that he had arrived *home*. Inside, his wife was preparing a supper she had not grown or picked or plucked. His children would get up tomorrow morning and walk a short distance to school, and afterwards would play with other children who lived only a few yards away. Tomorrow, his work would allow him to walk on pavement in shoes he normally wore only on Sundays. People would seek him out with their problems, or simply pass the time of day. People. He would see more people in a day than he normally saw in ten. He had a place, a position in other people's lives, for the first time. He would not disappoint them.

In one short day he had single-handedly captured two armed bank robbers in a manner that, if anyone other than Frank Mudter ever found out about it, he would never live down; he had almost seen his son kill his daughter with a pistol he himself had left loaded and within reach; and he had been knocked on his ass by the sheriff of Meriwether County. It was less than an auspicious beginning, but it was, by God, a *new* beginning.

He climbed the steps and went inside.

8 HOLMES closed the front door and carefully hung his coat in the hall closet.

"Hugh?" The call came from upstairs. "Is that you?"

"Yes, Ginny, I'm home." He heard her start for the stairs, and he waited in the entrance hall for her. He kissed her on the lips as she reached him, and they went into the small sitting room together. They had only recently completed the red-brick colonial house, and already they gravitated toward the "den," as Virginia called it, instead of the more formal living room, which was kept for occasions when company called. The den was oak-paneled and leathery, and in winter Virginia always had a fire going in the little fireplace by the time he arrived home. Here, too, was kept their dark secret. In a cupboard which was part of a bookcase, concealed by a door onto which was glued a row of book spines, rested a bottle of bourbon whiskey, one of Scotch, one of very good cognac, and a bottle of very dry sherry. Holmes had made the cupboard himself after the builders had departed. Neither he nor Virginia ever touched the whiskey or brandy. Those were kept for civilized and trusted visitors, none of whom had as yet appeared. But Holmes knew that, surely, the day would come when he would want to offer a man a drink, and he would be ready.

The cupboard was the only receptacle in a Meriwether

County home which had been consciously constructed for the
storage of alcoholic beverages, secret spirits usually residing in a
cellar or out-of-the-way kitchen cupboard. Alcohol was a religious issue in Delano, and there were many people who held the
belief that a man could not both drink whiskey and call himself
a Christian. Although he had been brought up in an abstemious
home, Holmes could see no logic in this viewpoint. He and Virginia had traveled widely in the United States and seen respect-
able people imbibing in hotels and restaurants without
debauchery. The summer before, in London, on their first trip
abroad, they had gone to Rule's, the famous restaurant in Covent
Garden, and Holmes had impulsively asked the wine waiter to
recommend a good half-bottle of wine. He had also accepted a
recommendation of sherry before the meal. He and Virginia had
returned to Brown's Hotel slightly tipsy, had had the best night
in bed of their eight-year marriage, and had smuggled a bottle of
sherry home.

Although the Eighteenth Amendment would not be declared
officially ratified until later that same month and would not go
into effect for another year, a man in Holmes's position did not
buy liquor openly. Instead, once a month, a small, extremely
well-dressed young man in a large Pierce Arrow called at the
Holmes residence after dark, filled a modest order, accepted cash
in payment, and continued on his merciful rounds.

Holmes poured them both a sherry and sank into the leather
sofa. He did not come home for "dinner," as most men did. He
had a sandwich at his desk and worked. Virginia prepared a
three-course meal for the evening—they had dinner later than
other people—and they shared half a bottle of wine with it.
When he arrived home at night, the day's news was fresh between them, and they always had plenty to talk about.

"You heard about the bank robbery and the arrest."

"Yes, in great detail, at least four times this afternoon."

"I swear, Ginny, it was the best thing that could possibly
have happened right at this time."

"You mean you're *glad* the bank was robbed?"

"Oh, no, not that, although it will teach us to be a little more
prepared for that sort of thing. What it's done is made this whole
chief-of-police situation so much easier to handle. We got a motion to build a police station through the council just like *that*,
and I think we'll get a police car through next meeting."

"Even Idus Bray went along?"

"Went along! He was leading the charge! I've never seen him so excited about anything! Will Henry handled the thing real well, too. Naturally, he was surprised, and I could tell he was nervous, but he stopped that car and arrested those two boys just as cool as you please. You know, I probably wouldn't have wanted Will Henry to have that job if there had been any kind of real choice, if there had been an experienced man available. Skeeter Willis still has a lot of reservations about him, I think, but he handled this thing real well, and he's anxious to get Skeeter's advice about everything. He may not know much about being a policeman yet, but at least he *knows* he doesn't know much. Thank the Lord for that. Can you imagine what somebody like Foxy Funderburke would be like in that job?"

They talked on for a while, then Virginia excused herself to finish cooking dinner. Holmes felt the sherry warming him and stretched out on the sofa, groaning with fatigue and pleasure. He closed his eyes and felt a sense of completion. With the new fire department and the appointment of the chief of police, he felt that the town had reached a milestone, that it now had the organization and staffing and equipment that it needed. The paving of the central streets, the waterworks, the telephone exchange had all been milestones. There were dozens of other things they would need in the future, but for the moment, everything seemed complete. Holmes dozed.

Unlike Will Henry and Carrie Lee, who had grown effortlessly into what they were, like healthy plants, the products of long and provincially selective breeding, Hugh Holmes had designed and constructed himself, brick by plank by nail. He was a farmer's son, too, but his father, who had been born to a starving sharecropper's family, had had only his own shrewdness, industry, and sense of timing to help him extract a prosperous farm and cotton gin from the shambles of Reconstruction. He had passed on to the young Hugh the notion of the self-made man, the idea that he could decide what he wanted to do and then do it. Holmes took the idea quite literally, and he began with one or two attributes which would be of great help. In addition to a remarkable native intelligence, nature had given Holmes a rare physical presence. He was six feet five inches tall and might have been thought of as Lincolnesque, if his posture had not been so erect. From his early teens he towered over everyone he met; indeed, he did not meet a man taller than himself until he was thirty, and the experience depressed him for a week. He learned early to use his height with subtlety and effectiveness, when to slump into a chair and when to rise and look down. To his imposing height was added the distinct advantage of early maturity. Grayness tinted his hair at nineteen, and his features had been large and craggy even before that, lending him an air of thoughtfulness and wisdom.

Holmes decided early that he wanted a career in business, specifically, in banking. He realized that banks were at the heart of every business transaction of any consequence, that they held the power to move a community or a state, perhaps even a country. He knew, too, that a good bank was a highly efficient intelligence-gathering organization, and he liked the idea of having a special knowledge of what was going on. He believed that with such knowledge and with access to capital he could achieve whatever he wanted.

There was not, however, a megalomaniacal bone in Holmes's body. He did not wish to be J. P. Morgan. He wished to be a big fish in a small pond and to gather to himself just enough power to shape his own destiny and that of the pond he chose. He wished to travel, to learn, to experience many things in the world, and he knew if he went into a big city bank he would have to devote all of his energies to climbing the business ladder and to surviving in intramural, political warfare. He did not doubt that he could excel in such circumstances, but they were not circumstances to his liking.

Hugh Holmes had constructed a set of circumstances exactly to his liking, and, at the time of Will Henry Lee's escape from the farm, at the end of 1919, those circumstances were the Bank of Delano. They were achieved with a combination of hard work, intelligence, and a stroke of luck, to which he had applied a finely developed sense of opportunism and a willingness to take, under the right circumstances, a major personal risk.

The first time Holmes had seen Delano, or rather, the place where Delano would soon be, was more than ten years before. He was the cashier at the Farmers and Merchants Bank at Woodbury, some twelve miles north, when on a Sunday afternoon he took the train to Warm Springs for a Sunday School Union picnic. Warm Springs was a prosperous and fashionable resort, attracting people from all over the South to bathe in the naturally warm waters and listen to music and lectures at the Meriwether Inn. It was also a favorite spot in the county for church outings, and Holmes was with a party of thirty who took the M&B to Warm Springs that day.

The Macon and Birmingham Railroad was misnamed, since it did not reach either Macon or Birmingham. The local name, Mule and Wagon, was more appropriate, owing to the slow speed at which the trains traveled. On this occasion, the train stopped for water at a country tank, and after a few minutes it was announced that there would be a short delay due to mechanical troubles, and that passengers were encouraged to stretch their legs. The whistle would blow when the train was ready once again.

Holmes got down from the train and looked about. They were in a pine forest—mostly young trees, but a few older, taller ones. There was a generous scattering of oaks and elms, as well, and the place was cool on a hot day. He strolled aimlessly away from the train into the woods, enjoying the scented air and the carpet of pine needles underfoot. Shortly, he came to a large clearing and was surprised to see a very new, white Cadillac touring car parked there. Three men, their dusters and goggles draped over a fender, stood talking, occasionally referring to a map and pointing in one direction or another. Holmes approached the group. "Good day to you, Gentlemen." The men responded. "I'm a little bit surprised to see a big car like that so far off the beaten track."

The shortest of the three men spoke up. "Well, it's only about a hundred yards through the trees there to the Atlanta highway. There used to be a sawmill here, and there's an old road to the highway." Holmes remembered that the train had just traveled under a rickety wooden bridge. The man stuck out his hand. "My name is Thomas Delano." Holmes recognized the name immediately. Delano, after a short, but successful career as a merchant, was becoming something of a tycoon in the textile business, based in Atlanta, but having mills in three smaller towns nearby. "This is Mr. Bill Smenner, of the M&B Railroad, and Mr. Svensen, a visitor from Norway, who is doing some surveying for us."

"I'm Hugh Holmes, from Woodbury."

"You the cashier in the bank over there?" Holmes registered surprise. "Oh, I do a little business over there, as you know." Holmes had had no idea that Delano had business in the county.

Delano exchanged a glance with Smenner. He turned back to Holmes. "You might be interested in what we're up to here, Mr. Holmes."

"Well, it looks like kind of a lonesome place to put a cotton mill."

"It may look that way, now, but in two years it won't. We're going to build a town here, Mr. Holmes. Have a look at Mr. Svensen's plan." He spread the map out over the hood of the Cadillac and pointed out various features. "As you can see, this is the spot where the M&B and the Atlanta–Columbus highway cross. That's pretty good transportation access to start with. I'm going to build a modern cotton mill right here, and Mr. Smenner has decided—you don't mind my mentioning it, Bill?—he's going to put the new repair shops for the M&B right up there, about where the water tower is. The two together will be a fine base of employment for a town."

Holmes was impressed. "What will you do for a water supply? Or will you have folks digging their own wells?"

"No, sir. There's a spring up on that mountainside over there that's got a flow rate that would supply a city of a much greater size than we're planning. We'll have a modern waterworks and a sewerage system, too, and we're going to pave the business district and four residential streets first thing."

Holmes noticed he was breathing faster. "What method of financing all this will you be using?"

"We're forming the Delano Development Corporation—the town will be called Delano; I'm not bashful about things like that. Our initial capitalization will be one hundred thousand dollars. Mr. Smenner and I will participate personally in that, in addition to our capital expenditure on the mill and rail shops, and we'll be inviting a limited number of other gentlemen to invest, men who have the personal resources and the kind of business experience to help the town grow. We're going to have a barbecue here on this spot the fifteenth of next month and sell three hundred residential lots for seventy-five dollars each and fifty business lots at two hundred dollars. Folks will pay their money in advance, and then there'll be a drawing for locations. The corporation will retain ownership of all the other prospective residential and business property until such time as it feels more should be sold."

Holmes was quiet. Delano was watching him closely. "It would be the finest investment a young man could make, Mr.

Holmes. It would be an investment with a future, and it would mean getting in on the ground floor. At this moment no more than a dozen men know about this, but our commitments are firm, Mr. Holmes. This is going to happen." The train whistle blew.

"Mr. Delano, this sounds like a very interesting idea to me. Could I get in touch with you at your Atlanta office?" Holmes shook hands with the three men and turned to leave. Delano stopped him.

"Mr. Holmes—Hugh, if I may call you that—I've already made proper application to the secretary of state for a bank charter, and I expect it to be granted shortly. This bank is going to have the mill and the railroad as depositors right off, and it's going to need the right man to run it. I've heard some good things about you, and I'd be interested in talking to you about it. There would be an opportunity for investment, and a chance for more later. Why don't you think about it for a day or two, then come see me in Atlanta?"

"I'll be in touch with you before the week is out, if that's all right, Mr. Delano."

"That's fine." They shook hands again, and Holmes hurried back to his train. The picnic at Warm Springs passed in a blur, and he did not sleep that night. The next morning he telephoned a man in Athens who had previously made him an offer for his recently deceased father's farm and cotton-ginning business and named a price. After the usual haggling, the man met it.

Within the week he had invested ten thousand dollars in the Delano Development Corporation. The following month he went to the barbecue on the Delano site and bought a residential lot and a business lot. He drew the land on Upper Third Street, where he would later build his house and the lot at the intersection of Main Street and the Atlanta highway, where the bank would be built. He suspected that he had been more than lucky in the draw, but he did not question it. Before the day was out, he bought two more business lots, one adjacent to his own, for three hundred dollars each from men who found a fast hundred-dollar profit more interesting than a long haul in a new town. He also renewed an old acquaintance with a prosperous farmer named Idus Bray and agreed to put up twenty-five percent of the capital in the new telephone company Bray was to build. He reached agreement with Thomas Delano on the bank. He would own forty-nine percent of the stock and supply that proportion of the capital. In five years he could buy the two percent that would give him control, and Delano would sell the remainder of the stock to local investors.

By the end of the day, he had committed all but two thousand dollars of his inheritance and savings. Still, two thousand dollars cash, three business lots, a residential lot, twenty-five percent of a telephone company, forty-nine percent of a bank, and ten percent of the Delano Development Corporation constituted an extraordinary collection of holdings for a man of thirty-four years, even if his holdings were mostly paper. He was very pleased with himself.

And as he responded to Virginia's call to dinner, he was more pleased with himself than at any time since that day.

9 TWO WEEKS PASSED. Work on the new jail moved rapidly along, now that the firehouse was finished. Holmes got the authorization of the council to buy a good secondhand car for the police department. A two-year-old Ford was found, and a clerk at Ralph McKibbon's hardware store painted Delano Police on both front doors in white paint. Will Henry began to establish a routine of sorts. When the stores opened at eight o'clock, he would make a slow tour of Main Street, speaking to those store owners he saw, and being seen by the others, just in case anyone had any loss or complaint to report. He would then go to the post office, collect any police mail and take it to the city hall, where, in Willis Greer's office, he would sort the various bulletins and wanted posters which came in. He would have a cup of coffee at about ten with a small group of merchants and businessmen who gathered every day at the Delano Drug Company's soda fountain to exchange gossip and opinions. He figured that if there were any dissatisfaction with the way he was doing the chief's job, he would hear about it at these daily meetings before it got to be a problem.

After coffee he would make a slow tour of the whole town, "showing the flag" on every street in both black and white sections. Sometimes he would stop and chat with someone, and most days he stopped in Smitty's Grocery Store in Braytown, the black section unofficially named after the white man who owned about a third of the property within its boundaries. Smitty's was the daytime social center of the black community, and Will Henry would have a cold drink and chat for a few minutes with Smitty and whoever else happened to come into the store. He began to know many of the black people by name.

After leaving Smitty's he would drive to the north side of town and park the police car in a conspicuous place near the city limits sign on the Atlanta highway. He did not arrest anyone for speeding. He wanted the truck drivers and traveling salesmen who drove regularly from Atlanta to Columbus and back to know that the town now had a police car, and the sight of the car was enough to slow anybody down. He stayed at this post for an hour or so, then drove back to the city hall to check in before going home for dinner. He spent an hour at dinner, fifteen minutes of it stretched on the living-room sofa in half a doze, then made another tour of the town, stopped at the drug store for an afternoon cup of coffee, and parked near the city-limit sign on the south side of town, the Columbus side, for an hour.

With all this routine he still had two or three hours of his day to spend looking for something to do. He passed it at city hall, making lists of things to do in the future, or at the firehouse, talking with Jimmy Riley and checking on the progress of the police station. He felt that when the building was complete he would not be at such a loss as to how to spend his time. After supper each night, just before bedtime, he drove to Main Street, parked the car, checked all the front door locks on all the stores, then got back into the car and made another quick tour of the town.

One rainy morning when the police station was nearly finished, a small man, neatly dressed in a brown tweed suit with a matching brown derby hat, walked in and introduced himself. "Chief Lee? Thought so." The man extended a hand which Will Henry found to be as soft as a child's. "T. T. Brown, National Law Enforcement Equipment Company, Incorporated. Sheriff Willis said to stop in and see you. Ah, I see you're making progress with your station. Mind if I have a look around?"

"Go right ahead, Mr. Brown." Will Henry followed him into the back of the building.

"Ah, see you took Skeeter's advice on making it roomy. Good, good. Oh, that won't do. Got to have a cement floor, no good putting bars around a pine floor, you'll have some booger prising 'em up and getting out of here, see what I mean?" Will Henry nodded. He was embarrassed that he had not thought of the floor.

"I suppose you're right about that, Mr. Brown. We'll need cement to set the bars in, too, I reckon."

"Now, about the bars, Chief, about the bars. You can't go having your local blacksmith make those, you know. Not that he wouldn't do his best job, of course. But you need a specially hardened steel for jail bars, and you need the right locks, too. We can make all that up for you at our factory."

"Well, now, I don't have approval from the city council for that sort of expenditure just yet. I'll—"

"Course you don't. Can't be expected to know about all this your first month on the job. Here, take this end of the tape measure, and we'll see what you've got here. We'll get you measured up, see how many locks and keys you'll need, and I'll get you an estimate drawn up right away so you can talk to your council. Just back right along there. Hold it." He scribbled in a black notebook. "Now, it's four cells, isn't it? Window in each. No, two against the firehouse wall. Tell you, though, I'd put a window in the end of the corridor there. You want as much ventilation as you can get in here. Now, that's four cells, two with windows, two extra windows; you can get one in over there, too, and four locks. Tell you, you'll want a door locking the whole jail area off, too. Basic security, that is. You going to screen one off for the ladies? That's one extra wall you're gonna need, too. There, I'll get that typed up in our Atlanta office and have it down to you all official in a day or two. Phone it in this evening. We're very quick about these things, Chief Lee, we know the needs of our Georgia law-enforcement officers, and we don't want the law waiting to be enforced, do we? No, siree. Now, you'll be wanting some personal equipment, I expect."

"Well, yes. Why don't we go around to the firehouse where we can sit down? Jimmy'll have some coffee over there, too."

"Fine, Fine. I'll just get my cases out of the car." The little man hauled two very large leather sample cases out of his car and deposited them on the firehouse floor. "I'll need a hand with the trunk. Two hands wouldn't hurt." Will Henry and Jimmy Riley helped Brown drag a small, extremely heavy, padlocked trunk into the building. "Thank you, Gentlemen." He began unstrap-

ping the two cases. "Now, let's start with some duty clothing. I'd
recommend three changes of uniform, summer and winter. You
can get by with two changes in the winter, but when the hot
weather comes in, you're gonna have to change every day if
you're gonna stay looking neat, and that's important to a law-
enforcement officer, of course. I'd say you're a stock standard
forty-two in the chest, am I right?" He whipped out a tape and
measured Will Henry's chest, waist, and trouser length. "Right,
thirty-four in the waist and thirty-one length. My trousers are all
thirty-two in the length, but no doubt your little lady can fix that
up for you. Now, I've got a real handsome uniform tunic here
that goes real well with a white shirt, but I'll admit that most of
my officers are happier with the heavy wool shirt without a
tunic. Suits real good for spring and all, and they wear the pea
jacket over it in the cold weather. What would be your preference, Chief?"

Will Henry, who had not seriously considered the wearing of
a uniform, was a bit taken aback, but he began to feel it would
be better to be properly uniformed. "I think the shirt should do
all right. I expect I can get by for now with just two changes,
though."

"Fine. Now you have your two shirts and two trousers there.
Here, slip into the pea jacket—that's what they call one something like this in the U.S. Navy, you know. There, that's a perfect
fit if I ever saw one. This is sure the cold weather for it, ain't it?
Now, here's your wet-weather gear."

Within a few minutes Will Henry was standing next to a pile
of clothing that reached his waist, and Brown was opening the
padlock on the trunk. Jimmy Riley, who had been watching the
uniform operation in a kind of trance, gasped. Will Henry reckoned Brown could arm a whole police force in a bigger town than
Delano with what was in the trunk. Brown took a green felt cloth
from the trunk and spread it over Jimmy Riley's firehouse card
table.

"Now," said Brown, lifting a large, squarish-looking pistol
from the case and polishing it with a corner of the cloth, "here's
your latest sidearm, the Colt .45 automatic pistol, as used by the
U.S. Army in the recent European war." He took an enormous
bullet from the trunk. "Fires a piece of metal that will knock a
man flat on his back if it only hits his outstretched hand. A big
wallop."

Will Henry picked up the pistol and held it gingerly. Brown sensed he had not yet suited his man to the weapon. He removed two more pistols, revolvers, from his trunk and placed them on the felt cloth. "Two very fine weapons, both from the house of Colt. A .32 revolver with a two-inch barrel, excellent piece for the detective or the officer who wants to conceal his weapon. Or your .38 revolver with your four-inch barrel. A fine police sidearm. I feel, myself, that this pistol will sooner or later become standard for most law-enforcement agencies." Will Henry picked up the pistol and pointed it at a spot on the wall. Then he quickly brought it down and fumbled for an entrance to the cylinder. He had had enough problems with "unloaded" pistols. Brown showed him the mechanism which allowed the cylinder to fall sideways. "I think this might be the best weapon for you, Chief Lee. Not as bulky as the .45, but a lot more impact than the .32. An excellent piece. Now, you're going to need an extra weapon around here, Chief. If you ever have to deputize a man you're going to have to arm him. You can't have a man showing up here with a .22 rifle or a .410 shotgun for police work. You ever shot much with handguns?"

"Not much."

Brown began hauling boxes of cartridges from the trunk. I'm going to leave you with a thousand rounds. That may sound like a lot, but you've got to go out in the country somewhere and practice a lot with the pistol. Not at all like using a rifle or shotgun. Different thing entirely. Now, you're going to need at least three pair of handcuffs. Hear you've already been in a two-cuff situation; handled it well, too. One key fits 'em all, so you don't have to worry about keeping track of a pocketful of keys." He held up a small blackjack similar to the one Skeeter Willis had shown Will Henry. "An officer's best friend." Brown dove into one of the other cases and came up with a holster and belt. "Handcuffs fit right in here; here's a place for a dozen extra rounds of ammunition; and your billy fits right here. All your equipment on one belt. Just buckle this on, and let's see how it fits." It fit.

"Now—"

"Let's see what all this comes to, Mr. Brown." Brown whipped out an order pad and began writing furiously. "I'm sure you'll find every item on this list absolutely necessary in time, Chief. I've been equipping peace officers for twelve years now, and I can honestly say that I've never overequipped one yet. Now, let's see. That's two winter uniforms, shirt and trousers, three summer uniforms—that's first-grade military khaki there, sir—shirt and trousers, one pea jacket, one winter hat, one summer hat, two black neckties, one holster and belt with attachmants for extra ammunition, handcuffs, and blackjack, one blackjack, two Colt .38 pistols, three pair of handcuffs, and one thousand rounds of .38 ammunition. That comes to exactly three hundred forty-nine dollars and forty-five cents."

Will Henry looked narrowly at the little man. "Couldn't you think of anything to spend the other fifty-five cents on?"

Brown grinned. "I always like to see a department come in under budget." He reached into an inside pocket and withdrew a thin leather case. "By the way, Chief. Just as a token of our esteem and congratulations on your new post, the National Law Enforcement Equipment Company, Incorporated, would be honored if you'd accept this little gift." He opened the box and set it on the green felt. Inside were three badges, large, medium, and small. Each bore the legend Delano Police Department and the designation Chief. "One's for your shirt, the middle-sized one clips onto your cap, and the little one"—he took a small leather wallet from his pocket and pinned the smallest badge into it—"this is for carrying when you're in civilian clothes. It's gold plated."

Will Henry picked up the order blank and signed it. "Mr. Brown, you sure come prepared, don't you?"

"Chief, I know my business, and I know my officers' business. I know what they need to do the job." He turned to Jimmy Riley. Now, just let me run out to the car for a minute. I've got a few things you're going to be needing."

Will Henry gathered his things and left Jimmy Riley to the tender mercies of T. T. Brown.

10 SINCE THE NEW police station was simply being added onto the already-planned fire station, building proceeded quickly. Will Henry had been chief for less than a month when it was completed. On the Saturday night before the Monday when the station was to be officially open, he and Hugh Holmes were hard at work in the new building. T. T. Brown's custom-made bars, doors, windows, and locks had arrived during the week, and their installation had been completed the day before. Holmes had purchased a roll-top desk, two filing cabinets, four straight-backed chairs, a swivel chair, and a hat rack. The cells had been furnished with wooden bunks, cotton mattresses, and army blankets, and a large potbellied stove was glowing in the office. Will Henry was tacking wanted posters to a new bulletin board, and Holmes, his shirt sleeves rolled up, was sweeping up excelsior, in which the new furniture had been packed. A man from the telephone company had just left. The new instrument had been hung on a wall next to a window opening into the firehouse, so that it could be answered from the other side. The telephone rang.

Will Henry put down his box of thumbtacks and answered it. It was Estelle, the night operator. "Is that you, Mr. Lee? Chief?"

"Yes, Estelle. How're you?"

"I'm just fine, but I've got a lady on the line who's nearly 'bout hysterical. She says there's something terrible happening over on Maple Street." The streets on the north side of the M&B tracks were all named after trees. They were lined with nearly identical white houses built by Thomas Delano to house his work force.

"Well, you better connect her with me, here. You can do that, can't you? I mean, the phone is all hooked up, isn't it?"

"Yessir. Here she is." There was a click, and Will Henry could hear someone breathing irregularly, as if trying to suppress sobs.

"Hello. Hello, this is Will Henry Lee. Chief Lee. What's the matter?"

"Oh, thank God!" a woman's voice said. "I'm so glad I got hold of you! The operator said there was a phone in the jail now. I'm so glad you was there."

"Yes, I'm here. Now what's the matter? What's wrong?"

The woman continued in a loud whisper. "You've got to come over here quick. He's going to kill her this time if you don't get here quick! I can hear him now, and she's crying again. I—"

"Who is this speaking?"

"I'm Mrs. Smith. My husband is James Smith. I'd send him over there to stop it, but he's on the night shift at the mill. He's stopped him before."

"Stopped who, Mrs. Smith?"

"That Butts man next door. He's beating her up again."

"I see. Now you're on Maple Street, is that right? Where is Maple Street?"

"On the corner. The corner of Poplar. They're right next door, at number four. We're number two. Can you come over here quick? He's going to kill her—"

"I'll be right there, Mrs. Smith. Now, you stay away from their house until I get there, you hear? Don't go in there" He hung up the phone and started to get into his coat. "Sounds like somebody's beating up a woman over in Milltown," he said to Holmes. Holmes reached for his coat.

"I'll come with you."

They started for the door. Will Henry stopped. He looked at the gun belt lying on his desk. He strapped it on and left the building.

Will Henry drove as quickly as he could through the Saturday-night shopping traffic. "I've got to get a siren for this car," he said, blowing his horn at a mule and wagon blocking his way.

"Get it," said Holmes grimly. "I'll fix up the money."

"You know a man named Butts?"

"Grady Butts? Works at the mill?"

"I guess that's the one."

"I know his wife, Mary. She saves a dollar a week at the bank. Never misses a week. Never met him. Don't think he knows she's putting the money away. She always comes in alone. Pretty, in a plump sort of way. She's got forty-two dollars in her account. Forty-two weeks, forty-two dollars."

Will Henry wondered if Holmes had every account at the bank in his head. "A Mrs. Smith who lives next door to them says it's happened before. The way she talks you're going to lose a customer unless this damn mule and wagon gets out of the way." He drove around the wagon, blowing his horn.

As they pulled up in front of the house a woman stepped from behind a tree and ran to the car. "Oh, hurry! It's getting worse! He's going to kill her!" They heard the noise of something being knocked over, and the light against the shades on the front windows of the house changed its angle sharply.

Will Henry ran up the front steps, closely followed by Holmes. He stopped at the front door. The noise inside had stopped. He banged on the door. "Open the door! This is the police." Now he could hear a woman sobbing.

"There's no trouble here," a man's voice said. The words were slurred. "Go on away from here."

Will Henry turned the knob and pushed the door open. The room was surprisingly neat. Will Henry had expected a shambles. A worn three-piece living-room suite occupied most of the room. A cheerful little fire was burning in the fireplace. Through a door at the back of the living room, he could see a dining table set for supper, and there was food on the table. The only upset in the room was a tiny table which had held a lamp. The table and lamp were sprawled across the floor, but the bulb was still burning. A small, plump woman stood with her back to the wall next to the fireplace. She was crying, and with every sob a spurt of blood came from her nose. The front of her cotton dress was soaked in blood, and it had begun to drip onto the floor.

Across the room from her stood a thin, wiry-looking man of medium height, dressed immaculately in a white shirt, necktie, and what must have been the trousers to his Sunday suit. His hair was slightly mussed, his face was red and twisted with anger, and he held a large lump of coal in his right hand. It occurred to Will Henry that the man had been about to hit his wife with the lump of coal. This thought so astonished him that he stood for several seconds without saying anything. The woman's sobs were the only sound in the room.

"There's no trouble here," the man said. He seemed to be drunk.

Will Henry said, "Put that piece of coal down." The man looked at the coal in his hand and seemed surprised to find it there. He dropped the coal onto the linoleum floor.

"This here's private property. This's my house. Get away from here. None y'business." Holmes stepped toward the woman, pulling a handkerchief from his pocket. "Stay 'way from her," the man said. Holmes took the woman by the arm and led her to a chair.

"Here, now, Mrs. Butts. You just hold this handkerchief to your nose." An eye was swollen shut. Will Henry thought it would be very black within hours. He began to grow angry.

"Get outta my house," the man said.

"Shut up," Will Henry replied.

"You got no right—"

Will Henry hit the man with his open hand. "I said shut up. Stand over there by the wall until I get ready to talk to you." The man backed up to the wall, holding his hand against his cheek. He looked like an outraged child who had been picked on by a bully. Will Henry went and looked closely at the woman's face. She rolled her eyes in his direction and mumbled something about everything being all right.

"You're not all right, Mrs. Butts. You've got a terrible black eye there, and your nose looks like it could be broken. Anyway, we can't fix that here, we're going to have to get you over to Dr. Mudter's and let him fix you up."

"Baby," the woman said through her sobs. She rolled her eyes toward a bedroom door.

Will Henry turned to the front door, where the petrified Mrs. Smith stood watching. "Ma'am, could you look after the baby tonight? I expect Dr. Mudter will want her to stay at his clinic tonight." The woman nodded and went to the bedroom. "Mrs. Smith from next door will take care of the baby until tomorrow," he said to Mrs. Butts.

"Now, listen here," said the husband.

"I told you to shut up. Hugh, could you get her into the car?

Put her in the front seat with us." Holmes helped the woman to her feet and led her out of the house. Mrs. Smith appeared at the bedroom door with a bundle. "Mrs. Smith, would you have a look around here and take what you need for the baby, and then close up the house and turn off the lights when we're gone?" The woman nodded. "And will you please call up Dr. Frank Mudter and tell him we're on the way over there?" She nodded again.

"Now, listen," said Butts. He was beginning to become agitated again. "You got no right."

Will Henry stopped himself from hitting the man again, but he wanted to humiliate him somehow. He reached behind him for his handcuffs. He knew there was no need for them, but he very much wanted to humiliate the man. "Come here," he said.

The man shrank back against the wall. "Now, listen—"

"Come *here*!"

The man edged fearfully over to him. "Hold out your hands."

"Now, listen—"

"Hold out your hands!"

The man held out his hands. Will Henry handcuffed him. "Now, go out and get in the back seat of my car. You won't get lost, will you? Just get in the back seat, and don't say anything to Mr. Holmes or your wife." The man started to speak. "If I hear one more word out of you I'm going to take this blackjack and do to you just what you did to your wife." The man turned and hurried to the car. Will Henry stood in the living room chewing his lower lip. He was breathing very fast; his lungs seemed too full of air.

The Smith woman was still standing there. "Will you be all right with the baby, Mrs. Smith? Can you take care of all this all right and call the doctor?"

"Yes, sir," she said. "I'll take care of everything here."

Will Henry left the house and got into the car. Holmes had the woman's head on his shoulder and was holding the sodden handkerchief. All the way to the doctor's house Will Henry was torn between his concern for the woman and his hatred of her husband. He said as little as possible.

Frank Mudter was standing shivering on his front steps in a bathrobe when they arrived. He helped Holmes put the woman inside. "You leave her with us, Will Henry. Martha and I will get her fixed up and put her to bed. Call me tomorrow."

Will Henry and Holmes walked back to the car. Butts was

huddled in the back seat, saying nothing. "Will Henry, I think if I'm ever at that jail again when you get a call, I think I'll pass up the opportunity to go with you," Holmes said. "I'm just not cut out for seeing things like that."

Will Henry had not realized how shaken Holmes was. He had handled the woman very well, but Will Henry could see that he was trembling. He hoped Holmes had not noticed how upset he himself was.

"I'm glad you did come, Hugh. I don't know what I'd of done without you tonight. I'm going to go downtown and inaugurate our new jailhouse now."

Holmes glanced into the car. "It couldn't happen to a nicer fellow," he said.

Since Holmes lived only across the street from the doctor, Will Henry left him there and drove to the police station. The lights were still burning. He took Butts into the jail area, took the handcuffs off, and locked him into a cell. "It's freezing in here," said Butts. He was beginning to sober up.

"There's four blankets in that cell, one on each bunk," Will Henry said to the man. "That'll have to do you, because I'm not about to start building fires for bastards like you. For all I care, you can freeze to death tonight." He slammed shut the main door to the jail area and locked it. "Tomorrow I'm going to see how many things I can charge you with. You've beat that woman up for the last time."

He locked the building and went home.

That night he had trouble getting to sleep. "I've got to learn not to get mad on this job," he told Carrie. "I swear, I hate being mad. I think it's punishing me more than that man down in the jail." He finally fell asleep in her arms, as she rubbed the back of his neck. It was another half hour before she fell asleep.

The following afternoon Mrs. Butts came to the jail in a taxi and told Will Henry she would not press any charge against her husband. She would not listen to any argument. Will Henry let the man out of his cell, and the couple went home together in the taxi. Will Henry was furious.

11 ON MONDAY MORNING Will Henry rose, bathed, shaved, and, for the first time, dressed in his uniform. Carrie had cuffed the trouser bottoms and pressed everything. He pinned the large badge to his shirt and affixed a second one to his cap. He had not worn a badge before, but he had kept the small gold one in his pocket.

"You look real handsome," Carrie said when he came down to breakfast. She handed him a small gift-wrapped box. "Here's a finishing touch to your uniform from the children and me." The box contained a gold tie clasp adorned with a tiny replica of his badge.

"Now where on earth did you get a thing like that?"

"I ordered it from the same company in Atlanta that made your badges." He kissed her and thought that the fine hand of T. T. Brown was evident here.

Will Henry arrived at the station at a quarter to eight and built a fire in the wood stove. He and Carrie had spent two hours after church the night before giving the place a final cleaning and putting it in order before its official opening. Idus Bray was the first to arrive, a few minutes before nine. He ambled in as though the thought had just struck him that he might stop by, and then he went over the building in minute detail. Finally, he seemed satisfied that the city's money had been properly spent. "Phone working all right?" he asked, patting the instrument.

"Just fine, Idus. Had our first call Saturday night, before we were even officially open for business."

"Yeah, heard about that. Man ought not to beat his wife like that. Still, seems like something our police force shouldn't have to spend its time on."

"Well, I guess that comes under the heading of keeping the peace. Can't let folks go beating each other up, even in their own homes."

Bray grunted what seemed agreement.

The other council members wandered in over the next hour, and a number of passers-by stopped in. All complimented Will Henry and Holmes on the thoroughness with which the station had been planned and equipped. Skeeter Willis put his stamp of approval on the jail and admired Will Henry's new uniform, much to Will Henry's embarrassment. He wondered how long it would take for him to become used to wearing it.

Finally, they returned to their businesses, and Will Henry was left alone. George Pittman, the postman, came by with the mail, peeked into the jailroom, and fled as if afraid that he would be held there if he stayed too long. Will Henry sat down and started to open the mail.

He heard the sound of someone vigorously opening the door and wiping his feet on the doormat just inside. He looked up from the mail in time to see Foxy Funderburke marching through his office toward the jailroom. He got up and followed. Foxy marched briskly in and out of each of the four cells, felt the mattresses, flushed the toilets, stamped on the floor, looked under the bunks, and tested the strength of the bars.

"Morning, Foxy."

"Lee."

Foxy stood in the aisle between the cells and looked about. He seemed irritated because he had found nothing amiss. He stalked past Henry into his office and gave the place a cursory glance. Will Henry was annoyed. "Can I offer you a cup of coffee, Foxy?" He could think of nothing else to say.

"Never drink the stuff. Eat your insides out." Will Henry felt as if he had spoken above his rank.

Foxy stared at him fixedly for half a minute without speaking. Will Henry felt forced to look away. He went to his desk and began shuffling through the mail.

"You're not the man for this job, Lee."

Will Henry looked blankly at Foxy, startled by the statement. "I'll do the best I can, Foxy. Look, I hope there's no hard feelings between us because I got this job. I—"

"You'll never survive. Somebody's going to kill you."

There was a brief silence while the two men stared at each other. Finally Will Henry spoke. "Well, if you hear about anybody planning to do that, I wish you'd tell me about it." Foxy stared coldly at him for another ten seconds, then executed a nearly military turn to the right and stamped out of the station.

Will Henry was baffled by the exchange. He was not accustomed to dealing with people who did not make sense, and there was something about Foxy which transcended the silly eccentricity most people ascribed to him. There was something angry and—menacing. It made Will Henry uneasy.

12 APART FROM the incident of the inept bank robbers, Will Henry's first month as chief had been free of any serious demands upon him as a policeman. He had had a period of adjustment, an opportunity to ease into the job, to begin to feel comfortable in it, without the pressure of major incident. On the Wednesday following the opening of the police station his period of adjustment came to an end.

He arrived at the police station on the stroke of eight, to find a young boy sitting on the doorstep, clutching a hound dog and weeping as though the end of the world were at hand. Will Henry knew the boy from church. He was called Brother, as his sister was called Sister.

"Good morning, Brother," Will Henry said as casually as he could. He didn't want to show too much concern for fear of increasing the weeping; it was a technique he used when his children came to him with stubbed toes. "What can I do for you? What's the problem?" Brother almost collapsed with relief, but every time he began a sentence his sobbing and gasping overtook his speech. Will Henry sat down beside him on the steps. "Now, just take it easy. Take your time and get your breath back. I've got all day, no need to rush." Brother gradually collected himself enough to speak.

"There's this fellow out in the woods." He stopped.

"Out in the woods."

"Yessir, right next to the Scout hut, right at the bottom of Hodo's Bluff."

"What's this fellow doing, Brother?"

"He's not doing nothing, sir. He's dead."

Will Henry took a quick breath. "You ever seen a dead person, Brother?"

"No, sir."

"Well, how do you know he's dead?" Will Henry thought maybe the boy had come upon a bum sleeping in the woods.

"Well, he's nekkid, sir. And there's ants in his eyes."

Brother Maynard had awakened with a start at exactly six o'clock on that morning. He did not need an alarm clock. He brushed his teeth and dressed, and then went to the kitchen. He fried an egg and two strips of bacon and made a sandwich of them, wrapping the sandwich carefully in waxed paper. His dog, Buster, who was almost a purebred beagle, watched with interest and earned a scrap of bread for his attention. Brother's name was John, but his parents had called him Brother and his sister Sister for all of their lives, and so had everyone else. Brother was fourteen.

He dressed warmly and rode his bicycle to the M&B depot, Buster trotting alongside. At near enough to six-thirty, the Atlanta train pulled into the station and dropped off 400 *Atlanta Constitutions.* Brother counted out 172 and folded each of them into a tight three-cornered hat, warming himself next to the pot-bellied stove in the stationmaster's office. He placed the papers in neat rows in the large grocery bike basket, then pedaled around virtually the entire "town" (as opposed to "mill town") side of the railroad tracks, tossing papers accurately onto front porch after front porch. He rarely tossed a paper onto a roof or under a porch any more. Finally, he pedaled laboriously up Broad Street, up the mountainside, where there were eleven more subscribers. He always saved this part until last, so that he could enjoy the ride down the mountain. His final delivery was invariably to the solitary mailbox which Foxy Funderburke had erected at the crest of the mountain, exactly on the city limit, so that he would not have to come all the way into Delano for his paper. Foxy's house was a mile further along, on the Talbot County side of the mountain.

When Brother had delivered Foxy's *Constitution*, he turned off the road onto the footpath the Boy Scouts had built from the crest of the mountain, past the Scout hut to the end of Fourth Street. The path was wide and smooth enough for his bicycle, and Brother relished the thought of the long, steep, practically straight coast down the mountainside. The sun had risen now, and half the mountain was in bright new sunlight, the other half in cold blue shadow. Brother began his descent, and his speed increased rapidly. He had never been able to bring himself to make the whole coast without once using his brakes, but this morning he was determined. The bicycle went faster and faster. Buster began to drop back on the path, too winded to bark more than once or twice. Brother's eyes were almost closed from the force of the wind. Tears streamed down his cheeks. His hands grew numb as the wind rushed through his woolen mittens. His forehead, cheeks, and the bridge of his nose hurt furiously from the cold. It occurred to him that if he struck a stone or a fallen limb his battered body would probably not stop rolling until it reached the Scout hut.

There was a jolt as the path turned slightly uphill, then leveled off as it approached the hut. Finally, he applied the brakes and brought the bike to a halt at the foot of Hodo's Bluff, which rose nearly a hundred feet straight up the mountainside. He leaned the bike against a tree and flopped down in the leaves and pine needles, his heart pounding wildly. Buster trotted up and dropped beside him like a stone. They both panted for a minute, before Brother regained enough strength to open his sandwich. Buster wolfed down his small piece and hoped against all odds for more.

Brother pushed back until he was resting against the foot of the bluff. He munched his sandwich and looked lazily around him. The early morning sun filtered through the pines and the haze. Everything more than a few feet away had a fuzzy, out-of-focus quality that Brother found particularly pretty. He especially liked the way the sunlight struck the smooth faces of a number of granite boulders which were embedded in the earth and pine needles around him. The low angle of the light and the smoothness of the stones gave them the texture of the hides of fallen beasts—elephants, maybe, felled by the gun of some mighty hunter. The texture of one smaller boulder in particular caught his eye. It was whiter than the others, probably from a covering of dead, gray moss. As he chewed his sandwich and stared at the rock it seemed to change in texture, as if his eyes had suddenly reappraised an optical illusion. There was something familiar about that texture, something he had seen only this morning. He recalled with an unpleasant jolt that it was the texture of his own skin, which he had inspected while dressing before the mirror that morning, longing for a summer tan.

He got slowly to his feet and approached the stone. He stopped chewing the sandwich. An acidic foreboding crept into his bowels. As he walked toward the boulder it became, unmistakably, a buttock, and as he drew closer the new angle revealed part of a back and a shoulder and, finally, a closely cropped head, turned sharply to the right. The nose and jaw were covered by leaves, but there was an eye, and it was open. A column of ants wound in and out of it. Buster came over and sniffed at the corpse. Brother dropped his sandwich and ran. Buster collected the sandwich before following.

Will Henry thought fast as he listened to Brother's story. He didn't want to spread news of this sort on the telephone. He might as well go to Atlanta and put it on WSB. "Tell you what, Brother. You run over to the funeral home and tell Mr. Maddox I said for him to come out to the Scout hut with his ambulance. I'll go pick up Dr. Mudter, and we'll meet you there in a couple of minutes. He's right at the foot of Hodo's Bluff, you say?"

"You say he's naked? In this weather?" Frank Mudter huddled down into his overcoat and put his hand under the dash of the police car to see whether any heat was coming out.

"That's what Brother said. He was pretty shook up, of course. He said something about the fellow having ants in his eyes, too. Sounds like he might be imagining the whole thing. I hope so."

Will Henry stopped the car as close as he could get to the Scout hut, and they walked the rest of the way.

Dr. Mudter knelt beside the corpse. "Well, Brother was right. He's sure naked. Right about the ants, too." Will Henry shuddered. "Give me a hand, Will Henry, let's turn him over." Will Henry was horrified at touching the cold flesh but tried not to show it. "Nothing but superficial wounds. No gunshot or stab wounds that I can see." A car door slammed in the distance. Dr. Mudter stood up.

"How did he die, then, Frank? Did he fall off the bluff?"

"I don't think there's any question about that, Will Henry. Question is, what happened to him before he fell down here? What was he doing running around up there naked as a jay-bird?"

"Well, first thing comes to my mind is, there's only one thing around here that's bizarre enough to go with this."

"Klan?"

Will Henry nodded. "They horsewhipped a man up at Greenville two years ago. White man fooling around with a colored girl. But this is just a boy. What would you say, eighteen, nineteen?"

Will Henry glanced at the corpse involuntarily. "Yes, I guess so. How long would you say he's been dead?"

"Well, the rigor's still there. Less than twenty-four hours, maybe less than twelve. We can take his body temperature as soon as we can get him back. That might help. Temperature was in the twenties last night. Can't be more than twenty-five right now, and he's not frozen. Tell you the truth, Will Henry, this isn't my line of work. I generally get to 'em before they go, you know?"

"Well, Frank, I've almost certainly got a criminal case on my hands. I mean, this doesn't look like any kind of accident to me, not like I've ever heard of, anyway. There's going to have to be a thorough investigation of this, and it ought to start with a medical examination. Hadn't we better get somebody down here from Atlanta to see about this? You know anybody?"

Lamar Maddox came striding through the leaves carrying one end of a stretcher. Brother Maynard trotted along behind with the other end, followed by Buster.

"Morning, Frank, Will Henry. What we got here?"

"You know as much as we do, Lamar. We just got here. I was just asking Frank if he knows somebody in Atlanta, an expert, who could do a thorough medical examination."

Brother interrupted. " 'Scuse me, Chief, but I'm already fifteen minutes late for school. Can I go now, please?"

"Sure, Brother, and thanks for letting me know about this. You did the right thing."

"Uh, Chief, could you give me a note or something? You have to bring a note if you're late."

Will Henry took out his notebook and wrote, "To whom it

may concern: Brother Maynard is late for school this morning because he was helping the police with a confidential matter. If there is any further question, please telephone me." He signed and dated the note and gave it to the boy.

"Listen, Brother. We don't know yet what's happened here. Word'll get around about this sooner or later, but right now I don't want any talk about it, all right? I don't want you to tell anybody about this until—until you read about it in the paper, all right?" Will Henry thought for a moment. "And even then, I don't want you to tell anybody, and I mean *anybody*, about his not having any clothes on. That could be very important, and nobody's to know about it but us, all right?"

"Yessir, I promise." Brother hopped on his bicycle and rode off to school.

"You think he'll keep this to himself?" Frank Mudter asked.

"Lord, I hope so. Frank, you and Lamar have got to help me keep this thing under control. For the time being, when it comes up, let's just say that it looks like a fellow got lost and fell off the bluff. This is going to be hard enough to handle without a lot of hysteria. All right?"

Both men nodded. Frank Mudter looked thoughtful. "Will Henry, I've got an old med-school friend in Columbus who's pretty much of a hotshot pathologist. He's done a job now and then for the Columbus police. I could call him up and ask him if he'll drive up here and do a postmortem. His fee could run to twenty-five or thirty dollars if you figure he's got to travel, but I think the council will sit still for that."

"That sounds good to me, Frank. Is there any reason we shouldn't move him now?"

"I don't think so. You reckon we can get him on the stretcher and in your hearse like he is, Lamar?"

"No problem, Frank." Lamar Maddox was, by profession, a stoic.

At the funeral parlor, Dr. Mudter telephoned Columbus. He came back into the workroom, where Will Henry was eyeing the syringes and tubing uneasily. "Well, I had to promise him a fried-chicken supper—he's a bachelor—but he's coming as soon as he can get away from the hospital. He figures to be here about four. In the meantime we're to take the temperature and then keep the body as cool as possible. Lamar, could we put him in your storage room and open a window?"

"Sure, I guess so. What are you going to take the temperature with? I don't get much call for thermometers from my customers."

"I guess I better run back to the office and get an anal thermometer."

Will Henry spoke up. "Frank, I don't think there's any more I can do here. I better check in at the station and see if anything's happening, then I've got some investigating to do, I guess."

"Why don't you come back here about four. He'll do his postmortem first, and then we'll have supper at my house. I'll get Martha and the children to go down and have supper with Carrie, and Nellie can leave as soon as she's cooked. That way we can talk about this by ourselves."

"Fine. Maybe I'll know a bit more myself by then."

13 WILL HENRY sat down at his desk and took a pad and pencil from a drawer. He noticed that his hand was trembling. He was filled with the most curious mixture of emotions. He was angry that someone had caused the boy to die; he was sickened by the thought of the boy wandering, probably pursued, through the woods; and he was terribly excited. He felt guilty about it, but he was excited that he suddenly had a major crime to investigate, to solve, so soon in his new job. He had no doubt that he could do it. He thought that a professional soldier must feel the same way about a declaration of war; regretful, but eager. He began to list the things that must be done.

1. Question everybody who lived anywhere near where the body was found.

2. Check with Atlanta for any persons recently reported missing.

3. Check the top of Hodo's Bluff for evidence.

4. Check on Klan activities.

5. Telephone Skeeter Willis.

6. Go see Harmon Everson.

He could think of nothing else to do, at least until the medical examination was done. He telephoned the state police in Atlanta. There were no missing-persons reports that matched his victim.

He telephoned Skeeter Willis. "Skeeter, you might want to drop by here today or tomorrow if you get a chance."

"What's up, Will Henry?"

"Interesting development. Not much more I can tell you right now."

"I get you." Skeeter had telephone operators to deal with, too.

"If I'm not here when you come, get Jimmy Riley to give a blast on the fire siren. We've got a signal worked out. I'll come back to the station."

"Probably be tomorrow morning before I can get down there. Can it wait until then?"

"That'll be fine. I'm here from eight o'clock."

He knew how to check on the Klan, but that would have to wait until he had questioned the householders near Hodo's Bluff. He would save Harmon Everson until last. He wanted to know as much as possible before he talked to the press, even to the editor of the *Messenger*.

Two hours later, he had talked with people at nine houses on the mountainside. Nobody had seen, heard, or noticed anything unusual the night before, except for one woman who had heard something crashing through the bushes sometime after midnight. She thought nothing of it; deer and other animals were about; she often heard them. There was nobody home at one house, and a neighbor said they were away for a week, visiting relatives in Waycross. Only the visit to Foxy Funderburke was left, that and the inspection of Hodo's Bluff. Foxy lived down the other side of the mountain and seemed the least likely of Will Henry's prospects to have seen or heard anything, but Will Henry was not looking forward to interviewing Foxy.

He drove slowly up the gravel road to the Funderburke cabin. The road wound back and forth up the mountain and was very steep in places, but it was well cared for, not rough at all. Foxy probably didn't get too many visitors, not with his personality, so the road didn't get worn down much from trafic. Still, Will Henry figured Foxy must be spending a good bit of money keeping it so well, since it was not a county road, but private. The road turned and fell away slightly downhill before the tall pines gave way to a large cleared space. The cabin stood squarely across the road, and on each side of the house were matching flower beds. There was nothing blooming this time of year, but Will Henry thought the place must look very pretty in spring. A profusion of azaleas formed a background for the beds, and two quite large dogwood trees faced each other in front of the house. He had expected something much rougher and was surprised that Foxy had spent so much effort to make the place beautiful. It was obvious how Foxy, who had no regular job and needed none, occupied much of his time. Still, in midwinter it failed to be beautiful. The place had an oddly regimented orderliness about it, as if it were part of some eccentric military reservation. It was a lot like Foxy. Will Henry immediately felt like an intruder.

He got out of the car and approached the house. The place seemed deserted. There was no answer to his knock at the front door. He walked around to the back of the house, peering into windows. The rooms seemed almost unnaturally neat. There was a large shed at the back. Will Henry peeked through the crack between the padlocked doors. Foxy's pickup truck stood inside. He walked back to the house and looked through a kitchen window. It was much the same as the other rooms—neat, cold, well equipped, orderly. Only in the kitchen was there a touch of disarray. The chairs surrounding the little kitchen table were in the process of being recaned. Two of them had complete new backs and seats, one was half done, and the fourth was stripped down to the bare wood, waiting its turn. Foxy seemed to have a number of manual skills.

Will Henry froze. There had been a tiny, almost surreptitious, sound, then silence. Then there was an explosive sound of something striking wood and the creak of metal. Will Henry spun to his right, clawing for his pistol. He found himself facing a large, placid golden Laborador retriever. The dog approached him, everything wagging. Will Henry sagged against the house with relief. He felt a complete fool. He scratched the dog behind the ears. Why had he drawn his pistol? Why did he feel threatened on Foxy's property? He realized he was, irrationally, still very afraid. His heart was pounding, and he was sweating in spite of the cold. There was more to it than being startled by the dog.

"How are you, old fellow? You scared me real good, there." There was another scraping. The dog turned to the back door leading into the kitchen and pushed the lower panel with her nose. It swung back, and five puppies tumbled through the opening. "Sorry, it's old girl, isn't it?" The puppies, which seemed to be five or six weeks old, surged around his ankles,

yapping and stumbling over his feet. He squatted and played
with them for a moment, and his anxiety ebbed away. The bitch
and her puppies made the place seem less threatening. He
walked to the door, tucked the puppies through the flap, gave
their mother a pat, and walked back to the car. She came with
him and sat in front of the cabin, watching, as he drove away.

Will Henry drove down the track from Foxy's cabin to the
main road, continued for a mile, then turned left up the Scenic
Highway, as the road was called which ran along the crest of Pine
Mountain, overlooking Delano. He drove another mile until he
came to the bottom of a steep dip in the road known as Hodo's
Gap, named for a reclusive old Cherokee Indian who had lived
in a shack near the spot until his death years ago. Hodo, said to
have been in his nineties, had fallen to his death from the bluff
which bore his name.

Will Henry parked the car and began picking his way through
the woods toward the bluff. Even in winter the going was slow,
and he moved clumsily through the thick growth. He looked for
signs that someone had been through these woods before him,
but he saw nothing. Shortly before reaching the edge of the bluff,
he thought he heard the sound of someone else moving. He
stopped for a moment and listened, but heard nothing; so he
continued.

Abruptly, he reached the edge of the bluff. He had been expecting the undergrowth to clear at the edge, but it did not. He
knew he had arrived there only because he could see a few feet
ahead to clear air, and because he knew the bluff was ahead. It
was easy to see how someone who did not know about the bluff,
traveling at night, could simply walk over the edge, especially if
he were in a hurry, if he were running from something. Looking
over the edge he could see nothing that would tell him anything
about what had happened. He was disappointed, for he had half
expected to find some obvious clue to what had happened—a
piece of clothing caught on a thorn which could be traced to its
owner; a footprint with a distinctive mark on the heel; some
small, personal item which would identify the pursuers or the
pursued. But there was nothing.

He began to work his way to the right, where the thicket appeared to be less thick, and he nearly ran head-on into Foxy Funderburke, standing with his feet planted apart, holding a 30-30
lever-action rifle stiffly at port arms. Even in the sudden shock of

finding Foxy there, Will Henry noticed that the hammer of the rifle was cocked.

"Good Lord, Foxy, you scared me half to death! What are you doing up here?"

Foxy's face was impassive, lacking even his usual tight-lipped grimace. "Hunting. What are you doing?"

"Having a look around. I stopped by your house to see you, but there was nobody there but your dog and her puppies. Nice animal." Will Henry thought he noticed some tiny reaction at the mention of the visit to the house. "The puppies for sale? I've been thinking about getting a dog for my children. None of the farm dogs could have lived in a house in town."

"Haven't given it much thought. Why did you want to see me?"

"I just wanted to know if you heard anything, anything or anybody, around your place last night."

"No."

"Nobody in the woods or anything?"

"No. What was I supposed to have heard?"

"I had a report the Klan might of been having a gathering up here somewhere last night."

"They get together in a pasture the other side of the road"—he pointed—"over yonder about half a mile. I generally hear the cars when they do. Didn't hear anything last night."

"Well, that's all I wanted to know. Is there a better way back to the road from here?"

"There's a path." Foxy motioned to his left. "After you."

Will Henry stepped past him and found the path. The going was much easier. It seemed to lead from the road directly to the bluff, then along the side of the mountain. It probably came out onto the Boy Scout trail further along. They walked single file, Foxy bringing up the rear. Will Henry thought about the cocked rifle at his back. He had not seen Foxy uncock it, and he began to feel uneasy with the man behind him. Neither of them said a word until they reached the road.

"Can I give you a lift back to your place?"

"I'll walk."

"Say, Foxy, what are you hunting up here with a thirty-thirty?"

"Bobcats."

"In the daytime, and without a dog?"

"I get one now and then."

Will Henry got into the car. "You let me know if you want to sell a puppy. I'd like a male. Billy and Eloise would be real glad to get one."

Foxy nodded noncommittally. Will Henry drove away. He watched Foxy in the rear view mirror until he crested the next hill. Foxy stood staring after the car, the cocked rifle in his hands, never moving.

14 WILL HENRY had one more stop to make, one more person to question, before he gave the newspaper his story. He felt that it would be the most important part of his investigation and that he must handle it well or perhaps lose all hope of solving the mystery of the boy's death and apprehending those responsible.

He entered the shop from the alley at the back. Even before he opened the door, the smell of leather reached him, and by the time he was inside it seemed to fill his lungs. It was not at all unpleasant. Tommy Allen was buffing a shoe on a large machine and did not hear him enter. Will Henry waited for him to finish before speaking.

"Tommy?"

Tommy Allen jumped. "Hey, there, Chief, you snuck up on me, there."

"Didn't mean to scare you. Think you might half-sole these shoes for me while I wait? They're my only black pair, and the city fathers might frown on brown shoes with the uniform."

"Be glad to. I'm not all that busy, anyway." He took the shoes from Will Henry and climbed onto his high stool and fitted the shoe over his last. "Might as well go ahead and let me put some heels and a whole sole on these shoes. They'll wear better and last longer."

"You're the doctor."

Tommy took a long-handled plierlike tool and began to expertly strip the soles off the shoes. "First I've seen of you since you got the chief's job. Haven't had a chance to congratulate you."

"Thank you, sir."

"I've been sort of expecting you to drop by, as a matter of fact."

"Oh? The Good Lord tell you when my soles are getting thin?"

"Come on, Will Henry, you look just like you used to look when we'd go down to the blacksmith shop and try to borrow Jesse Brown's new horseshoes to play with. Why, in a minute you'd of told me how it fascinates you to watch me fix these shoes." Will Henry was embarrassed in spite of himself. Tommy looked up from the shoe at him. "I reckon you want to know about the Klan, Will Henry."

"You always could see through me, Tommy. Yeah, I want to know about it. I know you never wanted to talk about it, but now I need to know, and you're the only fellow I can talk to."

"Well, I reckon it's not too big of a secret that I'm in the Klan, but like you say, I never talk about it to nobody."

"Why are you in it, Tommy? I never knew why. Always wanted to ask you."

"Well, a long time ago, old—well, a fellow took me to a meeting, and I was real impressed with the Bible reading and the praying. You know how daddy brought us up. And later on, when they got up to some high jinks I thought I'd get out, but I was able to hold 'em back a little bit, help keep 'em from getting out of hand. There's a few boys in there would be a lot of trouble to folks if there wasn't somebody to keep an eye on 'em."

"I expect there are."

"Yeah, and I figure with some older fellows to keep things in line, the Klan might get to be a little more responsible organization. There's a job to be done, you know. Somebody's got to keep the niggers in their place, and I don't know who else is going to do it, do you?"

Will Henry was silent.

"Well, don't get me started on that subject." Tommy was quiet for a moment as he brushed glue onto a strip of leather.

"Tommy, you wouldn't get mixed up in something really

bad, would you? You—" Will Henry stopped when he saw the expression on Tommy's face. "I'm sorry, I know you wouldn't. I was thinking about that story about the fellow up at Greenville last year getting horsewhipped for fooling around with a colored girl. Things like that."

"That was a bunch of Greenville boys, and I wouldn't of let it happen around here. I'd of seen that he got a good talking to, maybe scared him a little. Theatening to tell his wife would have been the best way."

Will Henry nodded, and they were both quiet again. The only sound in the little shop was that of Tommy's curved knife as he carved the leather to the size of the shoe.

"Tommy, something bad has happened, not in Greenville or Woodbury or Manchester, but right here in Delano. Last night."

Tommy stopped working. "Last night?" He looked worried. "There was a meeting last night, but it was a regular sort of meeting. Nothing unusual about it."

"This one got unusual, Tommy. Somebody got killed."

Tommy stared at him, frozen. "That's not possible," he said.

Will Henry slammed his palm down on the counter, and his voice became tight. "Dammit, Tommy, the boy's dead! He ran right off the bluff. The Maynard boy found him at eight o'clock this morning. He's up at Lamar Maddox's right now, and there's a doctor coming from Columbus this afternoon to examine him. Now, this thing has got Klan written all over it, and I want you to tell me anything you know about it."

Tommy was staring at him incredulously. "What bluff?"

"Hodo's Bluff, Tommy. It's no more than three hundred yards from the field. He ran, and he ran right off it. I figure he found an old path that leads down to the bluff and then turns toward the Boy Scout trail. He didn't turn. He went straight ahead." Will Henry paused for a moment. "How could this have happened, Tommy? How?"

"You mean the field on Pine Mountain? Will Henry, that field hasn't been used since we burned a cross last summer." Tommy reached under the counter, pulled out a Bible, and put his hand on it. "Listen to me, Will Henry, this is the truth, I swear to God. That meeting was held at somebody's house nowhere near Pine Mountain. All but one of our bunch was there, and he was home sick in bed. We were at that house 'til after midnight, and we left in ones and twos and went home. Nobody was excited about anything. Nobody was going after anybody. Everybody went home, and if it came to it, every one of us would be able to prove it."

Will Henry leaned forward and looked into the shoemaker's face. "You're sure about this, Tommy?" He said that because he couldn't think of anything else to say.

"Will Henry, that meeting was at *my* house."

By the time Will Henry reached the *Messenger* office it was late afternoon, and his excitement had soured. He had been almost certain that the Klan was connected with the boy's death, and now he was almost certain that it was not. His only hope of a quick solution now lay with the medical examination, and he could not imagine a doctor, however good, telling him much of great use in finding the murderers. He still thought there was more than one person involved. Perhaps it was the bizarre nature of the boy's death. It held overtones of a prank gone wrong, of a club initiation which had got out of hand. The killers, in his mind, were young, irresponsible. They had intended to frighten, not kill. But with the Klan out of the picture, he could not come up with a plausible substitute. If Delano had had a college he would have suspected some student group. The boy was not from Delano. Brother Maynard or one of the three men who had seen the body would have known him. He began thinking what colleges were within driving distance. There wa La Grange College, but that was a religious institution, not the sort that would have a student group that went in for violent hazing. There was nothing else at all near.

He walked into the storefront office of the *Delano Messenger* and closed the door behind him. Harmon Everson was sitting at his roll-top desk, his back to the door. He turned to see who had entered. The editor and owner of the weekly newspaper was wearing a green eyeshade, and black cuff guards protected his shirt. There was a smell of ink and paper in the air.

Everson looked up from his desk. "Evening, Will Henry, what can I do for you? If you want to place a classified ad, I'm afraid you're a little late."

"No, Harmon. I've got some news for you. Not very good news, I'm afraid."

"Pull up a pew. Something I should hold the paper for? We're just going to press."

"I expect you might want to." Everson walked across the

room and opened a door. The clatter of machinery came into the room.

"Henry, hold the paper for a few minutes. We might have something to go in." He returned to his desk, sat down, and waited.

"Harmon, you're going to have to exercise a little restraint on this."

"You trying to muzzle the press, Will Henry?"

"No, I want this in the paper, but I don't want my investigation hampered by a lot of sensationalism."

"You think the *Messenger* runs to sensationalism?" Harmon was shifting irritably in his seat.

"No, Harmon, I don't. But what's happened has some sensational aspects, and I don't want them in the paper."

"Well, you're just going to have to trust my judgment, Will Henry."

"No, I don't have to do that, Harmon. There's still time to get this in tomorrow morning's *Constitution*, and I'm sure the Atlanta papers would be happy to print it. Now, if you'd rather have it that way, you can pick up your story from them in time for next .week's *Messenger*. Or I'll write you out a short statement and won't answer any questions."

"Now, listen here, Will Henry—"

"I don't want to do it that way, Harmon. What I'd like to do is tell you what I know, every step along the way, but have you print just the basic facts for the moment, until I think it's time to print the whole story. Now, if you'll give me your word to print only what I authorize, then I'll tell you everything." Everson squirmed even more. He clamped his jaws together and stared angrily at Will Henry. "It's a murder, Harmon. A nasty case of manslaughter, at the very least."

"All right, Will Henry," Everson exploded. "You have my word. But you better not hold out on me. I want to know it all, theories and everything."

"I'll give you the facts as I know them. I'll keep my theories to myself." Will Henry squirmed a bit himself. "To tell you the truth, I'm a little short of theories."

"All right, all right, let's have it. We're holding up a press run."

Will Henry told him everything that happened, omitting only the identity of his Klan source.

"How much of this can I print?"

"For the moment, I think you'd better just say that the body of a young man was found at the foot of Hodo's Bluff and that he apparently fell off while walking through the woods the night before. You can say that we haven't identified him yet, but that we don't believe he's a local boy. You might say that if anybody knows of a young fellow missing from home they should get in touch with me right away."

Everson was scribbling rapid shorthand on a pad. "Description?"

"About five feet eight, a hundred and thirty pounds, sandy-colored hair." Will Henry paused for a moment, remembering. "Blue eyes."

"Age?"

"I don't want to be too specific about that until the doctor from Columbus has seen him, but I think you can safely say he's in his teens."

"Can I say you think somebody killed him?"

"For the moment say it appears to be accidental, but I'm investigating any possibility of foul play, if only to rule it out."

"Accidental! With the boy naked like that?"

"I don't want a word printed about his being naked, Harmon. That's the sort of thing that will get people a lot more upset than is good for anybody. Except for you and those of us who've seen the boy, nobody but whoever is responsible for this knows the boy was naked. I think it might be important to the investigation to keep it that way. Just print the straightforward story. You come meet the doctor at Lamar's and then have supper with us at Frank Mudter's tonight, and maybe you can say more next week, but I'm not promising anything."

"Do you think he was sexually abused?"

"What?"

"Did anybody cornhole him? There are people who do that kind of thing to youngsters, you know."

Will Henry was horrified. The thought had never even occurred to him. "How the hell should I know?" He was aware that he was blushing. "You can ask the doctor." He got up to leave. "He's due at the funeral home at about four. I'll see you there."

By the time Will Henry reached the front door, Everson was already banging away on his typewriter, and the chief was feeling a new kind of unease about his case.

15 ALTHOUGH WILL HENRY had had no real idea of the sort of man the visiting doctor would be, Carter Sauls surprised him. He was well over six feet tall and heavily built. Will Henry guessed he had been an athlete, probably a football player, in his college days, and he had only slightly run to fat. He was jocular and a bit loud, and he greeted Frank Mudter with gusto.

When the greetings were over and the small talk finished, Lamar Maddox ushered them into his workroom. A chemical smell, mixed with that of a kerosene heater, greeted them. The room was about twelve feet square and had a cement floor slanting into a drain in the middle. There was a large, deep sink on one side, beneath shelves stacked with bottles of chemicals and strange instruments. In the center of the room was a metal table, slanting slightly from head to foot, imprinted with a herringbone pattern of gullies, all emptying into a deeper one which ran down the center to the foot of the table. A large porcelain bucket stood ready to catch whatever might run from the table. The place was very neat.

"I think you'll find pretty much what you need," said Lamar Maddox, not without pride.

"Looks fine, fine," replied Carter Sauls. "Now all we need is a cadaver."

Maddox went into a back room and returned pushing a trolley containing the boy's body, covered with a heavy muslin sheet. A blast of cold air entered the room with him. "Had him in cold storage," said Maddox.

"He's not frozen, is he?"

"Oh, no. It's only about forty degrees back there."

The doctor had brought with him two cases; one a large black leather bag; the other an even larger wooden box with leather handles nailed to each end. He opened the box and began setting up a big bellows camera and a tin flood lamp.

"Thought we'd get a few pictures for both our files," he said to Will Henry. "I may do a book on forensic medicine one of these days." Will Henry nodded.

Lamar Maddox and Frank Mudter lifted the corpse from the trolley to the table and removed the sheet. Will Henry was again struck by the youth and vulnerability of the boy. He was lying in much the same position as they had found him, and the undertaker straightened his limbs and turned him onto his back. "Rigor's gone," said Maddox. Harmon Everson, the hard-boiled newsman, seemed frozen with pity. Sauls quickly took several photographs of the corpse from different angles, including closeups of the wrists, the rib cage, the buttocks, the neck, and the ankles. He began repacking the camera equipment into the wooden case.

"The boy was bound hand and foot and made to sit on something pretty uncomfortable," the doctor said to Frank Mudter and Will Henry, "and for quite a long time." Will Henry and Dr. Mudter exchanged a glance, but said nothing. "He was also beaten about the ribs and upper arms, but not, so far as I can see at the moment, about the face and head. Unusual."

Before Will Henry could question him further, the pathologist opened his bag and began to arrange his instruments neatly beside the sink. On the counter he placed three small scalpels of different sizes, large and small saws, forceps, a pair of heavy shears, scissors, and a large scalpel, the blade of which Will Henry nervously estimated to be at least eight inches long. The doctor also set out several gummed labels and a number of small fruit jars filled with a colorless liquid. Finally, he opened a leather notebook and placed his open fountain pen next to it. He began to pull on a pair of rubber gloves.

Will Henry felt uneasy about what seemed about to happen. "Uh, Doctor, are you going to do some kind of surgery?"

Sauls looked at him in surprise. "I'm going to conduct a thorough postmortem examination. I thought that was what you wanted. It's certainly what you need. You don't even know how he died, yet."

"Well, he fell—"

"Maybe he died from that fall, maybe he didn't. He could have died and then been thrown from that bluff. He could have died in any of a large number of ways."

Frank Mudter interrupted. "This is the way these things are done, Will Henry. This whole thing will just be a great big question mark until we have a postmortem. I've already told you about Carter's reputation in this field."

"Doctor, I'm sorry, I didn't mean to interfere with your work. I guess I just have a pretty sketchy idea of what goes on in these cases. Please do whatever you think is necessary."

Sauls smiled slightly, nodded, turned, picked up the large scalpel, inserted it at the point of the boy's chin, and drew it firmly down the abdomen, stopping in the scanty pubic hair. Harmon Everson made a kind of strangling noise. Will Henry was too stunned to make any sound.

Sauls made several quick incisions around the neck and chest, then picked up the shears, clipped the cartilages joining the ribs to the breastbone, and with both hands pulled away the entire front of the chest, leaving the abdominal cavity completely exposed, the boy's internal organs displayed. There was a loud dripping noise as the corpse began to leak into the bucket.

Sauls then cut around the lower jaw and freed the tongue muscle from its moorings. He took hold of the tongue and pulled downward through the open neck. Grasping the trachea and making deft motions with his scalpel, he pulled the attached heart and lungs from the corpse and dropped them into the sink.

Will Henry said dully, "I don't think you gentlemen need me for this," and repaired to the parlor of Lamar Maddox's funeral home, closely followed by a rather green Harmon Everson. The two men sank into the overstuffed furniture.

Everson's muffled voice came from between his knees, where he had placed his head. "Goddam butchers, all of 'em!" Will Henry was too weak to say anything.

There was a quiet moment after Carter Sauls had finished eating most of a fried chicken. Frank Mudter's house made tiny noises mixed with the muffled ticking of a huge clock in the hallway next to the dining room. A large crystal chandelier cast a weak light over the heavy dining-room table where the four men sat. Sauls had insisted on a supper uninterrupted by any talk of business. He and Frank Mudter had reminisced about their medical-school days and Sauls's football career. Dr. Sauls finally heaved a deep, satisfied sigh and began rummaging in a briefcase. "Frank, that colored woman of yours knows how to fry a chicken. And I never had a better biscuit in my life."

"You appeared to enjoy it, Carter. You can leave a little something for her in the kitchen if you want to."

"Hell, I may mention her in my will. Biscuits like that are a dying art." He straightened up a sheaf of notes and fished in a vest pocket for his reading glasses. "Now—" He looked at Will Henry and Harmon Everson, both of whom had eaten little and said less during the meal. Will Henry still felt weak.

"Fracture-dislocation of the cervical spine, at the level of the second and third vertebrae."

"We're laymen, Doctor," Everson said, pencil poised over notebook.

"The boy died of a broken neck, most probably suffered in the fall from the bluff."

"Probably?"

"I wasn't there, Mr. Everson. I can only surmise from the available evidence what happened to this boy. The injury is also consistent with hanging, for instance, but there are no other signs of hanging, either internal or external. If you'll permit me to continue without interruption until I'm finished, then I'll give you a better-educated guess than you'll get anywhere else in the southeastern United States, all right?"

"Sorry, Doctor, do go on."

"Thank you. I'll start at the beginning and give you the best summary I can of what I think happened to the boy. And I'll keep it colloquial for you, Mr. Everson." Everson nodded. "The boy was tied by the wrists and ankles to some sort of seat, something like an old-fashioned toilet chair, and beaten repeatedly with some sort of heavy whip, probably a length of ordinary rubber garden hose. At some time during this part of the beating, his hands were untied from the chair and retied over his head, and the beating resumed. I say this because there were fewer bruises on his upper arms than on his rib cage, and tying his hands above his head is the only way his arms could have been removed from the line of fire, so to speak. Also, either before or after the beating, he was made to kneel and he was beaten or spanked with a board or paddle. I've seen very similar markings and discoloration on boys who have been through fraternity initiations. In fact, I've seen worse on such boys. This was no initiation, though, no prank. This was an interrogation."

Will Henry sat upright. "Interrogation?"

"Nobody gets beaten with a rubber hose as a prank, and if the assailant's aim is simply to cause pain, he could have caused more with a buggy whip or a stick. The rubber hose is a police technique."

"Police?" This time it was Harmon Everson who sat upright. "I've seen it in Columbus and one or two other, bigger cities. It's what you might call moderate torture, to extract information as part of an interrogation. It's painful, but it doesn't break the skin or bones. The victim can take a beating one day and make a court appearance the next. It's illegal, of course, and a policeman could be charged with battery if he were caught at it, but cops don't like testifying against other cops, any more than doctors like testifying against other doctors.

"Incidentally, speaking of the police, the boy's wrists may have been handcuffed rather than tied. The marks on his wrists are somewhat different from those on his ankles. Could have been metal instead of twine or rope. Although I can't imagine how he could have escaped from his persecutor if he was handcuffed. But let me go on. There are scratches on his legs, indicating that he ran through some dense brush before his fall. His feet were rather badly cut, too, although they were heavily calloused, so I think he was probably running rather than walking just before his death. By the way, I'd say he was a poor farm boy. A kid eighteen or nineteen like that still with callouses on his feet. There were blisters, too. He had probably walked some distance in shoes he wasn't accustomed to. His hands were very rough, too, nails broken and some red dirt under them he hadn't been able to scrub out. I'll bet you he was doing farm work only a day or two before he got into this.

"Where was I? Oh, he probably stumbled over the bluff while running, rather than being taken there and thrown off. He landed near enough to head first, breaking his neck and his left forearm and dislocating his left shoulder. He didn't get up.

"He hadn't eaten for somewhere between twelve and twenty-four hours, although he had been given some water. It seems logical to assume that he hadn't been a captive for more than twenty-four hours. I think that, apart from the damage suffered in the fall, his injuries could be described as superficial and not serious. There is no indication whatever that whoever beat him intended to kill him or even seriously injure him, although a case could be made that his captor could hardly afford to let him go free for fear that he would inform the police. Also, we don't know what would have happened next if the boy hadn't escaped. His injuries up to that time may have merely been the preliminaries to something much worse."

Sauls shuffled through his notes in a silence that even Harmon Everson did not feel inclined to break, as they all tried to picture what had happened. "I think that's about it, except for one thing I'd like to point out. As far as I can determine, all the blows he received, both with the hose and with the paddle, were delivered in equal numbers and with equal force to both sides of his body. That's unusual. It would be more common if one side took more punishment, depending on whether his persecutor was right- or left-handed. It indicates to me that the beating was accomplished by only one person, because two or more persons wouldn't be so neat. Given that it was one man—or woman, we can't rule out a woman—I'd say he has an obsession with orderliness, specifically with symmetry. He *had* to deal an equal number of blows on each side. His life is probably full of expressions of this symmetry thing. I'd be willing to bet he parts his hair in the middle."

Will Henry said, "I part my hair in the middle."

"I noticed that. In fact, if you weren't so new to the police job and if Frank Mudter didn't know you as well as he does, I'd figure you for the chief suspect, Chief."

"What?"

"My first guess would be that whoever did this had a police background. The rubber hose isn't a common weapon. Its whole purpose is to extract information, not to maim or kill. It's the sort of thing that's passed by word of mouth from cop to cop and police force to police force. Your average member of the public wouldn't know about it and wouldn't have any use for it if he did. If two fellows get into a knockdown, drag-out fight, they'll hit each other with bottles or two-by-fours or whatever else is handy; but not with rubber hoses. A rubber hose is the sort of weapon that's chosen coldly, deliberately."

There was another silence, then Harmon Everson asked, "Was he sexually assaulted?"

Sauls shook his head. "He wasn't sodomized, if that's what you mean. There was no evidence of bruising in the anal passage and no semen present. But there's sex with a capital S written all over this thing."

"What do you mean?" asked Will Henry.

"I mean that whoever beat this boy up probably got a sexual thrill out of doing it, enjoyed it, and if the boy hadn't got loose, it might have gone further. That sort of psychology isn't really my field, but there are a couple of doctors in Europe could write you a book on the sexual ramifications of this one incident."

"It's hard to believe there could be anything like that in a place like Delano," said Will Henry.

The doctor took off his glasses and rubbed the bridge of his nose. "Chief, when you've been a policeman a little bit longer, you'll get to know that there is just about every possible kind of person in Delano, or in the county, anyway. You'll get to look under the rock and see what peculiar lives even perfectly ordinary people lead. I see it as a doctor and especially in my work with the Columbus police and the Muscogee County Sheriff's Office. I expect Frank sees it right here in Delano, because people will tell a doctor things they wouldn't tell their dearest friend." Dr. Mudter nodded agreement. Sauls heaved another sigh and put down his notes. "There isn't anything in the world that could happen in Columbus or Atlanta or New York or Paris, France, that couldn't happen right here. Believe me, there isn't."

Twenty minutes later Will Henry arrived home to find Billy and Eloise on the living room floor, playing with a golden Labrador puppy. Someone had left it on the doorstep after supper, with a note reading, "A gift from a friend for the Lee children."

That night Will Henry fell asleep quickly. A part of his mind knew part of the truth, and the rest of him could not accept it. The anxiety this condition produced affected him like a drug, and he slept like a stone, afraid to dream.

16 THE BOY was buried in the city plot, a part of the cemetery set aside for the indigent or the unknown. Only Lamar Maddox, Will Henry, and the Baptist minister, Howard Abel, attended; the two black men who had dug the grave did not seem to count, although they removed their hats and assumed reverent postures as Preacher Abel prayed for the receipt of the soul of the dead boy into Abraham's bosom. Not the early hour, the numbing cold, or the bleakness of the city plot inhibited the fervor of the minister as he shut his eyes tightly, tilted his chin toward heaven, and let his rich baritone roll over the bare earth toward the tall pines that watched over the family plots with their brown grass and wrought iron fences.

"And we beseech thee, O Heavenly Father, find a place for this young man in thy perfect paradise above, take him home to thee, and give him eternal rest." Abel shifted his weight and altered his tone to one of special pleading: "And we pray, dear Lord, for the parents of this boy. Comfort them in thy secret way, and prepare them for the time when they can no longer hope for the life of their lost son. Spare them needless suffering and make them ready for the day when they can be reunited with their child in thy heavenly host."

Will Henry huddled inside his pea coat and prayed for the

preacher to finish praying. The cold of the early hour made it difficult to concentrate on the service, and he was becoming tense and irritable as his thoughts began to shift from pity for the boy to hatred for those who had beaten him, who had allowed this thing to happen. Despite the depth of his personal religious feeling, he could not bring himself to pray for them, and he felt guilty.

"All these things we ask in the name of thy son, Jesus Christ our savior. Ay-men." Lamar Maddox stepped forward and touched a button on one of the four metal posts around the grave, and the coffin began to be smoothly lowered into the ground. Lamar watched carefully the inaugural performance of this ingenious new piece of equipment. He would give it its first large public display later in the morning at a more important and more profitable service.

Skeeter Willis was waiting in his car at the edge of the cemetery. "Morning, Will Henry. I saw your gathering and stopped. What's up?"

Will Henry climbed gratefully into the warm car. "Well, Skeeter, looks like I've got a murder on my hands." Skeeter did not respond. "Our paper boy found a dead body at the foot of Hodo's Bluff yesterday morning. Boy in his late teens. We just finished burying him."

Will Henry clearly had Skeeter's undivided attention. "Tell me all of it," Skeeter said. "Start at the beginning, and don't leave anything out."

Will Henry took the sheriff through the events of the last twenty-four hours, again omitting only the identity of his Klan source.

"What do you think?" Skeeter asked.

"I don't know what to think," Will Henry said. "I don't put much stock in the doctor's views about the kind of person that killed him. That seems like the wildest kind of speculation to me. If the Klan had anything to do with it I think this fellow I know would have told me or at least hinted at it. I don't know anybody around here crazy enough to do something like this. Foxy lives up there near where it happened, and he's a little strange, but I can't see any fair reason for suspecting him."

"Foxy's not your man, Will Henry. Granted, he's a little peculiar, but he's a good enough man. Not the Klan, either. In spite of what you hear sometimes. No, Will Henry, I'll tell you what happened, and I don't want you to think I'm jumping to conclusions. I'm just talking out of my own experience and the experience of a dozen other sheriffs I've talked to. Your killer's long gone by now. There's a lot of fellows on the road these days, what with the weevil and the times. Probably this boy was traveling with another fellow or two, and he had something they wanted—not much, maybe a little money or something—and they beat him up to get it, and he tried to run and fell over the bluff. These hoboes are always killing each other, fighting over money or whiskey or less. I'm not surprised the boy was naked. I've known 'em to kill a man for his shoes, nothing more. When they've been on the road for a while they start playing by their own rules, don't care nothing for what's right any more, just living from day to day."

Will Henry felt oddly relieved. "Well, that sounds pretty plausible. It hadn't occcurred to me, I'll admit. I'd begun to think it was somebody here in Delano, and that really worried me."

"I don't think you have to worry about that. This fellow isn't going to get caught, not for this, anyway. Somewhere down the line somebody'll do the same or worse to him, or he'll finally run afoul of the law. But you're not going to catch him, Will Henry. I know you'd like to, not just to get a feather in your cap, but because you're mad about this. I know how you feel. Now, if you don't want this kind of thing happening all the time, take my advice and don't ever let no hoboes get a jungle going around Delano. Just make sure they don't get off the train. You let 'em start camping around here, and you'll have one of these killings a week, you mark my words."

"I see your point."

"Another thing, Will Henry." Skeeter shifted in his seat and rubbed at his nose. "About the Klan. I think you'll find it's best to leave 'em be. Somebody calls you about a cross burning, you go out there in your own sweet time and poke around the ashes with your toe and look concerned and forget about it. They don't mess with nobody don't deserve messing with, and they'll take care of things you can't yourself sometimes. Like horsewhipping that fellow last year. He needed it, and I couldn't do it; so they did it."

Will Henry's surprise must have shown in his face, because Skeeter reddened slightly and went on, "There's some highly thought of people in the Klan, Will Henry. They're all that's going to keep the niggers in line, and I've got a lot of respect for anybody can do that."

Will Henry made an effort to keep his face expressionless and his voice calm. "Skeeter, I don't hold with horsewhippings or scaring innocent colored folks to death with cross burnings, and I don't have much respect for grown men who run around at night in bed sheets. If I catch anybody at any of that in this town I'll have 'em in jail on the best charge I can think of." He paused. "And you can pass that message on to anybody who's interested."

Skeeter reddened further and began to fumble with starting his car. "Suit yourself, Will Henry."

"Can you think of anything I should have done that I haven't already done, Skeeter?"

"Nope, you've covered everything I would of. I don't think you're going to catch any murderers on this one, though. Whoever did it is long gone." The car's engine clattered to life, and Will Henry got out.

"Thanks for coming down, Skeeter."

"Any time," Skeeter called back as he put the car into gear. "Shit," the sheriff muttered under his breath as he pulled away.

17 FOR A WEEK nothing whatever happened in Delano to require Will Henry's attention. He watched for speeders, checked locks, and patrolled streets, but nothing occurred that could take his mind off the boy. The story was run prominently in the *Atlanta Constitution*, and Will Henry hoped that someone might read it and come forward to identify the boy, but there was not a single phone call. He covered his steps again, talked to the people who lived on the ridge near the bluff, examined again the path to the bluff, and racked his brain to think of some other sensible step to take, but he could not. As each avenue of investigation proved fruitless, he turned more to Skeeter's theory of a murder among hoboes; it made sense; it fit the facts in every respect; but he could not drive the thought from his mind that there was a killer loose in town, and there was nothing he could do about it.

At home he had always been a quiet but affectionate father and husband, but now he was unusually silent, and the children tiptoed around him. Carrie did not. She bore his preoccupation for a day or two, bustling about the house in her accustomed manner, cooking, sweeping, dusting, scolding children; then she had had enough. When the children were in bed she removed his feet from the stool in front of his easy chair, sat on the stool, and looked at him closely. "It seems to me that if you are going to be able to live with this job you are going to have to maintain some detachment from it."

"I know it, but it's hard. Especially in this instance." He had told her little more than he had told the newspaper.

"You're new at the job, but it seems to me you've done everything any policeman could do under the circumstances. Would Skeeter Willis have done anything you haven't?"

"I asked him that. He said not." Will Henry also felt that Skeeter had now withdrawn any help he might have offered, because of their conversation about the Klan, but he did not say so to Carrie.

"Can't you find some peace in that?"

"I know I ought to be able to, but I haven't."

"Then I think you ought to pray about it. I'll pray for you, too."

"Thank you, honey. I know that will help."

"You haven't been paying much attention to me lately, you know."

He smiled down at her and pulled her into his lap. "Are the children asleep?"

"Like logs."

Will Henry finally found distraction from routine and from his state of mind when court met in Greenville, the Meriwether county seat. His testimony was required in the matter of the robbery of the Bank of Delano, since he was the arresting officer of the O'Brien brothers. The twenty-mile drive took nearly an hour over a pitted, badly paved road that was still the best in the county.

Greenville was a pretty town by Georgia standards. Dating from the 1840s, it presented a handsome, red-brick, white-domed courthouse set in a spacious square of neat stores and green grass, and out on the La Grange road there were graceful examples of antebellum architecture, set among carefully tended azaleas and tall magnolia trees. It was one of those rare Georgia towns which conformed to the southern myth. The streets in the square were twice the breadth of Main Street in Delano and offered ample room for the mule-drawn wagons of farmers and the cars of local merchants. As Will Henry drove into the little town, the square was teeming with people, for the opening of court was a semigala occasion, offering an opportunity to see distant neighbors, to window-shop on the square, and to transact a little business at the bank or at one of the cotton gins which still clung to existence despite the pestilence of the boll weevil.

Will Henry thought, as he pulled into a parking space reserved for court officials and the sheriff's department, that the lack of money showed in the crowd. Clothes were clean but patched; the women looked longingly into the store windows, but most remained outside; there were too many children selling sandwiches and fruit and homemade preserves to an unbuying crowd; and the men stood about in groups, a vacant, stunned look about them, talking, but not laughing much. Since the War Between the States, as it was called in Georgia, these people had had little, and had perhaps not had much before that. Only the land. During the boom that had come with the Great War they had hoped for a future; they had worked harder and borrowed more for seed and equipment. Unused land had been cleared and planted in more of the single crop, cotton. The war ended, and with it the boom, and meanwhile, out of west Texas a plague of Biblical proportions began moving east at the rate of sixty miles a year.

They saw it coming. Deputations were sent who looked, came back, and said, yes, the boll weevil was destroying cotton, something must be done. But no one knew what to do. Some tried to diversify, buying dairy cattle or chickens, but there was no market for these products, no economic system to connect farmer and consumer. And so, even when the weevil crossed the Chattahoochee from Alabama, men were still planting cotton and hoping. Nobody but a farmer can understand what it means to clear land, plow, plant, then come to harvest and find nothing but dust in his hands and the note due at the bank.

Will Henry knew, as he picked his way through the crowd, exchanging a greeting here and there, that all that stood between many of these people and starvation was the fact that a prudent farm family could produce much of what it needed, keep a cow and a few chickens, grow vegetables and put them up for winter, pick berries and crab apples and make preserves, make clothes from flour sacks and mend them repeatedly. And there were quail, rabbit, squirrel, and 'possum for the boys to shoot if enough preserves and sandwiches could be sold in town to buy ammunition. Will Henry thanked God it hadn't come to that for his family.

He found Skeeter in his office, a place of oiled floors, cigar smoke, and spitoons; it was filled with bewildered people waiting for justice for their kin, wondering whether their husbands and sons would come home with them that night or go with Skeeter to the county camp, and how it had come to this. The two men went together into the high-ceilinged courtroom, with its hard benches and yellowing paint, and chatted idly up front as the milling throng filed in, blacks in the balcony, whites downstairs. Skeeter excused himself and left through a side door to find his prisoners, and Will Henry seated himself on a front bench and waited to be called. He was not kept waiting long.

A clerk bustled in, dumped a load of papers on his table, and yelled into the din, "Order in the court! The superior court of the fourth district of Georgia is now in session, Hizzoner Roy B. Hill presiding! All rise!"

All rose, and Judge Roy Hill strode to his bench and rapped twice. "Be seated. Call the first case."

"The state of Georgia versus P. and R. O'Brien!"

A side door opened, and the O'Briens, accompanied by Skeeter Willis, entered, blinking in the sunlight which was streaming through the room's large windows. They were directed to face the bench, where they were joined by their attorney, Pope Herring, a courthouse fixture for twenty years.

"Read the charge."

"It is charged that on the first day of January, in the year of our Lord nineteen hundred and twenty, the defendants, P. O'Brien and R. O'Brien, did enter the premises of the Bank of Delano in Delano, in the county of Meriwether, in the state of Georgia, and did, by the use of force and with firearms, unlawfully take money in the sum of seven hundred and forty dollars and forty cents in violation of section five one five four of the penal code of Georgia!"

"How do the defendants plead?" asked the Judge, turning to Pope Herring.

Herring stepped forward and assumed an almost reverent tone. "Your Honor, the defendants both plead guilty to the charge as read, and, being unable to raise bail, request immediate sentencing. In sentencing I would ask the court to consider that these boys are from an honest farming family and that neither has ever been in serious trouble before. I would also point out that no one was injured in this incident and that very little damage to property occurred. When faced with arrest for their offense, the defendants readily surrendered and offered no resistance, and I submit that this incident occurred only because of a rare overindulgence on New Year's Eve, the night before. The defendants beg consideration of these circumstances and the mercy of the court."

The judge turned to the county attorney, Jesse Bulloch. "Does the state wish to comment before I sentence?"

Bulloch shuffled forward. "Yes, Your Honor. The Upson County Sheriff's Office has advised me that the defendants have on three other occasions been arrested on drunk and disorderly charges and on one occasion have served thirty days in the Upson County jail on such charges." Pope Herring shot an uncharacteristically sharp glance at the O'Briens, who blushed and looked guilty. Bulloch continued. "I would also point out that the car which they were driving and the weapons which they used in the bank robbery were stolen and that a warrant for their arrest in Upson County has been issued on charges arising from these thefts. The state cannot, therefore, join in a recommendation for clemency in this case." He handed the judge a sheet of paper. "This is a true copy of their record of prior arrests and of the Upson County warrants."

The judge read the sheet of paper, placed it on his desk, and directed his attention to the two boys, who stood with their hands cuffed behind him, staring at the floor. "The defendants will step forward." The boys moved toward the bench and looked sheepishly up at the judge. "The court accepts the plea of guilty to the charge and accedes to the request for immediate sentencing. After consideration of the defense request for mercy and the statements as to the past conduct of the defendants by the county attorney, I sentence both defendants to twenty years at hard labor in the county prison camp. However, in consideration of the facts that no one was hurt, that no resistance was offered to arrest, and the absence of any prior felony conviction, I will suspend the last two years of the sentences, on condition of good behavior." He rapped sharply with his gavel. "Next case."

Skeeter led the bewildered boys out of the courtroom, followed by their attorney, and the clerk began to call the next case over a hum of conversation in the courtroom. The whole process had taken less than three minutes.

Will Henry sat, nearly as bewildered as the O'Briens. They would pay at least eighteen years of their lives for fifteen minutes of drunken foolishness. He left the courtroom and drove back to Delano, his journey to Greenville wasted. All the way back he dwelt on the contrast between the imprisonment of the O'Briens and the continuing freedom of the unknown boy's murderer.

He is *my* murderer, Will Henry thought, and I am *his* pursuer. We belong to each other. I must find him, if it takes all of my life.

18 ABOUT THE TIME Will Henry left Greenville for the trip back to Delano, Hugh Holmes left Delano for Greenville. They passed each other in Warm Springs and exchanged waves. Holmes had business at the courthouse quite different from that of Will Henry. It was to be an important day for Holmes—a milestone day—and it was typical of Holmes that he had been preparing for it for the past ten years.

Holmes had, on settling in Delano, taken the trouble to learn how things were done, not just on the county level, but also on the state level. He had begun to perceive that there existed a complex pattern of relationships among the county bosses, a small number of large Atlanta law firms, small-town lawyers and newspaper editors, the railroads, and the Georgia Power Company. The law firms controlled the communications between the big-business community and the county bosses; the railroads were principal clients of many small-town lawyers, a group which dominated the state legislature; and the Georgia Power Company had become a major advertiser in many small-town newspapers, running large corporate advertising schedules and paying for their space in advance on yearly contracts, thus giving them a sympathetic ear among local editors.

The platform upon which this network of relationships rested was known as the County Unit System, established in the Reconstruction year of 1876 and designed to give the state's rural counties domination over state elections. Each county was given two unit votes for each representative it had in the General Assembly; thus, the 8 most populous counties had six votes each, the 30 next-most populous counties had four, and the remaining 121 counties had two votes each. Holmes's own senatorial district comprised the counties of Meriwether, Harris, and Talbot, also known as the Tri-Counties, which meant that if he could establish firm political control over those counties he could produce a county unit vote equal to that of, say, Fulton County, which included Atlanta, and enjoy commensurate political influence in the state. Only a handful of men could produce six county unit votes on demand, and Holmes meant to be one of them.

He would be aided in his quest by a condition he had helped bring about; indeed, Holmes had almost singlehandedly invented the tri-county idea, although he was pleased to let people forget it. The three counties had lacked sufficient population for each to support a county fair, so Holmes, using the Delano Kiwanis Club as his instrument, had brought about the Tri-County Fair, held each fall in Delano, which brought farmers and townspeople from more than two dozen small communities to Delano to have their crops, animals, and recipes judged and to fritter away a dollar or two on unaccustomed paid entertainment. Holmes had also lent support to various athletic competitions among the schools of the three counties, which fostered a feeling of community and further nurtured the tri-county concept. It was this concept which might give him the political clout he needed at state level in order to further the economic, educational, and social well-being of Meriwether, Harris, and Talbot counties, which was his long-term personal goal. It was not entirely an altruistic goal, though Holmes was extremely civic minded; the Bank of Delano was the economic cornerstone of the area, and what was good for the Tri-Counties was good for the bank.

And so, as Holmes entered the chambers of Judge Roy B. Hill, he was ready to make his first visible move from being a merely influential man to being an overtly powerful one. He was joining a coalition of men which ran things in the Tri-Counties. It was typical of his way of doing things that he did not seek admission to this group until he was in a position to command it, and that he took pains to see that commanding it was unnecessary. It was also typical of Holmes that he was joining the coalition at the top.

Present for the initiation were the judge, the county attorney, Jesse Bulloch; the sheriffs of Meriwether and Talbot counties, Skeeter Willis and Tom Erenheim; the representatives of Meriwether and Harris counties, William ("Tiny") Estes and Harold Whitworth, both lawyers; two newspaper editors, Harmon Everson of the *Delano Messenger* and Roz Hill, a cousin of the judge's, of the *Meriwether Vindicator*. The occasion was the confirmation of the candidacy of Holmes for the office of state senator in the Democratic primary. Considering the constitution of the meeting, this was tantamount to the appointment of Holmes as the Democratic candidate, which was tantamount to election. The current holder of the office was absent, being otherwise engaged at a private hospital in Atlanta, which specialized in the conversion of drunken citizens into sober ones, but Holmes was able to produce his written regrets, along with a statement of disinclination to seek reelection. Holmes's selection was unanimous, although at least two of the other men present had coveted the nomination for themselves.

As if to dispel any doubts about their harmony, Holmes quietly announced that a complete repaving of Highway 41 from the Talbot County line at Delano to the Coweta County line above Greenville would commence on the following Monday, to be completed by the end of the year. This announcement had the effect of producing respectful enthusiasm for his candidacy in quarters where there had been only regretful acquiescence, since no man or combination of men in the room had been able to achieve this coup in more than four years of assaults on the state highway department through every means at their collective disposal. When Holmes further stated that every mile of the repaving would be accomplished by professional contractors without the assistance of convict labor, respect turned to awe.

The judge recovered first. "Where, may I ask, will funds come from for this work?"

"From the governor's contingency fund," replied Holmes. "I've suggested that this project should be used as an experiment to demonstrate that a central state highway fund and competitive bids from contractors will produce cheaper, higher-quality road building in the state. The old way of having each county responsible for its roads using chain gangs just isn't sufficient any longer, now that we're making such a rapid transition to the automobile. We need a proper state highway system, now, and I'll be making that a cornerstone of my campaign."

There was a shifting and murmering in the room which said, "Of course," as if the group had been having weekly discussions on this very trend. Holmes restrained himself from bringing up any other of his goals in the state senate. He had already, with this single coup, established himself as the one person in the group whom anyone would have to consult before doing anything, and he knew this single idea would hold them for some time, without his having to expend any more political ammunition.

Holmes left the courthouse that day with what he wanted, or at least, as much of what he wanted as the group could give him. He began to look for the rest of what he wanted among the crowd still gathered around the square, exchanging a greeting here, shaking a hand there. It was not too early to begin.

In late September the Democratic primary took place, and Holmes won more than eighty percent of the votes cast, running on a platform of a state highway system, higher standards in education and better pay for teachers, and more help and advice for farmers from the state department of agriculture.

Shortly after the primary, a meeting of the courthouse group was called, and driving to Greenville, Holmes was annoyed by what seemed to be slow progress being made on the paving of the road. Just north of Warm Springs he stopped his car to allow a single lane of traffic to pass around a work site. Looking idly around him, he was surprised to see a gang of convicts swinging picks in a drainage ditch beside the contractor's work party. Two of the men looked vaguely familiar, but traffic moved on before he could place them. He was nearly to Greenville before recognition came with a jolt. They were the O'Brien brothers who had held up the bank, or rather, they were pale shadows of the husky farm boys he remembered from the day of their arrest. They were both pitifully thin and looked ten years older.

At the meeting Holmes accepted congratulations on the size of his victory and made sure it had sunk in well before changing the subject. "Driving up here today, I saw a chain gang working on the repaving of forty-one." He turned to Skeeter. "Why is that?"

Skeeter replied blandly, "Oh, the contractor said he could use some more muscle down there. I obliged him." Skeeter tilted his chair back and sucked on a toothpick.

The room became very still. Holmes leveled his gaze at Skeeter and waited for a moment before speaking in a tone that was quiet and cold. "You will oblige me by seeing that all convict labor is permanently removed from work on forty-one today." He looked around the room, then zeroed in on Judge Hill. "Judge, I understand that your brother-in-law was awarded the contract for the paving work." The judge nodded. "Tell him today that he had better have a full paid crew back at work by tomorrow morning if he wants to keep that contract. Tell him, too, that he's behind schedule, and he's got thirty days to catch up. If he has to hire extra men to do it, that's his problem."

Holmes once again addressed the group. "It was not easy to get twenty miles of pavement for this county at state expense. I will not see the plan for a state highway system fail because ground rules which I myself set were violated. Am I perfectly clear on this point?" Skeeter and the judge looked uncomfortable, but both nodded. Holmes turned back to Skeeter. "And while you're speaking with the captain down at the camp, you might mention to him that I'll be paying him a little visit next week to look at conditions down there. I might even have lunch with the prisoners."

Skeeter's eyes narrowed. "Now, listen, Holmes, the way that camp is run is none of your business, and—" Holmes cut him short.

"You had better accustom yourself to the idea that from now on everything that happens in Meriwether, Talbot, and Harris counties is my business. And if you can't arrange my visit to the camp I'll make my own arrangements. Clark Howell at the *Atlanta Constitution* might like to send somebody along with me."

Skeeter reddened. "All right, all right. I'll tell him you're coming."

The tone of the rest of the meeting was subdued. Afterward, Holmes reflected that he had rarely given anybody a direct order about anything, and he worried that perhaps he had used too much weight too soon with the courthouse bunch. But he was angry that such an important project had been jeopardized, and shocked at the appearance of two men who had been in perfect condition six months before. He wondered what he would find at the camp, and he dreaded the visit.

19 THE BITTER WINTER of 1919–20 gave way grudgingly to spring, in fits and starts. It was late March before the new season seemed in any way established, and mid-April before plowing could be well underway. Summer arrived well and truly in early May, and Will Henry was sorry. He liked a long spring, with time to savor the cool nights and pleasant days before entering the crucible of a Georgia summer.

Not until May did the pervading sense of ineffectualness finally leave him. The tedium of traffic violations and routine patrolling had been broken only by a cutting in Braytown. Will Henry had jailed the assailant and watched Frank Mudter put thirty stitches into a crescent-shaped wound that exposed the black man's skull, gleaming, Will Henry thought, like a silver dollar in the light on the examining table. The victim, who according to Dr. Frank's estimate, had lost two quarts of blood, had hopped off the table and strolled easily from the clinic, cheerfully promising to pay the doctor as soon as payday rolled around. Dr. Frank had allowed that he never ceased to marvel at the amount of abuse the black male could take without going into shock or, indeed, seeming much worse for the wear.

Shortly after the cutting, Will Henry's home telephone rang late one evening. The caller announced herself as Mrs. Smith and hurriedly asked him to come. Will Henry lost a moment before he remembered the Mrs. Smith at Maple and Poplar who had reported the wife beating some months earlier.

"He's doing it again," she whispered in half panic. "Please come right away, before he hurts her."

Will Henry pulled his pants on over his pajamas, strapped on his gun, and ran for the car, doing his best not to upset Carrie. He drove fast, unimpeded by traffic, taking the corners as fast as the old Ford allowed, fearful that he would not be in time. During the drive he could think only of the lump of coal Butts had been holding last time. The man could kill her with less. He screeched to a halt before the Maple Street house and ran for the door. The scene inside was much as before, domesticity undisturbed, except this time she was holding the baby, holding it seemingly as a buffer between herself and her husband. She was obviously frightened and her husband was obviously angry, but the only sign that anything was amiss was her swollen lower lip and a bit of blood.

Will Henry brought himself to a halt and took a deep breath. "Mrs. Butts, are you hurt anywhere besides your lip?" The woman shook her head. Her husband took a step backward and looked worriedly back and forth from his wife to the chief.

"Are any teeth knocked out? Are you sure you're not hurt anywhere else?"

She shook her head again and this time dislodged a pair of tears, which rolled down her cheeks. Tears of embarrassment more than anything else, Will Henry thought. He sat her down and looked closely at her.

"Now listen to me, Mrs. Butts. I'm going to take your husband with me for the night—" She started to interrupt. "No, it's best that he come with me. Now, I want you to put the baby to bed and then put some iodine on your lip where it's cut. I don't reckon you need to see the doctor tonight. You come and see me in the morning and let me know if you want to file charges against your husband." She shook her head again, and he knew she would never do it.

He turned to the husband and said with a gentleness that belied his anger, "Now you go and get in my car, and don't say a word." He turned back to the woman, who seemed to be collecting herself. "He'll be all right with me. Do you want me to get Mrs. Smith from next door to help you?"

She spoke for the first time, quietly. "No, I'll fix myself up.

I'll be all right."

He left her and went to the car, where Butts waited quietly in the back seat. He drove back to the jail, and not a word passed between them, but Will Henry felt exactly the way he had the time before: he seemed to have trouble exhaling; his lungs were too full of air. He unlocked the front door of the jail and allowed Butts to precede him into the building. Butts walked unhesitatingly toward the cells. Will Henry unlocked the outer door, then a cell door, and Butts walked in. They were alone in the cell block.

Will Henry hit him. The blow was delivered with his open right hand and struck high on the left cheekbone. Butts reeled slightly, but did not fall. Will Henry swung again, this time with the back of his hand. The blow straightened Butts, but still he did not fall or even attempt to stay out of range. The beating continued, deliberately, dancelike, around the cell. Butts clenched his fists and clamped his elbows tightly against his ribs, but made no attempt to shield his face or head; an involuntary hunching of the shoulders was his only defense. When Will Henry's right hand began to hurt he switched to his left, and still they moved together around the cell like dance partners with the floor to themselves, mutual participants, each assigned his role. When his left hand began to hurt, too, he stopped. Butts maintained his clenched position, standing, with his shoulders hunched. Tears were streaming down his face, and sobs racked him, air and spittle hissing through his clenched teeth.

"You won't do it again," Will Henry said, panting slightly. Butts sobbed louder and shook his head, his whole, tense body moving with it.

"Not ever again?" Will Henry asked, the way he might have asked Billy after a switching.

Butts shook himself again. His face was red and puffy, but there were no marks on him. He would look perfectly normal by morning, bar a bruise or two.

Will Henry stepped out of the cell and locked it. As he turned to switch off the light and lock the outer door, he noticed that Butts had not moved, was still sobbing. He turned off the light and left.

Driving home, he felt cleansed, with none of the guilt that remained when he punished his children. He felt, for the first time since having taken the job, that he had seen his duty through to the end, that he had done justice. He felt, at long last, *effective*.

At home Carrie questioned him.

"That Butts fellow was beating his wife again. Nothing serious, he didn't hurt her." He climbed into bed and snuggled against her. "He won't do it again."

20 WHEN WILL HENRY and Carrie had left the farm, only Flossie's sister, Nellie, and her husband, Jesse Cole, had remained working there. Robert and Flossie Dunn had followed the Lees to Delano, where Flossie gave Carrie part-time help in the house and, in the remainder of her time, began to establish a home baking business in her own kitchen. Robert, unable to find steady employment, turned to yard work and soon garnered half a dozen regular customers, giving him a modest but dependable income.

Jesse and Nellie Cole, perhaps because of their temperaments, had not been so fortunate as Robert and Flossie. Nellie lacked Flossie's natural charm and combined considerable intelligence with a tendency to speak her mind. Jesse's intelligence was the equal of his wife's, and if he did not often speak his mind, his reserve could sometimes be taken for sullenness. Jesse and Nellie Cole possessed between them more dignity than was good for a black couple in rural Georgia in 1920. They also possessed a son, Willie, who, even at the age of nine, would have elicited a one-word description from most white people: "uppity." Willie and Billy Lee had been playmates on the farm, and even Billy, with a generous nature and a child's lack of prejudice, sometimes found Willie a little hard to take.

When the Lees left the farm, Jesse and Nellie were secure for a while, because the bank continued Jesse's pay so that the place could be kept up until sold. When Hoss Spence leased the place and installed a foreman in the house, Jesse's money stopped, and he went to Hoss for work.

Hoss Spence farmed dairy cattle and, increasingly, peaches. He had appeared in Meriwether County some ten years before with a pocketful of money some said had been earned in the making and selling of corn whiskey. He had bought land and had shown talent and shrewdness in managing it and was now a principal supplier of dairy products to Delano and was contemplating the building of a packing shed to process his own peaches. He and his family were now prominent in the community, the church, and, some said, the Ku Klux Klan.

Jesse drove to the Spence place in the buggy that had been his father's, pulled by a small pinto horse he had traded a plowing mule for three years before. He inquired for Hoss at the kitchen door of the big brick house and was sent to a nearby pen, where he found Hoss overseeing the breeding of two of his herd. Jesse pulled up the horse far enough away not to disturb the proceedings, got down, and stood by the horse's head until the bull was done and Hoss noticed him. The white man walked over, his hands in his hip pockets, stopped in front of the horse, and began examining its teeth.

"Morning, Jesse."

"Mornin', Mr. Spence."

"Nice little animal."

"He ain't much good, but he get me 'round."

"You want to sell him?"

Jesse knew this was a test of his subservience. He could not flatly refuse to sell the horse; that would be a breach of etiquette, an insult. He did the best he could. "Well, suh, Mist' Spence, he ain't much good, but my boy, he real proud of him. Nellie shoot me if I sell him." The two men chuckled together. Apparently, Jesse had passed.

"You looking for work, Jesse?"

"Yessuh."

"I don't plant no cotton. Don't have no croppers."

"Nossuh."

"You know anything else 'sides cotton?" Hoss picked up a hoof and examined it.

"Well, suh, I grow up milkin' fo' cows evuh day of my life.

My daddy wuz on ol' Mist' Reynolds's place ovuh Talbot County. He have fo' cows. I'se a pret' fair carpenter, too. Fix things up 'round the place."

"How about your boy?"

"He ain't but jes' turn nine. His mama want him in school. But he chop wood."

"Nellie?"

"Nellie jes' 'bout the bes' washwoman they is, yessuh."

"Uh-huh." Hoss put down the hoof and stood up, stroking the horse's neck. "Can't offer you much in the way of money, Jesse. Times is hard. But there's a house empty over there." He pointed to a crumbling shack a couple of hundred yards away. "Needs some fixing up, but you say you're a carpenter. There's some scrap lumber in the tool shed. Roof's all right, I'd say. You can have a quart of milk a day and a pound of butter a week from the dairy. I grow my own wheat and mill it over at Luthersville. You can have a sack of flour every month. There's room for some vegetables behind the house, and there'll be some corn at harvest time and some peaches in the summer. Miz Spence'll give Nellie a few chickens that can scratch around your place. All right?"

"Yessuh."

"My niggers work hard, do what they're told, or I run 'em off, you understand me?"

"Yessuh." Hoss began to stroll back toward the main house. Jesse started to heave a small sigh of relief, but Hoss cut him off in midsigh.

"Folks say Nellie's got a sharp tongue. You see she keeps it in her mouth, hear?"

"Yessuh."

Hoss continued toward the house, and Jesse turned the horse, climbed into the buggy, and started back for his family and their few things. He was sweating heavily, and his hands were trembling. Soon the horse's trotting soothed him, and he reflected on his new job, their new life. It wasn't a bad deal. He knew he wouldn't see much money, but they could live. The milk and butter was a nice thing. It wouldn't be like working for Mr. Will Henry, but if he could keep Nellie quiet and the boy out of trouble they could live.

21 IN MID-OCTOBER of that year Billy Lee spent a Saturday afternoon that he would have cause to remember many times during the remainder of his life, partly because it seemed to embody the best of a long series of childhood Saturday afternoons and to represent them all in his mind, and partly because he was introduced to something new and, in many ways, disturbing.

He spent the morning raking leaves, for which he received his weekly pocket money, had a sandwich and a slice of cake from Flossie, because his father was too busy on Saturdays to come home for a proper dinner, and then he went to town. Town was a single block of Main Street, and it was only two blocks from his home, but for a child of eight during his first year as a town dweller it could not have been more fascinating if he had arrived from a great distance by magic carpet.

He began at the Delano Drug Company, on the corner, where he splurged a nickel of his fifteen cents on a root beer, a concoction made all the more exotic because he could watch it being assembled before his eyes—a splash of syrup, a dash of milk, then filled with soda water and, at the last moment, the handle reversed on the tap to produce a thin, hard stream that whipped the top of the drink into a creamy froth. He savored this over a copy of the *Police Gazette*, borrowed from the magazine rack, then carefully returned. Mr. Birdsong didn't mind if you didn't buy them as long as you put them back neatly, and Billy was not about to abuse this privilege, since it inflated his pocket money no end.

From there he went to another favorite place, McKibbon's Hardware, which smelled wonderfully of iron and rope. There he spent some time assessing the relative qualities of two dozen pocket knives and settled tentatively on one with a bone handle and four blades. A final selection would have to wait until he had saved the dollar and twenty cents.

Then to the feed store, which was the cleanest-smelling place in the world, with its powdery aroma of grain and flour. To Billy's mind, Jim Buce's feed store was also Delano's answer to a big-city pet shop, for there was a stack of deep trays holding dozens of baby chicks, which were as cute as kittens, until they got bigger. He cupped one of the fluffy creatures in his hands for a few minutes and wondered again how anything so lovable could grow up to be a chicken.

Finally, he dashed through the thickening shopping crowd to the post office, where he peeked through the little windows of the boxes in a private game to find the furthermost postmark. Birmingham was the best he could do. Once he had found a New York postmark; on another occasion, one from a place called Los, in California. He saved the wanted posters for last, imprinting the faces on his mind and trying to remember their crimes, so that he might someday recognize a criminal visage and turn the man in to his father.

From the post office he dashed across the street, nearly under the hooves of a team of mules, and through the passage next to the Toonerville Trolley, which was a real trolley car turned into a diner, and came to the most entertaining place in all of Delano, Winslow's Livery Stable. It sat behind the north row of Main Street stores, perhaps fifty yards away, on a bluff which fell to the B&M railroad tracks. Between the stores and the stables was a large open space, and this was now rapidly filling with wagons, which his father no longer permitted to park on Main Street on Saturdays, and with perhaps two hundred people, many of them leading or grooming mules, which would be auctioned that afternoon. He was darting through the milling crowd when he ran, forcibly, into Foxy Funderburke.

Foxy let out a loud grunt, then grasped him by his coat at

each shoulder and held him back at arm's length, a fierce scowl on his wizened face. The scowl softened slightly. "Young Lee," Foxy said, not unkindly.

"Yessir," Billy panted. " 'Scuse me, I wasn't watching where I was going."

Foxy still held him, still stared at him. "How's your dog?" Billy and Eloise had, at their mother's insistence, composed a thank-you letter when the puppy had arrived.

"Just fine, sir. We named him Pepper, 'cause Eloise spilled some pepper on him and he sneezed." Still Foxy held him. "He's on the back porch right now, 'cause Mr. Winslow doesn't like dogs around at the mule sales." Still Foxy held him and stared. "He's an awful good dog, and we thank you for him."

Foxy released him but continued to watch him closely. "Do you know about Labrador retrievers? Where they came from and all that?" Foxy spoke flatly, as if he were thinking of something else.

"Nossir."

"They originated in Newfoundland and Labrador. The fishermen there used them to help retrieve their nets in the cold water. They have such thick hair that the cold water doesn't bother them, and they like to swim. That's why they're such good duck dogs. Does your father take you duck hunting?"

"Nossir, he doesn't like shotguns much. He hunts squirrels and rabbits with a .22, though."

"Maybe I'll take you and your dog duck hunting sometimes." Foxy did not wait for a reply. He took a deep breath and released it, then walked away. Billy looked after him. He didn't understand Foxy Funderburke. He didn't talk like other people. You didn't know what you were supposed to say.

"Hey, Billy Lee!" A familiar voice spun him around.

"Hey, Willie!" Billy had not seen him since leaving the farm. The black youngster had grown at least an inch but was still very slender. "How you doing?"

"I'm doin' awright. Mama and Daddy's over to the buggy."

"They doing all right?"

"Yeah. Daddy, he milkin' for Mist' Hoss Spence and fixin' up 'round the place. Mama, she washin', and I chops a whole heap o' wood. How you like it in town?"

"I like it fine. We got a new dog; he's a Labrador 'triever. They used to pull in fishing nets in Labrador. Ol' Foxy Funderburke gave him to us. How you like it out at the Spences'?"

"It's awright. We don't git off much, but we git a whole lotta milk 'n stuff. Ol' man Hoss whup me onct fo' spillin' some milk. Mama like to had a fit, but I reckon I done had it comin'. Daddy say he reckon so, too." Willie Cole seemed older to Billy; quieter. Billy thought he liked the change.

"Hey, let's go watch Farrell do the shoeing!" The two boys cut through the crowd toward the smithy, which stood, not under a spreading chestnut tree, but under a tin roof at one side of the stables. They found a pair of nail kegs and settled themselves quietly out of the way, but in sight of the smith's hands and tools. Farrell Moran did not like little boys chattering and asking questions, not on a Saturday when there were a lot of mules to be shod and gossip to catch up on from the men who brought them. A man led up a mule, and Farrell tethered it to an iron ring on a post. He picked up a hoof and quickly pulled the nails and removed the old shoe. He handed it to Billy with a wink, then cleaned the hoof and, with deft strokes of a two-handled blade, cut away the excess hoof as easily as a man pared a fingernail. Billy cringed inside his collar, but the knife never seemed to hurt the animals. Farrell selected a shoe, compared it to the hoof, exchanged it for another, and plunged it into the coals, pumping the bellows with his foot to make the fire hotter. As the shoe began to heat, he quickly repeated his actions with each hoof. Billy and Willie exchanged a quick grin. Now came the part they liked best.

Farrell retrieved a shoe with his tongs, placed it on the anvil, and began banging it into the shape he wanted, sparks flying and the hammer ringing as it struck home. When it looked right to Farrell he plunged the red-hot shoe into a trough of water, and the boys laughed out loud as the water hissed and bubbled. He fitted the shoe to the hoof and nailed it home, clipping the ends of the nails, which protruded through the hoof. He picked up another shoe from the fire and began banging again.

"What about ol' Hugh Holmes gettin' that road to Greenville paved by the state!"

"What did Holmes have to do with that?" a farmer asked.

"Shoot, where you been? He talked the state into paying for the whole thing, and that was before he even got elected!"

"You hear about that business with the county camp?" somebody chimed in. "Mr. Holmes went up there and saw what they was feedin' those boys and pitched a fit. Cap'n had 'em eatin' fatback and dried peas three times a day! Mr. Holmes got the commissioners to let the prisoners build 'em a chicken house and plant some greens. And ol' Holmes just drops by now and then and has dinner with 'em on the road and makes the cap'n eat with 'em, too, and you know, they say those boys eating real good these days!'' Everybody had a good chuckle over that.

"Wonder what ol' Skeeter is doin' for pocket money nowadays, now that he ain't rentin' convicts to nobody? Shoot, I remember when some folks 'round here had convicts picking their cotton when I was payin' niggers to do it, back when there was some cotton to pick.''

"They say peaches is the thing of the future.''

"I don't doubt it, if you got the money to wait for the trees to grow up. It's all right if you're Hoss Spence, and you got the land and the money from a crop the weevil can't kill to see you through while the trees are growin', but I'll tell you one thing, there ain't goin' to be no little peach farmers around here, just big ones that can afford to pack 'em theirselves.'' There was a murmur of agreement.

The boys watched another two mules be shod, then wandered off toward the stables. The lofts were packed with new-mown hay, and they spent the better part of an hour climbing as high as they could and jumping into soft piles. They looked for peanuts clinging to the peanut hay and ate them greedily, even though it was said that raw peanuts would give you a stomach ache, just as green crab apples would. Gradually, people in the stables led their mules and horses outside for the sale, and it became quiet inside. Billy and Willie lay back in the hayloft, temporarily exhausted from their exertions, and fell into a kind of hazy doze, watching the shafts of sunlight penetrate the cracks in the side of the building, playing on the dust that hung in the air.

The stable door opened a crack and closed again. Footsteps were heard as someone walked to the center of the stable and stopped. There was silence for a moment. Willie tapped Billy on the arm and put a finger to his lips with an air of conspiracy. They would spy on whoever was alone in the stable. The footsteps were heard again, and they heard the creak of a stall door opening. It did not close. The two boys rolled carefully onto their bellies and slid silently to the edge of the loft, so that they could see over the edge. They saw Foxy Funderburke leaning against the side of the stall, in the shadows, illuminated only by stray shafts of light through the cracks. In the distance they heard Winslow's voice rise and fall as he pled for a better price for a mule. Foxy seemed to be fumbling with his trousers, and Billy wondered why he would pee in a clean stall instead of behind the barn. But something was unusual about Foxy's posture. His knees were bent, and he was hunched over, rocking back and forth through a small arc. They could hear his breathing grow quicker and deeper, and then there was some sort of frantic movement in the darkness. Suddenly, the air was pierced by a loud sound from Foxy, not words, but a sound. Billy thought he must be ill and looked at Willie in alarm. Willie motioned for him to remain still and quiet.

Foxy slumped against the side of the stall, and his breathing gradually returned to normal. There was a flash of a handkerchief and the rattle of a belt buckle; Foxy walked to the stable door, opened it a foot and paused. He looked back into the stable, glancing about until suddenly, his eyes seemed to lock with Billy's. Billy held his breath and prepared to run. But Foxy did not seem to have seen him. He stepped outside and closed the door.

They waited until they were sure he was gone before speaking. To Billy's surprise, Willie was laughing. "What's so funny? What was he doing?"

Willie laughed out loud. "He jackin' off. What you think?"

"What's jackin' off?"

"Don' you know *nothin*'? Well, I guess I better show you."

Willie showed him, and he tried it himself, but it had seemed a different thing when Foxy was doing it. It had seemed angry, and—Billy didn't know. Just angry.

22 THE EARLY 1920s passed quickly for all of the Lee family. They thrived, parents and children, in their community. Will Henry became an established local figure in his job, as did Carrie in church and community activities. Billy and Eloise made friends, did well in school, and pleased their parents. They felt as if they had lived in the town for all of their lives, and the town seemed to feel the same way.

Holmes continued to improve his political position in the Tri-Counties, and his solid local position helped him to establish himself as an effective force in the state senate. A force of another kind appeared in Meriwether County during this period, one which, in time, would have a hand in making Holmes even more effective, and which would change the face of the country. Will Henry was, by chance, the first to meet the man, something the family would always remember.

The chief was leaving his regular afternoon coffee klatch at the Delano Drug Company on a fine spring day in 1924, when a shiny new Ford coupe with the top folded down pulled into a parking space in front of the drugstore. "Excuse me, there, Officer!" the driver called out to Will Henry.

Will Henry walked to the car and said, "Yes, sir, what can I do for you?" He was greeted by a smiling, finely sculpted face on a man of some bulk. A straw hat crowned the large head. Will

Henry expected to be asked for directions to Atlanta or Columbus. The man's accent was clearly not local, not even southern. He looked familiar, Will Henry thought.

"I wonder if I could ask for your testimony on the quality of the chocolate ice-cream sodas in that establishment?"

Will Henry laughed. "Well, if the testimony of my children is worth anything, everything made in Mr. Birdsong's fountain is unsurpassed anywhere."

"Well, that is excellent testimony indeed! I wonder if I could impose upon you to go inside and order something for me?"

Will Henry hesitated a moment, then he saw the crutches propped in the back seat. "Be glad to. What was it? Chocolate ice-cream soda?"

That's it." He handed Will Henry a quarter. "If you could just ask the fountain clerk to bring it out when it's ready. I don't want to take any more of your time."

"Not at all." Will Henry went inside, waited until the drink was prepared, and brought it back himself, with the change.

The man accepted it and drew thirstily on the straws, while Will Henry stood by, smiling. "Ahhhh, that certainly hits the spot." He stuck out a hand. "My name is Roosevelt."

Will Henry accepted the hand, feeling a little foolish. "Of course, I should have recognized you. I guess it was the hat threw me off. My wife and I voted for you and Mr. Cox in 1920. Harding's not my sort of man. We're Democrats. My name's Will Henry Lee. I'm a little surprised to see you in Delano, Mr. Roosevelt. What brings you down this way?"

"My family and I have taken a house over at Warm Springs. We hope that the waters there might be good for what ails me. Swimming, not drinking, you understand." Will Henry nodded. "Lovely little town you have here. Rather like the name. Delano was my mother's maiden name, you know; my middle name. Think I'll just pretend it was named for me."

They laughed together. Will Henry found himself, somewhat surprisingly, at ease with a man who had run for vice-president of the United States. "Welcome to Meriwether County, Mr. Roosevelt. I hope your stay here is beneficial and that you'll come back to see us often. Is there anything else I can do for you? The fountain clerk will come get the glass if you'll just honk the horn."

"Thank you, Chief, there is something else you could do if I could trouble you for just a minute. I expect you know a Mr. Hugh Holmes at the bank? I wonder if you'd be kind enough to step over there and ask him if it's convenient for him to join me here in the car for just a few minutes?"

"Certainly." Will Henry crossed the street, went into the bank, and stuck his head into Holmes's office, where the banker was poring over a ledger. " 'Scuse me, Hugh. Mr. Franklin D. Roosevelt himself is parked over in front of the drugstore, and he'd like you to step over there and meet him, if you have the time."

Holmes's eyebrows shot up. "Oh, yes. He's a friend of Clark Howell, at the *Constitution*. Clark said he was coming down to Warm Springs. You know he had a pretty bad case of infantile paralysis since the election."

"I read about it in the paper."

"Clark talked him into coming down here for his health." The two men left the bank, and Will Henry stopped and watched as Holmes crossed the street, introduced himself to the man, then went around and got into the passenger seat. The two men fell into conversation. Hugh Holmes and Roosevelt seemed to be getting on like a house afire. Will Henry thought what a pity it was that a man in the prime of life could have such a brilliant political career cut short.

23 IT WAS shortly after the first visit of Franklin Roosevelt to Delano that the second murder occurred. Will Henry, at least, thought of it as the second murder. He learned about it, almost casually, from Skeeter Willis, who dropped into his office without notice one day.

"A nigger found him early yesterday morning hung up in a barbed-wire fence a couple of hundred yards from the Columbus highway, over the side of the mountain." The other side of the mountain was in Talbot County. "He'd been shot in the back with what Sheriff Goolsby reckoned was a .45 automatic. Little hole in his back, big one in his chest where it came out. Don't know much more myself. I saw one of Goolsby's deputies at a filling station in Woodland. I been down to Albany to deliver a prisoner."

"Was he wearing any clothes? Were there any marks on him?" Will Henry had a terrible sinking feeling already.

"Don't know. You're not thinking it had something to do with that thing of yours, when was it—two, three years ago?"

"Four and a half years." Will Henry got up and put on his hat. "I think I better go talk with Jim Goolsby."

He found the Talbot County sheriff at the Talbotton courthouse during a recess. Goolsby, an elderly man who had held office for more than twenty-five years and looked fragile and worn, was very pushed for time.

"Sorry, but it's always like this when court's in session."

"What was the man wearing?"

"A shirt and overalls, no shoes. Feet was tore up a little. Looked like he'd been running. Run into a bobbed-wire fence. Bullet went clean through him."

"Were there any other marks on his body?"

"Huh?" The sheriff turned to a deputy. "Carlton, are they back with that prisoner, yet? Well hell, go see what's keepin' 'em. The judge has already had to call a recess. He'll pitch a fit." He turned back to Will Henry. "What was that about marks?"

"Were there any noticable bruises anywhere? Had his hands or feet been bound?"

Goolsby looked at him incredulously. "Good Lord, I don't know. The coroner would ordinarily have done some kind of examination, but he had a funeral to do in Villa Rica, so I just talked to him on the phone. I put 'death due to a gunshot wound' on the death certificate, and he signed it when he come back."

"Can I have a look at him?"

"The dead feller? He's halfway to Waycross by now. There was a letter in his pocket with a return address on it. I called the sheriff down there, and the feller's daddy come up here with a truck and took him home to bury this morning."

"You got any suspects?"

"Hoboes, we reckon. We found an empty camp we didn't know about not very far away from where the nigger found the body. He didn't have no money or shoes, and I reckon that's what hoboes would take."

"Do you have any idea which way he was running?"

The sheriff thought for a moment. "The way he was hung on the fence he could have been running either away from the highway or towards it. Hard to say. My guess was towards the road, away from the camp."

"How old was he, could you estimate?"

"His daddy said he just turned twenty-one, but he looked younger than that to me. Listen, Chief, I'd like to talk with you some more, but I'm due back in court. Was there anything else?"

Will Henry got the name and address of the boy's father and directions to where the body was found. He thanked the sheriff for his time and asked to be notified if anything else turned up on the murder.

The spot was easy to find. He had only to follow the tire tracks where the sheriff's car had driven. They stopped at a barbed-wire fence on the edge of a pasture. There was a scrap of cotton flannel still hanging from the wire. Will Henry looked in the two directions in which the sheriff had said the man might have been running. The Columbus highway was in sight in one direction, and on a reciprocal course was Pine Mountain. There was smoke rising from the trees half a mile away. The smoke was from Foxy Funderburke's house.

Will Henry began to walk away from the fence, using the smoke as a mark to maintain his direction. He walked slowly, looking at the ground. There had been no rain for a while, and the earth was firm under the grass. There were no footprints. He had covered nearly forty yards when he found the cartridge case. He stuck a twig into the case and gently lifted it without touching it with his fingers. It was a .45 automatic, its size left no doubt. There were smudges that might have been fingerprints, but they were no longer identifiable. He had read enough about finger-printing to know that. He turned the case slowly on the twig, willing it to give up some other bit of identifying information, but it was bare of anything, even a maker's name. Only the numerals .45 were visible. He turned and looked toward the fence, measuring the distance in his mind. Forty yards, near enough. An amazingly good shot for a weapon which had a reputation for being difficult to fire accurately. He put the cartridge case in his pocket and continued toward the smoke.

He entered the trees on the other side of the field and soon found the camp, a clearing scattered with cans and bottles and with the remains of a fire, cold. The smell of burnt garbage hung in the air. He searched the ground carefully for several minutes, but found nothing else of interest. Then he walked twice around the perimeter of the camp to see if he could find signs of someone having entered from another direction from that which he had come. There was nothing. The woods were mostly pine, and a thick carpet of brown needles had absorbed any footprints without a trace. He could no longer see the smoke because of the trees, so he walked back to his car.

He drove to Foxy's house almost without thinking, nearly surprised when he found himself parked in front. Foxy's azaleas were in bloom, and the place was really quite lovely, with none of the cold foreboding of his earlier visit, more than four years before. Foxy was a bit easier, too, inviting him in and offering him a chair with an air that was very nearly like courtesy. They sat in cushioned wooden rocking chairs on either side of the fireplace. On the wall over the mantle there were a dozen rifles and pistols. One of them was a .45 automatic. Will Henry tried not to stare at it.

"What can I do for you?"

"Foxy there was a shooting about half a mile from here, day before yesterday."

"I heard about it."

"You see or hear anything around that time?"

"Not a thing."

There was a long pause. Will Henry hardly knew what else to ask the man. He looked up above the mantelpiece.

"That's quite a collection." He rose and reached for the .45. "May I?"

Foxy jumped up and got to the weapon first. "Let me unload that." He slipped the clip out and worked the action, ejecting a cartridge. Will Henry noted that the pistol had been ready to fire. Foxy handed it to him, butt first. It was oily to the touch.

"Been fired recently?"

Foxy waved a hand. "They've all been fired recently. I take good care of them."

Will Henry picked up the clip from the mantelpiece, where Foxy had laid it, and slipped out a cartridge. The name Remington, along with the caliber, was stamped clearly on it. The brass was a brighter color, too, than the cartridge in his pocket. "I hear this is a hard pistol to hit anything with."

"That's the case. I'm a good shot with almost anything, but I just barely qualified with that in the army. Lots of men never did."

There was a silence again. "Think you could hit a man at forty yards with this, Foxy?"

"I doubt it. You think I shot that fellow?" Will Henry handed the pistol back to him before answering. "I don't have any good reason to think that."

"Then what are you doing here?"

"You live nearby. I just thought you might have seen or heard something."

"Seems like you call on me every time somebody gets himself killed. I can't say I like that much."

"Just doing my job, Foxy."

"Seems to me like you're doing more than that. This fellow was shot in Talbot County, I believe. I live in Talbot County. Seems to me you're doing Jim Goolsby's job. Jim's a friend of mine. I think he'd like to know about this."

"By all means. This is purely an unofficial visit, Foxy. I'm sorry if I've troubled you."

"The only thing troubles me is that there have been two killings here and you've come to see me twice. Well, I've got nothing to hide. You want to search my house?"

"No, no, Foxy, I'm sorry I bothered you. I—I do want to thank you again for the puppy. The children just love him, we all do."

"Don't mention it."

Will Henry drove away from the house feeling he'd made a fool of himself. He went back to the station, wrote a note to Jim Goolsby about how and where he'd found the cartridge case, slipped the note and case into an envelope, stamped it, and put it with the outgoing mail. There was nothing more he could do about this. It was out of his jurisdiction, and there was nothing to connect the two killings, except their proximity to Foxy's house, and that was just a coincidence. The hobo theory held up even better in this case than in the last. He went home and made a determined effort that evening to put the thing out of his mind. He remembered how he had become obsessed with the last killing and what it had done to him. He slept well that night.

The following morning he went to the office as usual, opened the mail, and discovered that he was depressed. He stared at the wall for a few minutes, telling himself not to get involved with this one; then he picked up the telephone. "Estelle, could you talk to the operator in Waycross and get me the names and numbers of all the funeral homes in town, all the white funeral homes?" He hung up and waited impatiently for her to ring back.

There were four, and he found the right one on the second call.

"Underwood Funeral Parlor."

"May I speak with Mr. Underwood, please?"

"Speaking."

"Mr. Underwood, my name is Lee, I'm the chief of police up in Delano, in Meriwether County. Could you tell me if you're in charge of funeral arrangements for, uh, Charles Collins."

"Charles Collins is the father. Frank Collins is the deceased."

"Yes, the young man who was shot up in Talbot, County?"

"I buried him an hour ago."

Will Henry's heart sank. He thought for a moment. "Mr. Underwood, did you embalm the body yourself?"

"Yes, I do all my own work."

"Could you tell me, please, sir, apart from the gunshot wound, were there any other injuries or marks on the body?"

"Well, the feet had some cuts and bruises, as if he'd been running barefooted."

"Yes, that sounds right. He had no shoes on when found. But was there anything else, any sign of bruises on the body, as if the boy had been beaten?"

"No, nothing like that."

Will Henry slumped in the chair. He didn't realize how tense he had been. "Well, thank you for your help, Mr. Underwood, I—"

"There was something else a bit odd, though."

"Yes, what was that?" He was tense again.

"Well, I didn't notice it until I was dressing the body, but his wrists—his wrists were bruised, like he had been tied up. There was some skin scraped off, too."

"Mr. Underwood, I wonder if you'd do me just one further favor. Would you write down a description of the boy's injuries as you remember them, especially a description of his wrists, and send it to me?" He gave the man his name and address and hung up.

He was elated, but why? What did he have? Only one real connection between the two deaths, and all he could do was pass that on to Jim Goolsby, along with the cartridge case. He had nothing but his own reopened wound. He slammed his fist down on the desk nearly hard enough to split the wood.

24 WILL HENRY telephoned Sheriff Goolsby and told him about the marks on the Collins boy's wrists and that he was sending on the cartridge case. Goolsby, as Will Henry had feared, was as miffed by Will Henry's unauthorized investigation as he was glad to have the meager evidence, and he did not take kindly to the interrogation of Foxy, who had telephoned him immediately after the event. Will Henry apologized profusely, pointing out that his only interest in the case was in the possibility of a connection with the earlier murder, and he admitted that there was no significant connection, not one that any reasonable law-enforcement officer could proceed upon.

He hung up thoroughly humiliated and more depressed than he had been since the period following the first killing. Will Henry's depression was anger turned inward, and before the day ended he found an outlet for his anger in Emmett Spence, son of Hoss.

Emmett Spence had been a troublemaker most of his sixteen years. As a small child he had horrified his mother by burying two dozen baby chicks up to their necks in the front yard and running a lawnmower over them; on a later occasion he had managed to throw a switch in the M&B railway yard that, had it not been discovered in the nick of time, would have caused two switching engines to collide. His father had taken a perverse pride in many of these incidents, preferring to think that in committing them the boy had showed "spunk." The local populace thought of Emmett as not quite right in the head and tolerated him only because his father was a rich man in a poor county.

On this evening, after supper, Will Henry received a telephone call from Smitty, who ran the grocery store in Braytown, saying that a white youth was breaking windows in the colored schoolhouse. Will Henry arrived on the scene to find Emmett Spence firing through the school windows with a .22 rifle, while a group of black adults, who had been attending a club meeting, huddled inside, trying to protect themselves from flying splinters of glass.

Emmett froze when he saw the police car pull up; he was too frightened even to run. Will Henry strode to him, yanked the rifle from his hands, unloaded it, and battered it to pieces against a nearby telephone pole. That got some of the rage out of him, but not all. He whipped off his belt with one hand, grabbed Emmett's wrist with the other, and delivered a proper hiding to the boy, urged on by the blacks, who had recovered themselves and come outside to watch their juvenile tormentor running in a circle, chased by a wide piece of leather and screaming like a frightened chicken.

Will Henry apologized to the people, promised them that the damage would be paid for, and dumped the shrieking Emmett into the car. He drove the three miles to the Spence farm, dragged Emmett out of the car, and knocked on the kitchen door. Hoss Spence himself came to the door.

Will Henry was breathing hard from anger and exertion. He shoved the boy into his father's hands. "Hoss, I caught this boy of yours firing a rifle into the colored schoolhouse, which was full of people at the time. I broke that rifle into a lot of pieces, and I took my belt to him. I should have locked him up and thrown away the key, but I'm bringing him home to you instead. But I'm telling you right now, Hoss, if I catch him at anything— and I mean *anything*—again, I'll have him under arrest, and he's big enough for the county camp now. Do I make myself clear?"

"Shut up!" Hoss shouted at the boy, who was still sobbing loudly. "Now you get yourself out to the barn, and I'll tend to you directly."

"Daddy!" the boy shrieked hysterically. "He whupped me in

front of all them niggers!"

Hoss's eyes narrowed. "He whipped *you* in front of a bunch of niggers?"

"Yessir!"

"Get out to the barn right now, or I'll knock your head off!" Hoss yelled. The boy fled. Hoss wheeled on Will Henry. "You whipped *my* boy in front of niggers?"

"You're damned right I did, and I whipped him good! And I'll tell you something else. If you aren't down at the city hall before the close of business tomorrow with a checkbook to pay for the damage, I'll come out here with a warrant, and I'll throw his ass in jail! Do you understand me?"

Hoss's face glowed nearly purple by the back porch light, but he held himself in. "I'll be there," he said; then he turned on his heel and started for the barn, unbuckling his belt as he went.

Will Henry watched him go, surprised at his own behavior. He could not recall shouting at anybody in his adult life. As he drove away from the Spence house, he could hear terrible screams coming from the barn. Will Henry shuddered, his anger spent. "Lord, I hope he doesn't kill the boy," he muttered to himself. "But I hope he can't sit down for a month, either."

And as he drove toward home, he again felt the glow that came from having done justice, from having been effective.

25 JESSE COLE was wakened by Nellie at three-thirty in the morning; he struggled into his clothes, half-awake, while Nellie fried some bread in fat for him. This had been the hardest part of coming to work for Hoss Spence, this getting up in the middle of the night. He had risen at dawn all his life, but cows demanded to be milked twice a day, and that meant getting up at three-thirty, there was no way around it. He ate the hot bread and drank milk from a tin cup. There was no cash to buy coffee now, and Jesse missed his morning coffee mightily. Nellie was asleep again before he finished eating. Willie never cracked an eye.

He left the shack with a kerosene lantern and walked a quarter mile to the gate across the Warm Springs road, where the herd waited patiently to be let through to the dairy. He stood with the lantern while they crossed the road, then walked slowly behind the cows, their bells thudding softly in his ears. He was about as close to sleep as a man could get and still walk a straight line, and he did not hurry the animals.

The cows entered the dairy barn and went into their stalls like ladies arranging themselves at an ice-cream social. Jesse milked his dozen still half-asleep, resting his head against soft flanks while his hands automatically coaxed the milk from the teats. He and the others emptied their pails into the big, five-gallon cans, and he drove the emptied herd back to its pasture, with the sun rising before them, huge and red. Already the air was heavy and hot, and the day promised to be a scalder.

There were the cement floors of the dairy barn to be hosed down and disinfected, the stalls to be cleaned, then the milk to be fed into the pasteurizer, cooled and bottled, while a portion went into the big mechanical churn. By ten o'clock Jesse was replacing a rotting door jamb at the main house, by now fully awake and doing his carpentry steadily and skillfully.

When Hoss Spence came back to the house at noon for his dinner, Jesse was just finishing up with the door jamb. He did not speak to Jesse, and the black man was aware that something was wrong. He finished the work, packed his tools, and started home for his own dinner, and as he left he was aware of Spence staring at him. He had heard about the incident with Emmett and the chief the day before, and he suspected Hoss's attitude had something to do with the Cole family's having once worked for the Lees.

Jesse was still eating when he heard Hoss's truck pull up outside.

"Jesse!" Hoss had a tendency to yell when he was angry.

Jesse walked out onto the porch. The truck's engine was still running. "Get in. I've got some work I want done."

Jesse swallowed what he was chewing. He was annoyed. He normally got two hours for dinner and a nap, to make up for the early rising. What did the man want now? He reached for his toolbox on the porch.

"Never mind the tools. You won't be needing 'em." Jesse got into the truck and sat silently while Hoss drove down a rough dirt road toward the middle of the farm, then turned off across a field toward Pigeon Creek. Hoss said nothing, but Jesse knew he was mad as hell about something the way he jerked the truck around.

They drove over a small rise and started downhill. As they moved along there appeared ahead in the distance a small forest of tall, topless tree stumps, bare of bark, thrusting from water like elongated tombstones in a flooded cemetery. They were headed for several acres of swamp that bordered Pigeon Creek. Something inside Jesse recoiled. There were only two things on earth that truly terrified him, water and snakes, and a swamp was the worst possible combination of the two.

Hoss stopped the truck at the edge of the water, where there were two truckloads of sandbags stacked, waiting for drier weather before being fashioned into a levee which would allow the land to be drained. Hoss got out and motioned for Jesse to follow him. The white man pointed over the water.

"See that tall trunk there, and, on along, that one with the limb sticking out?" The two stumps were about where the creek bank would be in dry weather, and about thirty yards apart. "I want you to start laying them sandbags between them two trees. I want 'em a in straight line, stacked so they'll stay, you understand me?"

Jesse's breath was coming quickly now, and his words tumbled out. "Mist' Spence, don't you reckon be better to wait fo' the creek go down a lil' bit fo' stackin' them bags down there?"

Hoss turned his head slowly and stared at Jesse. "I don't want no back talk from you. I want them bags in there today."

Jesse was near panic now. "But Mist' Spence—" Hoss turned back to the truck, lifted a double-barrelled shotgun from a rack behind the seat, broke it and looked at the twelve-gauge shells inside, then snapped it shut again. He walked back to where Jesse stood and stopped, the shotgun held across his chest. "You and me are all alone down here," he said softly. "Now you start shifting them sandbags, or I'll blow your fucking head off right where you stand." His eyes were bright with something beyond anger.

There was something terribly wrong here, Jesse thought. He had done nothing to bring this man down on him. Nellie had been awfully quiet lately, and the boy had been on his best behavior. But he knew that this man would kill him, so he turned quickly and lifted a sandbag to his shoulder. Jesse couldn't count, but he knew it weighed nearly a hundred pounds. He waded into the water and started for the tall tree, picking his way carefully as the water deepened, feeling for a drop-off. There was mud—soft, sucking mud—under the water, and his own 220 pounds, plus the weight on his back, pressed him down into it as he struggled on, staggering toward the tree. The water was only waist deep when he reached the stump, and he heaved a sigh of relief as he dumped the bag and guided it into place as it sank. He started back for another bag, mosquitoes swarming around his head, biting every exposed bit of flesh.

More than an hour had passed, and only ten bags had gone into place in the deepening water, when Jesse saw the snake. He was struggling back in water to his chest, and the reptile's head and wake appeared in the corner of his vision, with three feet of writhing length following. Jesse uttered a strangled cry and changed his course abruptly for a log which stretched out from the water's edge, his arms flailing the water. He was nearly to the log, and suddenly there was no bottom. His forward progress took him away from his last contact with anything solid, and the snake became unimportant. All he wanted was a hand, a toe on something that would bear his weight. He surfaced, sputtering, water spewing from his mouth and nose; he could see the shape of the log through the liquid that filled his eyes, and he expelled all the air from his lungs in a final, pleading scream. Before he could inhale again, he was underwater, sinking, being drawn down by his sodden overalls, his empty lungs robbing him of any buoyancy. Some spark of survival instinct kept him from inhaling again as he sank, and after what seemed minutes of downward travel his foot touched a soft bottom. With all his will he resisted struggling until both feet were on the bottom and he had enough leverage to push off the mud. He shot upward, and as he broke the surface, gasping and flailing, his hand came into contact with something cold and hard, and he drew himself around until both hands could grasp it, taking great gulps of sweet air and shaking the water from his eyes.

Then he saw what he had grabbed. Somewhere behind him was the dreaded snake; beneath him was the black water; and at the other end of the shotgun barrel to which he held so tightly was Hoss Spence, braced on the log, with finger on the triggers. And all around him the air hummed and bit and stung.

26 SOME WEEKS LATER Carrie Lee was ironing on her back porch, the coolest place she could find, when she looked up to see Nellie Cole at the screen door. She had not heard the black woman approach; nor had Nellie knocked; she simply stood there, staring blankly ahead of her.

"Why hello, Nellie." She went to the door and brought her to a cane chair next to the ironing board. She was clearly distraught. "Would you like some iced tea? I was about to have some myself. It's awfully hot this morning." Nellie took the glass and drank deeply from it.

Carrie sat down next to her. "Nellie, what's wrong? Why are you in town the middle of the week?" Nellie took another swallow of the tea. "Is it Jessie? Is something wrong with Jessie?"

"Yes'm. And now the words began to come. "Nearly 'bout a month ago Mist' Spence put Jessie to work in the swamp. He been doin' the milkin' and carpentin' 'round the big house, and they seem like they real proud of his workin'. But one day he come and git Jesse, and when he bring him back in the evenin' Jessie soakin' wet and shakin' and cryin'. He won't tell me what happen, but pret' soon he git sick, and Mist' Spence he wait three days fo' he call the doctor, and Dr. Wilson from Warm Springs he come out there fin'ly and say Jesse git somethin' from the skeeters in the swamp." She struggled for the name.

"Malaria?"

"Yes'm. Malaria, thas what Dr. Wilson say, and he make Mist' Spence go down to the swamp and spread oil on the water to kill the skeeters."

"How is Jesse now?"

"He git better after Dr. Wilson give him the medicine, but then he git sick again, and Mist' Spence he come down to the house this mornin' and say we got to git off the place 'cause Jesse cain't work no mo'. Jesse, he try to git up and go to work, but he cain't, and Mist' Spence he say we got to git off the place right quick. I make Willie stay with Jesse to keep him in the bed, an' I hitch up the buggy and come to town." She had been staring ahead, but now she turned and looked at Carrie with defeated eyes. "Miss Carrie, what we gon' do? We ain't got no place to to. What we gon' do? We cain't go to Flossie. She ain't got no room for a sick man and a boy. She got to do her bakin' to get by. She cain't have nobody sick in the house when she bakin'. What we gon' do?"

Carrie patted her arm and gave her some more tea. "Nellie, you just sit here and cool off for a few minutes, and we'll see what we can do. Don't you worry, now. It's all going to be all right. I'll be back in a few minutes."

Carrie called Will Henry at the station, but he was out. She felt something had to be done before the day was over. She was very angry with Hoss Spence. It was shameful that he should treat his people this way, that he didn't have the simple Christian decency to take care of them. She cranked the instrument again and asked for Idus Bray's number at his store. It was typical of Idus that when he set up his office in a downtown building he should also run a shoe store in the extra space. Never waste an opportunity to turn a dollar. Idus ran his business and farming interests from a space at the rear barely eight feet square, containing a roll-top desk, two chairs, and a hat rack, and he did it all between waiting on customers up front. A stranger visiting the store would have pitied the man, wondering how he could possibly make a living in the tiny shop, not knowing that Idus owned half a dozen farms, a peach-packing operation, a majority holding in the telephone company and that, on the side, he lent money at high interest rates to people Hugh Holmes considered poor risks for the bank. He answered the phone on the first ring.

"Idus, this is Carrie Lee. How are you?"

Bray was immediately on guard, remembering the large lump of cash Carrie had extracted from him for the new pastorium. "So, so, Carrie. How you doing?"

"Just fine. Idus—" She stopped and rephrased the idea in her mind. "I've got a little business proposition for you."

"How much is it going to cost me?"

"Not a thing, not if you've got a colored house empty."

"I might have. I'd have to check."

"I understand the city council has been after you to fix those houses up."

"It was mentioned."

"Well, I've got just the man for you. Jesse Cole. Carrie's brother. Used to work for us at the farm?"

"I know him."

"He's a first-rate carpenter; cost you a lot if he were white. He needs a house, and I reckon he can work off the rent by fixing things at the other houses."

"What's he doing now?"

"He's been working for Hoss Spence ever since we left the farm, doing carpentry work and milking. When he got sick, Hoss said he didn't need him any more."

"He's sick, is he?"

"He's been sick, but he's getting better. Be up and around in no time."

"I don't know if I've got anything just at the moment, Carrie."

"His wife's a good washerwoman, too. I know Bess would be pleased with her."

Bray was silent for a moment. Carrie knew his wife had been asking around for a laundress. When he continued to be quiet, she knew she had him hooked.

"Well, there is a place, on D Street, second house from the corner. Might need a little work."

"Tell you what. Jesse'll give you a day a week for his rent, you supply the materials to fix up his own place. Nellie'll do your washing."

"Two days."

"Done, as soon as he's on his feet. Now, Idus, if you don't treat these people right you're going to have to answer to me, you know that?"

Bray laughed out loud. "Carrie, I'm not about to bring *that* on myself."

Carrie hung up and took a couple of deep breaths. She went back to Nellie and told her what she'd arranged. Nellie nearly fainted with joy. "Now, Nellie, you drive back out to Spence's, and you and Willie get your things loaded onto the buggy. Flossie and I will go look at the house, and I'll send Robert out there for you and Jesse this afternoon. Willie can drive the buggy in."

Carrie and Flossie drove out to D Street. The house was a shambles, but two hours of sweeping and dusting made it habitable. The stove was all right, and Carrie gave a neighborhood boy a quarter to chop some wood and kindling. There were two iron beds and a few sticks of other furniture, and Carrie contributed some linens. By the time Robert returned with Nellie and a very weak Jesse, the Coles had a home again, and Carrie left feeling that a great weight had been lifted from her. That night she related the whole incident to Will Henry.

"You know why he did it, don't you? It was that business with Emmett."

Carrie was shocked. "You mean Hoss was mad at you, so he took it out on Jesse? What kind of a man would do that?"

"Hoss Spence's kind, I reckon."

Carrie continued to send groceries out to the Coles via Flossie until they had some money coming in. In a week Jesse was pottering around the house, and soon after he was giving Idus Bray his two days a week on the other houses. Idus seemed pleased, but Frank Mudter wasn't too optimistic.

"It's a bad disease, Carrie," he told her at church one Sunday. "It comes and it goes, and you never really get rid of it. If Jesse's lucky he'll be able to make a living, but he's going to have a hard time. I'll look after him for nothing, but there's not all that much I can do. There's quinine and rest, and that's about it. And a man in Jesse's position can't afford much rest."

27 AS THE 1920s moved on, Franklin Roosevelt became a familiar sight in Meriwether County, and in Delano in particular. Hugh Holmes continued a series of personal conversations with the man in which, for the most part, Roosevelt asked questions and Holmes answered. Warm Springs agreed with Roosevelt, and the improvement in his condition seemed to whet his appetite for information about Georgia and the South. Holmes and others were invited to Warm Springs for a steak supper whenever Roosevelt arrived, and the banker sensed, perhaps before the others, that Roosevelt, who almost certainly did not consider any of these men his social equal, was seeking more than merely their company. His questions in the private conversations with Holmes became more and more pointed, and Holmes could only surmise that the man was planning an attempt on the presidency in 1928, a fact which did not entirely please him, for Roosevelt seemed to stand considerably to the left of Holmes in his politics. The banker was caught between his personal attraction and his philosophical antipathy for the man.

In the late twenties Holmes was a leader among a hundred state legislators who sponsored a young lawyer from McCrae named Eugene Talmadge to run against the incumbent state commissioner of agriculture, one J. J. Brown, who had built for himself something of a political empire at the expense of the state's farmers. Talmadge was a bit wild, but he was a mover, and he had caught the imagination of the state's farmers, who needed entertainment as much as they needed help from the state. Holmes saw a certain kinship between Roosevelt and Talmadge, as different as they were in background and philosophy. Ambition seemed to be their common characteristic, and Holmes had little doubt that each was capable of gaining much of what he sought. Now the little mountain against which Delano nestled was aflame with fall, the oaks and sweetgums and the occasional maple mixing with the evergreen of the pines and giving the crisp air of early November a companion in color. Crops were in, and a whiff of prosperity could be caught drifting in from the distant economic boom that had the twenties of the rest of America roaring. The mill was running three full shifts, six days a week, and the railroad was hiring; the ring of cash registers was heard more frequently in the stores on Main Street; at the bank, deposits were up, and Hugh Holmes thought that an ex-school-teacher named Irwin Dixon should probably be the bank's first vice-president. Because of this young man's stewardship, Holmes could now take increasingly more frequent absences from the bank for legislative sessions, political meetings, and foreign travel with Virginia; and when he returned, things were in order.

If prosperity was passing anyone by, it was Jesse and Nellie Cole and their son, Willie. They existed precariously, Jesse's illness ruling their lives. Jesse managed Idus Bray's two days a week, but little more. Robert, his brother-in-law, steered handyman and small carpentry work his way as often as possible, but too often Jesse would accept or even begin a job, only to fall ill and not be able to finish it. His pride prevented him from accepting pay for work he could not finish, even though he might have devoted some days to it; Nellie was often late when the white folks came to collect their washing, and she lost customers. Willie could find only occasional work, and then at such low pay that he could not contribute much to the household. Only the kindness of Flossie and the concern of Carrie Lee kept enough in the Cole household to keep body and soul together. Willie took his father's old single-shot shotgun and killed a rabbit now and then, and that was the only lean meat they saw, except when Carrie or the church provided a turkey at Christmas and Thanksgiving. It made him feel good to be able to bring something to the table, and such an event momentarily lightened the gloom that increasingly surrounded their lives.

By the autumn of 1927 Will Henry had found a kind of contentment, if not peace, in his life. The two murders had receded into the past, and time had mostly healed his personal, psychic wounds. Occasionally someone would mention the first murder, and that would be enough to remind him and send him into a mild depression for a day, but this happened less and less often.

The feeling of unease that Will Henry experienced on a Monday morning in November had no basis in reason, and he tried to put it down to the lingering effect of an already-forgotten dream. But it had increased by the time he arrived at the police station, and it did not dissipate as the morning wore on. Shortly after eleven o'clock two strangers entered his office, and, with a jolt of precognition, he knew who they were. They came to the window which opened from the waiting room, a middle-aged man and woman, both thin and worn looking, obviously dressed in their Sunday best. They might have been brother and sister.

Will Henry stood and went to the window, placing his hands on the sill to keep them from trembling. There was a terrible weakness in his bowels. He wanted to go to the toilet..

"Good morning, can I do something for you?"

The man extended a hard, dry hand. "My name is Holt, Julius Holt. This is my wife." Will Henry and the woman nodded at each other. "I'm Will Henry Lee. How can I help you?"

The man took a yellowed newspaper page from his pocket and unfolded it. Will Henry willed himself not to look at it. "We've been putting a new room on our house—I farm down near Americus, at Plains—and we got some old newspapers from our neighbors next door to put up for some insulation. We came across this article."

"Why don't you come around in here and have a seat?" He opened his office door and arranged two chairs for them. When they were comfortable, he forced himself to look at the newspaper page. The headline read, "Youth Found Dead in Delano. Police Search for Identity." The paper was dated the first week in February, 1920.

"This sounds like it could be our boy, James." He produced a photograph. "This was taken more than eight years ago, but it's the only picture we've got of him." There were three people in the picture, all sitting on the front porch of an unpainted farmhouse. The man and his wife were seated rigidly in chairs; the boy was sitting on the porch at their feet, his skinny legs dangling over the edge. His parents were posed with stern faces; the boy was grinning. There could not be the slightest doubt who he was. "He left home at the end of January, in 1920. The weevil had hit us pretty bad, and James had the offer of a job in Atlanta. He never showed up for it. We never heard any more from him. The law, uh, wasn't able to help us much."

Will Henry put the photograph down on his desk and took a deep breath. He forced himself to look directly at the man. "Mr. Holt, Mrs. Holt, I'm sorry to have to tell you that James is buried in our city cemetery here." The woman gasped and clutched her dress at the throat. The man looked as if he'd been struck.

"Are you absolutely sure? Look at the picture again."

Will Henry turned to his desk and pulled a file from the bottom drawer. With his body between the couple and the file he quickly selected a picture of the boy's head, one in which it looked as if he were merely asleep. He closed the file, turned and handed the picture to the boy's father. "That's James, isn't it?"

They both looked at the picture carefully. Tears spilled from the woman's eyes and rolled down her pale cheeks. The man looked as if he had been struck yet again. "Yes, that's James," he said, and handed the picture back to Will Henry. He put his arm around his wife and comforted her awkwardly. Then he turned back to Will Henry. "How did it happen?"

Will Henry made an immediate decision to lie to them. "It was only a few days after he left you. He fell from a bluff on the mountain over yonder. It was at night, and a stranger wouldn't of known about it. A newspaper delivery boy found him the next morning. He had no identification on him. We thought he might have been traveling with someone—a lot of people were on the road around then—and that they might have taken his things."

"Do you think somebody might have pushed him off that bluff?" It was the first time the woman had spoken.

"There was no indication of that at all, ma'am. These . . . traveling people he was probably with, they don't like to talk with the law much. If one of their friends dies they divide what he has among themselves and keep going. We're pretty sure that's what happened. No one would have had any reason to kill your boy." There was a silence, and he prayed they would accept the story.

"I see," she said weakly.

"We'd like to take him home with us," said her husband. "We've got a truck. Do you think you could fix that?"

Will Henry hesitated. He wondered if the cheap coffin would be intact after more than seven years. "Why don't you folks make yourselves comfortable here for a few minutes while I make some inquiries. There's some coffee on the stove, and the rest room is over there. I'll be back shortly." He went next door and telephoned Lamar Maddox, the undertaker.

Maddox did not like the idea at all. "Will Henry, I don't have any idea what's in that grave after all this time. I mean, that was a good pine casket, but there was no vault, and that's not the driest part of the cemetery down there in the city plot. And, you know, I'm real good at burying 'em, but I've never dug one up. I don't know what we can expect. Listen, you hang on there for a minute, and I'll come over there and talk to them."

Maddox arrived at the station a couple of minutes later, a little breathless. After introductions had been made, he sat down and composed himself into his most professionally soothing demeanor. "Now, Mr. Holt, I know what a grievous shock this has been for you, but I think we're going to have to look at this situation clearly. I think—it's my most considered professional opinion, that you are going to feel a lot better about this if you leave James to rest where he is and let me erect a real nice headstone there in his memory. Now, don't you think that would be the best thing to do?"

Holt and his wife exchanged a long look, and she shook her head. He turned back to the undertaker. "Mr. Maddox, we appreciate the advice you're giving us, we really do, but we'd like to take our boy home with us, and we'd appreciate it a lot if you could arrange it so we could do it today. Will you do that, please?"

Maddox sighed and clapped his hands on his knees. "Well, if you're sure that's what you want to do—" He called Will Henry into the hallway. "Listen, I don't even know what the law is on exhumations, but I reckon nobody is going to object. Why don't I just write out a kind of order and get the JP to sign it, and then, well, we'll just have to see what's in that grave."

Will Henry stood with the Holts at their truck, some fifty feet from where the two blacks were digging, supervised by Lamar Maddox. He was grateful for their silence, grateful especially that they had asked no further questions. It was taking a monumental effort on his part not to pour out the whole story, give them the medical report, take full blame for not having caught the murderer of their son. He was tightly wound, his jaws clamped together, his facial muscles hurting from the wretched expression frozen into his features.

"Will Henry!" Lamar Maddox was calling from the grave side. He walked quickly over to find the two blacks clambering out of the grave. "Take a rope, and help us, will you?" They hauled until the top of the coffin was at ground level. "Hold it right there!" Lamar said. They stopped, and Will Henry could hear water streaming from the coffin back into the hole. "The casket's in one piece, thank the Lord, but like I said, this isn't the driest part of the cemetery. Let's just wait a minute.

Soon the dripping sound stopped, and they manhandled the coffin away from the grave, where the two gravediggers began to wipe the mud from it with rags. The varnish was mostly gone, and the wood was pitted, but Maddox was right, it was a sturdy casket. Holt pulled the truck over, and the coffin was lifted onto the bed and the tailgate fastened. Holt turned to pass some bills to Maddox, while his wife looked forlornly at the casket; then he came and helped her into the truck. He thanked Will Henry profusely for his help, then climbed in and drove away. As Will Henry climbed stiffly into his car the two gravediggers were shoveling dirt back into the grave.

Will Henry went home for the noonday meal, but could not eat. Instead, he went upstairs and stretched out on the bed. He felt as if he'd opened the grave himself and filled it again. Every muscle ached, and the ache went to the heart of him. He dozed.

He was awakened by the ringing of the telephone downstairs. Carrie answered it. "Will Henry, it's for you," she called up to him. He struggled from the bed, got his shoes on, and staggered downstairs, hardly awake.

"This is Chief Lee."

"Chief, this is Ed Routon, out at the grocery store."

"Yes, Ed, what can I do for you?"

"Well, I hired a colored boy to sweep up this morning, and I caught him going out with a ham and a sack of beans. I guess you better come get him."

"All right, Ed," Will Henry replied, wearily. "I'll be there in about ten minutes. Uh, who is the boy? What's his name?"

"His name is Willie. Jesse Cole's boy. Lives down on D Street."

28 WHEN WILL HENRY arrived at Routon's Grocery Store, Ed Routon was sacking some purchases for a woman and laying on the charm. Will Henry looked around, but saw nothing of Willie. He waited for Routon to finish with his customer.

"Hello, Will Henry. Sorry to have to get you out here."

"That's my job, Ed. Where's the boy."

Routon turned toward the rear of the store. He chuckled. "Got him on ice." He unlocked a large padlock and swung open the thick door of the cooler room. Willie sat on the floor, hugging his knees, trembling violently. Will Henry shot a glance at Ed Routon; the man avoided his eyes. "Only place I had to lock him up."

Will Henry helped the boy up. He was surprised to find that he was nearly six feet tall, though still thin. It had been a while since he'd seen Willie. There was a swelling around one of the boy's eyes. "Willie, you go out and sit in my car and get warm. I'll be out there in a minute." The boy left.

Ed Routon looked concerned. "He's going to run off."

Will Henry shook his head. "I know Willie. His folks used to work for me when I was farming. He won't go anywhere. You roughed him up, did you?"

Routon still wouldn't look at him. "Well, I got mad. I give the boy a job, and then he starts walking off with a ham."

Will Henry nodded. "Ed, do you have to make a case against him? His daddy's been sick for a long time, and they've had a lot of trouble. You won't have any more problem with him."

Routon shook his head. "I've got to do it, Will Henry. If I let him get away scot-free every nigger in Braytown will be in here stuffing his shirt full of groceries. I have to be hard about this, or they'll steal me blind. You understand. He won't get much. Tell you what. I'll make the case on the minimum charge. What would that be, petty theft?"

Will Henry nodded. "That's a misdemeanor. At least he won't go to the county camp. Thanks, Ed." He walked out of the store and got into the car. Willie was still shivering. Will Henry got in and turned the heater on.

"Why did you do this, Willie? You know what this is going to do to your mother."

Tears began streaming down the boy's face. "Thanksgivin' comin' up. We don' have nothin' in the house." His voice was very small, but Will Henry could tell it had changed. Willie was becoming a man.

"You know you could have come to us. Or to Flossie. Anyway, the church would have got y'all a turkey at Thanksgiving."

Willie shook his head. "Mama say we ain't gon' take nothin' else from nobody no mo'. Mist' Routon jes' payin' me a dime a hour. Cain't buy nothin' wif' that."

Will Henry fished in his pocket and found two dollar bills. He stuffed them into Willie's shirt pocket. "Now, listen to me, Willie," he said. "Don't you tell your mother where you got this. You tell her you found an odd job. Now, if you get this way again, I want you to come see me, and I'll help. We won't tell anybody. Will you do that, now?"

Fresh tears welled up in Willie's eyes. "Yassuh. I do it. Yassuh."

"We're going to have to tell her about this business with Ed Routon, though. That's out of my hands. City court's tomorrow, and he's going to see you're charged with petty theft. Don't worry, though, you won't get sent to the county camp for that. Likely, you'll be sentenced to some time in the city jail. I'll be around there, and you'll be all right. Now you stop crying, and let's go see your mother."

Will Henry talked to Nellie on the front porch at the house on

D Street. Jesse was inside, suffering through another malaria attack. Nellie took the news in silence, but Will Henry could see that she was angry and terribly hurt.

"Now, Nellie, I'm going to leave Willie here with you tonight. City court meets tomorrow, and he'll have to be there at nine o'clock sharp, hear? Mr. Routon has agreed to make the minimum charge, and that means city jail instead of the county camp, so he'll be right here in Delano, and you can come see him. It won't be for long."

She nodded, her teeth clenched, jaw muscles working.

"I've already given Willie a good talking to, and he got a pretty good clout from Mr. Routon. He's learned his lesson, and he's getting too big to spank, anyway, so you take it easy with him, all right?" She nodded again. "Now, I'll see you both at nine o'clock tomorrow morning at city hall. I'll send Flossie to stay with Jesse. You remember, Nellie, that I'm leaving Willie in your custody instead of making him spend the night in jail, which I'm supposed to do, and if you aren't there on time I'll get in a lot of trouble."

"We be there, Mist' Will Henry," Nellie said. "And we 'preciate you lettin' him stay home." But her eyes didn't meet his, and her mind was somewhere else, in a dark and desperate place. From inside the house came a noise, a loud moaning. "I got to see to Jesse," she said.

Will Henry drove back to the station slowly, his heart filled with pity for Jesse and Nellie Cole. After all their trouble, now this. And it all went back to the Spence boy. His pity changed to guilt, and, on top of the visit from the murdered boy's parents, it was almost more than he could bear.

The telephone was ringing as he walked into the station. "Delano police, Chief Lee speaking."

"Chief? T. T. Brown here."

The salesman from the police equipment company. Will Henry had seen him regularly, twice a year, but Brown had never telephoned before. "How're you, Mr. Brown?"

"Just fine, just fine. I'm due down there next week. Stop in and see you, if I may."

"Well, yes, there are a couple of things I need."

"Reason I called, though, we got an order from Delano last week."

"I haven't ordered anything."

"I know. It's apparently from a civilian. We get them from time to time, but we don't sell to the public. If somebody wants something from our catalogue we tell 'em to order through their local police department; that way we don't have any problem."

"I see. Well, who was it, and what did they order?"

"No name. Just got an order for two pair of handcuffs, with a money order for the correct amount enclosed and a Delano post-office box number for an address. Box eighty-two. Probably a child, we get that now and then. They want to play cops and robbers, and they save up some money and want the real stuff. Still, I thought you ought to know about it. We've already returned the money order with a letter telling them to go through you."

"Well, thanks for letting me know, Mr. Brown, and stop in to see me when you're down this way." Will Henry hung up. He didn't know why Brown had even bothered to call. The money had been returned, that was the end of it. He doubted it anyone would be coming to see him to place an order for handcuffs. He turned to other work. Anything to occupy his mind. There was a letter from some women who wanted a stop sign at their street corner. He marked it for the attention of Willis Greer at city hall and put it in his out basket so he wouldn't forget to take it over.

At home that night he told Carrie about Willie's arrest.

"Poor Nellie," she said. "I'll see her name gets on the list for a turkey. I'll have a word with Frank Mudter, too, and get him to look in on Jesse. I'd go out and see her, but knowing Nellie, she'd be embarrassed. It took a lot for her to come to me when Hoss Spence threw them off his place. She doesn't like asking for help, not even from Flossie and Robert. You know, I'm going to have to give some thought to finding some regular work that she can do. Or maybe something for Willie, though it won't help when word gets around about this business at Routon's. She's tried so hard to keep him in school, and he'll graduate next year, if she can just hang on. Flossie says he's real smart. Head of his class."

"I'll mention that to the judge tomorrow; maybe it'll help."

They ate their supper and talked a little, but it was plain to Carrie and the children that Will Henry was again in the grip of his private demon.

Willie got ten days in the city jail. His mother testified that he had never been in trouble before and that he was a good student.

Will Henry testified that he had known the boy all of his life, that he was a good worker, and that his parents had brought him up properly. Willie himself apologized for his theft to Ed Routon, and Routon said he had no wish to punish the boy unduly. Justice of the Peace Jim Buce, who also ran the feed store, was sympathetic, but said that the boy had to be taught some sort of lesson. So it was ten days working on the streets under the supervision of the city manager. Will Henry turned him over to Willis Greer for work as soon as the court had adjourned. Robert drove Nellie home in the Lee's car, and Flossie was designated by the chief to bring the prisoner his meals, for which the city would pay. He would be the only prisoner in the jail.

Will Henry made his usual rounds without thinking, in a torpor of depression. He returned to the station to receive his prisoner at six o'clock. "How did it go today, Willie? What work did Mr. Greer have you doing?"

"I clean leaves out of some drains under the street. It wudn't hard. He say we do the same thing tomorrow."

"Well, it's only ten days. You'll be all done the end of next week."

"Yassuh."

Flossie brought Willie his supper and stayed to talk with him while Will Henry went home for his own meal. He left the cell door open, and reflected that Willie was probably eating a lot better than he would be at home. Driving back to the station after supper, Will Henry had the sudden notion that Willie would not be there when he arrived. But Willie was there, staring out the window, the cell door still wide open. Flossie had left. Will Henry wondered why he had doubted the boy.

"Everything all right, Willie?"

"Yassuh. You gon' lock me up now?"

"Yes, you can settle in now. There's plenty of blankets, and I'll put some coal in the stove before I leave. You should be real comfortable." Will Henry closed the door and began locking it.

Willie rushed from the window and grabbed the bars, his eyes wide with fright. "You ain't gon' leave me here by myself, is you Mist' Will Henry? You ain't gon' do that?"

Will Henry reached through the bars and put his hands on the boy's shoulders. "Now, son, I can't stay here with you all night. You're perfectly safe here. It's all right."

Willie grabbed Will Henry's wrists, and he began crying.

"Oh, no suh, I cain't stay here by myself! I'se skeered of it here!
Please, suh, Mist' Will Henry, don't make me do it! Don't leave
me here all by myself! Please!"

Will Henry hesitated. "Now, Willie—"

"*Please*, suh!"

Will Henry thought for a minute. He had a lot of leeway here.
Nobody had ever questioned his disposition of a prisoner. He
made up his mind. "All right, Willie, now listen. I'll let you go
home at night while you're serving your sentence. You'll come
back here after work every day and let Flossie feed you, and then
you can spend the night at home. But you have to promise me
that you'll be at city hall every morning at eight o'clock sharp to
report to Mr. Greer for work. Now, will you promise me that?"

Willie nearly wept again, this time for joy. "Oh, yassuh! I
sho' will! Thank you, suh!"

Will Henry drove the boy home and watched him run up the
steps and into his mother's arms. He drove away feeling better
than he had in days.

29 WILL HENRY was late to work the next morning, for the first time since he had taken the job. It was nearly twenty minutes past eight when he arrived, and there was someone waiting for him. A tiny old man with a pack on his back and a bundle under his arm stood on the steps and said, "Good morning to you, sir. Name's Dooley. I do basketwork, itinerantlike. Whenever I come to a new town I always visit police headquarters first and offer my services. That way, when I start knocking on doors the police know I'm not out to steal the silver. Is there any caning I can do for you, sir?"

Will Henry smiled at the man. "Matter of fact, there is. Kind of nice to have somebody turn up just when you need them. Come on in." He showed the man into his office and pointed at two sagging cane-bottomed chairs. "How much for the two?"

"I'd be pleased to do them for nothing but the good will, sir."

"Suppose we call it a dollar for the both?"

The old man smiled and doffed his hat. "As you wish, sir." He slipped out of his pack, tossed the bundle, which turned out to be strips of cane, onto the floor, and set to work on the chairs with a sharp knife, sitting on the floor as he worked, humming tunelessly to himself. The telephone rang. It was Skeeter Willis.

"Morning, Will Henry."

"Morning, Skeeter."

"Had a call from the sheriff of Fulton County last night, an old friend. Asked a favor. Friend of his wife's had a boy run away Sunday after he got into a little trouble and took a whipping. Sheriff figures he might be headed for an aunt's place in Florida and thought he might be hitchhiking down forty-one. He'd appreciate it if we'd keep an eye out for him. You still there, Will Henry?"

"Yes." He had been thinking about another boy, on the road alone for the first time, gone home, finally, with his parents in a box on the back of a truck. "Got a description?"

"Sure. Name, Raymond Curtis; age, fifteen, but looks older; height, five feet nine inches; weight, one forty-five; hair, brown; eyes, brown; has a one inch white scar on his chin; stutters a little. Got that?"

Will Henry jotted down the information. "I've got it. When did you say he was last seen?"

"Sunday afternoon, late. If he's headed for Florida he'd be past you already, this being Wednesday, but keep an eye out for him, all right?"

"Sure, be glad to."

"And Will Henry, if you come on him call me instead of Fulton County, if you would."

Skeeter wanted any credit coming. "Sure Skeeter." He hung up.

He sat, elbow on desk, hand over mouth, like a man about to throw up, frozen, staring across the room. It couldn't happen again. Why did he feel this way? Just a runaway boy. Then he realized he was looking at something familiar, something from a long time ago. His eyes focused on what the little man, Dooley, was doing across the room. Dooley's hands were flying about a chair, quickly weaving a seat of cane over the frame. The other chair, stripped of its seat, stood next to him bare, horribly naked, beckoning some memory. He went to his desk and heaved open the heavy bottom drawer, dug into a pile of papers, extracted the file he wanted. Setting the photographs aside, he turned to the neatly typed report. It was there, in bare detail: ". . . horizontal and vertical bruises, approx. eight-nine inches in length, one inch wide, on buttocks . . ." But there was something not in the report; something in Frank Mudter's dining room after an uneaten supper; something said. Dr. Carter Sauls's deep voice came to him: "He was tied to some sort of seat, something like

an old-fashioned toilet chair with nothing in the middle. . . ."
And now he remembered. His first visit to Foxy's house . . . nobody there . . . in the kitchen, chairs being recaned . . . one still bare. The dog had frightened him at that moment, when she and her puppies had made their appearance through the slot in the kitchen door, scaring him half to death, obliterating the memory of the chairs. He hadn't remembered when Sauls had brought it up. Something else Sauls had said: the boy's hands were tied or, perhaps, handcuffed. He picked up the phone and spoke a number into it.

"Post office, Pittman speaking."

"George, this is Will Henry Lee."

"How you doing, Chief?"

"Fine. Tell me something George, who has box number eighty-two?" He already knew the answer.

"Foxy Funderburke. Got it last year. We've got a waiting list, you know."

Will Henry thought for a moment. "Does Foxy pick up his mail every day, George?"

"Never misses. In here every morning as soon as I've got it put up. Except—"

"What, George?"

"Well, it's funny, but Foxy . . . hang on a minute, will you?

Will Henry waited, tapping his foot, knowing what was coming, frightened.

"Yeah, just like I thought. Foxy hasn't picked up his mail since last Saturday. Hope he isn't sick or something, up there all by himself on that mountain."

"Thanks for the information, George."

"Sure, Will Henry, but what's this all about?" But the chief had hung up.

Will Henry took a dollar bill from his pocket and handed it to Dooley. "Would you mind finishing up over in the fire station? I've got to lock up for a while."

"Not at all." Dooley gathered up his things and moved out the door. Will Henry locked the door and started to get into his car. The telephone rang. He hesitated, then got into the car and drove away.

With some effort he kept himself from driving fast through the town. No need to disturb people. Once past the last houses, he accelerated up the mountain, climbing fast until he reached the crest of the pass. There he stopped, forced himself to be calm, to slow his breathing. He had faced Foxy twice on the occasion of murders and got nowhere. This time he would do it differently. Instead of taking the road across the mountain toward Foxy's, he turned right, onto the Scenic Highway, and drove along the mountain's ridge until he saw smoke rising. He pulled over to the side and got out. A few hundred yards down the mountainside he could see a part of the roof of Foxy's house. A puff of wind blew the chimney smoke in his direction. Good. He would be downwind of the dogs. He started away from the car, then went back. He unlocked the trunk, took out a 30–30 rifle and loaded it. If it was still going on down there he might need it. He pumped a round into the chamber, eased the hammer down to half-cock and started down the mountain.

30

HE MOVED DOWNWARD through a riot of color, trees at the peak of their autumn, shimmering gold and flaming red, a carpet of the same hues under his feet. He did not notice the beauty which surrounded him, thinking only of what horror he might find at the end of his walk down the mountain.

As he approached the house, he slowed and walked carefully, wishing to make no sound that might disturb the dogs. Now he could see snatches of the house through the trees, log stacked on log, the garage to one side, doors open, truck inside. The trees ended in a clearing twenty yards from the house. The last yards before the clearing he moved stealthily, from tree to tree to bush, always keeping something between himself and the house. Near the edge he stopped and looked at everything again. Quiet morning picture, nothing unusual, smoke from the chimney, truck, garage. He sought to move around the perimeter of the clearing and looked down for a quiet footing. He stopped. Something wrong. Dirt on the leaves, on top of the leaves. He knelt. Red dirt, clay. Leaves undisturbed. He raked aside the leaves and dug at the earth with his hand. Black topsoil. Black topsoil under the leaves, red clay on top. All wrong. He looked around him. More clay, sometimes mixed with black dirt, scattered over several yards. He turned his attention to the clearing. There. Ten feet, maybe, into the clearing, the leaves. A large patch had been disturbed. He had to see.

The patch was well into the clearing. No shelter. He looked carefully from one window to the next. Nothing. He stood up, crooked the rifle in his arm, and walked, as casually as possible, toward the patch of disturbed leaves. From firm ground he stepped into a soft spot, in the patch. He looked at the house again. Still nothing. He raked at the leaves with his foot. Underneath, black soil mixed with red, tamped with something, a shovel. He forgot the house and raked more leaves away. An outline. Six feet long, maybe two feet wide. A hole dug, something buried, filled again, tamped with a shovel, extra dirt scattered into the woods to avoid a telltale mound, leaves raked back over the raw earth. New. This morning. He was too late.

In the house, Foxy, exhausted, was shaving. There was three days' mail in town, and he had to be presentable when he went to collect it. He turned and reached for a towel next to the window and froze. Will Henry Lee was standing in the back yard, exactly on the spot, moving leaves with his toe, looking. Seconds passed before he could move. Then he dropped the towel and ran, barefooted, naked, into the living room, clawed at the .45 pistol on the wall over the fireplace, ran into the kitchen, working the pistol's action, just to be sure, ran past the wet spot on the floor, scrubbed clean and drying, ran past the kitchen table, handcuffs, rubber garden hose, rope, ran to the kitchen door, threw it open, dropped to one knee, aiming. Gone.

The clearing was empty. He could hear Will Henry running through the woods, up the mountainside. He followed, running hard, past the disturbed leaves to the edge of the clearing, into the woods, stopped. He could no longer hear the steps. Lee had too much of a start, and he suddenly remembered, with the chill, that he was naked. He turned and ran for the house.

Will Henry moved quickly up the mountainside, running a few steps, walking fast, climbing, thinking. He had been too late. Too late. But now there was evidence to find, hard evidence in the cold earth. Out of his jurisdiction. He reached the car and tossed the rifle onto the back seat. He'd have to go to Sheriff Goolsby in Talbot County, tell him, convince him. Foxy's friend. No matter. When he heard what Will Henry had to tell him he'd have no choice. A search warrant. He got the car started, turned around, and roared down the mountain toward Delano, unaware that Foxy had seen him.

Foxy reached the house, sweating in spite of the cold, grabbed clothes, shoes. He had to reach Lee before he could tell anybody. Had to. He snatched a rifle from over the fireplace and ran for his truck.

Will Henry unlocked the door of the station and hurried for the phone, impatient while the operator connected him.

"Sheriff's office."

"This is Chief Lee, in Delano. Let me speak to the sheriff, please."

"Sorry, Chief. He's in the judge's chambers in a county meeting. Be in there the better part of an hour, I'd say."

"Good. Who is this?"

"Deputy Simpson."

"All right, Deputy. I'm on my way to Talbotton right now. I have to see both the sheriff and the judge, and I want you to be sure that neither one of them leaves until I get there, you got that?"

"Yessir."

"You camp outside the judge's chambers and tell them this is an urgent matter, all right?"

"Yessir. I'll tell them as soon as they get out of the meeting."

Will Henry hung up. Willis Greer was standing in the door. The city manager had a disgusted look about him. "Where's my prisoner?" he asked.

"What?"

"Where's my prisoner? I came to pick him up this morning, and he wasn't here. You take him someplace? I tried to call you a while ago, but there was no answer."

Damn Willie. "I let him sleep at home last night. He was supposed to be at city hall at eight this morning."

"Well, he wasn't. I hope he isn't long gone, I sure need the extra help this week. All the storm drains have got to be cleared of leaves."

"Well, look, Willis, I can't fool with this right now. I've got to get down to Talbotton on some important business. I don't think Willie would run off. He's probably out at the house on D Street now."

"Listen, Will Henry, I need him this morning bad. Can't you go and get him before you go to Talbotton?"

Will Henry thought quickly. "Tell you what. It's on the way, anyhow. You follow me out to Braytown, I'll get Willie, and you can bring him back with you while I go on to Talbotton."

Foxy got the truck started, roared down the road to the gate, turned left, and headed up the mountain. As he crested the pass he suddenly slammed on his brakes and pulled the truck to the side of the road. He tried to think clearly for a minute. Sweat was pouring off him, and he was breathing hard, his heart hammering against his chest. Not Delano. Talbotton. Lee would have to go to Goolsby in Talbotton. He started to turn the truck around, but something down the road stopped him. The Delano police car was turning off the road into Braytown, followed by a city truck. Foxy wrenched the pickup back toward Delano and Braytown. He made the turn into A Street in time to see the two vehicles turn right onto Bray Avenue. He followed at a distance and saw them turn left, again, into D Street. He approached the intersection cautiously. No one seemed to be about in the chilly weather. He turned into D Street and stopped. There were only two houses there, one on the corner, empty, and one at the end of the street. The two were separated by a long empty lot overgrown with brush. He drove a few feet into the street and pulled over. Up ahead he could see Will Henry Lee and Willis Greer getting out of their cars and starting for the house. He got out of the truck, taking the rifle.

In the house Nellie was sponging down Jesse's forehead and face. He had had a bad night, but seemed quieter and more lucid now. She and Willie had had a struggle keeping him in bed, he in the grip of some delirium in which Hoss Spence apparently played a part, for Jesse would mutter or shout his name from time to time.

Willie was worried. He was nearly two hours late being at city hall, and he didn't want to get the chief into any trouble. "Mama, he quiet now. I got to git to town."

Nellie spun around. "No! No suh! You gon' stay here where you needed!" She seemed half delirious herself.

"But mama—" They heard car doors slam outside. "They done come to git me, now. They gon' put me *under* the jail."

"Willie!" It was the chief's voice.

Nellie started for the door. "You stay here an' wash you' daddy's face. I'm gon' tell him you ain't goin' noplace!" She walked out onto the front porch. The chief and the city manager stood at the bottom of the steps.

"Morning, Nellie," said Will Henry, as pleasantly as he could. "I've come to get Willie. He has to go to work."

Nellie was trembling with anger. "You ain't gon' take him. I needs him here. His daddy sick."

"I'm sorry about that, Nellie. I'll send Dr. Frank out here this afternoon. But Willie has to come with me, or he'll be in a lot of trouble. You know that."

Foxy worked his way through the brush in the empty lot until he had a clear view of things. Lee and Greer were standing at the bottom of the steps to the house, talking to a nigger woman. Foxy wondered if the chief had told Willis Greer anything. Probably not. Lee was talking to the woman about taking her boy away. That's what Greer was doing here. He dropped to one knee and brought the rifle to his shoulder. He'd have to kill all three of them.

"No!" Nellie screamed at the top of her lungs. Inside, Jesse sat bolt upright in bed. "No! You ain't gon' take him. You jes' like the rest of 'em! You ain't no better than Hoss Spence!" Jesse pushed Willie aside and started for the door.

Foxy raised his rifle and drew a fine bead on Will Henry's right temple. The chief was standing stock still with his hands on his hips. It was an easy shot for somebody as good as Foxy. He took a deep breath and started to squeeze down on the trigger.

Jesse burst from the house, wearing only a pair of overalls, his eyes wild, a shotgun in his hands. Will Henry turned to look at him, his hands still resting on his hips. He opened his mouth to speak to Jesse, who ran across the porch and pushed Nellie out of the way. "Now, Jesse, you put—"

The shotgun roared.

Foxy watched in disbelief as Will Henry left his feet and flew backwards through the air. The black man dropped the shotgun and ran, jumped off the end of the porch, and headed for the woods behind the house. A black boy ran out the door after him. The woman was screaming something.

Before he heard the noise of the shotgun, Will Henry felt himself being slammed backwards by something heavy against his chest, then everything slowed down. He left his feet and floated briefly through space, then struck the earth with his shoulders. He seemed to slide a long way, bits of gravel and dirt scraping against his shoulders as he landed. As he came to rest, the roar of the shotgun filled his head, then he was looking up at the sky, and the sky was filled with Willis Greer's face. He struggled for what seemed like a long time to fill his lungs, which had been emptied by whatever had hit him.

Foxy changed his position, swung the rifle toward the running black man, took careful aim between the shoulder blades, then stopped himself. He had no reason to be here with a rifle. Besides, he had to find out if Greer knew. He started back toward the pickup truck, running low through the brush. The black woman was still screaming.

Willis Greer was on his hands and knees, bending over Will Henry. The center of the chief's chest was a mass of blood and pulp, an expression of astonishment was on his face. He drew a long, gasping breath and heaved it out. Bloody bubbles popped through the wreckage of his chest, and he sucked in air again. Greer seemed in shock, didn't know what to do. Foxy stopped his truck in front of the house and ran to them, pushing Greer out of the way. He bent over Will Henry, a strange expression on his face. "Can you talk, Lee? Can you speak to me?" Foxy's voice was a soft purr.

Then the pain hit Will Henry, and he fainted.

In the woods Jesse stopped next to a small creek to catch his breath, and Willie caught up to him. He grabbed Willie by the shoulders, gasping for breath. When he could speak he said, "Listen, boy, we cain't stay together."

"But, Daddy, you sick, you cain't—"

"No! You listen. You go to yo' Uncle Tuck in Columbus. He live at sixteen Camp Street. Say that to me."

"Sixteen Camp Street."

"He take care of you. I done kilt Mist' Hoss, and they gon' have the dogs after me fo' long."

"But, Daddy, it wudn't Mist'—"

"Don't talk no mo'. Ain't got no time. Now you run up that creek, right up the middle, 'til you get to the top of the mountain, an' then you git to Columbus. Don't take no rides from no white folks. You walk if you got to, and you go to yo' Uncle Tuck. He know what to do."

Willie nodded. "Yassuh." Jesse held him at arm's length for a moment, then crushed him in his arms. Willie hugged his daddy. Then Jesse was gone, running across the little stream in his bare feet and out of sight into the woods.

Willie watched him until he was out of sight, then turned and started running up the middle of the creek, up the mountain, away from Braytown and Delano, away, away.

Will Henry dove into the water, clean and straight. He opened his eyes and swam downward. Underneath him the thick weeds moved as if in the wind, and minnows darted here and there. He swam and swam, the cold water delicious against his naked skin, streaming over his shoulders and buttocks, stroking his penis, shriveling his scrotum. His lungs began to ache for new air, and still he swam. He stopped and looked around. Behind him the dog, Fred, was swimming, his four legs running through the water, churning it into bubbles. Will Henry laughed out loud, underwater, at the sight, expelling the air from his lungs. His feet found the weeded bottom, and he pushed upward, aiming at a point in front of the swimming dog. He broke the surface to his waist, gulping air, reaching for Fred.

He sucked in air and opened his eyes. Carrie's fingers were in his hair, Frank Mudter was sponging at his chest, Willis Greer, hat in hand, looked on, wide-eyed, and Foxy stood at the foot of the examination table, tense, his jaw working, sweat pouring down his face.

Carrie was weeping, trying to do it quietly. It was all clear to him, every sound, every sob, every movement, every drop of sweat on Foxy's face. He was numb, but when he inhaled the pain came in his chest. He tried to speak, but it got worse.

Frank Mudter drew back and looked at him, followed Will Henry's gaze to Foxy, looked back at him with curiosity. He was still trying to speak. The doctor leaned forward and looked into Will Henry's face. "Can you speak, Will Henry? You haven't got long, old fellow, I can't do anything for you."

Will Henry's lips formed a word, but no sound came out. He sucked in another painful breath and tried again, his eyes still riveted to Foxy, seeming to ignore Carrie, who held his head up in her hands. "Again—" he managed to whisper, still staring at Foxy. He bit at another breath, but it rattled from him in a long sigh.

Darkness came slowly. He closed his eyes. He could feel Carrie's cheek against his, her tears on his skin, her lips at his ear; she loved him, she was saying.

He knew it, and he was glad.

BOOK TWO

Sonny Butts

1 BILLY LEE, or more formally, Lieutenant Colonel William Henry Lee III, Army Air Corps, was in a daze, a mixture of simple relief, intense happiness, and equally intense fear. He was relieved that the Germans would no longer be trying to kill him, having surrendered just that day; he was very happy to be in the company of the girl he could just see disappearing toward the ladies' room of the crowded London pub; and he was terribly afraid that when she came back she would not agree to marry him.

Billy had had what he would later come to think of as a good war. He had already earned a junior partnership in a large Atlanta law firm when the Japanese attack on Pearl Harbor came, but he had unhesitatingly enlisted in the army, using Hugh Holmes's influence with the Roosevelt administration to keep him out of the judge advocate's clutches and get him into flight school. His age had kept him out of fighters, where he really wanted to be, but bombers were the next best thing, and his maturity had helped him earn responsibility when, after suffering a shrapnel wound in the seat of the pants on his thirty-eighth mission, he was able to return to his squadron as its executive officer. By assigning himself to fly whenever his commanding officer would look the other way, he had completed his fiftieth mission two days before the European war ended.

But if that would seem like a "good" war later, all that mattered to him now was that it was over and that he was alive and that, somehow, he might talk this girl into marrying him. He made an effort to stop rehearsing proposals and looked around for distraction; he would do better if he had to improvise. It had always been that way in court. A young infantry captain was slouched beside him, staring glumly into a pint of warm beer. A cane was hooked over the bar at his elbow.

"Where you from, Captain?" The young officer looked up. Billy thought he was probably a little drunk, but then so was he.

"Elmira, New York, sir."

"I guess you'll be going home pretty soon now."

"Yes, sir." He tapped the cane. "This'll keep me out of the Pacific. Nothing permanent, though. I was lucky."

"You don't look too happy about it. Aren't you ready to get back?"

"Oh, sure, I've got a wife and a kid I've only seen once. I'll find it real easy to be a civilian again—even one with a limp. I was just thinking, though, there'll be some guys who'll be sorry it's over."

"Sorry not to get shot at any more?"

The captain looked up from his beer at Billy. "You're a pilot?"

"B-17's."

"You've killed some people in this war, then."

"Not much doubt about that."

"Did you like it?"

"Flying bombers?"

"Killing people."

"I try not to think about it. Dresden, especially. I have a hard time not thinking about that."

"There are men who like it."

"Killing people?"

The captain shifted his weight painfully on his barstool and continued in the careful way of speaking of a man who knows he's drunk, but wants to be understood. "There was a man in my company, a kid, really, a sergeant." He paused and took a deep breath. "I promoted him to sergeant. In the worst of it during the Bulge he led a platoon when his lieutenant bought it. He loved it."

"Leading the platoon?"

"Killing. He loved making other men die. I think it made him feel—" His words trailed off.

Billy started to say something, to change the subject, but the captain continued.

"I found him . . . there was this big shell hole, and he had these German soldiers, really young kids and a couple of old men . . . we saw a lot of that, it was all they had at the end. There were eight of them in the hole, and I came up on him; I heard his Thompson firing and thought he needed help. I saw him shoot the last one. He was at least sixty."

"Well, one man against eight, he had to defend himself. They were armed, weren't they?"

"The one I saw him shoot, the last one, he was armed with a rifle with a fixed bayonet, and there was a handkerchief, a white flag tied to the bayonet. He didn't see me at first. He waited a minute; the man was begging. And then he shot him. He was grinning while he did it. He loved it. All eight of them."

"It's hard to know what a man thinks or feels at a time like that. It might have been different than you think."

"I know what he was feeling. His fatigues were wet. His pants. He came in his pants. It was all just a big wet dream to him."

Billy winced. "Did you . . . was he charged with anything?"

"Before I could do anything at all a mortar shell went off somewhere behind me. I woke up in a field hospital. I was in England the next day. I don't know if he's dead or alive, but I hope he's dead. At home they're not going to know what to do with somebody like that. He'd go back as a hero. He was the most decorated man in the regiment, and it was all because he loved his work. He'd been trained to kill people, and he learned to like it. I think I suspected it, but I couldn't relieve him; I needed him. All I could do in the end was to write to the new CO from the hospital, and I don't even know if he got the letter."

Billy looked up and saw her picking her way back through the crowd. "I hope he got the letter, Captain, and I guess that's all you can do, too. I hope you'll have an easier time forgetting it than I've had forgetting Dresden, and I wish you luck. Excuse me." He struggled toward her and took her hand. "Let's get some air, okay?" They headed for the door.

There was a bench in the mews, at the bottom of the pub's steps. They sat on the bench with their drinks; she pulled her knees onto the seat and faced him. Her name was Patricia Worth-

Newenam, and she was Anglo-Irish. He had met her at a general's dinner party at the Connaught and had shamelessly wooed her under the general's nose. She was a WREN attached to Allied headquarters in London, and they had spent every possible free moment together since then. They had slept in each others arms in her London flat and in country inns, but she would not make love to him. There was an old boyfriend in the Royal Marines, a childhood sweetheart, and he thought that must be the reason. He tried not to think about the marine.

He had pulled some strings and managed to visit her family home near Kinsale, in County Cork, for a weekend. Her family were Protestants, farmers for generations, who lived in a huge run-down Georgian house set in two thousand acres of Irish countryside. Her father was a small, handsome man who was a splendid host, but wary of him. He had lost a son and heir in the war and had only a remaining son and Patricia. He did not intend to lose her to some passing American. Billy had told him flatly that he would ask her to marry him if he survived the war. "You're a nice enough fellow," Worth-Newenam had replied, "and you're not the first to speak to me, as you might imagine. Colin Cudmore has wanted her all her life, and if I have my way he'll have her. She was brought up on a horse, and she loves this land. She'll not be happy as an American lawyer's wife."

"Mr. Worth-Newenam," Billy had replied, looking him in the eye, "I know I'm a foreigner to you, and I can understand how you must want to keep her here, but I love her, and I can give her a good life. There's land in Georgia, too, and I think that living in London has made her want more than just that. The thing that neither you nor I really knows is whether she wants me. If she decides she does, I hope you and Mrs. Worth-Newenam will give us your blessing."

"Since we love her, too, I don't see how we can do anything else. I guess you'd better find out if she'll have you."

Now he was about to do that, and all he could think about was how unbearably painful it would be if she didn't want him. The light from the pub's windows shone on her auburn hair, and though her eyes were in shadow he knew they were the same color. He took a deep breath and improvised.

"Listen, Trish, I think I want to be the president of the United States. Do you want to be the first lady?" In the brief silence that followed he wished he could see her eyes. Nothing else was moving.

"Oh, sure," she said, sounding oddly American, "but how will Mr. and Mrs. Truman feel about that?"

"I haven't mentioned it to the Trumans yet, but Harry understands that any American boy can become president, so I don't see how he can object."

"Do they promote thirty-three-year-old leftenant colonels directly to president in America?"

"There's a waiting period, usually. I thought I might go into the Congress or maybe be governor of Georgia in the meantime."

"Right."

"I mean, with my sterling war record and my wound and everything, how could they deny me?"

"Listen, buster, just because you got shot in the arse for Uncle Sam doesn't mean anybody's going to vote for you. Lots of other people got shot in the arse, too, you know."

"I love it when you talk dirty."

"Don't change the subject."

"What was the subject?"

"You were proposing to me."

"Oh, yeah. Did you give me an answer?"

"Yes."

"What was it?"

"That was it."

His mouth fell open. She put a knuckle under his chin and closed it.

"You mean it?"

"There are conditions."

"Your bargaining position will never be better. Name them."

"First, you have to ask me properly."

"Patricia Worth-Newenam, I love you, I really do, and I want you to be my wife and the mother of my children and all that. Will you marry me?"

"That was very nice. Second condition: I can't just be a politician's wife all day long. You have to buy me a farm."

"Anything to bring in the farm vote."

"I mean it."

"I mean it, too. The farm vote is crucial in Georgia."

"Done, then."

"No more conditions?"

"That's it for now."

"God, but I love you, Trish."

"I love you, too, Billy Lee. Take me home, and I'll prove it."

As they walked up the mews to find a taxi, she asked about the captain in the pub. "War stories," he replied. "He told me the worst war story I ever heard. You really going to marry me?"

"If you promise never to tell me war stories."

"Conditions, always conditions."

He put his arm around her, and they walked up the mews very close together.

2 TOP SERGEANT Homer Butts, known to all as Sonny, stood in the sunshine of an early spring day in 1946, at rigid attention, on the baseball diamond of Delano High School. Thirty-one other Delano natives, all in army, navy, or marine uniform, stood in ranks with him.

Sonny was bored. The banker, Hugh Holmes, was droning on about service and sacrifice and honor, and Sonny had had it up to *here* with service, especially, and all that other stuff, too. It had been okay, when the war was still on; there had been something to get your blood going, but for nearly a year the most strenuous thing he had done had been to play poker while he waited, waited, waited to get out of the army.

His eyes swept the crowded grandstand, the part of it he could see without turning his head. They were here to see *him*, not these other yokels. Hometown boy—the most decorated soldier in Georgia. Well, probably. He'd damn near had the Medal of Honor, damn near. Somebody had torpedoed him, though. A friend of his, a clerk in the company orderly room, had hinted as much. Shit, if he'd had that one he'd be as famous as Audie Murphy, maybe even have a movie contract like Murphy. He was good-looking enough, he knew, better-looking than Murphy, for sure.

He knew exactly how he looked, braced up on that baseball

field in that uniform the old German guy had tailored for two cartons of Luckies. Not as tall as he'd have liked, only five nine, but service had put some weight on him; he was 175 now. If he'd had that extra 20 pounds when he'd graduated from Delano High he'd have been a sure thing for a football scholarship to Georgia or Alabama or Auburn. He'd had the speed, but not the size, for college ball, the scouts had told him. He would let the blond crew cut grow out. The girls were getting tired of guys who looked like soldiers. He'd get a couple of sharp suits with the poker money, and there was enough for a good used car. A convertible, maybe.

Sonny heard his name mentioned. Holmes was reciting his list of decorations. Sonny tuned out again, then snapped back, alert. Holmes was saying something he wanted to hear.

"This morning the Delano City Council voted to give priority on all city jobs to returning veterans, and among veterans, to those with combat records," Holmes was saying.

Sonny clenched his teeth. The interview with Holmes the day before had not gone well, he thought. Holmes disapproved of him in some way, was suspicious of him. He'd known the feeling before; his company commander in Belgium had given him the same uneasy feeling. Sonny suspected the CO of torpedoing his Medal of Honor, even though the guy was in a hospital somewhere and had been replaced.

Holmes continued, "Today I can announce that the first of these openings has been filled by a veteran. From among the available candidates, Sgt. Sonny Butts is being hired to fill a vacancy on the city police force."

"Sergeant Butts, two steps forward, march!" The speaker was Billy Lee, Colonel Lee, the highest ranking of Delano's more than two hundred veterans, someone Sonny had known only as a high school athlete when he himself had been in grade school.

Sonny stepped forward, and Holmes shook his hand. "Congratulations, son. I hope you'll continue to make us proud of you. Report to Chief Thomas at eight o'clock Monday morning."

"Thank you, sir. I'll do a good job for you, sir." Sonny was weak with relief. He had been worried sick about work. His only job before the war had been jerking sodas and stocking shelves at the Delano Drug Company, and his only other prospect, apart from the police job, was the mill, and the thought of the mill depressed him. Now he had a job that would continue to command the respect he had earned by his deeds on the battlefield.

Colonel Lee formed up the group and marched them off the field in single file. As they passed through the fence next to the dugout, they broke ranks, and people came and pumped Sonny's hand and offered congratulations. As the crowd thinned out, Sonny found himself confronted by a wiry, wizened figure in the World War I uniform of a first lieutenant. The man had been pumping his hand for several seconds before Sonny recognized him. Jesus, it was Foxy Funderburke.

"Sergeant, you've done a fine job for your country," Foxy was saying, "and I expect you'll do a fine job on the police force."

"Thank you, sir, I'll do my best." When he was a kid he was scared shitless of Foxy Funderburke; they all were; he wasn't sure just why. Now here was the old fart shaking his hand.

"And I want you to know that my experience is always available to you. If you ever need any help, you just ask."

"Yes, sir, I sure will." What the hell was he talking about? What experience? But before Sonny could wonder any further, the tightly uniformed figure had spun about and marched away. Sonny stopped himself from laughing out loud.

Back on the field another group of ex-soldiers was forming. They were all black. Delano's black community was filling the stands. A few whites hung about to watch. Holmes repeated much the same remarks and singled out one or two men who had been decorated. Among them was Marshall Parker.

Marshall, who had been in some of the heaviest fighting during the D-Day invasion and had won a bronze star, noted that there was no mention of city jobs in Holmes's address to the blacks of Delano. Never mind, though; he had saved his money, and he had plans. Before the war he might not have dared to dream he could own a business, but his army service had changed him as it had changed his black contemporaries, and the war, he thought, had changed things for the better for all of them. Holmes had encouraged him, had indicated that a loan might be forthcoming for the right project.

As he stood in the sun and listened to Holmes's speech and accepted handshakes from the banker and Colonel Lee, Marshall Parker felt something he had rarely felt before—optimism.

Hugh Holmes and Billy Lee sat in Holmes's study and sipped bourbon. Billy laughed aloud. "You're pretty sneaky, you know. I never knew you had a secret stash of whiskey in this room."

"Last time you were in this room, you weren't old enough to know."

"Let's see, I was twenty-eight, I think."

"Too young to be trusted with my secret."

"I'm flattered to be trusted with it now."

"Well, if anybody ever had any doubts about you, and I don't think many folks did, your war record certainly has removed them. Your daddy would have been real proud of you."

"Thank you, sir."

"That's quite a girl you've got there."

Patricia was in the Holmes garden with Virginia, looking at azaleas and such.

"I know it, believe me. She'd rather be in here with you and me now than looking at flower beds, too. I'll have to square it with her tonight by telling her everything we've talked about."

"She's like that, is she?"

"Yes, sir, and I'm glad. She's smarter than I am."

"You're a lucky man, then. She can help you a lot. I don't think her being a foreigner will hurt a bit."

"Hurt?"

"You are still interested in politics, aren't you?"

"More than ever."

"Good. Have you made any plans? You going back with Blackburn, Hedger, etcetera, etcetera?"

"They want me. Partnership within a year, they're saying."

"What are you thinking of, Congress?"

"It crossed my mind."

Holmes shook his head. "The way I see it, only one Atlanta area seat is weak enough to change hands this year, and you've never lived in that district. There are at least two good men, veterans, who've already announced, and they both have roots there. You'd be at a big disadvantage."

"That's true. I'd thought, too, about moving back here and running."

"Against Joe Collins? Forget it. Not even I could support you against Joe. He's done too good a job for us, and he's a good friend of mine."

"What do you think I should do?"

"Are you only interested in going to Washington, or does Georgia politics have any interest for you? What about governor, eventually?"

"That interests me a lot."

"Good. I think it's a better goal, even if you want to end up in Washington. The Senate's the place, and Walter George is an old man now. Good for a few more years, I expect, and governor, or even lieutenant governor, would be a better springboard to that seat. Mind you, not for another eight years. Old Gene Talmadge is already running hard for one last shot at the office, and he'll win, I think. His health's not good, though. He might not live through a term. Melvin Thompson will probably be elected lieutenant governor and would succeed for the remainder of his term if Gene died in office, but I don't think he could be reelected on his own hook. I think Herman Talmadge will have it next time. By the time Herman finishes his term, you should be about ready, I'd think."

"Where do you think I should begin?"

"I think you should run for the state senate."

"Which district?"

"This district."

Billy swallowed hard. "You thinking of retiring?"

"I am. I'm seventy. I've been dealing with those scoundrels for thirty-five years. I'd stay on the state board of education and keep my hand in a number of other areas, but I'd be ready to leave the senate if I knew I were being replaced by the right young man."

Billy was quiet.

"Well?"

"It's a wonderful opportunity, Mr. Holmes, but—"

"What's bothering you? You think Patricia might not want to live in Delano instead of Atlanta?"

"Oh, no. In some ways I think she'd prefer it down here." Billy shifted uncomfortably in his seat. "Mr. Holmes, after Daddy died you were about the closest thing to a father I had. Even after Mama married Mr. Fowler, as good a man as he is, I still felt closer to you, and I want you to know how grateful I am for the advice you've given me over the years and your efforts on my behalf with the army and all—"

Holmes waved a hand. "Billy, you've never really needed my help in any important sort of way. You're going to rise to the top in whatever you decide to do. But I can help you now in many ways, and I want to. Ginny and I never had children, and I think of you as a son."

"Thank you, sir. I really appreciate that. But what I have to make clear to you is that . . . well, I have to be my own man right from the start if I'm going to really be effective in government. Forgive me for putting it bluntly, but I don't want to be elected to the state senate to represent Hugh Holmes."

Holmes grinned sheepishly. "Well, I guess I'm a pretty pushy fellow sometimes, and I'll admit I'd hope that you would pursue some of the same goals in the legislature that I did."

"I'm sure I would, sir, but you and I are going to disagree on some things sooner or later, that's only natural, and I want you to understand that I couldn't accept your help unless I felt free to follow my conscience."

"I have a feeling you have something specific in mind."

Billy shifted in his seat again. "I think the war has changed a lot of things irrevocably. I think we're going to be in for some upheavals in the South, things that a lot of Georgians are going to find distasteful."

"Billy, has the army turned you into an integrationist?"

"I think we have some painful transitions to make in this state. Those colored boys out at the school this afternoon fought and bled in the war just like everybody else, and they're entitled to the gratitude of their community. A lot of them were treated like grown men for the first time in their lives, and they're not going to forget it. They're just not going to accept things the way they were. And if I'm elected to the state senate I'm going to be representing those men."

Holmes grinned slightly. "That was a very politic answer to my question. Let me tell you where I stand on this. I think that for the races to start mixing and intermarrying would be the worst thing that could ever happen to this country, would ruin it. I don't want to see us become a nation of mongrels. But I think our colored people are entitled to things—education, work—just like white people, and I've always taken care to represent them in the senate."

"I know you have, sir."

"However, in spite of my views on miscegenation I know there are some important changes coming. My concern in all this is to try and prevent a confrontation which would be disastrous for all of us, white and black. One of the major concerns of my life has been education in this state, and that includes the education of Negroes, too. I think—and if you ever quote me on this

I'll call you a liar—we're going to end up being forced to integrate the schools in the next fifteen or twenty years by the federal government. I'll hate to see it happen, but I'll do what I can while I live to see that it doesn't destroy our public education system. So, you see, even though we might not quite see eye to eye on this question, we'll still have some common goals, and I think we'll be able to work together."

"I'm relieved that you feel that way, sir, because I don't think I could ask for or accept your help if I had to fight you tooth and nail on this issue. I want you to know, too, that I'm not going to lead any integration movements. I want a career in government, and to have that you have to keep getting elected. I'm enough of a realist to know that."

Holmes cocked his head to one side and examined the young man who sat across from him. "You know, I think you might be even more ambitious than I thought."

"I think governor is what I'll be aiming for. I don't want to get ahead of myself."

"Right. You'll run for the state senate, then? You'll have my full support, and I don't think we can anticipate any difficulties."

"Yes, sir, I will. And I can't thank you enough for the opportunity. I hope there's room for another lawyer in Delano."

"You know Harry Mix died three months ago?"

"Mama wrote me about it."

"The bank hasn't appointed another counsel yet. You've got all our work, so you'd better start reading up on your banking law—not quite the same as being a trial attorney."

"That's wonderful, sir. Thank you."

"You'll get some work from the mill, too."

"Doesn't Blackburn, Hedger still represent them?"

"Oh, yes, but I've already had a word with Tom Delano. You'll get whatever they need doing locally and maybe some of their trial work, too."

"Blackburn, Hedger won't like that, much."

"They won't have to."

"How is old Delano, anyway?"

"Eighty-two and still ruling with a steel-trap mind and an iron hand. I reckon that between the bank and the mill you'll get ten thousand a year in business. That ought to be enough to get a young lawyer started."

"That's business any lawyer would give his eyeteeth for."

"You'll need an office. There's space on the second floor of the bank building. Small, but it'll do for a beginning. You'll need a library, too. You save any money in the service?"

"All my flight and overseas pay, plus some. I've got about eight thousand in war bonds."

"Good boy. Still, you'll need more to get set up properly—you've got to have a place to live, too, and since there was no building during the war, housing is very short. I'd suggest we find you something temporary; then you build. That'll show folks you're serious about staying here."

"I've promised Trisha a farm, a working farm."

"Good, good. We'll find you some land hereabouts and work out a mortgage. Farmer-lawyer is a hard political combination to beat in this state." Holmes got to his feet. "I think this calls for another drink."

"I'm having a tough enough time keeping my feet on the ground now."

Holmes began to pour for both of them. "Nonsense. Since you were a small boy, Billy, your feet have never been anywhere but on the ground. You're going to do well, boy, really well." He sank back into his chair and looked at Billy appraisingly. "There's just a chance, with a lot of luck, that you could go all the way." He sipped his bourbon and stared into the fire. A tiny smile played across his lips. "The first southerner since the War Between the States. Wouldn't that be something."

As they drove home to his mother's house in his stepfather's car, Patricia snuggled close to him. "All right, then. Let's have a report," she said.

"Well, it appears I've just been appointed to the Georgia State Senate."

"Appointed? Don't you have to get elected?"

He laughed and put his arm around her. "Oh, I have to run. You're going to get to meet every storekeeper and dirt farmer in the Tri-Counties. But in this particular district one vote elects, and I've already got that vote.

"All right, start at the beginning."

3 SONNY sat at a table on the edge of the dance floor at Fletcher's, a road house five miles north of Delano, and watched the girl. A hillbilly band in cowboy suits was cranking out something mournful, the whine of the steel guitar leading the way, and the floor was crowded, but Sonny saw only the girl. Charlie Ward, Delano's only other police officer besides the chief, sat at his elbow and peered at Sonny through the thick glasses that had kept him happily out of the war.

"Jesus, Sonny, it's going to be great having you on the force, it really is. You and me together are going to snatch some folks sideways in this town, you wait and see."

"Yeah, sure, Charlie." Sonny signaled the waitress for another Pabst. He nodded at the girl as she drifted past in the arms of a beefy type in a sailor's uniform. "Who is she?"

"The readhead? She's from La Grange. Name's Charlene something. Not bad, huh?"

She was better than not bad. She was tall and had her hair swept back on one side with a flower behind her ear. Her angora sweater was pulled down tightly over her breasts and secured at the waist by a belt. "I love that," Sonny said. "I love slim girls with big tits." He took a short swig of the fresh beer and started toward the floor. Charlie grabbed his sleeve.

"Hey, listen, that guy's got a mean reputation around here.

You better wait 'til she sits down."

Sonny took hold of Charlie's wrist and squeezed until the fingers opened. "Don't crease the uniform, kid."

"Sorry, Sonny, I just—"

But Sonny was wading into the crowd. He caught the girl's eye over her partner's shoulder and held it as he approached them. She gave a little frown and rolled her eyes sideways at the sailor. Sonny read the look. You're cute, but watch it with this guy, it said. He stepped up to the couple and tapped the sailor firmly on the shoulder. The young man turned and looked at him, surprised. Sonny smiled. " 'Scuse me," he said, in his friendliest manner. "May I cut in?"

The sailor's eyes narrowed and his nostrils flared. "Fuck off," he said, and turned back to the girl.

Sonny grasped a fistful of navy uniform at the shoulder and turned the man slowly toward him. The smile left his eyes. "I don't think you understood me, swabby. The army is cutting in."

The sailor looked him up and down, took in the ribbons. He had a few of his own. "What the army is gonna do," he said, "is get cut up, not in."

Fletcher, the club's owner was suddenly present, towering over both of them, shoving his big belly between them. He held a child's baseball bat in one hand, its large end wrapped in black friction tape. "All right, boys, the back door is right over there." He nodded toward a fire exit in a corner of the room. "This discussion takes place outside." He slapped the bat into his left palm for emphasis. "Right now."

Sonny smiled again. "Yes, sir, Fletcher." He motioned the sailor toward the door. "After you, swabby." The crowd parted to let them through, then fell in behind. The girl leaned toward Sonny as he passed her. Her eyes were bright with excitement.

"He's got a knife in his sock," she whispered quickly.

Sonny nodded his thanks. "Come on, honey, I need an audience." As they moved toward the door Sonny slipped a ring from his left hand to his right. The stone moved back and forth easily, esposing the sharpened corners of the setting. He watched the sailor moving ahead of him. Lots of hard muscle there; the guy had thirty pounds on him, easy. No close stuff; stay back and cut him up; see how he likes the sight of his own blood.

The sailor shoved the door open and started down the short flight of steps to the parking lot, Sonny staying close behind. The sailor was starting to turn around. "Okay, soldier boy, how do you want—"

Sonny, pushing off the bottom step, had started to swing as the man turned. The blow caught him high on the cheekbone as he came half way around, and his own momentum helped spin him to the ground, hard. He started to his feet, swearing, but Sonny stepped quickly in and clipped him above the left eye, sending him down again. Now the sailor noticed that he was bleeding from both sides of his face, and as he rose his hand went to his ankle and began to come up with the knife, switching it open. Sonny took one long step forward and kicked him in the face, like a football player going for the extra point. The sailor's feet left the ground as he flew backwards. The knife fell from his hand, and Fletcher stepped on it, but there was no need; the sailor lay where he fell.

"All right, folks," Fletcher yelled to the crowd. "It's all over. Everybody back inside, the band's only playing for another half hour." He turned to Sonny. "You better scat before he comes to, or you'll have to kill him to stop him."

Sonny walked over to the girl, slipping the ring back onto his left hand. "Give me the car keys," he said to Charlie, who was standing beside her. She was breathing as hard as he was, he noticed.

"You're gonna come back for me, ain't you, Sonny?" Charlie asked.

Sonny took the girl's hand and started for the parking lot. "Why don't you get a ride with somebody, Charlie. I'll see you tomorrow. Don't worry about the car." He handed the girl through the driver's door and got the car started. "You're Charlene, right?"

"Charlene Pearl." She was still breathing hard. So was he.

"I'm Sonny Butts." He spun the car out of the dirt parking lot onto the highway and drove a few hundred yards to a dirt road that led to Fletcher's catfish pond. She slid over to him and put her hand on his thigh.

"You took real good care of Maxie, you know that? He never knew what hit him." She was up close, breathing into his ear. Her hand moved up to his crotch. "Hey, hey," she giggled.

"Take off your pants," he said, concentrating on driving fast.

She laughed and wriggled out of them. "And your sweater, and the brassiere."

"Is that all, hon?"

He whipped the car into a little clearing off the road and stopped. They got out, and the girl crawled into the back seat without a word. Sonny unbuckled his belt and shed his pants and uniform tunic; then he was on her and in her, driving, biting the big nipples, driving, driving. They came together in less than a minute, noisily. Spent, they lay in a heap on the back seat and fought for breath.

"It was the fight, wasn't it?" he said, finally, panting. "The fight got you going."

"Oh, yes," she said, panting herself. "It got you going, too, didn't it?"

"Yeah," he replied. "It always does. It does it every time."

4 HUGH HOLMES and Marshall Parker stood in the dim light of a disused barn on the outskirts of Delano.

"What do you reckon you'll need to fix it up, Marshall?"

"Mr. Holmes, I figure to patch up the roof and make the walls weathertight and to put in a couple of potbellied stoves and otherwise get it in shape to work in, that would take about fifteen hundred dollars—that's with me doing most of the work myself."

"How about tools and enough spare parts to get you started?"

"Another five hundred dollars, I reckon."

"And you've figured your expenses, your rent and things?"

"Yessir. And he'll give me a option to buy it at three thousand dollars. That's with just over two acres of land."

Holmes thought that sounded high, but it was a white man selling to a black one, and if Marshall did well enough to buy the place the bank might help him negotiate a better price.

"Marshall, I know you worked for Mickey Shelton before the war. That where you learned how to work on cars?"

"Well, sir, I didn't do much for him except grease jobs and oil changes and flat tires, like that. It was in the army I really learned about vehicles. We didn't have a proper motor pool in my outfit, and we found out we'd get things running a lot quicker if we did it ourselves instead of taking them to regiment."

Holmes nodded. He could understand how an outfit that came to be known as Eleanor Roosevelt's Niggers might have its problems getting help from an all-white unit.

"Then after we left Italy and went to England to get ready for the big invasion, we were stationed down in Cornwall, in the southwest part of the country. We were living in tents and on ships hidden and camouflaged up these rivers, and we had a lot of time on our hands, so I started going down to this little village, St. Mawes, and helping out this old gentleman, Mr. Pascoe, in his garage. I worked on Austins and Wolseleys and even Jaguars. Course, they were real short of parts, and we had to make do, and it was real good experience. I got so I could fix parts you'd usually throw away. That'll stand me in good stead around here right now, I reckon, since parts are still pretty scarce, and most colored folks like to get things fixed 'stead of replacing them."

Marshall did not mention the Sunday dinners at the Pascoes or the sailing in Falmouth Harbour with their daughter, Veryan, or how, for the first time, he had been made to feel like an equal by white people. They still corresponded. Holmes had noticed that Marshall spoke more like a white man than a black one and supposed that must have been the result of his English experience. He hoped the man's speech wouldn't cause problems for him.

"Good point. Tell you what, Marshall, we'll make you a loan of a thousand dollars to start—you say you've got some money saved up?"

"Yessir, over two thousand dollars."

"Well, you put half of that in a savings account at the bank, and you'll still be earning interest on it until you need it. Do you know about that?"

"Yessir. I got all the way through high school."

"And when you get on down the road a little bit, and we see how you're doing in business, maybe we can let you have more money to help build it up. That all right?"

"Yessir, that's just fine, and I sure appreciate it, Mr. Holmes, I sure do."

"Well, Marshall, you've always been a good fellow, and if you work hard and build up something for yourself here in your garage, folks'll have faith in you, and you'll be surprised what they'll do for you." Holmes looked at his watch. "You come on down to the bank tomorrow morning, and we'll fix you up. I've got another stop to make this afternoon, and I don't believe I'll get back before closing time."

Holmes left Marshall Parker at his new barn-garage and drove
to the other side of town. Idus Bray had shrewdly figured on a
housing shortage for returning veterans and had set up a trailer
park on a piece of his land there. Patricia Lee met him as he
drove up to the tiny box she and Billy were living in. Billy arrived
as Holmes was getting out of his car. There were greetings all
around.

"Well, Miz Lee, how are you appreciating Idus Bray's hospi-
tality? You enjoying your spacious new home?"

She kissed him on the cheek. "Mr. Hugh, he promised me
land, a farm," she grinned, tossing her head at Billy. "And look
at this—I'm living in something the size of a stall in my father's
stable. If Daddy could see this he'd horsewhip my husband."

"Listen to her," Billy said. "We've only been home a week,
and she's complaining already. I've bought meself an Irish
shrew, I have."

"Well," said Holmes, "we might be able to make a start getting you out of the grips of your wicked landlord. Come take a
ride with me." He looked at the rusty '38 Ford convertible Billy
was driving. "Let's take my car."

They drove north on Highway 41 for a couple of miles, then
turned east onto the unpaved Raleigh road for another two.
Holmes turned off the road and drove a hundred yards up a
slight rise and stopped. Billy stared ahead of them. A tall stone
chimney stood alone on the little hill. Cows grazed where the
house had been. Oaks, sweet gums, and a few pecans shaded the
area.

Billy got out of the car silently and walked toward the chimney, followed by Patricia and Holmes, carefully avoiding the
cowpats. He stopped and looked around him.

"No shortage of fertilizer for the grass," commented Patricia.

Billy nodded at a pile of manure near her feet. "That near
enough marks the spot where I was born." He pointed upward.
"Up one floor. Not exactly a marble monument, is it?"

Patricia's mouth fell open. "This was your father's place? The
cotton farm?" She looked around her. "You never told me it was
so beautiful."

"To tell you the truth, I never remembered it as being beautiful. I haven't been out here since I was thirteen. It is beautiful
though, isn't it." His eyes swept the trees and meadows. "My
God."

"It's for sale," said Holmes.

"Who owns it?"

Holmes looked embarrassed. "Well, I do."

"*You* do?"

"I bought it from the bank. Hoss Spence wanted it, but your daddy said to me once that he'd rather the bank have it than Hoss Spence. I leased the grazing rights to Hoss after Will Henry died, but I couldn't bring myself to sell it to him. He could never figure out why. He's mad at me for it to this day."

"How much land is there?"

"Six hundred and forty-one acres. Your great-granddaddy owned more than three thousand when the War Between the States started. Reconstruction was hard. You can have it for what your daddy owed on it, plus interest from that time. You'll be assuming his debt, sort of. Works out to about twenty thousand. I reckon a house will cost you thirty. Materials are short, but there's good timber on the place, hardwoods. There's a sawmill three miles down the road. I know a fellow over at La Grange has got a wrecking business. He's got a lot of old brick. Pretty when it's cleaned up. We'll find you some cement and copper pipe somewhere. Roofing's a problem, but we'll find some."

"Twenty thousand's too cheap."

"I'll have got a reasonable return on my investment. You forget, Hoss has been paying me for the use of the land. The bank'll be getting your mortgage business, too. I'm no fool."

Billy looked at Patricia. "Say yes to Mr. Hugh, or I'll divorce you," she said.

He turned back to Holmes. "The bank has itself a customer."

"There's just one condition," said Holmes. "I want to make you a wedding present of the brick. I want to give you something that'll last."

Billy started to protest. "Shut up, Billy Lee," Patricia said, then put her arms around Holmes and kissed him, making him blush. "Thank you, Mr. Hugh," she whispered in his ear. "Thank you so very much."

On the way back to town Holmes asked where Billy had found the Ford convertible. Billy told him.

"You should have checked with me," Holmes said reprovingly. "Still, I know a fellow could probably fix it up for you."

"I don't doubt it," Billy replied.

5 OFFICER SONNY BUTTS strolled out of the Delano police station and into the bright June morning. This was his favorite time of day and his favorite thing to do. He threw a leg over the big Indian motorcycle, flipped out the kick starter with a toe, rose into the air, and came down with all his weight. The engine roared the first time, and he throttled back for a moment as he kicked up the stand and adjusted the aviator sunglasses on the bridge of his nose. The black leather seat was hot from the sun and felt good against his genitals as he pulled smoothly from the station's parking lot into Main Street and headed unhurriedly through the business district. People waved, and he waved back or gave a little two-fingered salute from the bill of his cap, if the recipient was a city councilman or a storeowner.

At the traffic light at Main and Broad, Hugh Holmes waved him to the curb. A young man in a blue suit, very tall and skinny, stood with him.

"Morning, Mr. Holmes." Sonny was instantly on his most correct behavior. Holmes always made him a little nervous.

"Morning, Sonny. Meet the new preacher at the First Baptist Church. Brooks Peters. Preacher, this is Officer Sonny Butts, one of our combat veterans, joined the police force about three months back."

"Glad to meet you, Sonny." The preacher sounded as though he really were glad.

"Welcome to Delano, Brother Peters. My mother and I go over to West Side, so we're not in your congregation, but maybe we'll get to hear you at a revival sometime." Sonny knew exactly how to talk to Baptist preachers, just as he knew how to talk to most kinds of people.

"That's a powerful-looking machine you're riding, there."

"Yes, sir, I guess it is. We picked it up for just about nothing at a war-surplus sale down at Fort Benning last month. Only had seven thousand miles on it. Real good buy for the city, I reckon." He shot a look at Holmes, who said nothing, but gave a low grunt of indeterminate meaning. "Well, Preacher, Mr. Holmes, I better get going on my rounds. Nice to meet you."

Sonny pulled away from the curb and continued down Main, then up Second to Broad and on up the mountain. At forty miles an hour the breeze was downright cool. He felt wonderful. At the top of the pass he swung across the road and parked in the shade of a billboard for the Bijou Theater, advertising the current attraction, *The Best Years of our Lives*. Sonny had seen the picture the night before and had identified strongly with the Dana Andrews character, the former soda jerk who had come back to his home town and been unable to find work. He felt grateful again for his job. All through the film he had kept wanting to say to Andrews, "Apply for a police job, you stupid bastard, then you won't have any trouble holding onto your women."

He kicked the stand down and sat sidesaddle, waiting. A lone mailbox stood not eight feet from where he was—Foxy Funderburke's mailbox, he knew. He was surprised to recognize a piece of mail protruding from the box. Even though he couldn't read the whole return address, he knew what it was, because he had opened an identical envelope at headquarters only that morning. It was a catalogue for police equipment. That guy was a real cop freak. The back bumper of his pickup truck was studded with stickers and stars from various police and sheriff groups that solicited memberships from the public. People joined them because they thought they might not get arrested for speeding if a cop saw the stickers. Before he could think further about Foxy, a car flashed past the billboard doing at least fifty.

Sonny caught up with the car before it had gone a mile. It was one of the new '46 Fords, and it had a police-association badge stuck to the rear bumper. Sonny pulled up alongside and waved the surprised driver over. The man got out to meet him.

"What's the problem, Officer?" The man was grinning, friendly.

"I'm afraid I clocked you doing forty-five in a twenty-five-mile-an-hour speed zone, sir. Can I see your license, please?"

"Sure." The man pulled out a wallet and opened it. His driver's license was displayed opposite a card with a big star on it, a police-association membership card. He was still grinning. Sonny noted the license number and began writing out a ticket. The man stopped grinning. "Say, didn't you see my association card?"

"Oh, yessir, and I want you to know how much we appreciate your contributing to the association that way."

The man watched Sonny continue to write the ticket. "But don't members get some kind of special consideration?"

"Sir, we want to give you every consideration we can. So if you'll just follow me down to the station we'll try to have you on your way with the absolute minimum of inconvenience." Sonny handed the bemused man his license and got on the motorcycle. "Just follow me, sir." He kicked the machine to life and led the way.

At the station the man paid a twenty-five-dollar bond to Chief Melvin Thompson and left in a huff. "That's three this week, Sonny," the chief said. "Sure you're not cutting 'em too fine? The council likes the income, but they wouldn't want to get a reputation as a speed trap, like some of those south Georgia towns on U.S. 1."

"No, sir, Chief. That one was doing a clear fifty, and I only wrote him up for forty-five."

"Okay, then. You mind the store for a while. I'm going home for my dinner." It was only just past eleven, but the chief had a bad back and liked a nap at midday. Sonny knew he wouldn't be back before two. Thompson was relying more and more on him to run things, and that was just the way Sonny wanted it.

"Yessir, Chief. Enjoy your meal. Say, if I clean up that old roll-top desk, can I use it regular?"

The chief glanced at the disused piece of furniture across the room, piled with old notices and circulars. "Sure, Sonny. Time some of that stuff was cleared out of here, anyway."

Sonny spent half an hour sifting through papers, throwing

away most of them, then another ten minutes dusting and polishing the old desk and oiling the roll-top. Didn't look bad,
when it was done. He sat down and began rummaging through
drawers. The debris of half a dozen past small-town policemen
filled most of them—notebooks, wanted circulars, a rusty old
handgun taken from some drunk years before, some loose
rounds of ammunition, various calibers. Sonny dumped it all
into a cardboard box.

In the bottom drawer, though, he found a neat bundle of files,
tied with string. There was a note with them: "Files of Chief of
Police William Henry Lee, Deceased," it read, and was signed in
an indecipherable hand. Sonny was about to put the bundle on
the chief's desk for him to check before discarding, when the
aged string broke and, before he could recover, some of the files
spilled onto the floor. A corpse stared up at him from a photograph.

Sonny had seen many corpses in various attitudes, but he
could not remember ever having seen a photograph of one. There
were several photographs, in fact, taken from different angles.
The kid had been beaten up. Sonny noticed a quickening of his
pulse, then dismissed it. He started to read a typed report
clipped to one of the photographs. When he finished that, he
read another report, neatly handwritten on ruled notebook paper. As he read, he referred frequently to the photographs, con-
necting the boy's injuries to what had been written about them.

He looked at the signatures on the reports. He had never
heard of the doctor, but he remembered the chief—Colonel Billy
Lee's old man. He must have been six or seven when that nigger
killed him with the shotgun. He remembered that the nigger had
been tried two or three times before they finally got the conviction to stick. It had been the first execution in the electric chair;
he remembered talking about that at school.

He had no memory of them finding this kid, though. Shit, old
man Lee had had himself an unsolved murder on his hands when
he died. How about that? Sonny leaned back in his chair and had
a sudden fantasy about going around and checking for clues and
solving this old murder that went back to . . . when was it? 1920.
More than twenty-five years. There was no statute of limitations
on murder, he knew that. Maybe it was some solid citizen did it.
A headline: "Butts Pins Murder on Banker Hugh Holmes". He
laughed aloud. He'd be a fucking hero all over again, no doubt

about that. He stacked up the photographs and the two reports neatly and was just turning to a second report in the same handwriting when there was a commotion in the hallway outside the office. He stuffed the bundle of files quickly back into the desk drawer—he would keep them to himself—and walked into the hallway to see what was going on.

His fellow officer, Charley Ward, was pushing a black man, obviously drunk, down the hall toward the cells. It was a local, "Pieback" Johnson, so named for his reluctance to do any heavy work. The man was in jail overnight at least twice a month. Charley gave him a kick to move him toward the cells faster.

"Jesus, Pieback," Sonny said, "you getting tanked up in the middle of the week now? I thought you was a Saturday night special."

"Caught him panhandling right in the middle of Main Street at high noon," said Charley. "Can you believe that?" Pieback groveled his way into a cell, dodging another kick.

"Naw, suh, I ain't really drunk. I jes' had a little nip or two of shine; I ain't what you'd call true drunk."

Sonny slammed the cell door, not bothering to lock it. "Well, you can just get yourself true sober in there for forty-eight hours. The JP ain't holding no special sessions for something like you." Sonny remembered that Pieback had stayed out of the draft by showing up for his physical drunk as a skunk. He'd been classified a 4-F because of his chronic alcoholism. "You just sleep it off, and if you start snoring I'll come in there and kick your ass up around your ears, hear?" Pieback flopped onto a bunk and heaved a deep sigh. He might have just come home to his own bed after a hard day's work.

Then somebody came in about a lost bicycle, and there were a couple of phone calls, and Sonny didn't get back to the old files. The boy's murder stuck in his mind, but he had not read Will Henry's account of the second murder.

6   BILLY LEE sat on a Coca-Cola crate in the shade of a pecan
    tree and watched his wife charm and bully a variety of
    carpenters and other building tradesmen into doing
things exactly as she wished to their half-finished new home. He
had forgotten, after nearly four years in England, how hot it
could be in Georgia in July. Patricia loved the heat. She had been
cold all her life, she said, and it couldn't get too hot for her. In
the distance he could see two black men repairing a barbed-wire
fence.

He had not really had a hell of a lot to do with the planning
and building of the house, because his new clients, the bank and
the cotton mill, were working his tail off; because Holmes was
marching him to every Kiwanis, Rotary, and Jaycee meeting in
the Tri-Counties, and to every church social and barbecue they
could find; and because Patricia had said she didn't want him in
the way. She had, to his astonishment, produced a finely ren-
dered set of plans for a two-story Georgian house from her trunk,
based on one she had known in England, and had proceeded to
assemble the materials and people necessary to construct it in
record time, considering the postwar shortages. Thus, in a few
weeks more, they would be living in a four-bedroom, three-bath

house all out of proportion to their needs or income. When he had protested, she had, reluctantly, revealed to him that she had a bit of money of her own, that she would spend it as she pleased, and that she pleased to spend it on a house they could live in for the rest of their lives, since she had no intention of moving about like a gypsy. He had gone back to work and campaigning and left her to it.

Now, from far down the Raleigh road toward Delano, a column of dust arose, led by a small dot of a car. Soon it was visible as a police car, and it eventually turned into Patricia's newly paved driveway and pulled up before the house. Sonny Butts and Charley Ward got out.

"Afternoon, Colonel," Sonny sang out. A lot of people referred to Billy as colonel, and only partly because of his military rank. In Georgia, as in much of the South, attorneys were called that. Billy had never known why.

"Sonny, how are you?" He got up and shook hands with both officers. He had seen little of Sonny since their return from the war, only an occasional glimpse of him patrolling on the motorcycle or directing traffic.

"Just fine, Colonel. That's going to be some house." Sonny looked admiringly toward the structure.

"Yes, well, my wife never seems to do anything small. What can I do for you?"

Sonny handed him an envelope. "Got some good news for you. Fellow just showed up at the station with a brand new Chevrolet for you. Said he couldn't find you at your office or the trailer park, so he reckoned it'd be all right to leave it with us. Here's the papers and keys. We put him on the bus back to Atlanta."

"Oh, that's great." He took the papers. "Fellow I was in the service with has a dealership in Atlanta." Billy had sent him a large deposit a month before and agreed to take whatever he could get. "I appreciate your keeping the car for me and coming all the way out here."

"Glad to do it. Anyway"—Sonny nodded toward Billy's '38 Ford—"I wondered if you'd be interested in selling the convertible. I been looking for one."

"Sure, come have a look at it." They walked toward the car. "Wasn't much when I got it, but I've put some money into it—a ring job and some rewiring and four recaps. It's in good shape now, except for a little rust here and there. Spare's not so hot, but it's okay for a spare."

Sonny walked around the car, kicked the tires, asked some questions, listened to the engine. They haggled, agreed on a price. Sonny wrote a check. Patricia came down the temporary front steps and was introduced to the two policemen.

"Sonny's just bought himself a snazzy Ford convertible," Billy said to her.

"How much are you paying him to take it away?"

Billy looked pained. "He got it for a song. The two of them sandbagged me."

"I'll miss it, Officer Butts. You take good care of it. Billy'll never buy anything that romantic again."

"Don't you worry, Miz Lee. I'm going to fix it up even better." He turned to Billy. "Who did the engine job for you? Mickey Shelton?"

"No, it was Marshall Parker, the colored fellow who opened up over by Braytown. Did a good job, too. I recommend him. He's a lot cheaper than Micky."

Sonny shook his head. "Well, I never knew a nigger could fix any kind of machinery more'n a wheelbarrow. I hope you're right about him, seeing as how I've bought the thing."

Billy looked at the ground. "Marshall's good. He was pretty good in the army, too, from what I hear. He picked up a bronze star at Anzio." Billy wanted to change the subject. "I hear you were in the Bulge."

"Yeah."

"Pretty rough, I guess."

"Only for those guys who couldn't take it. I didn't have no problem. We got along without Eleanor's Niggers."

Billy could feel his anger rising. "Hope you like the car, Sonny. Stop by the office tomorrow, and I'll give you the registration."

"Sure thing, Colonel." Sonny got into the Ford and drove away, followed closely by Charley Ward in the police car.

"Funny," said Patricia. "He never even noticed you were annoyed about the way he talked about Marshall Parker."

"Yes, he did," Billy said, looking down the road after Sonny. "He was putting the needle in. I knew guys like him in the army.

They liked to see just how far they could go with you. He noticed."

Sonny turned off the Raleigh road onto Highway 41 and drove the two miles to Delano at seventy-five miles an hour. He took his hands off the wheel for a moment and noticed that it vibrated slightly at that speed. At sixty it was solid as a rock. Shit, he'd have gone another two hundred for the car if Billy Lee had pushed him. Stupid bastard.

As he approached the city limits he saw a sign he hadn't noticed before: "Parker's Garage—repairs on all makes & models." Billy Lee had said the nigger was a lot cheaper than Mickey Shelton. Sonny whipped into the bare dirt space before the converted barn and killed the engine. He could see a pair of feet sticking out from under an old Plymouth. He got out of the car and walked inside.

"Be with you in just a minute." The voice came from under the car. Sonny waited impatiently for a moment, then tapped the sole of one of the protruding shoes with his foot.

"Come on, I ain't got all day."

"I'll be with you just as soon as I tighten this bolt." There was an edge in the voice. Sonny didn't like that from a nigger. After another moment's wait Marshall pushed himself from under the car, riding on a slab of plywood mounted on casters. He stood up, wiping his hands with a rag. "What can I do for you?"

Sonny glared at him for a second before speaking. "You know how to balance wheels?"

Marshall waited a beat before replying evenly, "Sure do."

"Well, I got a little shimmy in the front end at about seventy-five. I figure it's a balancing job."

Marshall looked at the convertible. "You buy Colonel Lee's car, did you?"

"Well, I sure as hell didn't steal it."

"I balanced the wheels on it last week. You might have a little alignment problem, though."

"Listen, I'm due back at the station, I haven't got time to argue with you about it. Just get the front wheels off and balance them right this time."

"I balanced them right the first time. Them's recaps on there. They won't never run as true as new tires. But if you want to bring it back in the morning I'll check the front end alignment. I'm gon' be tied up 'til this evening on this job."

Sonny flushed. "Whose rattletrap is that, anyway?"

"Smitty's." Smitty ran the grocery store in Braytown.

"Well, you just call up Smitty and tell him you gotta work on Police Officer Butts's car. *He* can come back tomorrow."

"I don't have no phone yet—they bringin' it next week—and, anyway, Smitty's mama is sick up in Atlanta, and he's got to go up there tonight and carry her home. Now, it ain't gonna hurt it to drive it tonight the way it is, and if you bring it back in the morning I'll do the best job I can on it. Tell you what, I'll pick it up at the police station and fix it and have it back to you by dinner time if it ain't nothing serious and I don't have to order no parts." Marshall knew Sonny was getting mad, and he didn't want any problems with a uniformed policeman who was also carrying a gun, so he said all this as placatingly as he could manage, considering that he was getting pretty mad himself.

"You know," said Sonny, "I thought I'd see what kind of work you do and maybe let you do all my servicing for me, but I shoulda known better. I reckon I just better take my car on over to Mickey Shelton where I know it'll get done right." He turned and started for the car.

Now Marshall had to make a real effort to hold himself in. "Well, I 'preciate you coming to me, and I wish I could fix it right now, but I promised this man his car. I done all the work on that convertible, you know, and couldn't nobody do it no better, I reckon."

Sonny got to the car and opened the door. He turned back toward Marshall. "Shit. You'll be back to sweeping floors and fixing inner tubes for Mickey Shelton in a month, anyway. I don't know why I even thought I could do business with a nigger." He slammed the door, started the car, reversed into the road, and burned rubber driving away.

Marshall stood in the door of his garage, his jaw clamped tightly shut, looking after the angry policeman. Annie, his wife, came out of the little office cubicle at the back, where she had been working on the books.

"You shouldn'ta made that man mad, Marshall. You know what we been hearing 'bout him. He can make us a lot of trouble."

"Shoot, girl, I was just as polite as I could be to that white boy. You heard every word of it."

"You know how to talk right to white folks. You coulda been talking to a colored man the way you was talking to him."

"Listen, I'm a businessman now. I don't have to go Uncle Tommin' nobody no more. He can't do nothing to us. Don't you worry about it." He knew she would worry, anyway.

Sonny was still angry when he got back to the station. He'd fix that nigger. He'd get him in his jail some Saturday night, and he'd fix him.

7 ON AN EVENING in early August two meetings were held in Delano. Their purposes were disparate.

In an apartment over the garage of Dr. Frank Mudter, his son, Dr. Tom Mudter, hosted a group which included Billy Lee, Bob Blankenship, the new owner-editor of the *Delano Messenger*; Ellis Woodall, owner of a radio shop; and Brooks Peters, the new Baptist minister. They were all young and all veterans, with the single exception of Peters, who had been too underweight to pass his physical.

This was not their first meeting. Since returning from the war they had been laying plans to establish their generation politically in Delano and the Tri-Counties. For more than four years virtually every healthy adult male between the ages of eighteen and thirty-five had been absent from the community, and the natural progression of the young into positions of influence had been halted. Now, at the approach of the first state-wide election since the end of the war, they were working hard to make up for the lost years. Their efforts were not without resistance from an establishment that had hardened in their absence.

Among their group and among the candidates they supported, only Billy Lee seemed reasonably sure of election, and that had made him their unofficial leader. Now he called them to order. "Okay, gents, let's hear what's going on out there."

Bob Blankenship spoke up. "Why don't you start by telling us where you think the state-senate race stands?"

"Well, Mr. Holmes seems to think we're okay. Ward is a nice enough fellow, but he's not well known outside of Talbot County, and he was a 4-F, that's not helping him any. He could edge us out in Talbot, but we think we'll take Harris and Meriwether without too much trouble. God knows I've shaken hands with every man, woman, and mule in the Tri-Counties at least twice. Lucky we don't have any Republicans to worry about; the primary is tough enough without having to fight it all over again in a general election. Bob, you're about as objective an ear as we'll get. How're we doing in the other races?"

Blankenship, a short, heavy man in his early forties, had bought the newspaper from Harmon Everson some six months before, and had quickly settled into the town. "The way I see it, we'll get one seat on the city council pretty sure; maybe the second one, too, if we work hard. I think Tom is in better shape than Ellis right now, because everybody knows his daddy. I think we'd be safe in putting more of our effort behind Ellis in the five weeks we've got left. We ought to make a real effort with the American Legion boys. They could turn it for us."

"That's okay with me," said Tom.

"What about the sheriff's race?" James Montgomery, a veteran from Greenville, the county seat, was challenging Skeeter Willis.

Bob Blankenship spoke again. "A toss-up, I reckon. James has got the veteran vote for sure, but Skeeter's got a lot of friends in this county."

"A lot of enemies, too, I'd think," said Billy. "A lot of people suspect he's in the bootleggers' pocket, and everybody knows about the black-market stuff during the war."

Tom Mudter chipped in. "Yeah, and a lot of people were buying stuff from him, too, stuff they couldn't get anywhere else. They might be grateful to him."

Blankenship looked thoughtful. "You know, I haven't really written a lot about what went on during the war. Maybe a good, strong editorial on the black market—no names, mind you— might stir up enough guilt in some folks to sway their votes toward veterans."

Brooks Peters spoke for the first time. "Speaking as one acquainted with folks' guilt over their sins, I think that just might work. In fact, it might be worth a whole series of editorials. A little repentance at the polls could go a long way next month. By the way, the last Sunday before the primary, I plan to lean pretty heavily on our debt of gratitude to our veterans in my sermon. Having been a 4-F myself I don't think it'll look too self-serving." Peters felt keenly his guilt at not having been in uniform.

Billy spoke again. "Brooks, I think that's a good idea, but you've got to be careful. You're the first preacher the First Baptist Church has ever had under the age of forty, and I can tell you that in the deacons meetings, when we were deciding whether to call you, there was a lot of harrumphing going on among some of the old boys. You can go just so far with them, and they'll be on your neck like a dog on a coon."

"Billy, I made my decision about that when I accepted the church's call. I decided I was going to do the job the way I felt it ought to be done and then take the consequences. I told the board of deacons that, too, you may recall. You were there. Now, I think I established to their satisfaction that we don't have any theological differences, but I told them then that I expected to conduct the day-to-day affairs of the church without undue interference—gladly hearing advice, but reserving my decision on whether to take it—and that I would preach my sermons according to my conscience and my perceptions of what the congregation's needs were." He tilted his chair back and grinned. "Right now I perceive that the congregation needs some veterans helping to run things in this town and this county, and I'm going to tell them so."

"As long as you know what kind of opposition you're going to have."

"I know I'm going to have Idus Bray calling me up and telling me to keep my nose out of civic affairs, but he's already tried that, and he didn't get anywhere. I was real lucky that I had a professor at the seminary who got fired from a church in similar circumstances, and he gave me a pretty good education in church politics, and as long as I have the support of people like you and Tom on the board of deacons and the veterans and younger people in the congregation, I figure I can weather whatever storms I have to."

"You know you have our support," said Billy. Tom nodded.

"We've formed a ministerial association in town, too. There are eight churches in town with full-time ministers, and we're

meeting once a week to see if we can't kind of coordinate ourselves on some points—youth programs, opposition to Sunday
picture shows, and civic improvements being among the things
we're already talking about. I'll see if I can't get some of the others to make some timely remarks before the primary."

"Good, now let's get down to some specific items and see if
we can't use them to scare up some votes. I think the paving of
the new Fourth Street extention is something a lot of folks are
pretty hot about. They're all complaining about the mud when it
rains and the dust when it doesn't."

The group ran through their list of issues and opportunities
for another hour and a half and then began to make adjournment
noises. Brooks Peters held them back for another moment.

"I wasn't going to bring this up until I knew more about it,
but maybe it's something we should all keep our ears open
about." He had the group's attention. "Jim Parker—you know
him, he's the janitor at the church—Jim has hinted to me that
there's something wrong down at the police station."

"He's Marshall Parker's daddy, isn't he?" Billy asked. Peters
nodded. "How do you mean 'wrong'?"

"Well, Jim won't say much—he may not trust me completely
yet, and he's pretty tight-lipped anyway—but I gather it's something to do with race, with some colored prisoners being mistreated."

"Mistreated by who?" Bob Blankenship was showing particular interest now. Possible news story.

"As I say, I don't know much, but it seems to be going on on
weekends or at night, so Melvin Thomas wouldn't be around
then. That just leaves Sonny Butts and Charley Ward."

There was silence for a bit. Finally, Ellis Woodall asked, "So
what do we do?"

"I don't guess there's much we can do, now, with the information so vague, but I think we all ought to keep our ears open,
especially with the colored people we know. We don't want anything bad going on down there."

The other meeting, taking place simultaneously, was held in
a tar-paper shack just off the Scenic Highway atop Pine Mountain. It was lit by a naphtha lamp and lubricated by two cases of
Blatz beer. There were eight men at the meeting, among them
Emmett Spence, dairy farmer, son of Hoss; Tommy Allen, shoe-

repair-shop owner; Mickey Shelton, garage owner; and Sonny Butts, police officer. It was Sonny's first meeting as a full member after his solemn initiation into the Ku Klux Klan.

Although the meeting lasted as long as its counterpart in the town below, most of its time was taken up with an opening prayer and a lot of talk about fishing, guns, and dogs. The business agenda was short and was concisely phrased by Emmett Spence. "It's about time we started doing something about our nigger soldier boys," he said, and belched.

There was a chorus of assent.

"Any ideas?"

Mickey Shelton had an idea. "Marshall Parker," he said, flatly. "He's their number-one boy. We bring him down and we bring 'em all down."

"Whatsa matter, Mickey?" a voice chuckled back at him. "Ol' Marshall takin' too much of your business?" There was other laughter.

"You goddamned right, he is," Shelton shot back. "He ain't got no overhead out there in that shack, and he's fobbin' off used parts on his customers, too. He's hit me for about all of my nigger business and some white, too. Hugh Holmes loaned him the money to get started up, and he's taking his car out there. So is Billy Lee and some others I could mention."

There was a jumble of remarks. Sonny Butts silenced them. "Mickey's right. Marshall's the ringleader in Braytown. He's getting them all stirred up about registering to vote. If we can put him out of business the rest of 'em'll fold."

Emmett Spence proposed a solution: "Let's burn the black bastard out." There was a general murmur of agreement. Tommy Allen stopped it, abruptly.

"No! We can't go burning anybody out. Burning, horse-whipping, all that's out. We'll just end up in a lot of trouble ourselves, and we'll get the whole town stirred up against us."

Sonny spoke up. "Tommy's right. We've got to do this legal."

"How do you mean, legal?" asked Emmett.

"I can't tell you right off of the top of my head, but let me think about it a little bit, and I guarantee you I'll find a way to get Marshall in jail." Sonny paused for emphasis and looked around at the lamp-lit faces. "And once I get him in jail he won't be a problem to nobody no more." He winked at them. "I guarantee you."

A few minutes later, a couple of miles down the highway, a railroad crosstie fastened to a utility pole was erected in a clearing beside the road overlooking the town. The whole had been wrapped in burlap bags and soaked in kerosene. Somebody tossed a burning newspaper at it.

Down in the town, Billy Lee and his group were leaving Tom Mudter's house. Brooks Peters, about to get into his car, glanced up at the mountain. "Oh, my Lord," he said. The others turned and looked up at the flaming cross, floating in the night above Delano.

Billy Lee was the first to break their silence. "That," he said, "is all we need."

8

"SO, why is this man—what's his name?—why is he such a character?"

"Funderburke."

Patricia Lee and Eloise, Billy's younger sister, were driving through Delano in Patricia's "new" '41 Ford station wagon, which Hugh Holmes had found for her. Eloise had married a young man before the war, and he had been killed in the Pacific early on. She now worked in her stepfather's store, Fowler's.

"And he's called Foxy?"

"His real name's Francis, but I've never heard anybody call him that. He looks kind of like a fox, I guess. Kind of pointy faced."

"How old a person is he?"

"I don't know, really. Old. It's hard to tell, exactly. Between fifty and seventy, I guess. I remember him mostly as a child. All the children were afraid of him."

"Why?"

Eloise laughed. "Oh, no good reason. It's not as if he ever did anything to anybody. You know how children are. He just became kind of an ogre to us."

"I know. I remember people like that from my own childhood. There was a man, a neighbor, who terrified me. When I came back later, when I was all grown up, I sat next to him at a dinner party, and he was charming. How did you know Funderburke had a litter of Labs?"

"He's raised them for years. He gave Billy and me a puppy

when we were little, before Daddy died. We could never figure
out why. Did I tell you he was there when Daddy died?"

"No. At the actual deathbed?"

"Yes. In fact, it was Foxy who brought Daddy to the doctor's
office, along with a fellow who was the city manager at the time.
He just happened along right after Daddy was shot. I remember
Mama mentioning how scared Foxy was. She was surprised, be-
cause he always had made such a point of his service in the First
War, but he was nearly hysterical, just barely in control."

"Well, I suppose the circumstances were pretty awful." Patricia turned into Broad Street and started up the mountain.

"Yes, I don't think Mama has gotten over it to this day, even
after marrying Mr. Fowler. She has a different sort of marriage, I
guess, more like just good friends. I don't think anybody could
ever take Daddy's place."

"From what I've seen of Mr. Fowler, I'd say your mother has
done very well."

"Oh, she certainly has. He is a fine, fine man, and everybody
has enormous respect for him in the community and the church.
He's been a deacon practically since he moved here in . . .
twenty-eight, I guess it was." Eloise pulled her knees onto the
seat, turning toward Patricia. "You've been in Delano for six
months, now. What do you think of it?"

Patricia looked thoughtful. "It's funny, I'm more surprised by
the similarities than the differences. Oh, the landscape's different, and the heat certainly is, and the houses are different, but
apart from accents a lot of the people here seem very familiar.
Mr. Fowler reminds me of my father in a way, and your mother
is very much like an aunt of mine. I think farmers must be much
the same everywhere. Even the race thing doesn't seem all that
foreign. The white attitude toward blacks here is much the same
as the British attitude toward the Irish, especially before the rev-
olution." They crested the pass and started down the other side
of the mountain, toward the turnoff to Foxy's place. "One thing
I can tell you, Eloise, if that comparison holds true there's a lot
more resentment among your Negroes here than shows. You
mustn't believe that because they kowtow to you, they like it.
They're people, just like the Irish are people, and if you don't
pay more attention to being fair to them you could be in for an
awful time. Ask the British. I try to get Billy to understand that."

Eloise pointed. "It's just up here on the right." A sign appeared, "F. Funderburke, Breeder, Labrador Retrievers, By ap-

pointment only," and a phone number. "I called ahead. Word is
he doesn't like unexpected visotrs." Patricia turned into the road
and drove up the side of the mountain.

Sonny was covering the police station at noon, which, with
Chief Thomas's proclivity for a long dinner hour still ran from
eleven to two. Charley had been covering lately, but Sonny had
sent him to eat. Sonny had wanted a nap, but now he found
himself restless and bored. He was wondering how to pass the
time, when he remembered what was in his bottom desk drawer.
In a moment he had the files on the murdered boy spread out on
the desk.

He skimmed the two reports, the medical examiner's and Will
Henry's, then turned to the other files. They were routine, day-
to-day stuff for the most part, but then he came across a letter,
poorly typed on the stationery of Underwood's Funeral Home of
Waycross, Georgia. It was addressed to Chief Lee, of the Delano
Police Department and was brief:

> Dear Sir:
> In answer to your request via long distance telephone today
> about Frank Collins, deceased, the following are the details as
> best I remember them, which is good, since I only embalmed
> him last night. Frank appeared to be killed by a shot in the back
> from a heavy firearm, which shot went all the way through him.
> As to other injuries, his feet had some cuts and scratches like he
> had been going barefoot over rocks or rough ground. His wrists
> had marks like dents going all the way around and some skin
> had been scraped off. I would say he might have been tied up
> right before he died. I didn't notice any more injuries on the
> body.   Yours very sincerely,
>   C. V. Underwood, Proprietor

Sonny quickly noted that the naked boy's wrists showed such
marks, too. But who the hell was Frank Collins? There was no
report here on a Frank Collins. He shuffled quickly through the
papers. There was no report, but he found some loose pages of
notes.

7/10/24
Rep. from S. Willis. Man on fence. Goolsby says one shot .45.
Sent body Waycross. Checked area nr Columbus hiway, found

fence, hobo j., .45 casing, no markings. Spoke F.F. Has .45, shells marked. Spoke Waycross, promised description. Sent Goolsby casing. He and F.F. mad. Happened Talbot. No more go on! How many more?

The last words were heavily penciled and underlined, as if the writer had been angry. The notes fit the letter from the Waycross undertaker. It wasn't too tough to figure out that there had been a second murder, this one . . . four years, nearly four and a half after the first one, but this one was in Talbot County. Sonny knew a hobo jungle near the Columbus highway. He had knocked a couple of heads together and cleaned it out a couple of times. It was off his turf, but close enough to be a problem. The chief didn't like hoboes around.

Goolsby was sheriff in Talbot County years ago. F.F.? Foxy Funderburke's house was near that jungle. Chief Lee must have been to see him, and he had a .45, but what was that about the shells? The casing he found had no markings. That was the sort of casing somebody might use who was loading his own ammunition. Somebody who shot a lot and didn't want to pay retail for shells. But Foxy's shells had had markings.

Sonny quickly scanned the reports of the first murder. There was no mention of Foxy Funderburke specifically, but it did say that Chief Lee had questioned the residents of houses near where the body was found. Foxy's house wasn't all that far away. Lee must have talked to him. In his notes on the second murder Lee had said that F.F. was mad. Why? Did he object to being questioned when two murders happened less than half a mile from his house? He was the cop freak, wasn't he? Always wanted to help the police? Why was he mad?

Sonny opened his top right-hand desk drawer and took out an oily rag wrapped around an object. He removed a German Walther P-38 pistol. He slipped the clip out, emptied it, replaced it, and worked the action to eject the round in the firing chamber, then rewrapped the pistol in the rag. He heard Charlie Ward shuffle in the front door, coming back from lunch. He got up and walked past Charlie in the hallway and out to the motorcycle, slipping the P-38 into a saddlebag.

"Cover for a while, Charlie," he called back. "I got to go see a man about a dog." He switched on the ignition and kicked the machine to life.

9 PATRICIA'S CAR reached the top of its climb and began
to descend slightly. As it rounded a curve, she could see
the house, with its trees and neatly planted flower beds
and lawn. Foxy Funderburke was standing on the front stoop. As
they neared the house, he left the stoop and waved them around
to the back of the house.

Patricia had a brief moment to watch the man as Eloise
greeted him. Wiry, neat, a closely cropped fuzz of hair on a rather
large head. She thought he looked a bit like Mahatma Gandhi,
but with smaller eyes and a sharper nose. His nickname was apt,
and not just because of his physical appearance. He seemed instantly clever, alert, foxlike. He was awkward when she extended
her hand. She really must make an effort to remember that southern American men were not accustomed to shaking hands with
women. She looked about and remarked on the absence of kennels.

"I never keep more than two bitches," Foxy said. He walked
to a small, low shed built onto the back of the log house and
lifted the hinged roof. Inside were two compartments, both with
access to the house, one containing three sleeping puppies. As
he did so, their mother appeared through a flap cut into the back
door of the house and approached the visitors affectionately.
Foxy picked up the three puppies and set them on the ground.

Two of them immediately began to worry their mother for milk. The third, who was smaller, sat and looked expectantly at them. Patricia laughed and picked up the puppy. "He's the last male I've got left. The other two are bitches. Were you wanting a male or a female?"

"A male, I think. My, he looks the way I feel when I wake up."

"Oh, he's perky enough when he gets going. I think he'll be small, more like the breed in the British Isles. Ours are bigger."

"I don't mind that. He'd fit into the car more easily." She held him up and looked at him. He licked her nose. She put him on the ground and walked away. He quickly tottered after her. Memories of other puppies briefly made her homesick.

"He's cute as a bug," Eloise said, laughing. "He reminds me of the one you gave us a long time ago, Mr. Funderburke." Foxy nodded. "We sure got to love that dog. He lived to be fourteen."

"I came prepared to bargain with you Mr. Funderburke, but I'm afraid I'll have to pay whatever you're asking. I'm smitten."

"Well, I guess fifteen dollars'll do."

"Isn't that a bit low, now?"

"Well, he's the runt of the litter, after all. Seems to take to you."

Patrica wrote him a check, made her good-byes, and turned toward the car. She stopped with a start. The policeman Sonny Butts was standing at the corner of the house. He tipped his hat.

"Sorry to scare you Miz Lee, I just coasted down the hill, and I guess the cycle didn't make much noise. Miz Eloise, how're you?"

"Fine, Sonny. You scared me, too."

"Sorry 'bout that. I'll have to start making more noise, I guess." He shot a look at Foxy and noted that he, if anything, looked more surprised than either of the women. Worried, too. "I've just got a little business with Mr. Funderburke. I can come back if I'm interrupting anything."

"Oh, no, Sonny," Patricia replied, "I've just bought myself a puppy, and we're on our way home now. You go right ahead."

The women drove away and left the two men staring silently after them. "How you doing, Mr. Funderburke?" Sonny made a point of not sounding overly pleasant. He wanted to see how Foxy would continue to react. He had purposely cut the engine of the motorcycle and coasted the last, downhill part of the road.

"Just fine." Foxy was perspiring, which wasn't too odd, considering the warm day, but he was breathing a little fast, too. "Uh, what can I do for you?"

"Well," said Sonny, stretching it out, watching Foxy, "I just need a little information, and I thought you might be in a position to help me." He waited for a beat, then turned to the motorcycle and slowly unbuckled the saddlebag. He removed the bundle and walked back to where Foxy stood. He kept his voice flat, toneless. "I thought you might be able to tell me something about this." Foxy looked at the oily rag nervously. Sonny unwrapped the pistol and handed it to Foxy, butt first.

Foxy took the pistol as if it were a rattlesnake. Then he suddenly relaxed and licked his lips. "P-38. Walther. Good weapon." He removed the clip and worked the action to be sure it was unloaded. "Nice example. Want to sell it?"

"What do you reckon its worth?"

"Well, there's Lugers all over the place these days, but you don't see many P-38's. I've got one, but it's the only one I've seen up to now. I'd give you forty dollars for it."

"Well, no, sir, I didn't really come out here to sell it to you. I just wanted to get your opinion. From what I hear you're the authority around here." Sonny was smiling now, turning on the charm.

Foxy grinned slightly. "Well, I've owned a few handguns in my time."

Sonny looked around. "Nice place you've got here. First time I've been out here."

"Oh, well, let me show you around. I've got a few weapons around the place you might like to see, too." Foxy was completely at ease now.

"No, sir, thank you, I appreciate it, but I've got to get back to the station and spell Charley." Foxy seemed relieved, he thought. Sonny thought he liked him better nervous. "I'd really love to see your place some time, though. Tell you what, one day when there aren't too many speeders coming over the mountain, I'll just drop in and surprise you."

That did it. Foxy was all tight again. "Well, uh, I'd appreciate a little notice. I, ah, get pretty busy around here now and then, and I'd 'preciate it if you'd give me a call first. Be sure I'm available."

"Oh, yeah, sure Foxy, I could probably do that." Sonny

switched to the first name easily. He felt he was on top in this conversation, and he wanted to stay there. He wanted to keep Foxy nervous, too.

"Fine, that's just fine." Foxy put his hand on Sonny's shoulder and walked him toward the motorcycle. "Be glad to have you out here sometime. Just give me a call. I'm in the book."

Just before Sonny cleared the little rise and started down the mountain, he glanced over his shoulder. Foxy would be watching him leave, he knew it. He was right. There was something going on with that guy. Nothing urgent; he'd just check on him now and then, ask around, maybe drop in again, unannounced. Maybe he was connected to those old murders. That was a long time ago, though; why would he be nervous about something that far back?

Then Sonny felt his skin crawl, remembered something, something in Chief Lee's notes. What was it he said? "How many more?" That was it. He had underlined it. More murders? But there weren't any more murders, not in the files, not that anybody knew about.

Not that anybody knew about. Jesus.

10 BILLY LEE was just leaving for work when the phone rang in the trailer. He sank down in the dinette seat, where he could have a view of the house. They had moved the trailer out here as soon as the electricity and phone had been hooked up, so Patricia could be there all the time during the finishing work. He picked up the phone on the fourth ring.

"Hello?"

"Is that Colonel Lee?" A man's voice.

"Yes, this is Billy Lee." The voice was familiar, but he couldn't place it.

"This is Marshall Parker, Colonel, at the garage. How are you today?" Billy laughed at himself. He hadn't recognized a familiar voice, because he had identified it as white instead of black.

"Morning, Marshall, I'm just fine. How's business?"

"Just fine, just about all I can handle. I'm putting on some help next week."

"Well, that's good news."

"Yessir. Uh, Colonel, I think I've got a problem. I wonder if you could stop by here on your way to town for a minute?"

"What's the trouble, Marshall?" He looked at his watch; it indicated 7:45. He had a board-of-directors meeting at the bank at 8:00.

"Well, sir"—Billy noted an odd caution in Marshall's voice—
"I think it'd be better if I explain it here. Can you come by?"

"Is it urgent, Marshall? I've got a meeting at the bank at eight.
Could it wait until a little later this morning?"

"Well, ah, if you could just stop by here for just a minute you
might be a better judge of that than me. I, uh—" He stopped
talking, and Billy could feel tension in the silence.

"Sure, Marshall, I can stop by for just a minute. It's right on
my way in."

"Thank you, sir, I sure appreciate it." The relief in his voice
was obvious.

On the drive into Delano, Billy wondered about Marshall's
reluctance to talk on the telephone. Was somebody there with
him who inhibited his conversation, or was he worried about
the operator? Delano still didn't have dial phones, and all calls
were placed by operators. As he pulled up in front of the garage,
he was relieved to see that everything appeared normal. The
front doors were wide open, and Marshall came out to greet him.

"I'm sure glad you could stop by here, Colonel." Marshall
pointed to the rear of the building. "Could you step back here?
There's something I want to show you."

They walked out of the main building into a small storeroom
at the back. Billy immediately noticed that a window pane was
broken. The frame was new wood, unpainted, and stickers still
covered the other panes. "You had a visitor in the night, Marshall?"

"Yes, sir, I believe I did." He indicated two cardboard boxes
on the floor.

"Have you called the police? What did they take?"

"Well, sir, it's not what they took; they didn't take anything
as far as I can tell." He walked over to the boxes and pulled back
the flap of one. "It's more like what they left."

The box was a container of twelve Mason jars. Their shiny
new tops gleamed in the morning light. "You taking up canning,
Marshall?"

Marshall removed one of the jars from the box. It was filled
with a clear liquid. He handed it to Billy. "No, sir. I'm not taking
up canning. I'm not taking up this, either."

Billy unscrewed the top of the jar and sniffed the contents.
"Whew! That's powerful stuff! You a drinking man, Marshall?"

"Well, my brother-in-law gets down here from Atlanta 'bout

once a month, and he always brings me a bottle of Early Times. That's the only drinking I do."

Billy leaned against the door jamb and scratched his head. "Well, it looks like somebody's made you a gift of about a two-year supply. You know somebody in this business who might be using your place for some temporary storage?"

Marshall looked at him and shook his head. "No, sir, I sure don't."

"Well, why would—" Billy froze in midsentence. "Uh, oh." He looked at his watch. "Listen, Marshall, let's get this stuff in my car—you do that, will you? Just stick it in the trunk. I want to make a couple of phone calls."

Billy found the phone book and called a number. "Melvin? . . . This is Billy Lee. How you doing? . . . Good. . . . Yes, she's fine, working hard on the house. Listen, I wonder if you could meet me down at the station? There's something I need to talk to you about. . . . Right now, 'bout five minutes. . . . Good." He called Holmes and explained that he would be a little late for the board meeting; he'd get there as soon as possible. Then he started for the car. "You'd better lock up, Marshall, then come on and ride with me."

On the way into town Billy asked a few questions. "Marshall, anybody got anything against you?"

"I don't think so, I really don't."

"Haven't had any arguments with your neighbors or customers or anybody?"

"No, sir. I've been getting along real good."

"Nobody unhappy about the way you fixed his car, anything like that?"

"No, sir! When I fix something I guarantee my work!"

"Course you do." Billy thought for a minute. "You had any problems with any white folks?"

Marshall started to speak, then stopped. "Well—"

"Better tell me about it, Marshall, we haven't got much time."

"Sonny Butts might still be mad at me, I don't know."

"Sonny? What've you had to do with Sonny?"

Marshall told him about the incident with Sonny's car. "I would have been glad to work on it; I even offered to come get it when I was through with Smitty's car, but he wouldn't listen; he just went off. You reckon this is something to do with Sonny?"

Billy said nothing. They were at the police station, now, and he parked his car and got out. "Come on in with me, Marshall." The two men entered to find Charley Ward all alone. He seemed startled to see them.

"Hey, Colonel, you're up early." He looked quickly at Marshall. "What can I do for you?" Before Billy could answer Chief Melvin Thomas shuffled into the room looking sleepy.

"Morning, Billy, Marshall. Well, what's the problem, Billy?"

Billy walked him out to the front of the building and opened his car trunk. He pulled out a jar and handed it to Thomas. "Looks like somebody broke into Marshall's garage last night and left two dozen bottles of the finest moonshine, Melvin. What do you make of that?"

Thomas took the jar and laughed aloud. "Well, that's sure a new one on me. Folks usually take stuff when they break in, not leave it. You're sure a honest man, Marshall." He winked at Billy. "If somebody had left that at my house I'm not sure I'd of turned it in. You could have yourself quite a party with that much shine." He laughed again. "You serious about this, Billy? That really what happened?"

"Marshall called me about half an hour ago, just as soon as he found it. He didn't know what to do with it, so he called me. Somebody broke a window in the back of his place and left this there."

Thomas scratched his head. "Well, I'll come out there right now, and we'll take a look at it. I don't know what the charge would be if we caught somebody, though. It's not as though anything got stolen."

"Well, there's breaking and entering, and I guess if you found out who it was you could make a pretty good case for possession. They couldn't get it there without possessing it."

They unloaded the illegal whiskey and locked it in a cell, then proceeded to Marshall's garage, Billy's car leading the way, the chief following in the police car. As they came in sight of the garage, Billy said, "Well, now," and pointed ahead.

Marshall was speechless. Parked in front of the garage were two sheriff's cars and the Delano Police Department motorcycle. As they pulled to a halt, Billy could see the padlock and hasp hanging from a splinter of the front door. As they got out of the car he could hear somebody trying to raise the sheriff's car on the radio. He thought he could recognize Charley Ward's voice. Billy walked into the garage, followed by Chief Thomas and Marshall.

He could hear voices from the back room. "Hello back there!" he shouted.

Skeeter Willis, two deputies, and Sonny Butts all spilled back into the main garage. Skeeter recovered first. "Billy, I've got a search warrant here."

"Well, Skeeter, you better serve it, I guess."

Skeeter walked over to Marshall and shoved the paper at him. Marshall unfolded it and started to read.

"Have you conducted your search yet, Sheriff?" Billy asked innocently.

"We're . . . we were just in the middle of it."

"Keep going, by all means."

Skeeter motioned his deputies back to work. Melvin Thomas was next to speak. "Sonny, how'd you get in on this?"

Sonny was ready. "Well, Chief, I was just going off duty this morning—I had the night shift, you know, sir—and I got a call from Sheriff Willis. He said he had a tip that there was some whiskey being sold out of here, and he wanted the department in on the search as just a kind of courtesy, I guess. So I came on out here. We just got here a couple of minutes ago. I didn't call you, because it didn't seem like a big thing. I hope I did the right thing, sir."

"Well, yes, if Sheriff Goolsby called you, you did the right thing. Wasn't any need to call me on a thing like that."

The two deputies reported back to Skeeter. One of them shook his head. "Sheriff, there ain't no shine around here unless its buried."

Skeeter nodded and turned to Billy. "We had this call; we had to check it out. Looks like there's nothing here."

"It's down at the police station," said Billy.

Skeeter looked confused. "How's that?"

Chief Thomas spoke up. "Billy and Marshall turned in two cases of white lightning to me a few minutes ago. Marshall says somebody broke in here last night and left it here."

Skeeter snorted. "Well, that's pretty smart, Marshall. You must of knowed we had a tip."

"If Marshall had wanted to hide the stuff, he had plenty of time," said Billy. "Instead, he called a lawyer and asked advice on what to do. He took my advice and turned it in to the police. I think that demonstrates his innocence in this. Somebody planted it here and called you. That's pretty clear, I think."

Skeeter flushed and looked at the ground. "Yeah, maybe." He looked up at Marshall. "And maybe we just oughta keep an eye on you, boy."

Billy interrupted Marshall's attempt at a reply. "I think you'd spend your time better trying to find out who wanted to put the frame on an innocent man, Skeeter."

Skeeter signaled to his men. "All right, let's get outta here. We got work to do today." He nodded to Billy and Chief Thomas. "See you, gents." In a moment the two sheriff's cars were gone.

Sonny spoke. "Well, Chief, I reckon I'll go home and get some sleep if you don't need me."

"All right, Sonny, I'll finish up here." Sonny left, and the chief made a cursory inspection of the broken window. "Not much more I can do," he said. "I'll destroy the whiskey and make a note in the logbook about this, but unless you've got some idea about who might have done this, Marshall, I can't do any more."

Billy, out of the chief's line of vision, shook his head at Marshall.

"No, sir," Marshall said, "I don't know who would want to do it." The chief made his exit and left Billy and Marshall alone. "Marshall, you've been getting some of Mickey Shelton's business since you opened, haven't you?"

"Yessir, I guess I've got a lot of his colored trade. He was charging too much."

"Some of his white trade, too?"

Marshall nodded. "Yessir, I guess so."

"Well, that's what you're supposed to do in business, I guess. I sure won't advise you to stop doing that, but I tell you, Marshall, I'd be real careful where I stepped for a while. Mickey Shelton and Sonny Butts are pretty tight, I think, and I wouldn't be surprised if one or both of them was at the bottom of this thing. You just walk the straight and narrow. Don't get drunk, don't drive too fast, don't get into any arguments with anybody. There've been some rumors about Sonny, and you don't want to let him get you in jail. You see what I mean, don't you?"

"Yessir, I do. I'll watch my step."

Billy nodded. "And listen, if you even so much as get wind of anything else like this, or if you have any problems, you call me right away, hear? You did the right thing this morning."

"I'll do that, Colonel, and I'd like to pay you for your time."

"Well, I think my wife's station wagon could use a grease job and an oil change. That ought to just about do it."

Marshall grinned. "Yessir, you tell her anytime, just any-time."

Billy left and hurried to the bank for his meeting. On the way he thought about Marshall. He would not like to be in that man's shoes right now.

11 FOXY FUNDERBURKE woke about nine and took his time about rising, as was his custom. When he had shaved and dressed, he went to the kitchen, looking forward to what he would find there.

He felt the tiles first with his hand, then tapped them with a heavily shod foot. Dry. Firm. Foxy was delighted. He ate his breakfast quickly, anxious to finish with the floor. When he was done, he took a stiff brush and scrubbed down the whole surface to remove any vestige of dirt or cement left from his work, then attached a hose to the kitchen faucet and rinsed the floor. He watched delightedly as the water swirled, then inexorably flowed down the cleverly slanted surface to the drain he had installed in the center.

The stains in the old wooden floor had bothered him for years, and now he was rid of them for good. There would be no new stains, either. The glazed surface of the tiles would prevent that. Everything would disappear down the drain. Forever.

His task complete, Foxy went to his closet and pushed back the clothing hanging on the rack to expose another rack behind the first in the deeply built enclosure. From half a dozen things hanging there he chose a neatly pressed shirt and trousers of tan tropical gabardine and draped them across the bed. He dragged a stool over and, reaching to the back of the shelf above the rack, retrieved a peaked cap of matching material. He chose a black woolen necktie and from a box at the back of his sock drawer took two badges. He fixed one to the cap and pinned the other carefully to the shirt. Both badges bore the legend Chief of Police.

Foxy felt good about today. He had had a couple of false starts, lately, suspects who hadn't panned out, who'd been expected somewhere by somebody. Then Sonny Butts's visit had shaken him for a couple of days; he'd had to regain his confidence. Now that was back, and the pressure, which had been building for a long time, was nearly unbearable. He knew that because of the pressure he would have to be extra careful not to make mistakes. The need to act had done that to him before, had made him careless in his excitement, and he must not let that happen again. He was in control; he must stay in control. Balancing need against control was the essence of his crusade.

He stared longingly at the uniform. He wanted so much to wear it away from the house, but he controlled the urge. It was too dangerous. He would think of the preliminaries as undercover work, in plain clothes. He had his badge and gun and handcuffs, anyway, should he need them.

He left the house, double-locking the door. He wished, too, that he could have a proper police car, with a black-and-white paint job and a siren. The pickup would have to do.

Foxy was, in fact, a deputy sheriff of Talbot County. Goolsby had sworn him in properly and given him a badge. Honorary deputy, Goolsby had called it, but there was nothing about honorary in the oath, nor did the badge differ from that of other, full-time deputies. When Goolsby had retired, then died, nobody had ever asked him for the badge back. Everyone had forgotten. Everyone but Foxy. The badge had come in very handy.

Foxy knew he would make an arrest today, he felt it in his bones. He fought back the pressure. There must be no escaping. He had not had an escapee in a long, long time. He was too experienced for that now. He knew his work.

As he drove toward the main road, he began to anticipate. He fought the urge; he was superstitious about that; if you anticipated too much something might go wrong. He thought about the questions he would ask. He liked making up the questions.

None of his suspects had ever known the answers.

12 "HEAVENLY FATHER, we thank thee for this day, for the opportunity to worship which we have just enjoyed, and for the food we are about to eat which thou hast given us. We thank thee for our children, Billy and Eloise, for Billy's deliverance from the war and his return to us, and for the strength thou hast given Eloise in her grief. We thank thee, especially, for our new daughter, Patricia, and for the love she has given us. We ask thy blessing on this day of rest and for the days ahead. Give us strength to serve thee each day of our lives. We ask these things in the name of thy son, Jesus Christ. Amen."

H. W. Fowler performed each of his life's duties thoroughly and with care, and he did not exclude a blessing said over a Sunday fried-chicken dinner from these attentions. He would no more have recited a pat prayer than he would have skipped church or a revival meeting.

He had not the slightest difficulty in thinking of things for which to thank God; he found his life full of such things. He felt a visceral pleasure in the gleam of the mahogany dining table and the sparkle of the Waterford chandelier overhead, and in the heft of the sterling with which he now ate. He had chosen none of these things, but he had been thrilled to be able to allow his wife to choose them. His greatest personal satisfaction came from his ability to provide for his family, for his church, and for a long

line of Baptist preachers who had found their meager stipends
swelled by clothing from his store or cash from his pocket shyly
pressed upon them.

He was happy to have his family about him, his wife, his
stepchildren, and his daughter-in-law, but he was worried about
Billy. There had been something of a void in his life since Billy
had become a man and moved beyond his benevolence, and
since he could no longer buy him bicycles or send him to law
school, he could only worry.

"Billy, I've been hearing some talk about this business with
Marshall Parker. Eloise, will you pass the gravy, please?"

"What've you been hearing, Mr. Fowler?" They all called him
Mr. Fowler, even Carrie.

"I was selling a man a suit yesterday, and I heard two women
talking over behind one of the dress racks. Emmett Spence's wife
was one of them. I never liked that girl much. Never liked Emmett much, either. Maybe they deserve each other."

"What did Sylvia Spence have to say about it?"

"Oh, she was going on about you having a 'nigger practice,'
as she called it."

"Well, Sylvia's got a big chip on her shoulder, I guess. Emmett managed to stay out of the draft because he was a farmer—"

"A farmer's son, maybe. Not much of a farmer."

"That's the truth. But he and Sylvia seem to be real touchy
about veterans, and, Lord knows, they've got no love for colored
people. Word is, Emmett's in the Klan. Could I have another biscuit, Mama?"

"I've heard that."

"So I guess Marshall Parker represents all the things they hate
most—a Negro, and one with a good war record and a good business. You're not worried about my helping Marshall out, are
you?"

"Goodness gracious, no. I think Marshall's a good boy. His
daddy's been working at the church for years, and I think he got
brought up right. I let him have a charge account when he got
out of the service, and he's paid his bill better than most white
folks. I'm glad to see a colored boy working hard and doing well,
too. It just bothers me to hear folks trying to tear you down that
way. Pass the chicken, Carrie."

"Well, you can't please everybody, not even in politics. If I've
got to have enemies I'd just as soon Emmett and Sylvia Spence

were among 'em.'

Carrie Lee Fowler spoke up. "Now, Billy, you shouldn't have any man for your enemy if you can help it."

"Mama, I feel the same way, but what should I do to make Emmett Spence my friend. What do you think I should do?"

Carried laughed wryly. "Well, you've got me there. I guess anything you might do to make Emmett your friend might get you in trouble with the Lord. Can I serve you some more corn, Mr. Fowler?"

Patricia looked puzzled. "I don't undrstand why the Spences hate blacks so much."

"Well," said Billy, "from what I hear, Hoss Spence didn't have much, came from a family of dirt farmers, folks that might have had to compete with Negroes for sharecropping. Folks like that sometimes hate Negroes because they feel they're a threat to their prosperity. I guess maybe Emmett just inherited that view of things from Hoss. I expect his children will inherit it from him. It's a shame that sort of feeling has to go on and on. There's no reason for it."

Mr. Fowler spoke up again. "Billy, what do you reckon that was all about, out at Marshall's?"

"Well, it's pretty clear to me that somebody wanted to see Marshall in a lot of trouble."

"Who do you think?"

"Unless Marshall has a problem with somebody I don't know about, and I think he'd tell me if he did, then it seems to me that Mickey Shelton would make a good candidate. Marshall's giving him some unwanted competition, I guess. I think Sonny Butts could be mixed up in it, too. He and Marshall had some sort of argument, so Sonny's mad at him, and Sonny's in a position to handle the police side of a situation like this."

Mr. Fowler nodded. "I wouldn't be surprised. Sonny's always been a little too slick for my liking. He knows how to butter folks up, but I wouldn't trust him much. He ran up a big bill at the store, and I had to stay on him to collect it. I think he thought I was just going to mark it 'paid' because he's a policeman. I got that impression. I tell you, I'd rather have Marshall Parker for a customer than Sonny Butts."

Billy grunted. "I'd rather have Marshall Parker for a policeman than Sonny Butts, to tell you the truth. In fact, I suggested to Hugh Holmes that the city hire a colored policeman, one of the veterans. A majority of the actual peacekeeping the police do is in Braytown, anyway, and I think a Negro could do a better job over there."

"What did Hugh say?" asked Mr. Fowler.

"He seemed to think it was a good idea, and there was even some sympathy for it at the council meeting, I gather, but there was only enough in the budget to hire one new man, and they picked Sonny Butts. Melvin Thomas thought it might be a good idea, too, and he told me that when there was a need for a fourth officer he'd consider recommending hiring a Negro. I don't think Sonny would like that, though."

"Does it matter what Sonny likes?" Eloise asked.

"It matters to Melvin. He thinks Sonny has been doing a great job, and I guess he has with the traffic and such."

"Does Melvin know about the beatings at the jail, do you think?" Mr. Fowler asked.

"Brooks Peters talked to him when he first heard about it, and Melvin listened, although he didn't seem to think there was much to it. Sonny holds that he just uses necessary force, and that drunks get rowdy and have to be handled. There was another incident last night, apparently, although the man wasn't seriously hurt. Old Jim Parker came to Brooks about it before church this morning, and Brooks is going to talk to Melvin again tomorrow."

"Will that help?" asked Eloise.

"It's not going to get Sonny fired, but if Brooks can stir up Melvin enough, at least it might put a stop to what's been going on. It's not as though there was enough evidence, witnesses and all, to prosecute Sonny."

"Melvin's a good man," said Mr. Fowler. "He'll do what's right."

"Oh, he's a decent enough fellow," said Billy. "I just wish he was smarter. He lets himself get manipulated by Sonny Butts."

"That Butts family has never been much good," said Carrie. "His mother's nice enough, poor thing, but Sonny's daddy was always a problem. He was a drinker, and Will Henry had to put him in jail once or twice."

Across town, on the other side of the M&B railroad tracks, in Milltown, at the corner of Maple and Poplar, another family was having a Sunday fried-chicken dinner, a smaller family.

"Oh, Sonny, I'm so glad to see you. I wish you would come to see me more regular."

Sonny Butts wiped his mouth and sat back. "Mama, you know I'm on duty all the time. I wish I could get by here more often, but a lot of times when I'm off, you're at the mill, you know. Boy, that sure was good chicken."

"You look so nice in your uniform, Sonny. I'm real proud of you. Mrs. Smith next door said she saw you on your motorcycle the other day and you looked so dashing. That was what she said, dashing. Your daddy would be proud of you, too, if he was alive."

"Yeah, like he was proud of me when I was playing ball. I bet he got thrown out of half the games I played, the old rummy."

"You shouldn't talk that way about your daddy, Sonny."

"I don't know why you stand up for him, Mama. He never gave you nothing but a hard time, and he beat up on you 'bout every time he got drunk, which was regular." Sonny ground his teeth. "Beat up on me, too, until I got big enough to do something about it." Sonny remembered with some satisfaction the first time he had hit his father. The man had wilted like a flower, and he had never laid another hand on either of them again while Sonny was around. He drank nearly all the time, though.

"Well," his mother replied weakly, "In the beginning he was . . . I mean, he never did any of that before you was born."

"You think he got that way because of *me*?"

"It was like he was jealous of you, kind of. I don't know. I never understood it."

"Well, you're better off without him, I can tell you that."

His mother began to clear away the dishes. She still misses him, Sonny thought. He shook his head. The telephone rang, and she went to answer it.

Carrie found the buzzer under the carpet, and Flossie came to take the dishes away. "Now, who'd like some peach cobbler?"

Patricia glanced at Billy and smiled. "That sounds just wonderful, but . . . . I'm afraid I'm going to have to start watching my weight."

Carrie laughed. "Sugar, you're too thin as it is." Her eyebrows shot up. "Unless—?"

Billy laughed aloud. "Well, Mama, I guess you better start getting used to the idea of being a grandmother."

"That's right," Patricia said. "Next April. It's going to be a boy, I can tell."

In the excitement that followed no one heard the telephone ring. Flossie came back in. "It's for you, Mr. Billy." Billy left the room.

"When did you find out, Trisha?" Eloise asked.

"Just yesterday, when Tom Mudter confirmed it."

"Is everything all right?" asked Henry Fowler worriedly. "I mean, are you all right?" He was already thinking of what he could do for a grandchild.

"Of course, Mr. Fowler. Happens every day, you know. Nothing to be concerned about."

"Well, I'm just so happy, Patricia," Carrie said, beaming. "We're going to enjoy having a baby in the family. I'm just so pleased for you and all of us."

Billy returned to the room. Patricia noticed immediately that something was wrong. "What is it, Billy?" They all turned and looked at him.

"That was Hugh Holmes. Melvin Thomas collapsed and died on the steps of the Methodist Church about an hour ago, right after church."

"How awful," Carrie said. "He was such a nice man."

Billy stood with his hands in his pockets, looking out a window. Patricia wrinkled her brow. "Is there something else, Billy?"

He nodded. "Some of the council members got on the phone right away. Sonny Butts has been made acting chief of police. Mr. Holmes thinks they'll make it permanent tomorrow."

13 WHEN SONNY walked into the Delano police station after Melvin Thomas's funeral on Tuesday morning, he felt like a king newly crowned. The council had voted to make him chief of police the preceding day, although the announcement was being withheld until Thursday, partly out of respect for the dead and partly because the *Delano Messenger* was published on Thursdays, and that was a convenient way to announce his permanent appointment.

He had a girl, Millie, on loan from the city manager's office to answer the phone and handle the radio until he could hire another officer, and she was at work as he entered. He looked around the station room for a moment. The place was already the way he wanted it. Thomas had been content to let him arrange the station room, and Sonny was satisfied that he had done it efficiently. Now what he wanted was to get at the old man's office—now his office.

"Millie, I've got some work to do for a while. Don't call me unless its real urgent, okay?"

"Sure, Sonny." She giggled. "I mean, Chief."

He had been screwing her once a week for three months. Too bad there wasn't a sofa in the chief's office. Maybe he could wangle one. He went into the office, closed the door, and leaned against it for a moment. He was breathing hard with excitement.

Things had worked out so much better than he could ever have dreamed they would. After a whole war of being pushed around, first by NCOs, then by officers, now *he* was in charge. He had wanted a battlefield commission, but it had never come. Now he had better than a commission, he had a command. He was fucking *Eisenhower*, was what he was.

The office wasn't much—a small room that had been added onto the original building, furnished with a desk, a filing cabinet, a hat rack, and three wooden chairs. But it was the first office he had ever had, the sort of office a company commander might have had in the army. He walked around it slowly, looking into a filing cabinet, shuffling through the stack of papers on the desk. Christ, what a mess! Thomas had never let him get these files, this room, organized. He opened the top drawer of the filing cabinet and started.

Two hours later he had filled two large cardboard boxes with old files, circulars, papers, and just plain trash. The desk top was clean as a whistle except for a telephone and a calendar. He sank into the desk chair and opened a drawer. The drawers were all that was left. He began filling a smaller box with the old man's stuff—an electric razor, a Parker pen, a pistol, some personal bills, a few photographs of his family—there wasn't a hell of a lot. Then he emptied each drawer in turn on the desk top and filtered through everything to find out whether it was personal or police stuff and whether it was important enough to keep.

There were a few file folders. He put those aside for làst. At noon he sent Millie out to get him a sandwich, then he propped his feet up on the desk, ate his sandwich, and read through the files. They went back a long way. Thomas had been a sergeant on the Columbus police force when he had been hired to replace Will Henry Lee nearly twenty years before. At first, it seemed to Sonny, Thomas had been enthusiastic about his job and had stuck to the routines of a trained officer from a bigger town. The files were mostly collections of information on the same type of crime—there was a folder on stolen cars, for instance—and notes that, in cooperation with the state police, car thieves who had been working the area had been arrested and convicted. There was another file on a string of burglaries that had taken place over a period of months in the thirties, and a similar concluding set of notes. The files seemed to have been kept as much for sentiment as for records.

In the late thirties and during the war years, though, the files seemed to have been kept more erratically, and there were fewer notes. Thomas must have been getting tired of the work by then, Sonny thought. The last of the folders was one marked "missing persons." Sonny took a long swig of his Coca-Cola and opened it.

There were a dozen circulars put out by the state police, beginning in the late twenties and continuing into the war years. They were arranged more or less chronologically, as if they had been simply added to the file as they had come in, the more recent ones on top. Each sheet had a photograph, usually a family snapshot or a portrait by a two-dollar photographer, or, where there was no photograph, simply a detailed description. The missing persons, he noted, were all male and white. Nearly all of them were very young. As Sonny flipped through them, he noticed that the further down the stack he got the more attention seemed to have been paid to the circular. While the more recent ones on top were without notations, the older ones had comments and underlinings, mostly related to where the subject had last been seen. Greenville, Woodbury, and Waverly Hall had all been underlined on various sheets, and there were notations: "check jungles" or "seen hitchiking." Sonny viewed the lack of comments on the later circulars as typical of Thomas's waning interest in his job as the years wore on. There were no reports included of any of the subjects' having been located.

Clearly, though, Thomas had been interested in these missing young men, at least at first. He had obviously checked the hobo jungles and asked some questions, maybe showed the photographs around. Sonny picked up a pencil and started through the more recent circulars, underlining as Thomas had. When he had finished he found a road map and a grease pencil and started marking the towns where the subjects had last been reported. Five of the twelve had last been seen some distance away—Macon, Carrollton, places fifty or more miles from Delano. He removed them from the stack and did not mark them on the map. The remaining seven were represented by marks that formed an uneven circle. At the center of the circle, roughly, was Delano.

He read the seven circulars again. Five of them contained the supposed direction of travel of the subjects. In each case those last seen north of Delano had been traveling south; those seen south of the town had been traveling north. The likely route for each of them led through Delano.

Sonny picked up the phone and called a fellow he knew at the state patrol in Atlanta. "Hey, Tank, this is Sonny Butts."

"Hey, Sonny. Congratulations. Hear you got chief."

"Thanks, yeah. Nothing anybody couldn't do with good looks and hard work."

"Shit."

"Listen, Tank, I need you to look up something for me in the missing-persons files. Would it be pretty easy to find some old stuff?"

"We got 'em indexed by name and date of disappearance up through last month. You got that information?"

"Yeah." Sonny read him the names and dates. "How long you reckon?"

"Well, I finished my dinner. I'll do it now and call you back in a few minutes. Anything special you want to know about them?"

"Just whether they ever turned up."

"Call you back."

He read through the five circulars again. All the subjects were between sixteen and twenty-one years old. All were under five feet nine inches tall and slight. Four of the circulars displayed photographs. There was a sameness about them, Sonny thought, an innocence. He got up and went to his old roll-top desk in the station room and took the bundle of Chief Lee's old files from the bottom drawer. Back in the office he untied the string and fished through the folders until he found the photographs of the corpse. He chose the one that looked most lifelike, nearly as if the boy were sleeping. He placed it on the desk next to the four circular photographs. A shudder ran through him.

The phone rang. "Sonny? Tank. All your boys are still open files. Never found. Course, that don't mean a lot. They could all be in South America. Just means we never got no results from the circulars, and the families never reported them found. You got something on these cases?"

Sonny thought for a minute before answering. "Naw, Tank, I ain't got nothing. They just turned up in a file in Chief Thomas's desk, and I wanted to know whether to throw 'em away or not. I 'preciate you looking 'em up for me."

"Yeah, sure. Course, we don't usually hear much on these missing-persons things 'less it happens within a week or two of the disappearance. I guess you can throw 'em away. No use cluttering up your files."

"Yeah, Tank, I'll do that. Stop by here and see me some time. I'll get you drunk and laid."

"You know it, buddy." They hung up.

Sonny discovered that he was sweating, more than could be accounted for by the heat. He had something here, he was sure of it. Trouble was, it was all so cold. If it was new and fresh, that would be different, he might turn up something. He would be patient for a while. If what he thought had been going on was really happening, all he had to do was wait. Wait and watch. Keep an eye on the old son of a bitch. He would do that.

14 BILLY LEE and the Reverend Brooks Peters called on Hugh Holmes at home the evening after the funeral of Chief Melvin Thomas. Holmes settled them in his study and offered them some iced tea. The presence of the preacher precluded the offering of anything else.

There was some small talk, and then Billy came to the point. "Mr. Holmes, it looks like we might have a problem with Sonny Butts."

Holmes showed no surprise. "You mean about the beatings?"

"Yessir."

"Well, so far I haven't heard anything that couldn't be construed as the reasonable actions of a police officer to protect himself."

"We think there's more to it than that."

"I didn't say I believed what I heard. I wouldn't be surprised if there was a lot more to it."

"Didn't the rumors come up at the council meeting on Monday, when Sonny was confirmed as chief?"

"They came up. Matter of fact, I brought them up. I suggested that we leave things as they were, with Sonny as acting chief, until we had an opportunity to look for a more experienced man. There was no sympathy for that view at all. In fact, a number of voices spoke up for more hard handling by the police. They reckoned it would keep crime down in Braytown."

Brooks Peters spoke up. "There was another incident last Saturday night."

"Billy mentioned it to me on the phone Sunday, when I called to tell him about Melvin Thomas."

"Did that come up at the council meeting?"

"It got mentioned, but I take it that nobody is willing to make a complaint, and there weren't any witnesses—not any that would testify against Sonny, anyway. That's the trouble with something like this. There's nobody on the spot to determine whether Sonny and Charley Ward are exceeding the proper limits of their duty, nobody except the victim, anyway."

"But something has got to be done about this, Mr. Holmes," Peters said, with some passion. "There's enough resentment of white people in the Negro community without something as blatant as this going on."

Holmes nodded. "I agree with you. Something's got to be done, and if you'll suggest a course of action with a reasonable chance of success, I'll follow it. But I can't go down to the council and bring charges against the chief of police based on nothing more than rumors or, at best, the testimony of a colored man who got arrested for drunkenness and doesn't like the way he was treated."

"Mr. Holmes is right," said Billy. "We've got to have a case that will hold up in court before we can get the council to act on replacing Sonny. The city doesn't have any established procedures for dealing with a situation like this—no specific regulations, and no committee or review board to handle an administrative charge, the way a big city might have." He thought for a minute. "Mr. Holmes, is there some informal means we might use to bring pressure on the council, or directly on Sonny?"

Holmes shook his head. "Not unless you could bring public opinion to bear, and I tell you public opinion isn't going be on your side until there's a lot of less-disputable evidence than you have now. Sonny's riding high right now. He's organized the way the police department works, he's personally brought in a lot of money in traffic tickets, and he looks just like the model of what a police officer should be, and that counts for a lot with public opinion. No, sir, I think you're batting your head against a brick wall right now."

Billy and Brooks were both quiet. Peters rattled the ice cubes in his glass impatiently. "We've just got to think of something," he said.

Billy took a deep breath and spoke. "Maybe it's the colored community that's got to do something."

Holmes looked up. "How do you mean?"

"I don't know, exactly, but I think I'll have a word with Marshall Parker about this. They've got that colored veteran's group that meets regularly. Maybe they can come up with something."

Holmes looked alarmed. "You're not suggesting they try to fight fire with fire."

"Oh, no, sir. The last thing we need is a Negro Klan. I think the suggestion of what to do ought to come from them. If they could gather enough evidence against Sonny would you present it to the council?"

"Of course, but it's got to be strong and completely above board. Don't you let those boys go thinking of some way to try to trap Sonny into something. That would backfire right in their faces."

Brooks Peters stood up. "Well, that sounds like a good idea to me, Billy. You talk to Marshall, and then let's get together again and talk about this. Mr. Holmes, thank you for the iced tea. I'll see you in church Sunday."

Holmes shook hands with the preacher. "Well, I hope we can get something done about this, Brooks, and I'll help any way I can." He turned to Billy. "Can you stay for a few minutes? I've got some bank business to talk to you about."

They said their good-byes, and Holmes went immediately to his concealed liquor cabinet. "Can I force some whiskey on you?"

"You sure can. Bourbon and a little water."

Holmes mixed the drinks and made himself comfortable again. "Billy, we've got problems."

"At the bank?"

"No, I mean politics problems." He pushed an ice cube around his drink with a finger. "I don't know if you ought to get involved with Marshall and his colored veterans any more right now."

"I haven't been involved with them at all. Oh, I know most of them, but the thing with Marshall and his moonshine problem was the only thing I've been involved in."

"I know, but you get your car fixed out there, too, and—"

"Now, wait a minute. You get your car fixed out there, too, and we both do it because Marshall does good work, isn't that right?"

"Of course, and I'm not suggesting you ought to start going to Mickey Shelton. I just think you ought to leave things as they lie until after the primary. There's only three weeks to go, you know."

"What have you been hearing? You must have heard something to worry you."

"I have. This whole relationship with Marshall is getting blown all out of proportion, and it's hurting us. There's some question in my mind of whether we could carry Talbot County right now, and Harris County isn't looking too good, either. I think you're all right in Delano and Manchester and Greenville, but if the smaller communities and the farmers in Talbot and Harris go the other way, this thing could get too close to call."

"What do you think I ought to do?"

"Well, first of all I think you ought to make a big effort over the next three weeks to get out into Talbot and Harris and shake some hands and answer some questions."

Billy winced. "Boy, I thought I'd covered that every which way."

"You have, but you're going to have to do it again."

Billy sighed. "All right, I'll get out there starting tomorrow morning."

"Secondly, I think you ought to stay out of this thing with Sonny Butts and stay away from Marshall and his veterans until after the primary."

"That bothers me," Billy said. "I think something ought to be done about Sonny, and Marshall's people have been working to get more colored voters registered in Braytown, and I think I owe them whatever help I can give them."

Holmes leaned forward and rested his elbows on his knees. Billy recognized the stance as one that the banker adopted when he wanted to drive a point home. "Billy, I'm not suggesting for a moment that you should betray the trust of Marshall and those boys. All I'm saying is that you should wait until after the primary, at least, and probably until after the general election, before you get any further involved there."

"But I'm not all that involved. I—"

"It isn't a question of how involved you are. It's a question of how involved you are perceived to be. There is no point in going out and creating opposition for yourself where there was none before. If you want to help the colored community you can do it a lot better if you are elected. How can you help them if you lose?"

"I've already told Brooks I'd talk to Marshall."

"And you should. But Brooks is kind of a hothead, and you shouldn't let him push you into something at the wrong time. Timing counts for a lot in politics, and if you want to get things done you have to pay attention to it. Believe me."

Billy rubbed the back of his neck for a minute, and gulped down the rest of his drink. "All right," he said.

"And just let the Sonny Butts thing lie for a few weeks. Maybe we'll get lucky, and he'll make a mistake. Give him enough rope—you know."

Billy nodded.

The next morning, driving to his office, Billy passed Marshall Parker's garage just as Marshall was opening up. The black man waved at him and signaled for him to stop. Billy waved and drove past. By the time he reached his office, he was nearly sick with shame for having done so. He telephoned the garage.

"Marshall? This is Billy Lee. I had already driven past your place this morning when it occurred to me you might have wanted to talk to me. I'm sorry, I had a lot on my mind."

"Yes, sir, I did want to speak to you for just a minute. We're having a little get-together, our veterans and the wives early this Saturday evening. I was wondering if you could just come by and say a few words to us. It's at the Galilee Church, out on the highway."

Billy was gripping the telephone so tightly that his knuckles were white. "Oh, my gosh, thank you Marshall, but I'm going to be somewhere down in the depths of Talbot County Saturday night. Mr. Holmes thinks I need to get down there and mend some fences. We've still got another three weeks for me to speak to them. I'll call you next week."

"Yes, sir, that'll be fine." There was disappointment in his voice.

When Billy hung up he felt worse than before he had called.

[faded, illegible text from reverse side of page]

15 IN THE HEAT of Saturday afternoon, Sonny Butts stepped from the last rung of the ladder onto the hemp matting of the high-diving board at Pine Mountain pool. He looked idly around the handsome, bell-shaped, flagstone pool, built in the thirties by the Civilian Conservation Corps, and his gaze stopped at a blanket occupied by two girls. He had been watching them from a distance for an hour, as he lay in the sun and surreptitiously drank beer from a paper cup. Alcoholic beverages were prohibited in Franklin D. Roosevelt State Park.

One girl was fairly tall and slender and had ample breasts. She wore her hair pulled back into a ponytail. The other was shorter and heavier and had cropped blonde hair and powdery, freckled skin. Boyish but nice, Sonny thought. He had noticed the sort of attention the two girls had been paying to each other, slowly rubbing oil on each other's bodies, tickling, giggling. They made Sonny remember two girls in Belgium and what he thought must have been the wildest night of his life.

When he was sure they were watching, he walked to the end of the diving board and stopped, flexing his shoulder and leg muscles as if to loosen up. He took a couple of practice springs to test the board, then sauntered back and took up his position. He counted the steps, one, two, three, rose, and came down on the board. As he gained height he arched his body and fell backward into a perfect half gainer, his brown body and blonde hair flashing in the sunlight as he parted the water, making hardly a splash. For the next fifteen minutes he worked his way through a repertoire learned in many idle hours as a lifeguard, while the high school kids who had been using the board hung back and watched in awe. The girls were watching, too. They must be from Columbus, he thought. He'd never seen them before.

On his way back to his blanket he passed close to the girls and stopped, feet apart, hands on hips. "Hi," he said, careful to include them both. "I've got some cold beer over yonder. Why don't you girls come over and help me drink it?"

"Mmmmm," said the tall girl. "Maybe in a few minutes."

"Sure," said the shorter girl. She seemed to appreciate being included in the invitation.

He went back to his blanket, stretched out in the sun, and waited, sipping his beer. He dozed for a few minutes, and when he woke they were gone. He sat up and looked around. The girls were walking toward the chain-link fence that separated the pool area from the woods beyond. He wondered where the hell they were going. The girls' can was in the other direction, and the fence was eight feet tall. Then he saw the shorter girl step up to the fence and tug at it, revealing a gap. She held it for her friend, and as the taller girl stepped through, she looked toward Sonny and flashed him a smile. The two girls disappeared into the woods.

Sonny grinned. He'd been around; he knew what they were up to. He waited five minutes, then gathered up the beer and started for the fence. In the woods he found a path and padded along it, taking care to be quiet. A quarter of a mile along he saw a pair of sunglasses lying next to the path. He bent over to pick them up, and as he straightened he saw the top of a stone chimney behind a little rise through the trees. The glasses belonged to the tall girl, he remembered. He left the main path and followed another, slightly overgrown, toward the chimney. As he came silently to the top of the rise he saw that the chimney belonged to a disused barbecue pit which sat in a small clearing with a couple of picnic tables. He sucked in his breath and held it.

The tall girl was spread-eagled on her back on one of the picnic tables. The other girl was standing over her, stroking her breasts and belly. They were both naked. The tall girl's eyes were closed, and Sonny had approached from behind the other girl, so they did not see him. He stood, tensely, and watched. The short girl leaned over her friend and bit her nipples, which immediately came erect. Then she kissed her way slowly down the girl's torso and along the insides of her thighs. The tall girl moaned and opened her legs wider.

Sonny bent slowly and set the beer down, then slipped out of his bathing trunks and jock strap. He was fully erect, huge. The short girl now knelt and slowly spread her friend's vulva, stroking with her tongue. The tall girl came suddenly, making little noises and rolling her head back and forth. Both their eyes were closed now. Sonny walked softly over to them and placed one hand on the tall girl's belly, pinning her to the table, and the other hand on the back of the short girl's neck, locking his fingers in her short hair. They both started, but the tall girl was in too ecstatic a state to care what was happening, and he had a firm hold on the short one.

"Hey, now," he crooned to the short one, "why don't you let me do that, and you can suck this instead?" He thrust his swollen penis into her face. She pushed it away and began getting to her feet.

"No!" she said, backing away, assuming a fighting stance, her thick, muscular legs spread and slightly bent.

"Okay, okay," Sonny said, trying to placate her. "You just hang on there for a minute, and we'll have a real fuck, but right now I think your friend needs it more." He turned to the tall girl, who was trying to sit up, and pushed her back down onto the table. She attempted to close her legs, but he was already between them. He stepped in, guiding his penis with his free hand.

Behind him the short girl clenched her fists, stepped forward and kicked upward as hard as she could.

At the moment Sonny pushed into the girl the feeling of the wet, tight, heat of her was overtaken by another, overwhelming, sensation, the fiery shock of his testicles being driven hard up against his pelvis. He screamed and fell back onto the ground, curling into the fetal position, clutching his crotch.

"Come on!" the short girl hissed to her friend. "Get your stuff on, and let's get out of here." She was already half way into her own bathing suit.

The tall girl began struggling into her clothing. "Jesus, he'll kill us! Are you crazy!"

Sonny continued to yell with every breath. The short girl stepped behind him and kicked him again, this time in the kidney. He screamed again and fainted. The girls ran.

He came to in a few moments, but he was still in excruciating pain. He vomited a couple of times, and it was half an hour before he could get to his feet. The bitches had taken his bathing suit, but he found his jockstrap. He was filthy from rolling on the ground and cleaned himself up as best he could using the beer. He walked slowly and painfully up the path. He needed ice, he knew, but he dreaded the thought of holding it to his balls. The woods stopped a few feet from the pool fence, and he saw that they had left his suit hanging there.

It was late afternoon now, but there were still people about. He cursed the girls for putting him in this humiliating position. He waited for another half an hour before finding a moment when no one seemed to be looking, then he dashed for the fence, retrieved his suit, and got back behind a tree, whimpering at the effort. He got back through the fence, limped to the pool, and sank gratefully into the icy spring water. That would keep down swelling even better than the ice would.

In a few minutes he felt better, well enough to walk without limping noticably. He wrapped his blanket about him to hide the bruises around his kidney, went to the dressing room, and got his clothes on. He thought about looking for the girls, but he had no idea where they were from, didn't know what kind of car they were driving, didn't even know their first names. Still sick and trembling with anger and humiliation, he climbed gingerly into his car and headed back over Pine Mountain toward Delano. He got a pint of whiskey out of the glove compartment and started to drink.

When he got back to his boardinghouse he went through the back door to his room and collapsed on the bed. He dozed fitfully for the rest of the afternoon, waking now and then to take a pull on the bottle. His anger, like hot metal, cooled and shrank into something cold and hard, and a terrible pressure began to build inside him. As it began to get dark outside, he remembered it was Saturday night. He got up, found another pint of whiskey and, still dressed in jeans and a T-shirt, drove to the police station.

When Sonny entered the station room, Charley Ward had his

feet propped up on a desk, dozing. Sonny kicked his chair, sending him spinning across the room, nearly capsizing. "Jesus, Sonny," Charley whined, getting to his feet, "you scared the shit out of me."

"Listen, you're lucky it was me and not some council member."

"Yeah, well, there wasn't nothing happening."

"Well, you get your ass in the patrol car. You and me are gonna make something happen."

16 MARSHALL and Annie Parker stayed on at the church for a few minutes after the veterans group had wound up their Saturday picnic and dispersed. Marshall raked the small grounds, and Annie made sure there were no paper bags or cups left lying around. Since the event had been held on church grounds there were no beer bottles to worry about.

They drove back toward Delano at twilight, sitting close together in the car. "We have a pretty good week this week?" Marshall asked.

Annie smiled. "Sure did. You had that ring job, and Smitty paid off his bill. We took in nearly two hundred dollars, and I reckon a hundred and fifty after overhead."

"That's our best week so far?"

"So far."

"I saw in the paper there's a sale on down at Fowler's. You think I could make you buy a new dress?"

She laughed. "You might could."

Marshall drove on toward downtown Delano. "Looks like ol' Junior's going to work out all right, don't it?" Junior Turner was Marshall's new employee.

"Yes, and I'm sure glad we got him. Now you can stop working at nights."

"I guess I can get home a little bit earlier. You know, he can do 'bout anything I can, except maybe rebuilding some of those parts. But parts ain't so scarce now, so that don't matter much."

"He's a nice boy, too. Folks like him."

"You know, honey, if anything should go and happen to me, he could run it, with you keeping the books."

"Something going to happen to you?"

"Well, you know, if I got in a wreck or got sick or something. You have to think about things like that. You'd have my GI insurance, too."

"I don't even want to talk about that, Marshall. You too young to be talking like that."

"Now, honey, you have to think about the worst could happen, sometimes. If it happens, I want you to go see Colonel Lee. He'll straighten things out for you. You hear me?"

She put her head on his shoulder. "All right, now. That's enough about that. Talk to me about something else. Talk to me about building a house."

He talked to her about building a house all the way to town.

Henry Fowler stood on the sidewalk in front of his store and looked up and down Main Street with some satisfaction. It was nine o'clock, and still the block was busy with cars, wagons, and buggies. A reasonably cool evening and the late-summer sales were keeping folks out; he could judge that it would be ten-thirty before he closed. Not like the Christmas season, when he'd often stay open until midnight, but still good. He saw Marshall Parker and his wife drive past looking for a parking place and waved at them. They continued down the hill and out of sight in their search.

As he turned to go back into the store, he saw the police car, Charley Ward at the wheel, cruise slowly past. What caught his attention was an incongruity: Sonny Butts was sitting in the passenger seat wearing civilian clothes, not a uniform, a T-shirt, in fact. This offended Fowler's sense of propriety. He would complain to the first councilman who came into his store. Sonny leaned out the window and called out something to a girl walking down the other side of the street. Fowler left the sidewalk in disgust.

Shortly, Marshall and Annie Parker appeared in the store, and Fowler waited on them himself, flattering Annie on her choice of a dress and helping her talk Marshall into a new shirt and tie for himself. He took some pleasure in seeing a young couple so obviously happy and prospering in the community. It surprised him that he found himself thinking of them in just those terms, not considering their color, as a couple like Billy and Patricia.

Fowler waved aside Marshall's check and charged the purchases to their account. As he bade them good night, he looked forward to having them as good customers for many years to come. The next time he saw Jim Parker, he would have to mention to him what a fine boy he had raised.

"Turn around. Drive back up Main Street." They were at the grammar school, and Sonny had not found what he was looking for. Charley obeyed. As they started up the hill in front of the post office, Sonny suddenly said, "Ahhhhhh, look at that." He nodded to his right. Marshall Parker and his wife were walking down the hill carrying some packages. Sonny looked at his watch, then up and down the street. It was after ten, and the Saturday night crowd on Main Street had thinned markedly. This downhill end was deserted except for the two late shoppers.

"Pull over, Charley." They got out of the car.

Sonny motioned Charley behind the couple and walked toward them, smiling. "Evening, Marshall." His voice was casual, even polite.

Marshall and Annie stopped. "Evening," he replied tonelessly.

"I'd like a word with you, Marshall."

"Go ahead." Annie was clutching at his sleeve.

"Well, I think it might be better if we talked about it down at the station."

"What's this all about?"

"We got some new information about that moonshine out at your place. Why don't you send your wife on home with your stuff. We'll see you get a lift after while." Sonny could see the tenseness in the nigger. His wife was scared stiff.

Marshall hesitated for a moment, then turned to Annie. "Here's the car keys. You go on home and wait for me. I'll be on later." She was wide-eyed with fright. He leaned over and kissed her on the cheek. "Call Colonel Lee," he whispered without moving his lips. He stood back and looked at her. "Go on, now. It's going to be all right. These men just want to talk to me for a little bit." She took the keys and hurried to the car.

Sonny stood without moving on the sidewalk and waited for her to drive away. As he heard the car pull out, he said, "You black son of a bitch. You're mine now." His eyes flicked over Marshall's shoulder, and Charley hit Marshall hard from behind with his blackjack. Marshall staggered forward, reaching for Sonny, then fell to his knees.

"C'mon, Charley! Get the goddam cuffs on him before he comes around. We can't do this on Main Street, for crissakes!"

Annie drove as fast as she dared and tried to keep calm, but her breath was coming rapidly and in gasps. She made it home in little more than five minutes and ran for the door, leaving her packages in the car. She grabbed the telephone book and searched it fruitlessly. Then she remembered that the Lee number would not yet be in the book. She snatched up the receiver.

"Operator."

"Please, ma'am, can you give me Colonel Lee's telephone number out to his new house?"

"Sure, Annie,"—the operators knew everybody—"they're still in the trailer out there. The number is 120-W. You want me to ring it for you?"

"Oh, yes, please ma'am."

The phone rang, then rang again. Annie stamped her foot in impatience. Five rings. No answer.

"No answer, Annie, but they could be over in the new house. They've got a loud bell outside the trailer. I'll ring a few more times."

The phone rang ten times, fifteen.

"Looks like they're not at home, Annie. Billy's probably out campaigning somewhere. Better try later."

"Thank you, ma'am." Annie collapsed into a chair and tried to think. Then, in rapid succession, she tried Hugh Holmes's and Brooks Peters's numbers. No answer from either of them. In desperation she ran for the car and started back to town.

Marshall Parker came to, face down on the back seat floor of the police car, his hands handcuffed behind him, Sonny Butts's foot on his neck. The car squealed to a halt, and Marshall heard the front door open and close. In a moment the two policemen were dragging him roughly from the car.

He was still dazed, but he knew he was at the police station.

Billy and Patricia Lee were returning from Talbotton, where Holmes had arranged a barbecue at the home of a supporter. Patricia was driving and had pulled ahead of the Holmeses shortly after leaving the event.

Billy was slumped in the passenger seat, tired, but not sleepy. "What do you think of all this campaigning, all these country people?"

"Well, it's hardly a new experience, you know. Nobody loves politics better than the Irish. Being the candidate's wife is new, though, gives one a different perspective."

"How so?"

"I'd never thought much about the differences in the ways people react to politics. At home, everybody talked about it, and some were more interested than others, but standing next to you at these gatherings, like tonight, I can see the differences."

"Go on."

"Some are just there for the fun of it, for the party. Others support you personally, maybe because you're a veteran or because they knew your father or your family, or because you're Hugh Holmes's candidate. Others want something. They're putting their support in the bank now, and they're going to want to have something in return later. I wonder how much of a problem that will be for you."

"I've talked about that with Mr. Holmes. Most of those who want something later don't have anything definite in mind, now. They want to have an in just in case, and the things they want will be small—help with some state department, something like that. They'll be easy to accommodate."

"What about the ones with larger expectations?"

"I don't know how large their expectations can get with a state senator. If I were running for governor, they might want all sorts of things. Still, I'll help them if I can, I guess, unless they want something they're clearly not entitled to, and then I guess I'll turn them down."

"I'm going to remind you that you said that one of these days."

He grinned. "Okay."

"By the way, have you thought about what we'll be doing on election night?"

"Lord, no. You think we ought to have a victory celebration or something?"

She laughed. "Well, if Mr. Holmes's concerns about the election mean anything, planning a victory celebration might be presumptuous."

"You've got a point, there. Still, he thinks we can pull it off without too much trouble. He just doesn't want to say it out loud for fear of making me cocky."

"Why don't we have a housewarming, an open house?"

He straightened in his seat. "Are you really that far along with the place?"

"Not far enough along for a proper housewarming, but the work will be essentially finished by then. We can clean out the place and wait until afterwards to finish the floors. That way, everybody will get a good look at the house, and we won't have to worry about their tracking mud in. We can have the refreshments outside and let them wander around the house at will. If it rains, we can all go inside and stand around."

"Sounds good to me. Maybe we can get somebody to phone in the results from each district during the evening." He lay back again.

They were over the mountain now, and driving through town. Patricia saw a car, apparently in a hurry, run a stop sign ahead of her, crossing the street on which she was driving.

"That looked like Annie Parker," she said.

Billy lifted his head, but the car was gone.

"Just Annie," she said. "I didn't see Marshall."

Billy lay back again. "Yeah, well, she's probably picking him up somewhere." He looked at his watch. "The stores might still be open. I'll bet Mr. Fowler is."

Patricia laughed. "I'll bet he is, too."

They continued toward home.

Brooks Peters and his wife left the Rialto Theater after seeing a rerelease of *Guadalcanal Diary*. At the entrance they ran into Dr. Tom Mudter, who was alone. They walked together for a block, before separating to go to their respective homes.

"You were in the Pacific, weren't you, Tom?" Peters asked.

"Yeah. Hospital ships during the island invasions, then when we had essential control of an island, regimental field hospitals ashore."

"Was it bad?"

He nodded. "A lot worse than in that picture. I don't think

anybody can ever make a picture that'll show it as bad as it really was."

"You get shot at any?"

"We had kamikazes on the ships, and a strafing once in a while ashore, usually a single plane, but nothing like the guys on the beaches took. It amazes me to this day that troops could go up a beach like that. It was both inspiring and frightening. I still don't think that people at home have any idea of the resistance those boys met. The Japanese simply would not give up, wouldn't surrender. We'd invade an island with twenty or twenty-five thousand Jap troops on it and end up taking two or three hundred prisoners. It was unbelievable."

"I expect your experience out there has got something to do with your enthusiasm for veterans' rights."

"Sure has. I figure that after what those boys went through—and that's what they were, boys—they're entitled to the best their country can give them."

They said good night at a corner and parted.

Annie Parker drove slowly past the police station, then turned around and parked. The police car was there, so she knew, at least, they hadn't taken Marshall out in the woods someplace and shot him. She tried to think what to do. She had already called everybody she could think of except Marshall's father, Jim, and she didn't want to frighten him. What could he do, anyway, that she couldn't? She decided to go into the station.

There was no one in the station room, and she stood, uncertain what to do. She was afraid to go looking around a jailhouse. Then she saw a button and a sign asking visitors to ring. She pressed the button and heard the bell answer somewhere at the back of the station. There was silence for a minute or two, and as she was about to press the button again, she heard a door slam down a hallway and footsteps approaching.

Charley Ward rounded a corner and stopped as he saw her. He was sweating heavily, and his uniform was wet around the collar and under the arms. "What do you want, Annie?" He was nervous, she thought.

"I came to get Marshall," she said, her voice trembling.

Charley laughed. "Shoot, Annie, Marshall's already asleep. We got to talk to him some more in the morning. He ought to be home for Sunday dinner. You go on home, now. We'll bring him home in the morning."

"What you have to talk to him tonight for? Why's it have to be on Saturday night?" She was gaining courage now.

But Charley suddenly turned ugly. "Listen, I told you to get yourself home, didn't I? Now, unless you want to get locked up for obstructing an officer, you just get on home, right now."

She nearly took him up on it, insisted on being locked up with Marshall, but if they were both in jail, who would know where they were? Who would help them? She turned and went out of the station.

Back in the car she decided to go home and get on the telephone again. Those folks had to come home sometime. She'd call all night if she had to.

17 DR. TOM MUDTER felt the intense exhaustion that depression brings. The film had brought back too much of his war; he should never have gone to see it, but he had been lonely. He was a bachelor, there was a shortage of women his age in Delano, and there were times when he just could not spend the evning alone in his tiny garage apartment behind his father's house and clinic. He was about to begin building his own clinic, and he looked forward to the activity. His parents were old now, and his father was looking forward to retirement. Dr. Frank had only kept the practice going so that Tom could have it after the war.

Half asleep already, Tom got slowly into his pajamas. He switched off the bedside lamp and stretched out on the bed with a groan of relief. It was a warm night, but a breeze blew through the open windows. As he was about to lapse into unconsciousness, he heard a car door slam, then another, then voices from the street. He held himself back from the brink of sleep and hoped against hope that the voices would go to the house next door or the one across. He did not think he could face a Saturday night cutting or such, not the way he felt.

The loud buzzer brought him immediately upright. It always had that effect on him, even when he was expecting it. He had installed the buzzer in his apartment, led from a button at the clinic door, so that he could take night calls without disturbing his father. He pressed a button beside his bed which lit a small sign at the clinic door saying "doctor coming" and struggled into his clothes. Perhaps three minutes passed before he could dress, let himself in through the back door, walk through the darkened clinic, switch on the front-porch light, and open the door.

The three figures who stood at the door were blacklighted by the porch light, and for a moment he did not recognize any of them. The one in the middle was bent half over and was being supported by the other two. One of the others was dressed in a khaki uniform, without a hat, and for a moment he thought the man was a soldier, but then he recognized Charley Ward.

"Evening, Doc." The voice belonged to Sonny Butts, who was not in uniform. "We got a customer for you here."

The man in the middle gave a grunt and threw his head back, and the light fell on the nearly unrecognizable face of Marshall Parker. Both eyes were swollen nearly shut, and there were cuts on his forehead and cheeks. His nose was broken.

"Good God!" The doctor took an involuntary step backward, then recovered himself. "Bring him this way." He walked rapidly down the dark hallway and switched on the lights in the examination room, thinking ahead. If the man was that badly beaten he probably had internal injuries, as well.

Tom went immediately to the sink and started to scrub his hands. The two white men struggled into the room with their charge. "Put him on that table," the doctor called over his shoulder. "What happened?"

"We were questioning him, and he started fighting with us," Sonny said quickly. "Then he tried to grab a knife that we had taken off another prisoner, and Charlie had to shoot him."

Tom whirled around. "Shoot him?" He walked quickly to the table and ripped open Marshall's shirt. "Jesus Christ in heaven."

"Hell, Doc, I had to do it," Charley Ward whined. "He woulda killed Sonny."

"Yeah," said Sonny, "he was fighting like hell." He pulled up his shirt to reveal a large bruise over a kidney. "Look what he did to me. He kicked me in the nuts, too. You wanta see the damage?"

"I've got all the damage I can handle right here. Now both of you get the hell out of here." He turned back to his patient, who was unconscious, and felt for a pulse. Weak and thready. Profuse sweating. He cranked on the table to elevate the lower body. The man was clearly already in shock.

Sonny came and looked over his shoulder. "How bad is he hurt?"

Tom turned and shoved him backwards with his elbows, trying to keep his hands clean. "I told you to get out of here you stupid son of a bitch, now move it! Get all the way out of my clinic, goddam you, and shut the door behind you! This is out of your hands now." As he pushed them into the hallway and shut the door, he caught a strong whiff of alcohol.

He went back to the table and began checking for wounds. One small, neat entry wound, midline, upper abdomen. He got a grip on Marshall and turned him onto one side. Large exit wound, left flank, near the kidney. Not much blood from either wound. He rolled him onto his back again and felt the abdomen. Massive internal bleeding. The bullet, judging from the placement of the entry and exit wouds, had hit and probably nicked the aorta. Tom looked helplessly around the little room, wishing for a trained army surgical team. Even if he woke his father he would have too little help and too little time.

Marshall suddenly groaned loudly and sat up, clutching his middle. Tom turned and quickly drew morphine into a syringe, found a vein in the man's arm and injected it. Almost immediately Marshall began to relax and Tom was able to make him recline again. He bent low over Marshall and looked into his face.

"Open your eyes, Marshall, open your eyes and listen to me." Marshall slowly opened his eyes. Swollen as they were, Tom could hardly see them. "Don't fall asleep, Marshall, listen to me. Can you hear me? Can you talk?"

Marshall nodded and swallowed. "Yeah."

"Marshall, there's nothing I can do for you, except give you morphine, and I've already done that. You're going to die, Marshall, you've only got a few minutes. I wish I could help you, but I can't. Do you understand me?"

After a pause Marhall nodded again. "Yes."

"Listen, Marshall, I can't save you, but if you'll tell me what happened—tell me the *truth*—I promise you I'll see that the right thing is done. Tell me what happened, Marshall."

Marshall began to speak. His breathing was shallow, but his words were intelligible. Tom held his head and listened, trying to memorize every word. "Me and Annie was at Mr. Fowler's

. . . bought her a dress . . . Butts and Ward stopped **me on the**
street . . . want me to come to the station . . . **something about**
the moonshine . . . next thing, I'm in the jail, **handcuffs . . .**
Butts beat me . . . beat me bad . . . I said take off **the handcuffs**
. . . I'd fight him . . . Ward took them off, held a **gun on me . . .**
I knew they was going to kill me . . . I grabbed a **knife . . . not**
my knife . . . they shot me . . . Annie . . . **where's Annie at?"**

"She's not here yet, Marshall, she'll be here, **don't worry. Did**
you ever hit Butts or Ward?"

"No, sir . . . never once . . . my hands were **behind me."**

"Did you do anything that might make Butts **and Ward have**
to arrest you? Tell me the absolute truth, now, Marshall."

"No, sir . . . bought Annie a dress, that's all . . . ask Mr. Fowler. My hands was behind my back, and they beat me . . . . He's
crazy, Butts is crazy. Annie . . ." Marshall drifted off, and Tom
let him go. He sat by him for a few minutes more, monitoring
his pulse, until Marshall's breathing became irregular, then
stopped. No pulse. Tom pulled back a swollen eyelid. No pupil
contraction. He listened for a moment with his stethoscope. Marshall Parker was dead. He noted the time, then began looking for
pen and paper.

He found a pen, but no paper, and went to the reception area
to look for a pad in his secretary's desk. Sonny and Charley were
sitting in the waiting area. Sonny was idly flipping through a
magazine. "Hey, Doc, how's he doing?" he asked.

"I thought I told you to get out of here."

"Listen, now, I got a prisoner in there, you know."

"Yeah? What's the charge?"

"Resisting arrest," Sonny said easily.

"That's only a secondary charge. What was the charge you
arrested him on?"

Sonny froze for a moment. "Now, listen, Doc—"

"Come on, Butts, let's hear the charge. What was it?"

Sonny was clearly in a corner and thinking as fast as he could.
His face hardened. "I don't have to discuss official police business with you. It'll all be in my report."

"Yeah, I thought you'd say something like that. Now, go on,
get out of here."

"What about my prisoner?"

"You don't have a prisoner anymore. He died a couple of
minutes ago."

"Gee, that's too bad."

"You said he kicked you in the crotch. Show me." Tom switched on a desk lamp on his secretary's desk and swiveled it toward Sonny. "Come on, drop your pants."

Sonny unbuttoned his jeans, held his penis aside and stepped close to the light to display his bruised scrotum.

"Okay, let's see the kidney area again, in the light."

Sonny buttoned his jeans and pulled up his shirt.

"What time did this happen?"

Sonny looked at his watch. "Oh, not long before we brought him in here. Say, half an hour, forty-five minutes."

"You're lying, Butts. Those bruises are hours old. I don't know where you got them, but Marshall Parker didn't give them to you half an hour or forty-five minutes ago."

Charley Ward spoke. "Jesus, Sonny, what's going to—"

"Shut up, Charley," Sonny said. "You just keep your mouth shut. He don't know what he's talking about."

"We'll see about that," Tom said. "Now the two of you get out of here. I've got a postmortem to do, and you've got a story to make up. And it would be really stupid of you to try and leave town." He turned on his heel and left them standing in the waiting room. He had phone calls to make and work to do.

18 THE PHONE was ringing as Billy got out of the car, the loud, outdoor bell echoing over the farmland and the nearly finished house. He caught it, somewhat breathlessly, on the fifth ring.

"Hello."

"Colonel Lee, this is Annie Parker. They got Marshall down to the jail." The words rushed out.

"Annie? What was that again?"

"That policeman Butts and that other one got Marshall down at the jail, and I'm afraid what they might be doing to him. Can you go down there, Colonel? I sure would appreciate it."

"Of course, I'll go down there, Annie. Tell me what happened."

She told him as quickly as she could of Marshall's arrest and her visit to the police station.

"I'll go right now, Annie, and I'll call you as soon as I find out what's happened. Now, don't you worry, I'm sure Marshall's all right. He's probably asleep, just like Charley Ward said." He hung up and turned to Patricia. "I've got to go down to the police station. Sonny Butts has arrested Marshall Parker, and Annie's frantic. I'll be as quick as I can." The phone rang again.

"I'll get it," Patricia said. "You go ahead."

He was already in the car when she ran out.

"That was Tom Mudter. Don't go to the jail. Go to the clinic. Marshall's there. Sonny Butts and Charley Ward brought him there with a gunshot wound."

"Is he all right?"

"He died a few minutes ago."

Billy rested his forehead on the steering wheel. "Oh, my God in heaven, Trish. Marshall wanted me to meet with his veterans' group tonight, and I wouldn't. If I had been there this wouldn't have happened."

She opened the car door and took his head in her hands. "Now, you listen to me," she said. "This isn't your fault. You did what you could to protect Marshall, and this just isn't your fault. What you've got to do now is find out what happened and do something about it. You go on to the clinic, and I'll go to Annie. Go on, now."

He started the car. "You're right, I've got to do what I can now. Call Marshall's father, it's Jim Parker, should be in the phone book. Tell him as much as you know, and ask him to meet you at Annie's. Tell him I'll come out there and tell them everything as soon as I've seen Tom. Don't let them come to the clinic. Tell them to wait there for me." She nodded. He pulled away from the trailer and started for Delano, driving fast.

Billy sat with Brooks Peters and Tom Mudter in the waiting room of the clinic. Tom had told them everything, reading from the notes he had written. He had confirmed the severed aorta and the cause of death as massive loss of blood and shock.

"Have you told anybody else about this?" Billy asked.

"I reported it to Skeeter Willis."

"What did our good sheriff have to say?"

"Sonny had already called him about it. He said he'd look into it tomorrow, but it sounded pretty straightforward to him."

"Sounds like we're not going to be able to depend on Skeeter to do a serious investigation."

"Maybe we ought to go to the state police or the Georgia Bureau of Investigation," suggested Brooks.

Billy shook his head. "We can't expect any help from them until we can demonstrate that local and county authorities are mishandling the investigation. Even then, they're going to do their best to stay out of it, you can depend on that."

"One more thing," Tom said. "I've taken a sample of Marshall's blood. I'll send it to a lab in Atlanta in Monday morning's mail, and we'll know for sure if he had been drinking."

"Good idea," said Billy. "I have a feeling we're going to need all the evidence we can get if we're going to do anything about this."

Brooks Peters looked up, surprised. "I would have thought that the deathbed statement would be all we needed."

Billy shook his head. "In some circumstances it might be enough, but what we've got here is a Negro prisoner killed by a white policeman who claims he did it in the line of duty. Marshall's statement is a start, but we're going to have to back it up with everything we can find."

"Do you mean you think that Butts and Ward might get away with this?"

"That's exactly what could happen, Brooks. I think we can get an indictment easy enough, if the blood test and other evidence back up Marshall's story. I mean, the county prosecutor, Bert Hill, is a good enough fellow, and if there's evidence, he'll present it to a grand jury. There's one meeting now. But we're going to have a mighty hard time getting a conviction. It's hard to say whether Bert's heart is going to be in a trial like that, and a smart lawyer on Sonny's side will play hard to a white jury on the black-white thing. A trial is going to be touch and go."

"So what do we do?" asked Tom.

"I think we start by letting Skeeter Willis and the prosecutor know that we're not going to let this thing dry up and blow away, that we expect a thorough investigation and a strong presentation to a grand jury. The first step is an indictment."

"Well, I can give them medical evidence about the nature of his injuries, apart from the gunshot wound. He'd clearly been beaten badly, and he'd been handcuffed. And we'll have the lab test, assuming he was sober."

Billy nodded. "That's fine. In fact, why don't you put the whole thing in writing as soon as possible?"

Peters spoke up. "I'll call a meeting early tomorrow morning of the ministerial association. We've got nine ministers, and I might be able to get them stirred up."

"That's the sort of thing we need," said Billy. "I'll talk to Mr. Holmes, too, and see what he can do quietly behind the scenes. We should fill in Bob Blankenship tomorrow, so he can have as full a story as possible in Thursday's paper. That might help stir up public opinion. Anything else?"

Tom and Brooks shook their heads.

"Well, I guess we've done all we can here. All that's left is to break the news to Annie and Jim Parker. I'm not looking forward to that. Brooks, will you come with me?"

"Of course, but I think I ought to call Preacher Wright, too. They're going to want their own minister."

Brooks made the call, and they broke up, agreeing to meet the following afternoon to compare notes on their various efforts.

At the Parker home everyone knew the moment Billy and Brooks walked in that Marshall was dead. Billy told them, as gently as he could, what had happened and what he, Peters, and Mudter hoped to do about it.

"I can promise you," he said to Annie and Jim Parker, "that Butts and Ward are not going to just walk away from this." He meant what he said, but later, at home, he admitted his worst fears to Patricia.

"This is going to be hard, Trish, and I want you to know what's ahead, because you're going to hear about it from everybody, and what you'll hear may not bear much resemblance to what really happened."

"How do you think this is going to affect the election?" she asked.

"Mr. Holmes isn't going to like it much, but I'm not going to worry about that any more. This might have happened because I was too worried about getting elected, so except for the commitments I've already made and can't gracefully get out of, from this moment I'm through campaigning. I've said all I have to say, and I think folks know where I stand. They can take me or leave me, but I'm going to spend my time for the next few weeks doing everything I can to see that Sonny Butts and Charley Ward go to jail for as long as possible. I don't think I'd be able to live with myself if I didn't do that."

19 BILLY CALLED Hugh Holmes early on Sunday morning, and they met before Sunday School. Holmes listened without expression to Billy's account of the events of the night before. Billy kept looking for a reaction, but found none. Finally, when the lawyer had told him everything, including the steps he proposed to take, Holmes spoke.

"Billy, there's no advice I can give you that would do you any good. A bad thing has happened, and you feel morally bound to do something about it. I can't advise you not to do what you propose, even though it might cost you the election. I think you understand the political risk you're running, don't you?"

"Yes, sir, I do."

"Well, then, damn the torpedoes, and I'll do my best to minimize the damage."

"Thank you, sir, I appreciate that." Billy left Holmes's house relieved that he had the banker's support rather than his opposition.

Brooks Peters was on the phone at seven on Sunday morning, and at eight the Delano Ministerial Association met in his dining room. He told them what had happened, and they prayed together for a few minutes. When the meeting was over, he had their unanimous support for a resolution addressed to the city council in the form of an open letter.

He preached the sermon he had planned for that Sunday, and at the end he read the resolution, virtually at the same moment that it was being read in eight other churches, as agreed. The resolution read, "It has come to our attention that the death of a prominent member of our Negro community has occurred as a result of an incident at the Delano city jail. We call upon the city council to conduct a thorough investigation of this incident to determine whether the police officers involved were acting properly in the line of duty, and whether the death of this man was justified."

It wasn't a very tough resolution, Brooks thought, but under the circumstances it would serve the purpose. There would be talk of nothing else at Sunday dinners all over Delano.

Early Sunday afternoon Billy telephoned Bert Hill, the county prosecutor. Hill had already heard about the killing.

"Skeeter Willis called me half an hour ago. He's already been down there and taken a statement from Butts and Ward, and he says he'll have a report for me tomorrow."

"Bert, did he give you any idea of what the statement consisted of?"

"None at all. He didn't make an arrest, though. That ought to tell you something. Mind you, I'm not going to rely entirely on Skeeter's report in deciding whether to pursue an indictment. Billy, do you think you could do me a favor and take some statements from the other people involved? Annie Parker and the doctor and anybody else who has any information?"

"I'll be glad to, Bert. Tom Mudter is already writing up his report."

"That would really help me out a lot. This grand jury is probably going to be finished up this week, and I know you want a quick resolution to this situation."

"I sure do, Bert. We all do down here. I'll take statements tomorrow morning and have them typed and to you by evening. There'll be three witnesses: Annie Marshall, Tom Mudter, and H. W. Fowler. They'll appear on request; you won't have to subpoena them."

"Good. That'll save time. I'll tack this business on the end of their work load. They should get to it this week, but it's possible it could run over to next Monday or Tuesday."

"Thanks, Bert."

On Monday morning, Sonny Butts and Charley Ward met with the city council, a meeting called at the request of the police officers. As soon the meeting had been called to order, Sonny was given the floor. Dressed in a freshly pressed uniform, he stood erect before them, commanding their attention.

"Gentlemen, Officer Ward and I asked for this meeting because of rumors circulating in town about an incident that took place at the police station on Saturday night. This morning I want to read a statement to you which describes the events of Saturday night."

There was a general nod of agreement.

Sonny began. "Last Saturday night, at approximately ten o'clock, Officer Ward and I approached one Marshall Parker on Main Street. We wished to question him informally about events which occurred some weeks ago when a report of illegal whiskey at his place of business was telephoned to the sheriff's office.

"Parker became hostile and abusive, and it became necessary for us to subdue and handcuff him before removing him to the police station and booking him on a charge of assault. The station logbook will show such a booking.

"At the station his handcuffs were removed and questioning proceeded, but Parker remained hostile and became violent and wild. Officer Ward and I tried desperately for several minutes to subdue Parker, using reasonable force, but as we were about to handcuff him he produced a knife and came at me. Officer Ward then had no other alternative but to draw his service revolver and shoot the prisoner.

"Even after he had been shot once in the abdomen, Parker continued to fight, but we were able to subdue him. We then took him immediately to the office of Dr. Thomas Mudter for medical attention, where he died a short time later of his wound.

"We wish to stress that at no time did we use other than reasonable force in dealing with the prisoner, and that a firearm was used only when all other methods had failed.

"Immediately after the incident I informed Sheriff Willis of what had happened and requested an immediate investigation by his office. He has informed me that his investigation supports my actions and those of Officer Ward, and that his report has been forwarded to the county prosecutor.

"Since that report is still subject to grand-jury action, Officer Ward and I request that Officer Ward and I not be required to comment beyond this statement until the matter has been resolved by the grand jury. This will protect our legal rights in the meantime.

"We further request that the city council delay any further action in this matter until the grand jury has met on it."

Sonny knew before he finished that he had them. By taking action first, before they did, he had effectively stalled them. Within a matter of minutes the council had voted to suspend the officers only if indicted and fire them only if convicted.

Now he had to worry about the grand jury, and that worried him a lot.

Billy had finished taking statements from Annie Parker, Tom Mudter, and Mr. Fowler and was waiting for them to be typed, when he heard of the council's decision. He had thought the least that would happen was that Butts would be fired, but now it would take an indictment just to suspend him.

Billy had lost the first round without throwing a punch.

20 BOB BLANKENSHIP sat alone in the offices of the *Delano Messenger* and pounded out a final sentence to a blistering editorial on his Remington Noiseless. The editorial would cap the front-page story of Marshall Parker's arrest and death at the hands of the Delano police. It was the first time since he had bought the paper that he had run a front-page editorial, and he looked forward to the commotion it would cause.

He stacked the pages neatly in his out tray, from which they would be collected the following morning to be set in type, and switched off the desk lamp. The newspaper office was now lit only partly by the street lamp.

Blankenship stretched and took a deep breath. He loved the smell of ink that permeated his place of work. It smelled, well— *professional.* He rolled down his sleeves, retrieved his seersucker jacket from the hat rack in the corner, checked the lock on the front door, and walked out the rear entrance. As he turned to insert his key in the back-door lock, he heard the scrape of a shoe on the gravel of the alley behind him. As he turned to see who was there, something hard was rammed into the small of his back, shoving him against the door.

"Ain't no need to turn around," a voice said, low and menacing. "Just stand right there if you don't want to get blowed in half." A hand took him by the back of his shirt collar and moved him roughly away from the door, against the brick wall of the building. He heard the sound of other feet. "Go on in there and see what you can find," the voice said, apparently addressing someone else. Blankenship heard someone open the door and enter the building.

"Look, we've got maybe fifty dollars of classified-ad money in a tin box under the front counter. Just take it and go, okay?" He said it without moving. He was being pressed hard against the brick.

"You just shut up, Blankenship."

He was quiet. After a couple of minutes he heard the second man walking toward the door.

"Looka here," the second voice said. "A front-page editorial. How 'bout that." Blankenship heard the paper being ripped to shreds.

The gun was pressed even harder into his back. Oh, Jesus, he thought, they're going to shoot me right here. A weakness started to come over him, and his bowels felt loose. He sagged against the wall, but the hand at his neck held him straight.

"Now, you listen here," the voice said. "There ain't going to be no editorials, you got that? You take sides with the niggers and you won't write nothing no more, 'cause you'll be dead. There ain't going to be no editorials, and what you write better sound right to white folks, you hear me?" the gun jabbed him in the back harder.

Blankenship nodded weakly.

"What's that? Speak up."

"I hear you," Blankenship said.

"No editorials?"

"No editorials, no sides. Don't shoot me, please."

The hand yanked him away from the wall, shoved him through the back door into the building, slammed the door, and locked it behind him with his key. "We'll be looking for the paper on Thursday to see what you print, you hear? And if you don't want your brains blowed out, you don't say nothing to nobody about this." He stood still until he heard footsteps away from the door and, a moment later, a car door slamming further down the alley. An engine started, then faded away.

Blankenship sat down heavily at his desk and reached for the phone. He banged on the receiver to get the operator to answer faster, then he stopped and hung up the phone. Who was he calling? The police? The sheriff? The phone rang, and he picked it up.

"Mr. Blankenship, this is the operator. Did you want to make a call? I'm sorry, I was tied up on long distance."

"No," he said wearily. "I don't want to make a call. Never mind." He hung up. Who would he call? Brooks Peters? Could a Baptist preacher help him? Billy Lee? Who would Billy call? What could he prove? Nothing. He hadn't recognized either of the voices.

He was ashamed of the fear he felt. He had spent most of the war editing a camp newspaper for basic trainees at Fort Dix, New Jersey. Nobody had ever pointed a gun at him before. He rested his head on the desk in the crook of his arm, like a schoolchild taking a nap.

On Tuesday, Marshall Parker was buried at Galilee Baptist Church, the little frame building in the countryside bordering Braytown. Billy and Patricia, Eloise, Henry and Carrie Fowler, Brooks Peters, Tom Mudter, and Hugh Holmes were the only white faces in attendance, a pew having been reserved for them.

Annie Parker conducted herself with the same stoicism she had shown since the moment she had learned that Marshall was dead. Marshall's father, Jim Parker, wept quietly through the service.

Holmes, who had attended many black funerals in his time, was surprised at the restraint shown by the congregation, which overflowed into the outdoors. There was none of the wailing and open display of grief he had expected. A heavy sadness seemed to press upon the congregation.

Billy Lee could not have felt worse if he himself had been the murderer.

Late Thursday afternoon, Patricia Lee answered the phone at the new house. The extention had just been put in.

"Is that Miz Lee?" It was a woman's voice, white, country.

"Yes, this is Patricia Lee."

"They gon' come out there tonight."

"What? Who's coming out here?"

The woman's voice sounded very far away, and frightened. "I don't want you to get hurt. They gonna burn it; he said they gonna burn it."

"What? Burn what? Who is this?"

"It ain't nobody. I just wanted to tell you. I don't want nobody to get hurt." The woman hung up.

Patricia put the phone back on the cradle and looked at her watch. Nearly five-thirty. Billy had gone to Greenville to talk with Bert Hill; then he was speaking to the Rotary Club in Warm Springs on the way back, after that there was a meeting at somebody's house. These were meetings he had committed himself to long before. If she called him he would cancel and come home immediately. She didn't want that. He needed to be campaigning, if things were as close as Mr. Holmes thought they were. She left the house, got into her car, and drove to Delano.

She parked in the alley behind McKibbon's Hardware and went in. She walked to the sporting-goods department. McKibbon finished with a customer and followed her.

"Hey there, Patricia. How you doing? You looking for something in a fishing rod?"

"I'm fine, Mac. I'm looking for something in a shotgun."

He went to the glass gun case and slid it open. "Something for Billy? His birthday or something?"

"Something for me, thank you. Billy hates shotguns."

McKibbon peered at her over his glasses. "For *you*?"

She laughed. "Mac, I've shot more birds than you've had hot dinners. Let's have a look at the twelve-bore, there."

"The double-barrel?" He fished it from the rack and handed it to her, looking doubtful.

She broke the gun, peered down the barrels, hefted it, held it against her shoulder, and aimed.

"That's a Browning, prewar. Fellow sold it to me last month. It's in real nice shape, real light, too."

"Well, it's no Purdy, but it's all right, I suppose. How much?"

"Have to get a hundred and twenty-five for that one. You picked the best one in the store, right off."

"Throw in a couple of boxes of shells and done," she said.

"Fair enough, I reckon."

She began writing him a check. "Let me have a box of number-nine bird shot and one of double-aught buckshot."

He plunked the boxes down onto the counter. "Double-aught, huh? You must have some pretty big birds out there on your place."

"The biggest," she said, crooking the shotgun under her arm and scooping up the shells, "white-sheeted yellowbellies."

"Huh?"

She paused at the back door. "And Mac, if you tell Billy I bought this, I'll come back and use it on you."

He held up his hands in mock surrender. "Mum's the word, Patricia. Mum's the word."

It was just past eleven o'clock before she heard the cars. She hadn't really believed they would come, but she was glad they had. She was mad as hell.

She slipped out of and behind the darkened trailer, as the cars turned into the drive and stopped, dousing their lights. They didn't need the headlights, because she had turned on every light in the new house, including the outdoor flood lamps that illuminated the drive.

She knelt behind the trailer and set both boxes of shells on an upturned cement block. She loaded with the number-nine bird shot and snapped the gun shut, slipping off the safety. She stretched out prone. The double-aught buckshot stood open and ready, just in case they came at her.

She could see the men now, lighting torches. My God, they were really wearing bed sheets, she thought. How absurd. The men, eight of them, spread out and walked abreast up the newly planted lawn. They stopped short of the driveway, and one of them stepped forward of the others. "Billy Lee," he shouted, "come out and answer the justice of the Klan."

Patricial judged that about sixty yards separated them from her. She cradled the shotgun in her left hand, her forearm vertical, her elbow well planted. She aimed low at the speaker and squeezed off a round. The shot scattered, as she had thought it would, and the leader and one other man caught some pellets. There was a roar of cursing and yelling. She shifted her aim to the right a bit and fired again, peppering another man. They were running now, one of them clutching at his backside. She stood up and quickly reloaded.

She stood at the corner of the trailer and fired both barrels into the air. The noise was tremendous. She managed to reload and fire two more rounds before they were able to reach the cars and tear out of the drive.

She sat down on the steps of the trailer. She was trembling, she noticed, but she had never in her life felt more jubilant. She did not notice another car drive past, driven by Ralph McKibbon of McKibbon's Hardware, who was laughing so hard he was crying. On the front seat beside him was an unplugged pump shotgun, loaded with buckshot, which he was glad not to have had to use. He could not wait to tell his wife about this.

After a few minutes Patricia went into the trailer, cleaned the shotgun, and hid it and the shells. When Billy came home she was in bed reading.

"Hello, how did it go?"

He leaned over and kissed her. "Pretty good, I guess. Sorry to be so late. The meeting after the dinner dragged on a little."

"Did you get any questions about the police thing?"

"One. All I could say was that it would go to the grand jury, and we'd see what happened there. As a lawyer, I can hardly let myself get in a position where I'm seeming to go outside the legal process."

"I suppose not."

"Did the *Messenger* come? I want to see Bob Blankenship's editorial."

"It's on the kitchen table. I haven't had a chance to look at it myself."

Billy retrieved the newspaper and searched the front page. There was a short article in the bottom right-hand corner laying out the bare facts of the case. There was no mention of Marshall's statement to Tom Mudter. Confused, Billy looked for an editorial inside, but found nothing. "I don't understand this," he said. "Bob took all these notes and promised to run a big editorial. He was mad as hell when the council didn't suspend Butts and Ward. I'm going to call him."

"It's a little late, isn't it? Why don't you talk to him in the morning?"

"Dammit," he said, "I was counting on Blankenship to help get opinion stirred up. There's no chance of that now. Bert Hill says the way his calendar is moving, it's going to be Tuesday before this reaches the grand jury, and the paper doesn't come out again until next Thursday."

"And Tuesday is election day."

"Yeah."

21 FOXY FUNDERBURKE hated to go to town on Saturdays. The streets were crowded, it was difficult to find a parking place, and it was hard to get waited on in the stores. But this Saturday he had a broken toilet, and he had to have a part from town. After circling the block twice, he found a parking spot in front of McKibbon's Hardware.

He was right, the store was crowded. Rather than wait for help, he began rummaging about, looking for the plumbing he needed.

"Lord, Harry, you should have seen it." It was Ralph McKibbon's voice, coming from behind a row of shelves. "Earl Timmons's sister-in-law is a nurse over at LaGrange hospital, and she said four fellows showed up there at one o'clock Friday morning, said they'd been in somebody's watermelon patch, all of 'em had a butt full of bird shot, more or less. They didn't give their right names, but she recognized one of 'em—it was Emmett Spence!" He dissolved into laughter, then recovered himself. "Lord, if Hoss ever hears about it, he'll kill that boy!" He was overcome again. Foxy moved on down the shelves until he found what he wanted.

Another ten minutes passed before he could get somebody to charge his purchase, and Foxy was getting more fidgety by the minute. He had been hunting for some weeks now, without success. Every time he spotted a likely quarry there was something wrong—somebody nearby or something. He had actually picked up two boys, but they had revealed in their conversation that they were expected shortly somewhere, and he had reluctantly let them out of his truck. The pressure was building unbearably now, and he was afraid he'd rush into something and make a mistake. He couldn't let that happen.

He was out of town and over the mountain before he saw the boy. Foxy's heart leapt. He slowed down and coasted, taking a long look at him before stopping.

"Hey, there, son. Where you headed."

"Florida, sir," the boy answered, smiling. "You going that way?"

"Well, that depends on how much of a hurry you're in."

"Oh, I'm not in that much of a hurry. I'm kind of enjoying the trip."

"Nobody's looking for you to be down in Florida, then?"

"No, sir, I reckon they're not."

Foxy smiled. "Well, if you don't mind waiting just a little bit while I run by the house, I might give you a ride all the way to Daytona Beach. That do you?"

"Yes, sir! That sure would!"

"Get in, then."

The boy got in, and Foxy drove away. He had not seen Sonny Butts coming up the mountain, driving toward Delano in his own car.

Sonny's mind was on his own problems, and he paid little heed to Foxy. It would be some time before he remembered.

At church on Sunday morning Brooks Peters preached on the subject of justice, and no one in attendance could have doubted his purpose.

Brooks stood at the Church door and shook hands with the members of his congregation as they left. Some, Billy noticed, had words of encouragement for the preacher, others muttered a brief greeting and hurried out. Billy noticed that Patricia seemed to be drawing a lot of attention, too, and not a few broad winks. "What's all that about?" he asked her.

She seemed momentarily flustered, then said, "Oh, word's getting around that I'm pregnant."

"I thought the whole world already knew about that. Lord

knows, I've been telling everybody."

They had Sunday dinner with the Fowlers; then Billy joined Brooks Peters and the other veterans at Tom Mudter's. Billy opened the discussion.

"I've talked at length with Bert Hill about the grand jury. He says he thinks there's a good chance for an indictment. There certainly wouldn't be any question about it if Marshall Parker had been white, but there are some crusty old rednecks on the grand jury, and Bert won't make any firm predictions."

He paused and looked around the room. "I don't see Bob Blankenship here. Anybody know what's happened to him?"

Brooks Peters spoke up. "Something funny going on there. First, Bob backs out on running an editorial about Marshall in Thursday's paper, then he goes to his in-laws' in Brunswick today. Looks like he's not with us any more."

"I can't believe he'd change sides," said Billy, shaking his head. "I think somebody's been bringing pressure to bear on Bob. I couldn't get him on the phone all day Friday, and when I went by the newspaper office, he had already left for Brunswick. Strange. Anybody else having problems?"

There was a general negative muttering. "I'm surprised that nobody has said anything to me," said Brooks Peters. "I guess having the ministerial association behind me has helped, but folks have long memories. Those who are against what I've been saying from the pulpit will get around to letting me know about it sooner or later."

Billy leafed through some notes. "Okay, status on the races. From what I can gather we're in pretty good shape for the city council. James Montgomery in Greenville is neck and neck with Skeeter Willis for sheriff."

Tom Mudter spoke up. "Skeeter has been mending fences and keeping his head down. He went to a lot of trouble to seem to be doing the right thing in the Parker incident, but he's backing Sonny all the way."

"Right," said Billy. "About what we would have expected. Skeeter's no fool. Well, in my race, Mr. Holmes thinks we're down a little. We'll be lucky to pull it off."

"Oh, I don't know, Billy," said Brooks Peters. "From what I hear, things are looking up for you." He was smiling slightly, and so were some of the others.

Billy was puzzled. "You know something I don't?"

Brooks sat back, looking smug. "Oh, it's just what I hear. You're going to the fair tomorrow night, aren't you?"

The Tri-County Fair opened its week's run the following day. "Sure, we'll be there. I guess every other candidate in the area will be, too. Can't pass up an opportunity to shake that many hands."

"How did your meeting go?" Patricia asked. They were driving home late Sunday afternoon.

"Well enough, I guess. Brooks and some of the others seem more optimistic. Seems he's been hearing something, but he wouldn't say what."

Patricia blushed. "Ah, Billy—"

He turned and looked at her. "Yep?"

"There's something . . . oh, damnit, I'd better tell you about it before you hear it from somebody else!"

"Tell me about what?" He felt vaguely alarmed.

"Well, Thursday night, while you were in Warm Springs, we had some visitors at the house."

"Visitors?"

"The kind in bed sheets."

"Are you talking about Klan, Patricia? Are you kidding me?"

"No, they dropped by, all right."

"Well, what happened? What did they do?"

"They . . . ran, mostly."

He stared at her for so long he nearly ran off the road. "Trish, come on, tell me what the hell happened."

"Well, I had this telephone call—anonymous—Thursday afternoon. A woman, somebody's wife, I think. She said somebody was planning to burn the place."

Billy whipped the car to the side of the road and stopped in a spray of gravel and dust. "Why didn't you call me?"

"You had your speech, and I thought you needed to go."

"All right, all right, so what happened?"

"Well, they arrived, all right, all in their ridiculous bed sheets, with torches, and marched up to the house. I waited behind the trailer."

"You waited behind the trailer," he repeated tonelessly. "Then what happened?"

"I, ah, dispersed them."

"Yeah? How did you do that?"

"With a shotgun."

"*What?*"

"Well, it was only bird shot," she said defensively. "I didn't fire any buckshot. I was saving that for if they came at me. They never did. They ran."

"Where did you get a shotgun?"

"I bought it. At McKibbon's."

"Ralph McKibbon sold you a shotgun?"

She whirled to face him. "And why the bloody hell not? I'm damned good with a shotgun; I grew up shooting on my father's land."

"But Trish, you can't go shooting shotguns at people. Was anybody hurt?"

"Of course, they were hurt! You think I'd miss with a shotgun at that distance?"

"Jesus Christ, did you kill anybody?"

"No, just wounded some pride, I think. I heard this morning that somebody answering the description of Emmett Spence turned up at La Grange Hospital with three other men and some story about stealing watermelons. They had an amount of birdshot tweezed out of their arses, I believe."

"Jesus Christ. I don't believe it." He shook his head. "My wife taking a shotgun to the Klan."

"Well, it needed doing. You'd have just tried to reason with them."

He began to laugh, and she joined in. They became hysterical, rolling about the front seat of the car, tears running down their faces. It was some minutes before Billy could speak again.

"So that's what all the winks and nudges were about at church this morning. That's what Brooks was so amused about, too, I guess. God, I wish I'd seen it happen. Emmett Spence, for God's sake." They both began to laugh again.

22 THE DOG woke Foxy, nuzzling him behind the ear. He jerked upright for a moment, looking sharply about him, then relaxed and lay back on the grass again. A light breeze wafted over the back yard, stirring the pines over Foxy's head. He stretched luxuriously, feeling pleasant and secure. It was Monday afternoon, and the boy was holding up very well, even seeming to like it once and a while, Foxy thought. It had been quite a weekend, and the boy was good for another day, at least.

Foxy got up, put on his uniform cap, and went back into the house through the kitchen door, whistling a little tune.

Sonny was up, bouncing on his toes, in high spirits. He had already had a couple of snorts; he had never felt so good. He stopped by the station house to make sure Charley Ward was awake and on duty. Charley was on nights for the week.

"Hey, Sonny."

"How you doin', sport?"

"You're looking real sharp tonight. Gonna take in the fair?"

"You better believe it, buddy. You stay on your toes tonight, hear? Don't go screwing up right now."

"Listen, Sonny, about tomorrow—you think we're gonna come out of that grand jury thing okay?"

"Charley, I told you a hundred times, there ain't a thing to worry about. Emmett Spence's daddy is on that grand jury, and a couple of his friends. They ain't never going to do a thing to a white cop for killing a nigger. So you just suck up your guts and hold still for another twenty-four hours, and we'll be in the clear. It'll be nothing but smooth sailing."

"Gee, I sure hope so, Sonny, this whole thing worries me sick."

Sonny spun around. "*Shut up, godammit!* I'm sick and fucking tired of your whining!" Sonny caught himself and settled down. He'd have to watch his temper. He was as nervous as Charley, but he wasn't about to show it. He'd blow off a little steam at the fair, and tomorrow he'd be terrific.

On the way he stopped by the hotel and paid the porter ten dollars for another pint of Early Times. Fucking nigger, charging him that price. He'd have to do something about him and his little bootlegging business later on, when things had quieted down a bit.

"Jesus, Mary, and Joseph, where did all *that* come from?" Patricia asked, pointing through the windshield at the bright lights and rides as they approached the fairgrounds in the September dusk. "Did the Kiwanis Club buy all that?"

Billy laughed. "No, no, that's a traveling carnival. The Kiwanis Club sponsors the fair, and they arrange all the exhibits and award prizes, but they hire a traveling carnival to provide the rides and games. They get a cut of the proceeds, I guess."

"I was expecting something like an English village fete, I suppose. Just a lot of mince pies and pin the tail on the donkey."

"Don't worry, there won't be any shortage of pies. I'm judging a contest, remember? And, by the way, don't forget to ask for the recipe."

"You said you'd never eat my cooking again as long as you live."

"And I won't, not as long as we can afford a cook. But the ladies don't know that, and they'll be flattered if you ask how they do it."

"Will there be any livestock?"

"Sure there will, a whole building full. Dammit, why didn't I think to get you a job judging cattle. You know as much about it as anybody here, and the farmers would have loved it."

"Maybe I can buy a few head for the farm. We're going to need a bull."

They bought tickets at the gate and entered the first of the exhibit buildings, wandering up and down the rows of displays, the pickles and pies, the science exhibits from the school. They shook hands and flattered exhibitors and accepted congratulations on their coming parenthood.

They ran into Hugh Holmes and Dr. Frank Mudter. Dr. Frank wasn't holding up as well as Mr. Holmes, Billy thought. He looked quite frail. Holmes called Billy aside.

"What do you think about the grand jury tomorrow?"

"Touch and go, I think. If we'd had some kind of a break, some witness besides Marshall's statement, something else on Butts and Ward, maybe, we'd be in a better position. What do you hear on the election?"

Holmes smiled. "Your wife's marksmanship is the best thing that's happened yet, you know. That's the stuff legends are made of. That story will stand you in good stead for more than just this election. Makes me wish I'd bought Ginny a shotgun forty years ago."

"I didn't buy her that shotgun. She bought it herself. She never even told me about it 'til it was all over."

"Just as well. You'd only have stopped her."

"That's what she said."

"You know Hoss Spence isn't exhibiting any livestock this year? First time since we started the fair. He's really humiliated over this thing and mad as hell at Emmett."

"Couldn't happen to a nicer fellow. I hope Emmett can't sit down for a month. I wish Hoss wasn't on the grand jury, though. He won't do us any good."

A little girl came and tugged at Billy's sleeve. " 'Scuse me, Colonel Lee," she said. "My mama says it's time for you to judge the pies."

"Careful," grinned Holmes. "A wrong step there could cost you the election."

Billy gathered up Patricia and followed the child to the exhibit of pies. For twenty minutes he wandered among them with a fork, testing, judging, licking his lips, and rolling his eyes. Patricia, at the edge of the crowd that had gathered to watch, could hardly keep from laughing aloud.

Finally, he stood before the crowd with a pie in each hand

and addressed them. "Only my political enemies could have put me in this position the night before an election," he said, and the crowd laughed with him. "I believe Abraham Lincoln once found himself in this situation when he was running for Congress in Illinois, and I surely do wish I could remember what it was he did about it." The crowd laughed again. "I'm faced here with the best peach pie I ever tasted and the best sweet-potato pie I ever tasted, and I'm supposed to choose between them. It just isn't fair."

Billy looked up and saw Sonny Butts, in civilian clothes, walking through the building toward the midway. He brought his mind back to his task.

"The peach is such a beautiful fruit, and, of course, it's the symbol of our state, and Meriwether County produces more peaches than any county in America, so I guess a case could be made that a decision against the peach would be downright unpatriotic. That being the case, I hope you can all appreciate what an act of political courage I'm committing when I say I just have to give it to the sweet potato, because any cook who starts out with a sweet potato starts out at a terrible disadvantage. Anybody who can make something as ugly as a sweet potato taste as good as this pie just has to get the blue ribbon." He kissed the flushed winner on the cheek, presented the ribbons, and fled.

"That was very slick," Patricia said, when she caught up with him outside the building.

"Never mind that. Did you get the recipe?"

"Both of them," she laughed, triumphantly holding up two scraps of paper.

"Let's go look for a bull for you, before the lady who baked the peach pie catches up with me."

Sonny floated down the midway in a haze of bourbon. He winked at the girls, joked with their boyfriends, rode the rides, and rang the bell with the mallet. He had never felt like this, never, he thought, and he had never felt so horny, either. He had been out of action for more than a week, while his bruises from the encounter with the two girls at the pool were healing, but he was fine now. More than fine.

When he saw the girl he had an instant erection. She stood on a midway stage with two other girls, doing some mild dancing to a record that blared over loudspeakers. The girl was young, clearly not more than eighteen or nineteen, but tall and big breasted, just Sonny's type. A hawker droned on about the show inside, and male customers started to file into the tent behind the stage, leaving half-dollars with the hawker. A couple of beardless youths were cheerfully turned away. Sonny flashed his badge at the hawker and strolled into the tent.

Almost immediately, a man appeared at his elbow. "Could I have a word with you, Chief?" He nodded toward a flap at the other side of the tent.

Sonny went with the man.

"Listen, Chief, this is our first night, and we want to give the boys a good show, you know? But we don't want any problems."

"Sure, sport, I get you. I'm here for the show, myself."

"Ah, that's just fine," the man said, and Sonny suddenly found a wad of folded bills in his hand. "I hope you'll pass that on to your favorite local charity. I'm sure you have some fine youth organization that could use the help." He winked slyly at Sonny and left the tent.

Sonny rejoined the crowd. The show began, to the hoots and hollers of the audience. The three girls worked methodically through their dances, teasing, stripping, but not all the way. Each ducked into the wings at the climactic moment, leaving the crowd begging for more. Then the hawker appeared and started a pitch for the "insider's show," and most of the men paid another fifty cents to stay.

There was no stage, simply a two-by-four separating men from girls. Now the girls came back and bumped their way close along the fence, just out of reach, naked except for G-strings and pasties. Then they worked in even closer, allowing a feel here and there.

The young girl stopped before Sonny, dancing just for him. She came close and allowed him to get an arm around her waist and his hand under the G-string for a moment before slipping away, grabbing briefly at his crotch. Then the show was over, and after a lot of fruitless calls for an encore the men slowly filed out of the tent. Sonny stayed, unsatisfied, throbbing all over.

He ducked under the two-by-four and walked quickly to the flap where the girls had disappeared. He found himself outside, behind the tent, facing a small trailer. The manager, the man who had given him the money, was quickly beside him.

"Can I help you, Chief?"

"Where's the girl?" Sonny demanded.

"Well, she's resting 'til the next show. Come back for that one. Glad to have you."

"I think I'd like a little private show, is what I'd like. Where is she?"

"Now look, Chief, the girl's awful new at this, and besides, she's married, just been married a couple of months, you know?" He slipped his arm through Sonny's and began steering him back into the tent. "Listen, I tell you what, come on back around here when we close down for the night, 'bout twelve, and I'll introduce you to the little brunette, remember her? You'll have a real good time, believe me."

Sonny jerked his arm free and headed for the trailer. "Not later, and not the brunette," he said. "The tall one, and now." He opened the trailer door and stepped in. The girl was sitting at a tiny dressing table in a dirty terrycloth bathrobe, eating chocolates from a box.

"Hey, there, sweetheart," Sonny purred, walking toward her. "You don't want to go ruining your figure with all that candy."

The girl stood up and backed away from him. The robe fell open to reveal a large, beautifully formed breast. She quickly snatched it shut and tied it. The manager was quick into the trailer behind Sonny. "Cherry, this here's the Delano chief of police, uh, he admired your performance, and—"

"Get him out of here, Jimmy," the girl said quickly.

"Now, Cherry, you want to be nice to the chief, this being our first night and all."

"Yeah," said Sonny, unbuttoning his pants, "be nice to me, Cherry."

The girl turned and pushed open a window behind her. "Danny!" she yelled at the top of her lungs. "Danneeee!"

The manager was trying to quiet her and get Sonny out of the trailer when the door was yanked open and a short, heavily muscled young man barged in. He looked at Sonny. "Okay, Hiram, the show's over, now get your ass out of here." He grabbed Sonny's arm and started dragging him toward the door. Sonny whipped out a blackjack and swung wildly at the young man, grazing the bridge of his nose. He tripped and fell down the trailer's short steps into the sawdust, and Sonny was all over him.

"Hey, Rube!" the man screamed, shielding himself from the

blackjack with his arms as best he could.

"Shut up, Danny," the manager whispered loudly. "The guy's a cop! He's the fucking chief of police, for crissakes!"

Billy and Patricia were walking down the midway with Tom Mudter when they saw people running toward the lower end of the fairgrounds. They followed quickly and came to the edge of a crowd of at least fifty people. There was something going on, but they couldn't see well.

They burst onto the midway, swinging wildly, Sonny using the blackjack, the manager holding back a group of carnival workers who had responded to Danny's call for help, saying, "Stay out of it, the guy's a cop, and Danny's on his own."

Sonny was in a kind of frenzy. He was taking some punches, but the blackjack hurt where it hit. His opponent was bleeding heavily from the nose. Sonny stayed back, jabbing with his left hand, keeping the man away from him, using the blackjack with his right. He loved the feel of it when the leather billy struck home. He used it on the man's upper arms and on his ribs, he didn't want him going out too soon; this was too good. Danny fell to one knee, and Sonny lashed out with his foot, catching him under the chin, unaware of the crowd quickly forming around him.

Danny sprawled backwards, and Sonny followed, kicking the semiconscious man wherever he could, in the ribs, in the face. Something wonderful was welling up inside Sonny, something more powerful than anything he had felt since the war. He was on the verge of release, when suddenly he was yanked backward by the collar and sprawled, full-length, in the sawdust. He was back on his feet instantly, the excitement pouring from him; then he stopped. Colonel Billy Lee was standing between him and his victim.

"That's enough, Sonny," the colonel was saying quietly, but urgently. "Give me the blackjack."

Sonny looked around him and saw the crowd for the first time, looking at him in horror. He tried to speak, but failed. Finally he was able to say, "Resisting arrest."

The colonel took the blackjack from him and flung it away. "Butts!" Another voice from behind him. He turned and faced Hugh Holmes. "Now, listen to me. I want you to go home right now." Sonny started to speak again, but Holmes waved him quiet. "No, I don't want to hear it. You just go home and stay there. I'll talk with you tomorrow."

Sonny looked around at the crowd again. Women were hustling their children away from the scene. No one was saying a word. They were just staring at him. He realized that his fly was open, and he quickly buttoned it. He flushed. The front of his trousers was soaking wet. He turned and started up the midway, and the crowd gave way before him. He was confused. It must be the booze. He had to go home and think.

While Tom Mudter bent over Sonny's bloody victim, Billy watched the policeman half walk, half run, up the midway, but his mind was not at the fair. He was in a London pub on V-E Day, listening to a young infantry captain tell him a war story, the worst war story he had ever heard.

23

HOLMES put down the phone. Billy realized that it was the first time he had ever seen the banker truly angry.

"That's the last one," Holmes said. "The full city council will meet at noon tomorrow."

"Do you think there's any chance at all they'll back him?" Billy asked.

"They'll back him over my dead body," said Holmes, and Billy felt that they might finally be about to see the last of Sonny Butts. Holmes got up and poured Billy and Patricia a drink. They had arrived at his house only as he was finishing with his calls.

Holmes sat down again. "I've got the carnival manager to agree to press charges for assault and battery, if necessary, though he was afraid to do it at first, and he told me Sonny extorted some money out of him to let him keep the hootchy-kootchy show open, too. If the council shows any resistance at all to getting rid of Sonny I'll plunk down that complaint on the table, and we'll see what happens then. In anticipation of Butts's going I've already asked the governor for some state-patrol help while we look for a replacement."

Patricia spoke up. "I suppose it doesn't matter, now, what the grand jury does."

"Oh, yes, it does matter," said Billy. "Butts has to go to jail, or maybe to a mental hospital."

Holmes looked surprised. "You think he's crazy?"

"Didn't he look crazy to you tonight? The man's a menace to civilized society. He's got to be put away."

Holmes took an unusually large pull at his bourbon. "Billy, I owe you an apology."

"How do you mean?"

"It's my fault that this thing has gone so far. I had a lot of reservations about Butts from the beginning, and I should have spoken up."

"You had no way of knowing what would happen."

"No, but when the rumors about the beatings down at the jail started, I should have known they were true, I should have stepped in. Marshall Parker would still be alive today if I had done something about that early on."

Billy shook his head. "No, sir, you can't blame yourself." Billy could not absolve himself, though. If he had been quicker to understand, if he had taken responsibility sooner. . . . Well, he would have to live with that; he would have to find a way to make up for it.

Sonny was late getting to the station. He was hung over as hell, and Charley would just have to work a couple of extra hours. He wondered why Charley hadn't been on the phone, complaining.

But Charley wasn't at the station. When Sonny walked in he found a uniformed state-patrol sergeant sitting at Charley's desk.

"Chief Butts?" The patrolman stuck out his hand. "Morning, I'm Dave Barker, from the La Grange post. My commander sent me down here to give you a hand, seeing as how you're short an officer. I relieved your other man, Ward. Hope that was okay."

"Yeah, sure, uh, Dave." He motioned toward his office. "I'll be in here if anybody needs me." He started toward the door.

"Oh, Chief."

"Yeah?"

"There was a message from a Mr. Holmes about half an hour ago. He says you're to be at City Hall at twelve-thirty today for a city council meeting, without fail. He says just to wait in the city manager's office until they're ready for you." The patrolman seemed to avoid his eyes and turned quickly back to his newspaper.

Sonny stood frozen in the doorway. "Yeah, okay," he was finally able to say. He went into his office and closed the door.

In Greenville, Bert Hill called the case against Sonny Butts and Charley Ward before the grand jury. His first witness was Annie Parker.

"Annie Parker, you are the widow of Marshall Parker?"

"Yessir."

"What did your husband do for a living?"

"He had a garage. He was an automobile mechanic."

"His own business, was it?"

"Yessir."

"Where did he get the money to start this business?"

"He saved most of it up in the army, and he borrowed some of it from Mr. Holmes at the bank."

"Marshall served in the army, did he?"

"Yessir. He got some medals, too. The biggest one was a Silver Star, in Italy."

Hill let that sink in with the grand jury for a moment, before continuing his questioning.

Sonny sat at his desk for nearly an hour, staring straight ahead of him. He had to think of something, had to think of a way out of this, but his mind wouldn't work. He dug a bottle out of a desk drawer and took a long pull. After a moment, he took another one.

"Mr. Fowler, what is your business?"

"I have a dry-goods store in Delano, on Main Street."

"Were you acquainted with Marshall Parker?"

"Yessir, he was a customer at my store, a good customer, paid his bill on time every month. Better than a lot of white people."

There was a small stir among the grand jurors. Bert Hill was sorry Fowler had said that. He hurried on to his next question. "Did Marshall Parker come into your store on Saturday night a week ago?"

"Yessir, he did. He and his wife, there."

"Did you smell any liquor on Marshall Parker?"

"No, sir, I did not. He was as sober as I was."

"How would you describe his frame of mind."

"He was in a real good mood. He said he'd had his best week since he opened his business, and he wanted to buy his wife a new dress."

In the back of the room Annie Parker began to cry. It was the first time she had let anyone see her cry since Marshall's death.

Sonny paced the office like a caged animal, thinking, thinking. He needed a good arrest, something to make him look good to the city council, but what? Traffic tickets wouldn't do it this time. He thought about the porter at the hotel, the bootlegging business. Not good enough. Besides, half the council probably bought liquor from him. Sonny needed something bigger, more important. The phone rang in the station room. The patrolman stuck his head in the door.

"Phone for you, Chief."

Sonny snatched up the instrument. "Chief Butts."

"Hey, Sonny, it's Tank Talbot, up in Atlanta."

It took Sonny a moment to concentrate. Oh, yeah, Tank was in state-police headquarters.

"Yeah, Tank, how you doing?"

"Not bad. Listen, you know those missing persons cases you called me about a little while back?"

Sonny sat up straight. "Yeah, sure, what about them? You got something new on 'em?"

"Naw, not on them ones, but I got a fresh one for you, might be down your way."

"Yeah?"

"There'll probably be a bulletin in your morning mail, but I thought you might miss it."

"Yeah, Tank, thanks a lot." Sonny quickly found the bulletin in the mail on his desk. Tank read aloud from it.

"Name, Harvey Charles Mix; age, seventeen; five eight; hundred and thirty-five; blonde hair; green eyes; no scars or markings. Sounds like them others, don't it?"

"Sure does, Tank. Got anything else?"

"He's from Chattanooga; his folks think he might be headed for Florida."

"That might bring him through here, all right."

"Damn right, listen to this. This is new. He called home Friday night, and his daddy got the operator to check on it. He called from Newnan."

"That's forty miles north of here."

"Right, and if he was hitchhiking to Florida he'd have to take Highway 41 south, there's no other road, and that brings him right to you."

"That sounds good, Tank. Anything else"

"That's it."

"Okay, I'll check it out and let you know if I find out anything." Sonny hung up. His hands were trembling. His mind flashed through the file in his bottom drawer, the missing boys, the circle of marks around Delano, Foxy's nervousness when he visited unannounced. Then Saturday morning came back to him. Somebody getting into Foxy's truck over the mountain. He tried to remember. Did he see a blond head? Yes. Yes!

He quickly slipped the bulletin into the file and started for the door. Optimism flooded through him now. This was all he needed. Before the day was finished, he'd be a hero again. They wouldn't be able to lay a finger on him. He charged through the station room, startling Sergeant Barker.

"Be back in a while, Sarge," he shouted over his shoulder. In the parking lot he paused at his car and turned instead to the motorcycle. It started on the first kick, and he roared up the hill toward Broad Street, revving flat out through the gears.

Barker got to the front door in time to see him take the corner at Broad Street and turn up the mountain.

"Dr. Mudter, have you attended dying men before?"

"I was a medical officer in the army, in the Pacific, the island invasions. I saw them by the hundreds."

"Those that were able to speak before they died. What did they have to say."

"They had messages for loved ones. If they felt guilty about something they wanted to confess."

"Has it been your experience that men in those circumstances tell the truth?"

"Yes, it has. Why would a dying man lie?"

"Did you feel that Marshall Parker told you the truth?"

"I very definitely did. I told him how important it was for him to tell me the truth. He knew he was dying."

Sonny flew up the mountainside, over the crest, and down the hill to the turnoff to Foxy's house. He shifted down and drove more slowly. The motorcycle could be very quiet at low speeds.

Further up the dirt road, at the top of the hill, he cut the engine and coasted silently down toward Foxy's house. It appeared around a bend, seeming quite normal, its flower beds and trees laid out in perfect symmetry. He bore down around the house, heading for the rear. Beyond the detached garage he could see something, someone.

As Dr. Tom Mudter finished his testimony, Skeeter Willis entered the grand-jury room and whispered something to the prosecutor. There was a brief exchange between them, and Bert Hill nodded. Skeeter went to the door and beckoned to someone. A tall, thin black man entered, and Skeeter pointed him toward the witness chair. He was sworn in, and Bert Hill addressed him.

"Walter Johnson, is that your name?"

"Yassuh. They calls me Pieback, though." The man was sweating and trembling slightly.

"What is your occupation?"

"Well, I cuts some grass and does some odd jobs."

"Where were you on Saturday night, a week ago?"

"I was in jail, suh."

"In the Delano jail?"

"Yassuh."

Sonny got off the motorcycle, walked as quietly as he could to the corner of the garage, and looked around. Foxy was standing with his back turned, some ten yards up the hillside, stripped to the waist, leaning against a shovel. There was a mound of fresh red Georgia earth beside him. He was sweating profusely.

Sonny felt like a balloon that had been filled with an intoxicating gas. He stepped out from behind the garage. "Hey, there, Foxy baby!"

Foxy whirled, astonished, his eyes bulging.

Sonny threw back his head and laughed loudly. "Hey, I didn't mean to scare you, buddy. Just paying another friendly little call. Told you I would, didn't I?" He laughed again.

Foxy looked wildly about him. He seemed to be trying to gather his wits.

Sonny threw up a hand. "Hey, now, buddy, don't get nervous on me. Just a friendly little call. Am I interrupting something?" He began to walk slowly up the hill toward Foxy, who began backing away.

"Hang on, there, don't run off on me. I want to see what you're planting there." Sonny continued up the hillside. He looked quickly around to be sure that Foxy had no gun. He walked past the mound of earth and stopped, looking down into the hole. The corpse of a teenage boy lay pitifully before him; the eyes seemed to stare at Sonny's belt buckle.

"Well, looka here," he said, half over his shoulder to Foxy, half to himself. "Look what we got here." He threw back his head again and laughed wildly. "Foxy, you old fart, do you know what you've done? You've went and saved my ass, do you know that?" He looked around him. "And when I get some niggers up here with picks and shovels, I bet you're gonna make me fucking *famous!*"

He put his hands on his hips and rocked up on his toes. A rush of joy pounded through him, and he had a split-second fantasy of some sort of presentation ceremony, where Hugh Holmes and Billy Lee were pinning a big medal on him. He rocked back on his heels and up on his toes again, sucking in a huge breath, and then the back of his head seemed to explode. The wind flew from him in a garbled noise, and he pitched forward into the yawning red hole before him.

Foxy had swiveled nearly a full 360 degrees in swinging the shovel, and he sat down abruptly, his legs in a tangle, the long-handled shovel over his shoulder.

Sonny swam in a sea of black-and-red semiconsciousness for what seemed like several minutes, unable to sort his thoughts or make sense of what had happened to him. Then he was suddenly brought to a level of alertness by something striking him sharply across the shoulders. He opened his eyes, trying to orient himself, and pushed upward just far enough to focus on a pair of dead eyes six inches from his own. He realized he was lying face down in the grave on top of the boy's corpse.

He was struck again from behind, and this time he noticed dirt trickling down around his neck and onto the body beneath him. Christ, the old bastard was burying him alive! He struggled to get his arms beneath him in a better position to rise, and as he did, Foxy stepped into the grave, straddling him, and ripped his service revolver from its holster.

Sonny, still struggling, heard the pistol being cocked, but never heard the explosion that followed the bullet as it smashed into the back of his skull. Nor did he feel the pistol land on his back, nor the earth that followed it.

Billy could see Patricia standing behind the house, waving to him, as he tramped across the pasture, the dog at his side carrying a stick in his mouth, begging for Billy to throw it once more. Patricia was holding her hand to her head as if it held a phone. He walked slowly across the last few hundred yards to the house, in no hurry for news.

He had gone out at midmorning, taking a sandwich and a bone for the dog. He had relished the solitude and the company of the retriever, knowing that he had done all he could do on every front, that everything now depended on others. He had walked over his fields and through his woods—places he had not known since he had last walked this way with his father. He had thought a lot about his father during the day, wished he could be here, wished that Will Henry had lived to see the grandchild that would be born the following spring. Wished he could tell him the things he had learned as a man, things he could not tell Mr. Holmes, nor even Patricia—not yet, anyway.

"Will you hurry up, for God's sake!" she shouted across the last hundred yards. "It's Bert Hill, in Greenville."

He wiped his feet on a burlap bag at the back door of the new house and walked over the bare floors and through the empty rooms to the front hall and the phone.

"Billy?"

There was regret even in the way the man spoke his name. "Yes, Bert."

"Billy, the news is bad. I'm sorry, I've been had on a platter."

"What happened, Bert."

"Skeeter fed me a witness at the last minute, and I bought it, and put him on."

"A witness? Who?"

"Do you know a colored fellow called Johnson? Pieback Johnson?"

"Sure, he's the town drunk. One of 'em, anyway."

"He claimed to have been in jail that Saturday night on a drunk charge and to have seen everything. He backed Sonny's story to the hilt. The grand jury wouldn't indict."

Billy sank down onto the marble floor.

"Billy, you there?"

"Yeah, Bert, I'm here. Look, there was no way to see that coming; it's not your fault."

"I still feel rotten about it, though."

"Butts is going to get fired anyway, he beat up a guy at the fair last night, and Holmes took it to the council. I'm sure he'll be able to dump Butts."

"He'll still be a free man, though."

"Yeah, but at least he won't be a cop any more. Nobody'd ever hire him again after what's happened. We might even be able to get him on an assault with a deadly weapon. He had a blackjack. There's some talk about extortion, too."

"Anything I can do, Billy, please believe that. I'd love to nail the bastard."

"I'll let you know after I've talked with Holmes, Bert."

"Any news on the election yet?"

Billy looked at his watch. "The polls close in half an hour, at eight. We're having an open house down here after that. We'd love to see you."

"Thanks Billy, but I'm whipped. This isn't the best day I've had for a while."

"See you soon, then."

Patricia was standing next to him. He told her the news.

"Never mind. Mr. Holmes called earlier, said he had good news. He ought to be here in a few minutes. Why don't you get changed?"

It was half past eight before Holmes and his wife arrived, and a number of guests were already drinking punch and wandering through the nearly completed house. He pulled Billy aside into what would be Billy's study.

"First of all, I know about the grand jury. Bert Hill called me. It's a shame, but it probably isn't going to matter much after what's happened."

"What happened at the council meeting?"

"It went well. There was a resolution to fire Butts. There was no reason to do anything about Charley Ward until after we heard from the grand jury, but I had a little talk with him this afternoon, and he's quit, resigned."

"What about the carnival manager? I've been thinking about that. Those people will be on the road again next week, and we'll have one hell of a time getting him back here to testify."

"It looks like that won't be necessary. Sonny Butts took off this morning?"

"Took off?"

"Left town, apparently, ran. Damndest thing, he didn't go in his own car; he took the police motorcycle!"

"But that doesn't make any sense. Why would he do that?"

"The way I figure it is Butts was so scared about the grand jury and about the council, that he didn't wait around for the news; he just bolted. But the state patrol has been to his place, and he apparently didn't take anything with him, clothes or anything."

"But if he were going to try and run for it he'd surely take what he could, and he wouldn't run on something as conspicuous as a police motorcycle. That would be completely crazy."

Holmes shrugged. "So is Sonny Butts."

Billy nodded. "You've got a point there. He must have just popped his cork."

"That's what I think." Holmes grinned. "And if he ever does turn up, he'll have to face a charge of stealing the motorcycle."

Some time later Holmes was called to the phone. Billy watched as he stood in the hall and talked. Holmes returned to the bare living room, and called for silence. "Ladies and Gentlemen, as you may have heard, there has been a Democratic primary in the state of Georgia today, which is as good as an election. As a result, you will, early next year, experience a change in your elected officials. I have some results here." He consulted a small notebook.

"Sheriff Skeeter Willis has been reelected." There was a murmer of disappointment. "In the city council races, Ellis Woodall and Dr. Tom Mudter have been elected, you veterans will be glad to hear, and, perhaps more important to those here, the state-senate seat heretofore occupied by your humble servant has been handily won by our host." He raised a hand toward Billy and Patricia. "Senator Lee, come over here and make us a speech."

That night Billy and Patricia dragged their mattress from the trailer over to the new house, up the stairs, and into the master bedroom. Billy opened all the windows to let in the cool night air, and they slept in each other's arms.

Billy woke in time to watch the sun rise over the woods and fields behind the house, and though he was no more a farmer than his father had been, he felt that he had returned to the land.

He tiptoed down the stairs, walked to the trailer, and, rummaging in his tiny desk, found the family Bible. He opened it and ran his finger slowly down the generations of his people to the point where his marriage to Patricia was recorded, and to the blank space where his child's name would be written.

He walked back to the house, into his new study, and placed the Bible carefully on the walnut mantelpiece. Then he climbed the stairs, crawled into bed with his wife, and quickly fell asleep again.

BOOK THREE

Tucker Watts

1 AN INDIAN SUMMER DAY gave way to the cool of an early-autumn, New England evening in 1962. As the sun sank into the sea, the small group moved closer to the driftwood fire they had built on the beach at Gay Head, on the island of Martha's Vineyard. The women were getting ready to steam clams and left the men to their conversation, which, as always, concerned politics.

"All right," one of them said. "Let's not labor the point. Let's just assume for the sake of argument that he does decide to dump Lyndon. Who do we want, and why?"

"You mean who does *he* want, don't you?"

"No, I mean who do *we* want. He's going to ask, you know, and we'd better have an answer when he does."

"A southerner or a westerner," somebody said.

"Yeah, but a liberal southerner or westerner," somebody replied.

"I didn't know there were any."

"Comparatively speaking, then."

"Yeah."

The conversation continued for a few minutes, and names were bandied about.

"Those are the names I heard before the convention, before Lyndon," said the senior man, the one who had first asked the question. "Isn't there somebody new, fresh, that we haven't considered? Can't we apply some imagination to this problem?"

"How about the lieutenant governor of Georgia?"

Heads swiveled. The voice belonged to a member of the group who had not yet spoken at all.

"What's his name—Lee? Well, that's imaginative, David. Tell us why," said the senior man. Kass was New York, Jewish, NYU, instead of Boston, Catholic, and Harvard. It intrigued him that the suggestion had come from that quarter.

"Okay," said Kass. "Forget for a moment that he's only a lieutenant governor and not nationally known. I'll get to that in a minute. He's an interesting man."

"What's his background like?"

"Born on a farm, son of a failed cotton farmer who became a small-town chief of police and got shotgunned for his trouble; Andy Hardy upbringing, law school, the war. Bomber pilot in England, pulled down a DFC and a purple heart. Not exactly PT-109, but he got a B-17 that was all shot up and the crew back in one piece when most guys would have abandoned. Married an Irish girl he met in London, one son, good law practice, cattle farmer. He established a reputation early on for defending blacks in tough cases."

"Now he's beginning to sound interesting."

"Several terms in the state senate, effective there, in spite of a reputation for being soft on segregation. Ready for this one? Supported JFK for vice-president at the '56 convention."

"Applause, applause. Prescient, wasn't he?"

"Not exactly. Elected lieutantant governor in '59, supported Lyndon in '60."

"Oh, shit."

"Not necessarily. He came over quickly when we got the nomination and worked his ass off in the general election, when people like Herman Talmadge were sitting on theirs. Instrumental in our taking Georgia."

"That's better."

"Moderate to conservative on fiscal matters. You don't get elected in Georgia if you're not. But he's been a leading voice of moderation and compromise on race issues. Pushed for better jobs for blacks, backed desegregation of public facilities. There's a story, apparently true, that his wife once fought off a bunch of Klansmen with a shotgun."

"No kidding? That's terrific. Imagine what you could do with that in a campaign."

"Yeah. As I say, he wouldn't pass for a flaming liberal in Massachusetts, but he'll do, for a southerner."

"Sounds like you've been doing some research on him, David. Maybe you can tell us why he went with Lyndon in '60, when he supported JFK for VP in '56?"

"Remember a guy named Hugh Holmes?"

"Uh, something with Roosevelt, wasn't he?"

"Informally. Roosevelt saw a lot of him on the Warm Springs visits. Apparently had a lot of respect for him. Anyway, Lee is a protégé of Holmes, and Holmes and Lyndon have known each other for a long time. I suspect that influenced Lee's judgment at the time. He's firmly in our camp now, though."

"How's he come off, personally?"

"He's no redneck. Pleasant southern accent, clean-cut, forty-eight, but looks younger, in good shape—tennis player. Dresses conservatively. He's no intellectual giant, but he's bright. Well traveled, knows a few politicians in England and Ireland through his wife's family."

"Is the wife Catholic?"

"No, Protestant family. Goes to the Baptist Church with him. She's the cattle farmer, apparently, and good at it. Handsome woman, good campaigner."

"Okay, what's the catch. Booze? Women?"

"Light drinker, straight arrow, from all accounts. If he fools around, he knows how to keep it quiet."

"Does JFK know him?"

"They've met a number of times. Got along. Bobby spent a day with him in Atlanta during the campaign. He was impressed."

"Sounds too good to be true."

In the firelight, Kass could be seen to grin. "Did I mention that he's a brigadier general in the Air National Guard? Commands an air-transport group."

"Come on, David, you're making this up."

"I kid you not."

"Barry Goldwater would shit in his pants. Okay. what's the catch? Why isn't he better known?"

"The catch is, he's only a lieutenant governor. Can you name one lieutenant governor of any state except Massachusetts?"

"No, now that you mention it. So how does he overcome that?"

"He runs for governor in '63. Georgia governors are elected in off years. But there's still a catch."

"Yeah?"

"The race question has hardened up now. If he runs as a liberal he'll have a tough time winning."

"And if he backs off on race we can't use him."

"Right."

"What do you think are his chances?"

"No better than even right now, and they could get a lot worse. A wrong move, a misstatement, and he's down the tube."

"Then why are we even talking about him this early?"

"You asked. And he's worth it."

"What can we do to help him?"

"I'll have a look in the pork barrel."

"Careful, now, we don't want to put some congressman's nose out of joint. Tell you what. Send his file to me Monday morning—I'm assuming you've collected a file, or you wouldn't know so much—and I'll slip it to the boss when the time is right."

"Okay."

The senior advisor grinned. "Oh, David?"

"Yeah?"

"How does he get along with Georgia's Jews?"

"Just dandy."

"I thought so."

2   BILLY LEE arrived at his office in the Georgia Capitol
    shortly before nine, having picked his way through the
    heavy traffic from Dobbins Air Force Base in Marietta. It
was mid-November, and his group had been on alert, ready to
be called to active duty, since mid-October, when the Cuban
missile crisis had taken place. Billy had been working since that
time to ready his unit for call-up, and he was relieved to be going
back to a normal schedule, now that the crisis had abated.

His mail was stacked neatly on his desk in two piles, one of
letters which his secretary, the formidable Sarah, had opened
and screened, and one of those which appeared personal or of
sufficient importance to be seen first by him. He was continually
amazed at her uncanny ability to decide in which stack a letter
belonged. He could not remember her ever having erred in that
or any other regard, and he once again blessed the day that the
Georgia civil service had disgorged her into his office on the occasion of his inauguration.

He hung up his overcoat, turned to his desk, and was immediately transfixed by the sight of a pale, green envelope resting
on top of the "private" stack. He had received one or two letters
from the president before, routine notes prepared by some anonymous White House staffer and, probably, signed by a machine;
what struck him about this one was that it had been addressed

by hand, and not the perfect hand of a top-notch secretary.

He picked it up and stared at it for a moment. It had been addressed to his home and forwarded. He had not been home for a month. He gingerly opened the envelope and unfolded the paper.

Dear Billy

I heard on the grapevine that on the recent inspection tour the 109th came out head and shoulders above any other ANG group in readiness. I've sent my official thanks to the unit, but I wanted to let you know personally how much I appreciate your doing such a fine job. I know it took you away when the legislature was in session, and I'm glad we didn't have to call you to active duty in the end.

Next time you're up this way, let me know you're coming, and let's get together for a chat.

With best regards,
Jack Kennedy

Billy read the letter again, then placed it carefully in his brief case. He was astonished that the man had taken time to write the note, and he was giddy with flattery. He had been hearing a lot from the administration lately. That fellow Kass had been down in early October, and if Billy had read him correctly, he could expect an endorsement, perhaps even personal campaigning from the president when he ran for governor, although nothing had been promised, and the man had made it clear that the administration was looking to him for progressive action in race matters. Kass had also brought him confirmation of some mass-transit money for Atlanta from the federal government, something the city had not hoped to get for months. The governor was still wondering how Billy had done that. Billy hadn't done it at all, really. It had just fallen into his lap.

He was pondering all this when Sarah came on the intercom, and if he hadn't been preoccupied, he might have paid closer attention to the telephone conversation which followed.

"Chief Breen on the line, Governor."

"Who?" He struggled to concentrate on the name.

"The chief of police. Of Atlanta. You asked his help a few weeks ago, remember?"

"Oh, sure, put him on." It had been more than a month since he had talked with the chief.

"Morning, Chief."

"Morning, Governor. You asked me a few weeks ago to keep an eye out for a man for you, a chief for Delano." Breen never wasted time with pleasantries.

"Yes, Chief." Billy was surprised to hear from the man. They had bumped heads a couple of times on the question of more black officers on the Atlanta force.

"I've come across a man who seems very well qualified. He's a major in the army, commands the MP unit out at Fort Mc-Pherson. Retiring next month."

"Retiring? How old is he?"

"Only in his early fifties. Joined real young, apparently. He applied to us, but we have a policy of promoting from within, and we couldn't offer him anything anywhere near the level he'd want. I mentioned Delano to him, and he seemed interested. He's from Columbus, originally, and knows the town from driving through."

"Sounds like an interesting fellow. I'd like to meet him."

"I'll send a man over with a résumé he left with me, and your secretary can set up an appointment for him."

"Sounds good. What's the man's name?"

"Ah," Billy heard some papers shuffle. "Tucker Watts."

"Chief, I appreciate your remembering about this."

"Oh, glad to do it, Governor, glad to do it. Any time."

As they hung up, Billy thought the chief had delivered his last statement with a lot of relish, more than he would have expected, but his mind was again occupied by the signals coming out of Washington, and he thought no more about it.

He buzzed his secretary. "Sarah, Breen is sending over a résumé on a major out at Fort Mac named Watts. Will you set up an appointment with the man as soon as possible, please? It's about the job in Delano."

"Certainly, Governor. Mr. Holmes is calling from Delano."

He picked up the phone. "Mr. Hugh, how are you?" He knew why Holmes was calling, and he was relieved that Breen had called first.

"I'm just fine, Billy." He sounded fine, too, Billy thought. The man was, what—eighty-six, eighty-seven? He was still chairman of the state board of education, still chaired the city council, and still ran the bank. His wife had died of a stroke in 1948, and the event had seemed to concentrate his dedication to work. His only concession to age was a hearing aid. "Billy, I'm sorry to bother you, but we're beginning to hurt for a new chief of police down here. Have you heard anything from your sources?"

"Yes, sir, I have. Chief Breen of Atlanta has recommended an MP major who's about to retire from the army. I'm seeing him tomorrow."

"Good. All of our force down here are pretty young and inexperienced. None of 'em is really responsible enough even to be an acting chief. The city manager is tearing his hair out. How soon you reckon we can get this fellow?"

"Well, now hold on, I haven't even talked to him yet. Breen says he's good, though, and he expressed an interest in the job."

"Tell you what. We've got a council meeting at six o'clock on Friday. You coming down this weekend?"

"Yes, first weekend in a month."

"Well, if you like the looks of this fellow, why don't you bring him down here to meet the council? We're ready to move; if he's any good, we'll take him. Might even pay a couple of thousand more than we'd planned on."

"Sounds good to me. I'll call you as soon as I've talked with him and let you know if he can come. How's Patricia? You've seen more of her than I have, the last few weeks."

"Thriving. Will, too."

"Glad to hear it. See you this weekend, then."

Billy hung up and mopped his brow. He'd almost dropped the ball on that one. Imagine being saved by Breen, who didn't even like him, much.

3 SARAH'S VOICE came over the intercom. "Governor, Major Watts is here to see you."

"Ask him to wait for just one minute, would you, Sarah?" He had not had time until this moment to look over the résumé Chief Breen had sent him, but from what he saw now, the man had an outstanding record. Enlisting at age seventeen, he had finished high school, earned a degree while in the service, and attended a number of military police courses, in addition to the FBI training program for police officers.

Billy immediately thought that he would never find a city policeman so well qualified who would take such a job as that in Delano. He wondered why Major Watts was interested; then he remembered Chief Breen's remark about promotion from within, and how it would be difficult to hire Watts into a police force at a level in which he would not be overqualified. At least Delano could offer the job of chief.

"Send him in, Sarah."

As Major Tucker Watts strode into Billy's office and toward him, Billy was immediately struck by a number of things: the man's size, for he was six feet three or four, well over two hundred pounds; his bearing; his confident manner; the rows of ribbons on the perfectly pressed uniform. Most of all Billy was struck, forcibly, by the color of the man's skin. He was black.

During the time it took to make introductions and shake hands, Billy fought the wild urge to laugh aloud. Breen, from his office at city hall, had fired an ironic arrow into the air which, Billy felt sure, could be seen at this moment protruding from his back.

"Major, I want to thank you for taking the time from your duties to come and talk with me." After a year of baiting Breen about an insufficient number of blacks on the Atlanta police force, Breen was inquiring, through the presence of the man before him, about the number of blacks on the Delano police force. Billy wondered whether Breen had also called the press, whether they were waiting outside his office at that moment.

"Thank you for seeing me, sir. I was glad to come."

The major's speech was precise, perfectly enunciated. There was the musky, black intonation, but it seemed very unsouthern, almost West Indian. Billy thought it a pleasant sound.

Billy glanced at the man's résumé. "I see you're out at Fort Mac. Been there long?" He was beginning to overcome the distraction of what Breen had meant as a practical joke. He wanted to know more about Major Watts.

"I'm just finishing up a two-year tour. My last one, in fact. I'll complete thirty years this month."

"How did you get to know Chief Breen?" Watts seemed completely at ease. Billy wondered whether he knew why Breen had sent him.

"I command the MP detachment at Fort Mac. We liaise closely with the Atlanta police. I've met him several times in the line of duty."

"Like him?"

There was a tiny pause before Watts spoke. "I'm sure he's a competent police chief."

Billy smiled slightly. "Yes, I'm sure he is." He glanced at the résumé. "You saw combat in the war?"

"Yes, sir. 761st Tank Battalion."

"I've heard about the outfit."

"Yes, sir. Eleanor Roosevelt's Niggers."

"That's the one. We had a man from Delano in that outfit."

"Who would that be, sir?"

"Marshall Parker."

"He wasn't in my company."

"You were in Korea, too?"

"Yes, sir. That was when I transferred into the military police."

"You're married, I see. Any children?"

"No, sir. We married late."

Billy shifted in his seat. "Let me be direct with you, Major. I have no doubt that you are very well qualified for this job by training and experience, but let's talk about temperament. We're talking about the job of chief of police in a small southern town. There's never been a black policeman in Delano. There are bound to be a lot of pressures involving race. Do you think you could handle that?"

"I've thought about the problems involved. What you have to understand, sir, is that an army base, wherever it is, is a small southern town. The army is disproportionately southern. I serve under white southern officers, and white southern boys serve under me. I can't say that the situation has never caused friction. I think, for instance, that if I had been white I'd probably be a full colonel by now instead of a major, but I've never had any problems handling that. Ten years ago I was a master sergeant, so I can't really complain about promotion. I've always had outstanding efficiency reports from white southern officers, and I don't think there's a white boy who's ever served under me who would say he was been treated anything but fairly."

"Well, you'd have a force of six men, all white and all southern. Handling them would be your very first problem. Tell me, what sort of social life do you have in the army? Do you think you could adapt socially to a place where virtually all the black people are less well educated and less affluent than you?"

Watts smiled, revealing white, even teeth. "That's the first thing my wife asked me. But I reminded her that we're not all that social, anyway. We've gotten used to moving every couple of years, like everybody in the army, so what friends we have are pretty scattered. If we want a big night out we go to the officer's club, and living in Delano we'd still have PX and club privileges at Fort Benning and Fort Mac. We've always talked about buying a place in the country when we retire, and that would mean a pretty quiet life, too."

Billy nodded. "Well, there's no shortage of country around Delano. What sort of money do you think you'd need?"

"What's the budget for the job?"

"About ten thousand."

"I think that would do us very well. I'd have my retirement pay, too. I'd like to think that if I did a good job there would be more later."

"I should think there would be. There are some insurance benefits, too, I think."

"That's fine, but what would concern me most would be the budget for the department and my authority as chief. I don't want to run a force that isn't properly equipped and manned—that's a losing game—and I'd want absolute authority to hire and fire."

"Well, those seem like reasonable requests to me, but you'd have to take them up with the city council." Billy gazed across the room at a painting of a sailing ship. He had begun to see an opportunity in Tucker Watts. "Major, would you be available to come down to Delano on Friday afternoon? There's a council meeting at six o'clock."

"Yes, sir, I could do that."

"Let me talk with a couple of people, and I'll get back to you tomorrow, then." He stood up and stuck out his hand.

"Thank you, Governor, that will be just fine."

When Watts had gone, Billy picked up the phone and began dialing Hugh Holmes's number at the Bank of Delano. He broke the news as gently as he could.

"I don't know about that, Billy. We've talked about hiring a black policeman, as you know, but a black chief?"

"Mr. Holmes, I want to bring him down there on Friday, and have the council meet him."

"Well, I guess we owe you that, Billy, after you've taken the time to find this fellow. Do you want them to know he's colored?"

Billy thought for a moment. "Yes, but not until they arrive at the meeting. You're meeting at six. I'll try and have him there at six-thirty. All right?"

"All right, son. Do you think the press will get wind of this?"

"I don't think so, but if they do, everybody will come off a lot better if they've given the man a hearing."

"I suppose so."

Billy hung up and made a mental note to ask Watts to be sure and wear his uniform.

Tucker Watts left the meeting with the lieutenant governor half elated and half afraid. Might this really happen? If it did, could he bring it off? He tried to imagine what might lie ahead, but all his excited mind could conjure up was the image of a tightrope stretched before him, so high that it was impossible to see what lay below. He knew that he would not hesitate to walk it if the opportunity came. He was drawn irresistibly toward it, helpless to stop himself.

Delano. Of all the places in the world, Delano, Georgia.

4 TUCKER WATTS hated lying to his wife, because she read him so easily. He had thought carefully about how he would explain things to her, in order to keep the lies he would have to tell her at an absolute minimum. As soon as he came into the house he went into the kitchen, where she was preparing dinner, and mixed them both a gin and tonic.

"I had an interesting job interview today," he said, squeezing lime into their drinks.

"Oh?" She knew already just how interested he was.

"With the lieutenant governor, William H. Lee."

"A state job?"

"No. You remember a little town called Delano?"

She furrowed her brow.

"You remember. We've passed through there driving back and forth to Columbus. You always say how pretty you think it is."

"Oh, that one. Yes, it is pretty. Is the job there?"

He nodded. "Chief of police."

Her eyebrows went up. "What does the lieutenant governor have to do with that?"

"It's his home town. He's helping them find somebody. Breen on the Atlanta force recommended me."

"I thought Breen didn't like colored folks."

"He doesn't. I don't think he told Lee I was colored."

She laughed. "That must have come as quite a shock."

"Didn't seem to. I think he's going to recommend me to the city council."

"Is Delano someplace you think we ought to go?"

"Well, look at it this way. We already know by now that I'm not going to get hired at any sort of rank by any big-city police force because of seniority problems, and I'm too old and too mean to start somewhere as a patrolman."

"Lord knows that's true."

"Careful how you agree with me." He slapped her on the bottom.

"Mmmmm. Do that again."

"Later. Now, we're looking to retire, right? But we both know I need to work to keep from going crazy. Well, this might just give us everything we want. We can buy a few acres in the country near town, and you can do some gardening. We might even build us a house if things work out."

"Being chief of police isn't exactly retirement, is it?"

"Shoot, I can run that department left-handed, once I get the little white-boy cops to understand who's boss. Nothing happens in those little towns that even gets you out of bed more than a couple of times a year."

"How about money?"

"Pays ten thousand, and with our retirement pay and PX privileges at Benning, we could live right well, you know?"

"You make it sound good." She paused. "Is there something you aren't telling me about it?"

Jesus, the woman was psychic. "What's not to tell? You know everything I know. Lee wants me to go down there and meet the city council Friday evening."

"You think they'll hire a colored fellow?"

"I don't know, but I figure Lee wouldn't want me to go down there if he didn't think so. He's going to run for governor next year, you know, and it would be a feather in his cap with the colored vote, to have a black chief in his home town."

She nodded. "Guess so. Don't you have an aunt or a cousin in Delano?"

"Aunt. I haven't seen her in years. Don't even know if she's still alive."

"Well, if it looks good to you it's all right with me." She opened the oven and took out a meatloaf. "Drink up your drink; supper's about ready."

5 AS THE Delano City Council convened on Friday night, Hugh Holmes found himself wondering at exactly what point he had begun doing things Billy's way instead of the other way around. Early on, he decided, while Billy had still been in the state senate. The boy had always learned quickly. Now Holmes found himself leading the charge in a delicate matter, trusting Billy's judgment entirely. He had not met this Major Watts, but he knew that Billy wouldn't be bringing him to this meeting if he didn't fully expect Holmes and the rest of the council to approve his appointment.

"Did you know I was black before you met me?" They were driving south in Billy's car, a state-patrol vehicle leading the way and another state trooper following behind in Tucker Watts's car.

Billy smiled. "No, I didn't. I think that was Chief Breen's idea of a joke."

"You seem to be taking his joke seriously."

"Oh, I'm not taking you to Delano to waste your time, Major. I think you could be very good in this job."

"Do you think the city council is going to agree with you?"

"Well, there's a man named Hugh Holmes preparing the way for us. They're going to have a hard time disagreeing with him. He's been on that council since there was a council, and he knows how to get his way."

"How did he get convinced?"

"He isn't convinced, but he's impressed with your record, and he's willing to talk with you about it. He'll convince the others to listen, too, I reckon. Did I tell you that my father was the first chief of police in Delano?"

"No."

"Back in the twenties. He was killed in the line of duty, when he went to get a young boy who was serving a short sentence in the local jail. He let the boy go home for the night, and he didn't show up the next morning. His father was in a malarial delirium and came out with a shotgun. Thought he was somebody else, apparently."

"I'm sorry to hear it."

"It was a long time ago. My mother took it pretty hard, but she wrote a letter to the governor asking him to pardon the fellow. He should never have been convicted in the first place. He was out of his head at the time."

"That must have been tough on your family."

"Yes, but not as tough as it was on the fellow's family. His son was about my age. He ran. It was stupid, but he was charged as an accessory. My mother was trying to get the charges dropped against him, when he was killed, hit by a truck over in Alabama. Hitchhiking, I think. The father was finally sent to the electric chair, in spite of my mother's efforts. It was a tragic business. Couldn't happen today, at least I hope not."

They were both quiet for a few minutes. Tucker turned toward him. "You mentioned a fellow in my outfit in the war, Marshall Parker?"

"That's right."

"I heard about him at a battalion reunion, I think. Didn't he get shot at the jail?"

"That's right. He was beat up by two police officers and then shot. He told a local doctor about it on his deathbed—Dr. Tom Mudter, you'll meet him tonight at the council meeting—and the two of us and some others tried to get the cops convicted for it, but we couldn't even get an indictment. One of the cops resigned under pressure, the other one ran. Damndest thing, he stole the police motorcycle and just disappeared."

"On a police motorcycle? I wouldn't have thought he'd get far on that."

"We thought he had some help, that he must have been planning it. He ran before we heard from the grand jury. Never been heard from, as far as I know."

"Sounds like the Delano Police Department has had a pretty turbulent history."

"Oh, it's been pretty quiet for a long time now. The Parker incident made the city council much more sensitive to the treatment of black prisoners. I don't think there have been any serious abuses since that time. Hugh Holmes has always kept a pretty close eye on the police. He felt very badly about having had a hand in hiring this fellow Butts, the one who disappeared. I think his attitude will stand in your favor." Billy opened his briefcase on the seat between them and fished out a large buff envelope. "By the way, Mr. Holmes sent these up. The departmental budget and an inventory of equipment. He thought you might like to look it over before the meeting."

Tucker began reading through the material, and they were quiet for the remainder of the trip.

Holmes began the meeting by asking that all other business be postponed, in order to address an important matter; then he began a recital of attempts, all unsuccessful, to hire a qualified chief of police for the town. For a moment he felt transported to another council meeting more than forty years before, when he had made substantially the same remarks. Then his mission had been to get the council to hire a farmer to be a policeman. Now it was to persuade them to give a black applicant a hearing.

He read through the man's résumé, and as he did a murmur of approval and enthusiasm ran through the meeting. Then he told them, bluntly, that the man was black. This announcement was greeted with silence.

"Now, before we get into a discussion of whether it is appropriate for Delano to have a Negro chief of police, there are some things I would like to say." Everyone settled back to listen to him. "There are a number of points we have to consider that are new, that have never been necessary to think about before. You are all aware that, at the last council election, a Negro candidate ran and was nearly elected. I believe a colored candidate will be elected at the next election. Now, I am not saying that we should consider hiring a colored chief because we might someday have a colored councilman. I bring this up as an example of changes that are coming to us. I believe that many of these changes are inevitable. It is only a matter of time. I also believe that we can make these changes easier to accept without unnecessary conflict by anticipating them. Enough said about that. I think you all understand me." The council members knew that Holmes, as chairman of the state board of education, was talking about the integration of Delano's public schools.

"Now, let me be even more pragmatic. This community is engaged in an energetic, and so far fruitless, search for new industry. It is likely that any new manufacturer we are able to attract will come from a northern state. They want to come south to get nonunion labor. I believe you are all aware that earlier this year we came very close to finding our first new piece of industry and that the deal fell through, at least in part because the company had a key production employee who was colored, and they found another community where they felt he and his family would settle in better. I checked into this, and I discovered that the other community was no more integrated than ours is, but that there were some highly visible Negroes employed by the city, and this bore weight.

"Looking at it from another point of view, it is historically true that a large majority of violent crimes, of felonies, in Delano are committed by colored people, and if there is to be an effective crime-prevention program in this town, it will have to begin in Braytown. I think there exists the possibility that a colored police chief might be more effective in implementing such a program than a white chief.

"Finally, we have to consider Billy Lee and what he means to this community. I think it is no secret that Billy will run for governor next year, and I think you know what his election could do for Delano." There was an affirmative stir among the councilmen, and Holmes knew he had them. "This is going to be a difficult race for Billy. He will be running at a time when things are in a state of flux. He will be running on a platform of orderly change, and tonight he is bringing us an opportunity to show that orderly change can work. I think we owe it to Billy to give this man careful consideration."

Holmes took a deep breath and, as casually as he could manage, played his last card. "Now, I am not asking this council to accept this man sight unseen or *because* he is colored. What I am asking is that we consider him on the basis of his record and on our impressions of how he might behave in a sensitive job, and I would like to put that in the form of a motion. Do I hear a second?"

Dr. Tom Mudter seconded. "In favor?" A chorus of ayes. "Opposed?" There was silence. He had left the unconvinced councilmen an opportunity to object to the man, but he had effectively removed race as a subject of discussion. Now the council could reject Watts only if they found him personally wanting in the interview. Holmes knew from what Billy had told him that this was unlikely. It was 6:30. He rose and went to call Billy and Major Watts into the meeting.

Tucker Watts sat comfortably and looked around the conference table. He had been answering questions for half an hour. He had outlined his military record, his police training. He had been respectful in his answers and addressed each of the councilmen as "sir," without being servile. After years of dealing effectively with white commanders, this came naturally to him and without resentment. He had made the men feel comfortable and unthreatened. He had been asked to leave the room and had been called back after only a couple of minutes. Now the old man, the banker, Holmes, spoke.

"Major Watts, the job pays ten thousand dollars a year, plus a city employee's insurance program and pension. Will you accept the job?"

"Mr. Holmes, Gentlemen, I'm honored to be offered the job, and I believe I would like to accept it, but there are some points I think I should cover first."

Holmes nodded. "Go ahead."

"I'm satisfied with the terms you are offering me personally, that is, if I can expect salary increases if I am effective."

"You can." Holmes already had another two thousand dollars in hand, approved by the council.

"I would want it stated in my contract that I have full authority in the department with regard to personnel and expenditures."

"You mean you want to be able to hire and fire?"

"Yes, sir."

"You realize this will be a sensitive matter."

"I hope you will trust me to exercise good judgement and to deal fairly with personnel, but I could not function without complete authority."

Holmes nodded. "And what was that about expenditures?"

"I want to agree an annual operating budget with the council, and I want authority in my contract to make expenditures in accordance with the budget, without further council approval. So much for personnel, so much for equipment—but I decide which personnel and what equipment."

Holmes looked around the table and saw no disagreement. "I think that seems reasonable."

"I've looked through the departmental budget and equipment list, and I think you're not too badly off. I think you can get by for the time being with the six officers now on the payroll, but they're underpaid. I think an additional three thousand dollars in the personnel budget would bring salaries up to a good standard and improve morale. I also think the department is going to need a full-time clerk, but I won't know for sure until I see the state of the paperwork."

Another half hour passed before Tucker worked through his list of requests and reached agreement with the council. Billy spoke for the first time. "Gentlemen, if you'll all trust me as an objective party, I'll draw up a contract. I have notes on what you've agreed."

"That should be all right," said Holmes, noting no dissent. "Major, when do you think you could start?"

"My retirement date is the second of December. I should think, if we can find a house, I could start by the fifteenth. Is that soon enough?"

"That will be just fine. I might be of some help to you in finding a house. Now Billy, if you and Major Watts—perhaps I should say Chief Watts—will excuse us, we have some other council business to attend to." Hands were shaken all around, and Billy and Tucker left. Holmes turned back to the group. "Gentlemen, if it's all right with you, I'll write up something for the paper. I'd like to hold the news until just before Watts arrives, and I think it would be best if we kept his color quiet until that time. Agreed?"

Billy and Tucker shook hands in the cold night air outside city hall.

"Well, Chief," Billy said, "congratulations. If there's anything I can do for you to help you get settled just call me at the

Capitol or at home. We're in the book."

"Thank you very much, Governor. I appreciate your bringing me into this. Chief Breen is going to be a very unhappy man."

Billy laughed. "Oh, I hope so. I'll send you a contract to look at first of the week."

The two men parted. Tucker made a show of looking for something in the glove compartment of his car to give Billy time to drive away first. Then he started his car and drove away in the opposite direction—not toward Atlanta, but toward Columbus, to a point where D Street turned off the Columbus highway. He followed D Street past a number of ramshackle houses and stopped at the end of the street, in front of a house which seemed in better repair than the others, which had even been painted white.

He switched off the engine and sat quietly in the car, looking at the house, until it began to get cold in the car. Finally, his heart pounding and his breath coming quickly, he got out of the car, climbed the front steps, and knocked on the door. He looked around him in the frosty moonlight; it was so much the same. The door opened, and Nellie Cole peered into the night.

"Yes? Who is that?"

Tucker looked at her, clutching her quilted bathrobe about her in the cold. He took off his hat. "Mama," he said, "it's me. I'm home."

Nellie looked for a moment as if she had received an electric shock. Her hand went to her mouth. "Willie? Is that you? Is it Willie?"

He put his arms around her and held her tightly. "Yes, Mama, it's me." Willie Cole was home.

6 ON SUNDAY Billy, Patricia, and son Will Lee played host to H. W. and Carrie Fowler and Eloise Lee for lunch. This meal, which was always fried chicken when at the Fowlers', was always roast beef and Yorkshire pudding when at the Lees'. Wine was not served, only in deference to the Fowlers.

It seemed to Billy that, after an absence of a month, he drew as much sustenance from the presence of all the living members of his family as from the excellent food before them. He watched as they chatted among themselves: young Will, fifteen and still boyish and slight, with his mother's dark red hair; Eloise, still a widow and indispensable in the management of both Mr. Fowler's store and Billy's campaign organization; Mr. Fowler, plumper and grayer, but seemingly otherwise unchanged for twenty years, though he was now seventy-five; Carrie, the same age, but infinitely older, suffering always from an undiagnosed illness Billy felt to be his father's death; and Patricia, still beautiful, still alluring, aging slowly and improving like a fine wine.

They spent a drowsy hour together, shuffling through the Sunday papers, before the Fowlers excused themselves to go home for their nap. Eloise left with them. It began to rain. Hugh Holmes arrived, and Billy met him on the steps with an umbrella and brought him into the study, where Patricia had coffee waiting. Will excused himself to work on a school project.

Billy went to a cupboard under a bookcase and brought out an unopened bottle of brandy. His liquor was not as carefully concealed as that of Holmes, but it was concealed nevertheless. "Patricia's father sent us a case of this for Christmas. He always allows six months for anything to be shipped." He broke the seal and uncorked the bottle. "It's a *Fine Champagne* 1928. I'm not waiting until Christmas."

"I concur in your impatience," said Holmes, reaching for a glass. He sniffed the brandy and tasted it. "This is definitely an old man's cognac, my boy. I don't know if you're ready for this."

"I'll take a chance," said Billy. He sat back and sipped his brandy.

"Well, now that you've set us on the road to perdition by sending us this colored gentleman for the police force—"

"Now, now, now. This is a good move for the city, and you know it very well."

Holmes took a large sip of the brandy. "I suppose it is, but I know where it's leading, and I'm afraid."

"There's nothing to be afraid of."

"It's change, I guess. I never thought I'd be afraid of change—not change I could control. That's what bothers me. This thing has begun to control us, instead of we it. It's the first time in my life I've had the feeling of having to run to keep up."

Billy looked into his brandy glass and knew that no reasoning would make it any easier for Holmes. This was too fundamental. "You're doing the right thing," he said finally.

"The right thing under the circumstances, I suppose. I guess that's the best you can do when you're running to keep up." He heaved a deep sigh. "Now, what's this business with the White House?"

"Not much business to it," Billy said. "Just the mass-transit money. That came by an unusual route. Apart from that it boils down to one visit from a presidential aide—David Kass, his name is—and one personal note from Kennedy. But I can't help feeling something's stirring."

"Could be," Holmes said, rather sadly. "There's all this 'Dump Lyndon' business in the press. Maybe it's true."

"You know, if he asked my advice—not that he's going to—I'd say keep him on."

"So would I, but then I'm not John Kennedy. Neither are you. He can do it if he wants to, and nobody can stop him. He'll be reelected with any vice-president he wants. Who's going to beat him? Richard Nixon? Barry Goldwater? Not likely. He's annoyed at not being able to get so much past the House Rules Committee. Dealing with Congress is supposed to be Lyndon's great strength. Maybe Kennedy's blaming him for the problem."

"Maybe. I think they're just different sorts of men. Not comfortable with each other. Suppose all this does mean something. How should I handle it?"

"Handle what? There's nothing to handle unless they become direct. All you can do is continue business as usual. I think business as usual for you is compatible with the aims of the administration, anyway." Holmes sipped his cognac. "Tell me, would you have brought Tucker Watts down here if you hadn't thought the White House staff was keeping an eye on you?"

"Yes," Billy said without hesitation. "I think he could be a really good thing for the town, for the state. If he works out, it could show a lot of other small communities that they have nothing to fear from giving their blacks responsible public jobs."

"And if he doesn't work out?"

"I don't think it would be that much of a problem. A small hitch. Unless he failed publicly in some important way, if he turned out to be dishonest or made a complete fool of himself. That could set things back quite a lot."

"It could set *you* back quite a lot. This election is going to be a near thing. You can't afford a public embarrassment. That's why I did some further checking on Major Watts."

Billy looked at Holmes in surprise; he was suddenly tense. "How did you do that? More important, what did you find out?"

"A friend in Dick Russell's senate office had a word with somebody in the Pentagon who went through his record."

"And?"

"It seems Tucker Watts was something of a problem for the army in his youth. He went in as a kitchen helper, you know. Never even went to basic training. He did a lot of hell raising, it seems, got into some fights. Fortunately for him the army didn't pay much heed to blacks fighting amongst themselves. He managed to stay out of the stockade, but he was broken twice, once from corporal, once from sergeant, during the thirties. It wasn't until the war broke out and he got into a Negro combat unit that he seemed to take hold. After that his record was excellent. His early problems were overlooked when they needed leaders in his unit. And after Truman desegregated the services he was in a good position for promotion."

Billy heaved a sigh of relief. "I thought for a moment you had come up with something really bad."

"No, he's apparently all he seems to be. I have hopes for him. I'm not looking forward to telling six young white policemen that they have a new, black, chief, though. All of them have been in the service. I hope that will help them adjust to the situation."

The doorbell rang. Patricia, who had seemingly been dozing in her chair, got up. "I'll get it."

Billy slapped his knee. "That will be this reporter—new fellow down here with the Atlanta bureau of the *New York Times*. I told him he could drop by for a talk this afternoon and completely forgot about it. His name is John Howell, Trish." Patricia left the room and returned shortly with a slender, sandy-haired man in his late twenties. Billy made introductions.

Holmes shook the young man's hand. "Well, I'll leave you gentlemen to it. Rainy Sunday afternoons make old men sleepy." Patricia showed him out while Billy showed the journalist to a chair and offered him coffee and brandy. He accepted both.

"This weather is more like New York than what I expected in Georgia," he said.

"How long have you been down here?"

"Just a couple of weeks. I appreciate your seeing me on a Sunday. I was down in Columbus on something else, and it was on the way back."

"Not at all."

Howell opened a stenographer's notebook and produced a ballpoint pen. "I'm really just after background. Being the new boy, I need to get around the state and meet as many people as possible. That was the legendary Hugh Holmes, was it?"

"In the flesh."

"His name seems to keep coming up, no matter who I'm talking to. Is there anybody in the state he doesn't know?"

"Probably not."

"I spent two years in the Washington bureau before coming down here. He wasn't unknown up there. For that matter, neither were you."

"Oh?"

"I had lunch with a guy at the White House before I left. David Kass. He suggested I see you early on. Tell me, what do you think of the rumors about Kennedy dropping Johnson from the ticket in '64? We can go off the record about this if you like."

Billy hoped he didn't show the jolt he felt at the question. Was the White House planting rumors about him? Howell hadn't quite said that Kass had mentioned him in that regard, but the implication was there. "I'm perfectly happy to be on the record about that," Billy said smoothly. "I think Lyndon Johnson has been a tremendous asset, both in the campaign and in the vice-presidency, and I expect he'll continue to be that kind of asset on the Democratic ticket in 1964. I certainly hope so."

"You think Kennedy will stick with Lyndon, then?"

"The President hasn't confided his views on that subject to me. Or on any other subject, for that matter. The lieutenant governor of Georgia sits a long way from the White House. I'm amazed you would even ask my opinion."

"You have no contact with the White House, then?"

"My wife and I had dinner there early last year, an intimate little group of about seventy, as I recall. We had a Christmas card from the first family."

"How about David Kass?"

"He was down here on some business or other a few weeks ago and paid me a courtesy call. The governor was out of town. I bought him a cup of coffee."

"He seemed impressed with you."

"He must've liked my coffee."

To Billy's relief Howell dropped the subject of the White House and moved on to his gubernatorial ambitions. Billy admitted his interest but did not commit himself. The conversation wandered over a wide range of subject matter for more than an hour; then, as Howell was making to leave, Billy had a thought.

"There's something coming up that might interest the *Times*."

Howell opened his notebook again. "Shoot."

"You'll have to hold it until the middle of next month, and I'll have to ask you not even to talk about it until then."

Howell paused. "I don't know."

"You can read about it in the *Constitution* then."

"All right, all right."

Billy told him about the appointment of Tucker Watts, the whole story from Chief Breen's phone call to the present, asking only that the story not be attributed to him. Howell scribbled rapidly, asking an occasional question.

"Will this be an exclusive?"

Billy shook his head. "I'll have to give it to the Atlanta papers on the day, but at least you can run it simultaneously. You'll have time to talk with Watts, too."

Billy walked the journalist to his car with an umbrella and bade him good-bye. On his way back into the house he reflected that at the White House they might get around to the *Atlanta Constitution* now and then, but they saw the *New York Times* every day.

7 BY TUCKER'S retirement date of December 2, 1962, a contract between himself and the city of Delano had been agreed and signed, and a chief's badge sent to him by Holmes via Billy. Holmes had also sent him a clipping from the *Delano Messenger* announcing his appointment to the job and giving a detailed summary of his military career. Tucker was amused that no photograph illustrated the announcement. He visited a uniform store and outfitted himself, bought a .38 service revolver, and had a laminated identification card made.

On his retirement day there was a small party for Tucker and Elizabeth at the Fort McPherson Officer's Club. Tucker was given a Rolex wristwatch and Elizabeth a set of gardening tools, the best the post exchange had to offer. They were very pleased. The base commander had some nice things to say about Tucker's work, and then, suddenly, they were civilians. That evening, as they were trying to get used to the idea, Hugh Holmes telephoned.

"Major Watts?"

"I guess it's just plain Watts, now."

Holmes laughed. "Chief Watts, I reckon. I've got a house I think you ought to have a look at. Can you and your wife come down here tomorrow?"

"I expect so. Do you want us to come to the bank?"

"The house is on the north side of town, about three miles out. Why don't we meet there?"

"All right."

"After you pass through Warm Springs you drive for about ten minutes, and you'll come to a country grocery store and barbecue stand on the right-hand side of the road."

"I remember that. Smoky's it's called, isn't it?"

"That's the place. Just past a big dairy farm. You'll see a lot of cattle. Well, after the barbecue stand it's the first road to your left, a dirt road. There's a mailbox says 'Worth' on it. The house is about a quarter of a mile from the road. Say, about ten o'clock in the morning? That too early for you?"

"No, that'll be fine."

"Good, see you then."

They drove to Delano in bright, cold weather, enjoying the ride. Elizabeth was excited, and Tucker knew the place would have to be really unsuitable for her not to want it. They had never owned a house. A few minutes past Warm Springs they came to the gate to the Spence farm, and had to stop for a herd of dairy cattle crossing the road. They were coming from milking, Tucker knew. He had walked behind them so many times with his father. He felt a prickle of something as he looked up the hill at the Spence house and the shacks beyond. Anger? Fear?

Past the barbecue stand they found the Worth mailbox and turned into the road. The house soon appeared from behind a grove of pecan trees. It was frame, white, with green shutters; not large, but not small, either. Hugh Holmes was standing on the front porch, rubbing his hands together.

"Come in out of the cold," said Holmes. "I've got the heat running. It should get warm shortly."

They walked slowly through the house. A living room, separate dining room, three bedrooms, one of which could be a den, large country kitchen. Out back were a garage and another outbuilding which had once been a barn.

"Worth built this house in the early thirties. He was farming then, but not long after that he went to work for the railroad. Retired this year. He and his wife bought an apartment down in Panama City. Moved last month. There's a little over five acres with the place. Hoss Spence, the dairy farmer up the road, bought seventy acres from Worth, but he didn't want to give him anything for the house, so Worth held that back, along with the land on this side of the creek, yonder. The property's bounded by the creek, the highway, and the railroad right-of-way, back there in the trees. You get a couple of trains a day, but apart from that it's pretty quiet."

"What's he asking?"

"Twenty-eight. I think he'd take twenty-five."

"How's he feel about selling to black people?"

"All he's worried about is selling. He replaced the coal furnace with a heat pump a couple of years ago. There's a well and a septic tank. Worth was pretty handy; kept the place up. You could find some boys to pick the pecans on shares. There's half a dozen peach trees over there, too. Keep you in preserves and ice cream."

"How about financing?"

"I can fix up twenty thousand for twenty years at six percent. That'd leave five down."

Tucker looked at Elizabeth. She was practically vibrating. "I love it," she said.

"Well, you can tell Mr. Worth he's got a buyer, Mr. Holmes."

"That's just fine. If you want to give me five hundred in earnest money we can close next week. A lawyer here has got his power of attorney."

Tucker wrote him a check. Holmes handed him a bunch of keys. "There's a front- and a back-door key there. You'll have to figure out the rest. I've got to get back to the bank, so I'll leave you with your new place. Worth says that whatever's here goes with the place. I think there's a lawnmower and some other stuff. I think you got a good buy."

"I'll start to work on the fifteenth, then, as agreed."

Holmes grinned. "You're already on the payroll. Take the time until the fifteenth as a Christmas bonus. Come see me whenever you like; let me know if I can be of any help."

Holmes shook hands and left them. Elizabeth ran around the house, looking into closets. She came back with a broom and a dustpan. "Come on, Tuck, let's get it cleaned up."

He laughed at her. "Why don't we figure out what we have to do to the place, first." They walked through the house. The paint was mostly in good shape. Elizabeth didn't like the wallpaper in the master bedroom. Tucker pulled at it, and it stripped off easily. "Why don't we just paint in here?" Elizabeth said.

"Okay with me".

"Well, don't just stand there, go buy some paint."

"Right now? We don't even own the place yet."

"Just as good as," she said. She picked up a piece of the wall-paper and pointed at a cream color between flowers. "Get a gallon that's exactly this color, and brushes and all that. By tonight we can have this place ready to move into."

Tucker kissed her and left the house, turning onto the highway and driving in a leisurely fashion toward town in his brand new Oldsmobile 98, a retirement present to themselves. As he crossed the bridge that marked the Delano city limits, he slowed to thirty-five. To his surprise, a police car pulled up next to him and the driver motioned him to pull over. There had been no flashing light or siren.

Tucker pulled over and sat quietly in the car. The police car stopped ahead of him, and a large sandy-haired young police-man hefted his bulk out of it and approached. Instead of stopping, he walked slowly all the way around the car, looking it over. When he finally arrived at the driver's window, Tucker pressed a switch and the window slid silently down. Tucker sat slumped in the seat, looking straight ahead.

"Well, now," said the young cop, "electric windows, too. Boy, this sure is some car you got yourself."

Tucker said nothing.

"This is your car, of course. You didn't just swipe it out of somebody's driveway, did you?" It wasn't quite a question. "Okay, sport, outta the car."

Tucker slowly turned his head and looked at the policeman. "What for?" he asked evenly.

An astonished look came over the cop's face. "What for? Why, because I told you to, that's what for."

Tucker shook his head. "That's not a good enough reason. I ʾasn't speeding. You've got no cause to believe I've committed any crime."

The cop stared at him incredulously. He reached to his side, pulled out a large pistol and pointed it at Tucker's head. "How about this? Is this a good enough reason? Now you get your black ass out of that car, you son of a bitch, and do like I tell you."

Tucker uncoiled himself from the car and stood up, towering over the policeman. He was wearing a blue suit and a necktie. The cop patted him under the arms for a gun, then stepped back and holstered his pistol.

"Why, don't you ask me for my license and registration?" Tucker asked.

"I'll ask the questions here, boy. Now, lemme see your license and registration."

Tucker gave them to the cop, who glanced at them.

"Awright, Marvin", said the cop, "I'm going to get back in my car and drive down to the station, and you're going to follow me real easylike." Tucker's name was written on the license as Marvin T. Watts, in the military fashion. "Then we'll see whether you own this car. And by the way, I clocked you doing fifty-five in a thirty-five-mile-an-hour zone."

"Horseshit".

"You mouth off to me one more time, and I'll blow a hole in you, you hear me? Now you get in that pretty new car and follow me, and don't you even think about going anywhere else." The fat young man hitched up his pants and walked to his car. Tucker got into his car and followed him to the police station.

There were two other police cars parked in front of the station, and when the policeman and Tucker entered the building, there were three other officers in the main room. One was talking on the telephone, his feet up on a desk, picking his teeth; the other two were running around the room shooting at each other with water pistols.

"Whacha got, Tub?" the one on the telephone called out.

"Speeding, resisting arrest, Bobby. Maybe a stolen car."

Bobby turned back to the phone. "Listen, honey, I gotta go book a colored gentleman on a number of charges. I'll be by there around noontime. You keep your motor running, hear?" He hung up, got to his feet, stretched and yawned, ambled over to the counter that separated the waiting area from the squad room, and dug a form out of a drawer. He tugged a ballpoint from his uniform shirt and looked at Tucker, bored. "Awright, high roller, what's you name?"

Tub slid the license and registration across the counter. "His name's Marvin, Bobby. That's nice, ain't it? Marvin."

"My name is Tucker Watts," said Tucker, tossing his open wallet with his badge and ID card onto the counter. "But you can call me chief."

Hugh Holmes left the bank and headed for the police station with some trepidation. He had been putting off meeting with the members of the police force to tell them about their new chief, but time was growing short now. It was time to spread the word, and the police station was the place to start.

As he approached the building, he acquired a queasy feeling in his stomach. Tucker Watts's shiny new Oldsmobile was parked in front of the station, along with all three police cars. Holmes hurried through the entrance, but stopped in the entrance hallway when he heard Tucker's voice coming from the squad room. The new chief was not actually shouting—indeed, he was speaking at a quite normal volume—but there was an edge in his voice which made Holmes not want to interrupt him. Instead, he leaned against the wall and listened.

"I noticed in your records that you have all served in the armed forces at one time or another. Good, because you will all know what I mean when I say that this police force is a military organization and from this minute forward it is going to be run like one. Do you understand me?"

There was an affirmative mumble from several voices.

"Do you understand me?"

"Yes, sir!"

"That means military courtesy, military bearing, and, for the time being, military procedure. It is very clear to me that none of you knows the first goddamned thing about police procedure. We're going to change that, but for now military procedure will do. Just pretend that you're back in the army and that I am your commanding officer. If that doesn't work for you, pretend I'm God. Do you understand me?"

"Yes, sir!"

"Starting right now, nobody on this force has any rank at all. You're all patrolmen. There is no seniority. I'll decide, based on your performance, who will get promotion and responsibility. Which one of you is Strickland?"

"I am, sir."

"You were an orderly room clerk in the army, a buck sergeant, is that right?"

"Yessir."

"Then maybe you have, at one time or another, made out a duty roster?"

"Yessir."

"All right, I want you to make out a duty roster for the six men on this force. I want one man in the station to handle the phone and the radio, and I want two cars in motion at all times, is that clear?"

"Yessir."

"Until I come on full time duty, every man will work seven eight-hour shifts a week, with thirty minutes for lunch—no coffee breaks. Shifts will rotate—every man will pull both day and night duty. All leaves are canceled. Anybody who calls in sick had better be in the hospital. You got all that, Strickland?"

"Yessir."

"And make sure that information is communicated to the two officers not present, who I assume are home sleeping because they were on duty last night. If there's any deviation from those instructions, I'll have your ass, boy, and the ass of the deviator. I'm going to be floating in and out of here for the next couple of weeks, and around town, too. Don't any of you let me catch you in an unguarded moment. Is that understood?"

"Yes, sir!"

"Now, I'm going down to the hardware store and buy a bucket of paint, and I'm coming back down here at noon sharp. Strickland, you take the first station shift and schedule the others from there. When I get back I want to see that roster posted and this place looking like an army orderly room, and everybody else better be on the street."

Holmes heard footsteps crossing the squad room and Tucker's voice again, quieter.

"Now, you. Which one are you?"

"Murray, sir."

"Newton Murray?"

"Everybody calls me Tub, sir."

"Well, Newton, that nickname is soon going to be a thing of the past. What do you weigh?"

"About two-fifty, sir."

"You're a liar as well as a bad police officer, Newton. You weigh closer to three hundred. Well, Newton, I want you to see your doctor today and ask him for a diet and a prognosis on how much weight he thinks you can safely lose per week. You bring it to me here tomorrow, with a note from the doctor. I'll give you an exercise program at that time. We're going to make a new man of you, Newton."

"Yessir."

"And another thing, gid rid of that .357 magnum you're hauling around. The standard sidearm on this force is now a .38 service revolver with a four-and-a-half-inch barrel, and I don't want to see any pearl handles, either. You're lucky I didn't take that cannon away from you and feed it to you, Newton. That little patdown you gave me was no body search, and you never even knew about the .38 in my glove compartment. And when you bring a citizen in here on a speeding charge you better have something to back it up."

"Yessir."

Holmes winced. Had Tub Murray arrested Tucker Watts? Good God!

"Any questions?"

Silence. Holmes strolled into the squad room. "Good morning, Gentlemen. I see you've met your new chief. Officer Strickland, would you please telephone the *Messenger* office and ask Bob Blankenship if he could come over here with his camera right away? Thank you. Chief Watts, I've had the telephone connected at your new house." He handed Tucker a piece of paper. "Here's the number. Worth has accepted your offer on the place."

"I'm glad to hear it, Mr. Holmes. The wife is just delighted." He looked at the phone number and handed it to Strickland. "Memorize this, and see that everybody else does."

Holmes and Tucker chatted briefly; then Bob Blankenship arrived. He took a photograph of Holmes shaking hands with Tucker, with the patrolmen in the background. "Bob," said Holmes, "if you'd just run that in Thursday's paper I think that would communicate some additional information about our new chief. You might just mention, too, that Chief Watts paid his first visit to the police station today to meet his force, and that a good time was had by all."

8 EARLY on the morning of the fifteenth of November, Billy was awakened by a telephone call from the Associated Press in Atlanta, which was closely followed by calls from *Time, Newsweek,* the three Atlanta television stations, a Columbus station, the *Washington Post,* and the *Los Angeles Times.* After that he persuaded Patricia to take all the calls, except one from Hugh Holmes.

"Billy, all hell has broken loose," said the banker.

"I know, they've been calling me; too. I talked with three or four of them and then stopped taking calls. The story was in the *Constitution* this morning, I'm sure you've seen that, but it was the *New York Times* story that attracted all the attention, I suppose."

"I haven't talked with any of them, yet. What do you think I should do?"

Billy thought for a moment. "Mr. Holmes, I think the best thing to do would be to call the Associated Press in Atlanta and announce a press conference at, let's see . . . say, one o'clock. They'll get it on the wire right away. That'll give the TV people time to make the six o'clock news. I'd do it at the police station with you and Watts, and I'd make sure that all the patrolmen are out on duty. It's hard to say how they'd react having a microphone stuck in their faces and asked how they like their new chief."

"All right, but I want you there, too, Billy. I hope it goes well. The council members are going to be pretty nervous about this."

"I'll be there, and I think you ought to present this to the councilmen as an opportunity to get some favorable publicity for Delano. That's what it is, you know. I had no idea it would stir up as much interest as this, but now that it has, you should make the most of it. Tell you what, why don't you get the secretary of the chamber of commerce to put together some press kits—just a brown envelope with one of those brochures that Bob Blankenship printed up, and a map of the city. Hand them out to whoever shows up. Don't forget to call Blankenship. He can do a story for the *Messenger* about all the attention Delano is getting."

"Sounds like a good idea. Anything else?"

"Might be a good idea to instruct all of the patrolmen to politely decline to answer questions and to refer the press to you, just in case some reporter hunts one of them down."

"Right. Why don't we meet in the chief's office about 12:45."

"Fine." Billy hung up and turned to Patricia. "This thing has mushroomed into something a lot bigger than I ever expected."

"Is that good or bad?"

"We won't know until we see what sort of press this generates."

"Good luck."

At the police station Billy shook hands with Tucker. They had not met since Tucker had signed his contract.

"I hear you're getting settled in real well, Chief."

"Yes, sir, our furniture's all down, and we've done a little redecorating. The wife can't wait 'til spring to get a garden started."

"Have you met many people yet?"

"Mr. Holmes took me up and down Main Street this morning, and we met all the merchants. Lot of people on the street, too."

"The TV people are already at work," said Holmes. "One crew followed us the whole way and interviewed whoever they could get their hands on."

"I understand you had an unexpected introduction to your men."

Tucker smiled. "I guess you could put it that way."

"Any problems with them?"

"One or two haven't decided yet whether they can handle it, but most of them seem to be getting used to the idea."

"I saw Tub Murray in the drug store the other day. Looks like he's lost some weight."

"He'll be losing some more, I expect, if he stays with us."

Holmes looked at his watch. "Well, it's one o'clock. The squad room's full of folks. We'd better get out there."

Billy was delayed in town giving personal interviews at his law office, long enough to miss the six o'clock Atlanta news, but he got home in time for the NBC network report. He watched as Chet Huntley gazed into the camera and said, "There has been much turmoil in the South as old laws and customs have given way to the new and court orders have enforced integration of schools and public places. But one small southern town has taken an unexpected step, entirely of its own accord. Delano, Georgia, a town of about six thousand people just a few miles from Warm Springs, where Franklin Roosevelt vacationed and, finally, died, today hired a black chief of police."

Tucker's face filled the screen, filmed at the press conference, as Huntley's voice continued: "Tucker Watts, a Georgia native who recently retired from a thirty-year army career, became the first black chief of police in any town of the Old South. He seemed to think it was pretty routine."

"I've received a courteous welcome from the people of Delano that I've met, and I don't anticipate any special difficulties in doing my job here," said Tucker, in response to a reporter's question.

"City-council chairman, and one-time Roosevelt confidant, Hugh Holmes, said that Watts was by no means a last resort."

"Quite to the contrary," Holmes said to a reporter, "Mr. Watts was the most highly qualified candidate we could find for the job. We have a very high-quality community in Delano, and we want the best public servants we can attract, just as we want the best new industry we can attract."

Billy started as his own image filled the screen and Huntley talked on: "This all came about, apparently, because of this man, William H. Lee, the lieutenant governor of Georgia, a likely candidate for governor next year who has a reputation as a moderate and an active peacemaker in racial matters. Delano is his home town, and it was he who suggested that Watts be hired."

"Chief Watts came highly recommended and was obviously well qualified by his experience in the military police, and I was very pleased to recommend him to the city council," Billy heard himself say.

Then there were quick cuts to other faces, shot on Main Street, and their comments.

"I read in the paper that he has a lot of experience, so I guess it's all right."

"He has a fine war record, from what I hear, and he was an MP for a long time. I think we ought to be glad to have him."

"If he can do the job, who cares?"

Then Patrolman Bobby Patrick's face appeared. Someone had hunted down a cop, after all. His expression was sour. "I don't have nothing to say about that," he said, and drove away quickly in his patrol car, the camera catching his hurried departure.

Huntley came back onto the screen. "The White House Press Office issued a statement today commending the Delano City Council for its hiring of a black chief and hoping the town's action would serve as an example to other communities, both southern and northern, surely the first time the White House has ever taken note of the hiring of a small-town policeman. More news after this."

Billy turned to Patricia. "I don't-believe it," he said. "I just don't believe it. I spent the afternoon with a reporter from *Time*, and with John Howell, the fellow from the *New York Times* who was down here a couple of weeks ago. It was his story that kicked all this off, and he wants to do an article for the *New York Times Magazine*, to run after Tucker has had time to do the job for a while."

Patricia snuggled up to him on the couch. "All this should be a big help in the governor's race, shouldn't it."

"It seems that way, now, but all this favorable stuff is just going to harden the resistance of the people who are against me, anyway, and make them tougher to beat. I'd sure like to know how this is sitting with the undecided voters."

"It can't hurt with the White House, though, can it?"

Billy slumped into the leather cushions. "Not unless it goes sour in some way."

"In what way?"

"I'm not sure. But the whole situation, as good as it looks, makes me nervous."

9 TUCKER'S second morning on his new job was quieter. As soon as he had checked the roster and confirmed that all his men were at their assigned duties, he turned to the filing cabinets along the back wall of the squad room. He had planned to wait before going through the files, but he had an unreasonable urge to look through them for a piece of paper with his old name on it. He had no idea if Will Henry Lee had kept records of arrests, but he had to find out. If it existed, such a document would be the only written record anywhere that Willie Smith had ever lived, and for his own peace of mind he must destroy it. Patrolman Wendell Bartlett, known to all as Buddy, was doing his tour as radio operator.

"Chief, was there something special you were looking for?"

Buddy Bartlett was a fair-haired, sunny-faced man in his midtwenties, who looked younger. Of all the patrolmen, he alone had shown something most resembling a desire to be helpful to his new boss, and Tucker was grateful for it. Of necessity, though, Tucker felt he must keep some distance until he was sure of all his men.

"No, Bartlett, nothing special. I just want to see how they're set up."

Bartlett rose and crossed to the cabinets. "I'm afraid they're pretty much a mess. There was a fire here six or seven years ago, and stuff just got thrown out the windows, and a lot of it got wet. Whoever rescued it just threw it into the new filing cabinets any which way. The files after about 1950 were in colored folders, so they were easy to find and sort, but everything before that was in plain manila folders, and there it sits, right back to the beginning of the town, I guess. If we ever needed to find something specific we'd have a real hard time doing it."

Tucker grunted. "I guess we would at that."

"Everything from 1950 is cross-indexed by name and crime." Bartlett pulled open a file drawer to demonstrate. "On every arrest we fill out the form in duplicate and file one copy by last name and the other one by the charge. If there's more than one charge we file it under the most serious one."

"We really ought to have a copying machine so that we can file multiple charges," Tucker mused. There was a footstep in the entrance hallway, and he turned. A tall elderly, heavyset man in tan gabardines and a Stetson hat was standing at the counter. He took off his hat and ran his fingers through a thatch of snow-white hair.

"Morning, Buddy."

"Morning, Sheriff. I don't reckon you've met Chief Watts yet. Chief, this is Sheriff Willis."

Tucker would have recognized Skeeter Willis anywhere, in spite of his age. He was probably ten years older than he looked. "Nice to meet you, Sheriff," he said, sticking out his hand. "I would have gotten up to Greenville to see you sooner or later, I expect, but I'm glad you dropped by. Can we get you a cup of coffee?"

Skeeter shook the offered hand as briefly as possible. "No thanks, I've got business to tend to."

"What can we do for you?"

"I hear you got a fellow, Wilkes, in your jail."

Tucker looked at Bartlett. "Yessir," the young officer said. He went to a filing cabinet and retrieved a folder.

"I want him on a liquor charge," said Skeeter. "I found a still on his land, the other side of Warm Springs."

Tucker took the folder from Bartlett and glanced quickly at the record. "He got ten days from city court for reckless driving and damage to city property. H 's only done six. Have you got a warrant with you?"

"Does that matter?" Skeeter was looking impatient.

"Well, if you can show the justice of the peace a warrant, he might reduce the sentence to time served. Then I can release him, and you can arrest him."

"Look, why don't you just turn him out here, and I'll take him off your hands. I don't want to have to make another trip down here to get him."

"Sheriff, I'd like to help you, but I can't release him without the JP's okay. That would be illegal. And if you took him without a warrant and got a conviction, he'd have a basis to overturn it on appeal—improper arrest. I think everybody'd be a lot better off if you got a warrant and then saw the JP."

Skeeter was now red in the face. He leaned forward and rested his palms on the counter. "Now, listen, boy, I don't care how long you was a MP, you're doing business in *my* county now, and if you don't watch out how you talk to me you're gonna find out just what that means."

Tucker said nothing for a moment; then he spoke quietly, and his voice dropped to a dark rumble. "Sheriff Willis, you're welcome to a cup of coffee and a place to take the load off your feet. Any time. But if you want somebody in my jail, you're going to have to show me some paperwork. That's the way business gets done in *my* jurisdiction."

Skeeter's face turned a darker shade of red. He turned on his heel and walked out without a word.

"Whew!" whistled Bartlett. "I've never seen old Skeeter that mad before."

"He made an unreasonable demand. I couldn't accommodate him."

"I know it, Chief, but that man's been sheriff in this county longer than anybody can remember, and he's somebody you want to get along with.

"I'll meet him halfway."

"Well, sir, I hope you get the chance. You can believe me when I tell you that he's not gonna let that pass."

"I appreciate the advice, Buddy, I really do." Tucker was impressed by the boy's concern and found his statement easy to believe. Just to cover himself he telephoned the justice of the peace and casually informed him of Skeeter's request, his own refusal and his advice to the sheriff. Then, after thinking carefully for a moment, he called Billy Lee and explained the incident.

Billy heard him out, then said, "Buddy Bartlett is right, Tucker. You watch yourself. I think you were right to call me rather than Mr. Holmes about this. If you have any problem with Skeeter, you call me right away, whether I'm at a home or in Atlanta, hear?"

"I'll do that, Governor, and I appreciate your concern."

Foxy Funderburke didn't know what to do about the Kudzu. He had tried everything. Like many southerners, he had looked upon the broad-leafed, ivylike vine as an ideal, almost miraculous, ground cover. It had been imported from the Philippines in the twenties and touted as an agricultural cure-all. The state had planted it along roadsides to cover the bare red-clay banks where roads had been cut through, for both beautification and erosion control. The trouble with kudzu was that it didn't know where to stop. It climbed the banks and took over adjacent fields, choked out crops, and covered trees, utility poles, and eventually houses. It was said that the home of the Alabama man who had first brought the vine into the country had finally been eaten by kudzu. Poetic justice, Foxy thought.

Foxy had desperately needed ground cover on the clearing behind his house. He had hauled in topsoil, even gravel, and still the rain ran down the mountainside and took the soil with it. He had had nightmares about what might be uncovered there. So he had turned to kudzu, and now he regretted it bitterly. He had hacked away at the stuff for two years now, barely saving his garage, and although it looked dead in the wintertime, he knew it would resurrect itself in the spring and threaten the house. Foxy was nearly eighty now, and although he was remarkably healthy and strong, he was weary of his annual physical contest with the kudzu. Burning it out seemed the only answer. He poured the gasoline into a three-gallon insecticide spreader, slung the tank over his shoulder, walked up the incline, and began spraying.

Tucker took a quick turn up and down Main Street after lunch, noting the number of nonworking parking meters. He had already heard from a couple of merchants about the problem— people were parking in the same spot all day, some of them store employees, taking parking space from shoppers. He would have to move on that one quickly.

At the corner of Main and Broad he flagged down Tub Murray, patrolling in a squad car, and got in. "Show me the town, Newton," he said. They drove around for half an hour, and Tucker started to try and program some proper police procedure into the fat patrolman's work. As they stopped at the intersection of Fifth Street and Broad, a tan Cadillac passed, headed up the mountain. "Notice anything about that car?" Tucker asked.

Murray looked perplexed. "Well, he ain't speeding."

Tucker reached above the driver's sun visor and took down a Telex list of stolen cars, received that morning from the Georgia State Patrol. "Tan '62 Caddy, stolen in Atlanta yesterday. Hang a right, and let's look at him."

Murray turned up the mountain and accelerated.

"Easy, now, let's don't scare him just yet." Tucker peered at the car as they began to catch up and consulted the list. "Right color, wrong license plates. Well, he could have swapped with somebody along the way. Okay, Newton, let's see you handle this like I told you. I'll back you up."

Murray switched on the squad car's flashing lights and gave the siren switch a quick on and off. The driver's head jerked as he looked into the rearview mirror. He pulled over and Murray pulled in behind him. The patrolman got out and walked to the driver's window. Tucker got out and stood by the squad car, his hand near his pistol. He could hear Murray politely asking for the driver's license and registration. Some papers were passed through the window. Murray looked at them, comparing the description on the license with the driver, then walked to the rear of the car and checked the license number against the registration. He handed the papers back and walked back to the squad car. The Cadillac moved away and continued up the mountainside.

"College kid from Columbus, on the way home for the weekend. His daddy's car. He matched the license description and the plates matched the registration."

"That's just fine, Newton. Now you see how easy that was? Nobody got rousted, nobody got mad. Your blood pressure's okay, and the citizen is on his way, right?"

"Yessir." Murray was subdued, but seemed proud of his performance.

"What's that up there?" Tucker pointed up the mountain. Black smoke was boiling over the treetops. "Let's take a look."

Murray pointed the car up the mountain, and as they neared the crest of the pass they could see that the smoke was coming from the other side. "Looks like Foxy Funderburke's place," said Murray.

Tucker picked up the microphone and instructed Bartlett to call the fire department. "Step on it, Newton, we won't wait for them."

Murray gunned the car over the mountain, turning right into Foxy's private roadway. Tucker had never seen the Funderburke place, although he had heard about it as a boy, and he was impressed when the house with its neat flower beds came into view. "Looks like the fire's out back," he said. "Follow the road around there." They could hear dogs barking.

As they rounded the house they could see a blackened Foxy Funderburke beating at the flames with a burlap bag. A garden hose lay on the ground beside him, apparently abandoned in favor of the burlap. Foxy looked at them in surprise and relief.

"There's some more bags in the garage, there, grab some, quick!"

The fire was spread over a quarter of an acre of ground behind the house, and a couple of pine trees were already on fire. The two policemen jumped from the car; Murray ran for the garage, but Tucker went to the trunk of the car and found a fire extinguisher. He skirted the burning area quickly and directed the bottle at the trees while Murray beat at the flames near the kennels. Tucker was thinking they should probably let the dogs out, when he heard the fire truck's siren.

Twenty minutes later the fire was extinguished, but an oily pall of black smoke hung over the place. Foxy was grateful to the policemen and firemen, but seemed anxious for them to leave. Tucker immediately felt himself in the presence of a man with something to hide, a policeman's instinct developed over long experience. He looked about the place at the house, the garage, the kennels. It all seemed so perfectly normal, except for the burnt ground. What could an old man like Funderburke have to be so nervous about? His mind flashed back to a day in his childhood, a Saturday afternoon spent with Billy Lee at the livery stable, an image of a much younger Foxy in a dimly lit stall, watched from a hayloft by two boys.

Still, that was irrelevant. Maybe he was interpreting Foxy's concern with nearly losing his house as something completely different. As he and Murray drove down the mountain to the main highway, Tucker thought he might come back to the Funderburke place again, just for a chat. It just didn't feel right.

"They'll send him a bill," Murray said.

"What?"

"He's outside the city limits here. Outside Meriwether County, really. The Talbot County line is right at the city limits, at the top of the mountain. He's not entitled to fire service. They'll send him a bill."

10 BILLY SPENT most of his time before Christmas in Delano, seeing to his law practice. There would be little for him to do in Atlanta until the state legislature convened after the new year. In mid-December he was working in his office in the bank building, when there was a gentle knock on the door. Hugh Holmes stuck his head in. "Busy?"

"Not too. Come on in. Can I get you a cup of coffee?"

Holmes settled into a chair. "No thanks. I just wanted to touch base with you, find out what's happening."

"Well, in the month since Tucker Watts was appointed, I've had about thirty speaking invitations." He thumped a stack of correspondence on his desk.

"Where from?"

"Just about everywhere but Georgia."

"I'm not surprised. We've had a couple of strong nibbles on some new business for the town, too. An outfit from Pennsylvania that makes work clothes is thinking pretty seriously about us." He paused. "The Tucker Watts thing is going to help you nail down the black vote, but it remains to be seen what the white vote is going to do."

"To tell you the truth," Billy said, "I don't think it's going to cost us much there. Mullins has already got the hard-core anti-integration vote sewed up." State Senator Jackson Mullins would be his principal opponent in the Democratic primary the following September.

"That's certainly true. It's the middle ground that's going to swing things. If Mullins can scare some of those bad enough, or if he can make you look bad enough, you'll be in trouble."

Billy knew Holmes well enough to know that he had something specific in mind. He waited for the banker to go on.

"Skeeter Willis is a big Mullins man, you know," Holmes said.

"I know."

"I've had some indications that Skeeter and Mullins may be cooking up something."

"Something to do with Tucker?"

Holmes nodded. "You know about the run-in at the police station between Tucker and Skeeter."

"Tucker called me about it right away. I told him to let me know immediately if Skeeter gave him any problems."

"That's good, but I have an idea that when Skeeter moves, he's going for the home run. Remember the thing with Marshall Parker back in '46? When somebody put the moonshine in his place?"

"I sure do. Skeeter and Sonny were in that together, I reckon."

"Not much doubt about it. I think Skeeter might go that way again; what is it they call it at the picture show?"

"Framing."

"That's it. Skeeter'll try to frame him if he can."

"I'll have a talk with Tucker, tell him to be especially careful."

"He'd better be. Skeeter's already had somebody in the state police running background checks on him, his childhood in Columbus. I got a call." Holmes shifted in his seat. "Did you know that Tucker is Nellie Cole's nephew?"

Billy sat up. "Are you serious?"

"Tucker's mother was Jesse's sister. They think that after Jesse shot your daddy, when he and the boy, Willie, ran, that Willie might have gone to them. It seems logical. He was killed by that truck over in Alabama, and Columbus is on the way."

"Well, I'll be damned. He never mentioned a thing about it to me. I told him about Daddy on the way down here, when he came to meet with the city council."

"Course that's nothing against him. Even if Tucker's family

hid Willie, they're all dead now, and Tucker was only a couple of years older than Willie. That was nearly thirty-five years ago."

"I don't see how Skeeter can make anything of that, do you?"

"No, especially since Skeeter never even bothered to go down there looking for Willie."

"I guess nobody ever really looked for him. He was just an innocent bystander to the whole incident."

"Not entirely innocent. Technically, anyway, Willie had escaped from jail. Will Henry wouldn't have gone out there if he hadn't been looking for Willie."

"You know, it's just as well Willie's gone. We played together a lot as children, when Daddy was still farming. I didn't see much of him after we moved to town. I hate to think what could have happened to him if they'd caught him and laid some of that on him."

"Skeeter sure isn't the sort to have gone light on him, if he'd of caught him. Are you going to mention this to Tucker?"

Billy was quiet for a moment. "I don't think so. I'll just tell him to be extra careful with Skeeter. There's no point in embarrassing him. He wasn't under any real obligation to bring up a connection with something that happened so long ago. I can't say that I blame him."

Holmes got up. "Well, we'll leave it at that, then. I better go get some work done."

Billy sat for a while, thinking about Willie Cole. He hadn't thought about Willie for a long time.

Willie Cole sat a mile across town in his mother's living room. "Did they ask specifically about Willie Cole or Tucker Watts?" he asked.

"Both," Nellie said. "But they seemed to mostly want to know whether you might have hid out at Tuck's and Sarah's in Columbus. It was like they wanted to blame you for hiding . . . yourself. I told them I never heard another word from Willie after he ran, not 'til I heard he got killed over in Alabama."

"Well, now, listen; don't you worry about this. There's a birth certificate for Tucker Watts in the records down at the Muscogee County Courthouse, and I've got a thirty-year military record to back up that identity. No photographs and no fingerprints exist for Willie Cole. I'm four inches taller and a hundred pounds heavier than the last time anybody saw him.

They don't care anything about Willie Cole. Whoever's doing this just doesn't want Tucker Watts around. They might be trying to make Billy Lee look bad. I'll talk to him about it."

"Have you told Elizabeth yet?" The two women had met twice, the last time two weeks before.

"No. You're still Aunt Nellie, and I think it's best if we keep it that way." Tucker hadn't told Elizabeth, simply because he had no idea whatever how she might react. Her unpredictability had always both charmed and puzzled him.

He left the house and headed for the bank building.

Tucker looked steadily across the desk at Billy. "I'm sorry I didn't tell you about this at the beginning," he said. "It just didn't seem important."

"It wasn't important at the time. The important thing now is that you be very careful. I'll do what I can to keep Skeeter off your back."

"I can handle the sheriff."

"Don't be so sure about that, Tucker," Billy said. "Skeeter has a lot of clout in this county, and he's not a stupid man. He tried to nail Marshall Parker on a trumped-up charge once; he and Sonny Butts, I think, planted some white lightning in Marshall's place. If he wants to nail you badly enough he'll probably find a way. Unless he knows we're expecting it. I'll see that he knows."

Billy fumbled for a moment with a paperweight. "Did you know Willie Cole?"

"Our families visited a few times when we were kids."

"Did you see him after he left Delano? This is just between you and me."

"He came to our house one day while I was at school. Daddy sent him over to Alabama, down in the country someplace, to work on a farm with a sharecropping family. I never saw him. A couple of years later we heard he was dead. I had just joined the army down at Benning. I never even knew he had been to the house until then."

"I'm sorry things went so badly for Willie. We played together as children. Mama tried to help his folks when his daddy lost his job. Daddy did his best to help Willie when he got into trouble. It didn't turn out well for anybody, I guess."

Tucker was silent.

11 TUCKER went from Billy's office back to the police station, where he was startled to find Buddy Bartlett sitting on the floor, sorting files. He had not had a moment to go through the scrambled paperwork to look for Will Henry Lee's records, and he didn't want anyone to come across them before he did.

"What the hell are you doing, Sergeant?" He had promoted Bartlett and put him on permanent day shift at the station. The young man had a talent for organization, and things were running more smoothly now, with a responsible man always in the station. Tucker felt he could get out and around more.

"Oh, hi, Chief. I was having kind of a quiet day, and I thought I might get started on these records."

"You got the time for that sort of thing?"

"Well, like I said, it's been a quiet day. Anyway, they're not as mixed up as they could be. They're in chunks, sometimes three or four months together." He pointed to a bundle tied with string, set on the floor beside him. "This bunch here looks like several years' worth. All of it is Chief Lee's stuff—Billy Lee's daddy—from back in the twenties."

"You been through it?"

"Naw, it's all together. I'll just file it like it is, I reckon. We're not going to need anything that far back. You reckon we need it at all, Chief? Looks like we could have some sort of cut-off date—ten years, or something. Sure would give us a lot more filing space if we could store this old stuff over at city hall, or even throw it away."

Tucker picked up the bundle. "Not a bad idea. I'll have a look through this stuff and see if there's anything of any historical interest. He was the first chief, wasn't he?"

"That's right. My daddy remembers him real well. Says he was a good man."

"You carry on, then. Try to get two or three years of the most recent stuff—the time right before the fire—try to get that in some kind of shape, and I'll see about finding us some storage space at city hall for the rest."

Tucker went into his office and laid the bundle on his desk. He struggled out of his coat and hung it up. He sat down at the desk and untied the string on the files. His hands were trembling. He found what he was looking for almost immediately. On a plain sheet of paper with yellowed edges was written, "Arrested Willie Cole, age 15, on a charge brought by E. Routon, grocer, that Cole had stolen a ham and one sack of beans. Cole pled guilty in city court and was sentenced to 10 days, city jail. Assigned to city manager for street work." It was dated and signed.

That was it, the entire criminal career of one Willie Cole, now, through the grace of his uncle Tuck, deceased. Tucker was surprised that he had thought this piece of paper could ever have harmed him. He started to destroy it, then changed his mind, folded it carefully and buttoned it into his shirt pocket.

He sat composing himself for a minute or two, taking deep breaths until he could relax again. He felt foolishly relieved. He leaned forward in his chair again, rested an elbow on the desk, and began flipping idly through the files. It was mundane stuff—small theft, a wife beater, a stolen car. There was a brief but interesting account of a bank robbery early in January of 1920, apparently the new chief's first day on the job. Tucker chuckled. What a way to begin! And then he came to the photographs.

They were striking. His first thought was that they should be in a museum someplace. The youth and vulnerability of the boy, the starkness of the surroundings, the shock of his injuries—everything was accentuated by gorgeous lighting and the density of the prints. He thought they must surely be contact prints from one of those old-fashioned 8 x 10 bellows cameras. He read through the autopsy report and marveled at its expertness and clarity. He read the new chief's brief notes on his investigation, including an encounter with Foxy Funderburke, and the correspondence relating to the second murder—the young man found shot, hanging on a barbed-wire fence. It was obvious that Lee had thought the two murders related.

He read the whole thing twice, then came to a newer-looking folder. On the file tab were the words "Butts—Personal." That must be Sonny Butts, the one who disappeared. He wondered why it was filed with these records of twenty years earlier. As soon as he had leafed through the missing-persons bulletins he knew why.

Spread out in a row on the desk, next to the photographs of the corpse, the photographs of the missing youths had an eerie similarity. He noted that on each of the bulletins the names of towns had been underlined, and that an X had been drawn on the accompanying road map, forming a circle around Delano. He read Sonny's line of thought as though the man were sitting there explaining it to him. Two young men had been murdered in Delano or its environs and five others had disappeared in the same area over a period of what—twenty-five years? And now another sixteen years had passed.

"Bartlett, come here a minute," he called out. The policeman came to the door. "While you're sorting through those files, I want you to keep an eye out for old missing-persons sheets and pull them."

"Every single one of them?"

"Make that every report on a male missing person. And keep it to yourself, hear?"

In the late afternoon Tucker took a patrol car and slowly cruised the town, occasionally penciling a note on where a stop sign or a parking notice might be needed. He started with the "town" side of the city, then moved on to the "mill town," and finally to the major colored district, Braytown. The place was little different from when he was a boy; the streets were better graded now, though they were still unpaved; there were utility poles for electricity and telephone where there had been none; and though there was an occasional neatly painted and planted house, like his mother's, most were still ramshackle.

As he turned a corner into a side street, he spotted another patrol car parked in the barren front yard of one of the unpainted shacks. His first thought was that one of his officers might need backing up, but then he thought it more likely that somebody had a black girl friend in Braytown. He picked up the microphone. "Station, this is mobile one."

Bartlett's voice came back. "Chief, this is station."

"Who's patrolling in mobile two?"

"Patrick, Chief. He's due in right now. Any problem?"

"No problem. Over and out."

Tucker eased his car quietly in behind the other vehicle and got out. As he was about to climb the rickety front steps, he heard voices from the back of the house. He walked toward the back yard and stopped at the corner of the house, listening. He could hear Bobby Patrick's voice, angry, demanding, alternating with that of a frightened black man.

"You ain't paid, Roosevelt, and Mr. Cox wants his money." Cox, Tucker knew, ran a furniture and appliance business in town.

"I done paid him more'n what that stuff cost," complained the black voice, which was followed by the sound of flesh striking flesh.

"You ain't paid the carrying charges, Roosevelt. You got to pay the carrying charges. Now, are you going to get it up, or am I gonna have to hurt you?"

As Tucker stepped around the corner of the house he saw a black man cowering on the ground. Bobby Patrick, his back to Tucker, stood over him, unsnapping a leather blackjack from his pistol belt. A woman and three small children stood on the back porch, clutching at each other, terrified.

Tucker stepped into the back yard, grabbed Patrick by the shoulder strap of his Sam Brown belt and yanked hard. Patrick left his feet as he traveled backward, sprawling in the dirt and chicken droppings. "Officer Patrick, go and stand by your patrol car and wait for me."

The outraged policeman got to his feet, protesting.

"Shut up," Tucker commanded. "Just go and stand by your car. Don't say another word." Patrick turned and stumped off around the house. Tucker turned to the black man. "What's your name?"

"Roosevelt Hawkins."

"What did you buy from Cox?"

" 'Bout ninety dollars worth of stuff—a ironing board, some po'ch furniture. He send that poh-liceman around when I gets behind on my payments."

"Does Cox send the policeman around to see everybody who gets behind?"

"Yessuh."

"Just that policeman?"

"Just that Patrick. He the only one do it."

"Did you sign a contract with Cox?"

"Yessuh."

"Go and get it." The man went into the house and came back with a long piece of paper. Tucker skimmed through it. "How much have you already paid him?"

" 'Bout a hundred and thirty bucks."

"Don't pay him any more. This is unenforceable."

"But he might come after me."

"He won't come after you. I'll talk to him. Just forget the whole thing. Now, do you want to press charges against that policeman for beating on you?"

Hawkins shook his head hard. "No, *suh*! I don't needs that kind of trouble."

"If you want to press charges there won't be any trouble."

Hawkins shook his head again. "Nossuh, you just keep him off me, and I be happy."

"All right, I'll keep him off you, but I want you to do something for me. If you have any more of this kind of trouble, I want you to call me or come and see me. Will you do that?"

Hawkins looked at the ground. "Well—"

Tucker put his hand on the man's shoulder. "Now, listen to me, Roosevelt. If you'll trust me and let me know when things like this happen, I can do something about it. But I can't do anything if you don't tell me about it."

Hawkins nodded. "Awright."

"And tell everybody else that I want to hear from them. I'll see that they get treated fairly if they'll come to me."

"Awright, I tell 'em. And I sure 'preciate what you done."

Tucker left the back yard relieved. His reception among the local blacks had been cautious at best. He thought this incident might loosen them up a bit. He smiled; now the incident was going to solve another problem for him. Bobby Patrick had been resentful, insolent, and an all-around pain in the ass ever since

Tucker had taken the job, and now he was about to be rid of him.

Patrick was leaning against his patrol car, sulking. Tucker went and hiked himself up onto a fender next to the man. "Listen, I'm sorry about bringing you down back there, but I had to make it look good. You've bought yourself a real problem here; Roosevelt says he's going to press charges."

Patrick's head snapped around. "You going to let him do that to one of your own men?"

Tucker spread his palms. "What can I do, man? He's mad as hell, and he says he can get a lot of other people to testify who've had the same problem. He wants to see you in the county camp."

Patrick's eyes widened. "I can't go up there. Shit, I wouldn't last a week up there before somebody stuck a shiv in me. You know what it's like for a cop on the inside."

"I know, but what can I do? I saw the whole thing myself, and if I testify for you on the stand they'll get me for perjury. There were five witness there, man!"

Patrick was frightened now. "Listen, Chief, you can't let 'em do this to me. You gotta help me."

Tucker tried to look as if he were thinking hard. "Look, Bobby, I can't see but one way out of this, if we're going to keep you out of jail. You're going to have to resign. If you do that, maybe I can talk Roosevelt out of pressing charges." Patrick looked pained. "I know it's rough, man, but what else can you do? You could even end up in Reidsville on this one if enough other people testify." The mention of the state prison sent a shudder through the policeman. Tucker pressed. "They might even bring other charges. I don't think you want to let this get into court. They'd have some NAACP lawyer down here like a shot. You'd be lucky to get off with five to seven."

Patrick looked at Tucker pleadingly. "Listen, if I resign, will you get the bastard to back off? You promise me that?"

Tucker squeezed the man's shoulder. "I'll do everything I can, but we've got to move fast, before this spreads."

Patrick nodded. "Yeah, right."

"Tell you what. You go back to the station right now and get Bartlett to type up a letter for you. Say you're leaving for personal reasons, something like that; make it sound real sincere. Then tell Bartlett to put it in my safe, and you leave your badge with him and go straight home. I'll call you the minute I know something, okay?"

Patrick nodded. "Right, yeah, I'll do that." He grabbed Tucker's hand and wrung it. "And listen, Chief, I sure do thank you for squaring this for me. You won't regret it." He jumped into his patrol car and spun away in a cloud of dust.

Tucker stood in the road looking after him, chuckling to himself. "Oh, I sure won't regret it, Bobby, I sure won't."

Tucker stood in Elmer Cox's office and waited while Cox dug out Roosevelt Hawkins's contract. The merchant came back to his desk, nervously picked up a rubber stamp, and marked it "paid." He signed and dated it and handed it to Tucker. "Chief, I sure appreciate your handling this quietlike."

Tucker took the paper and folded it into a pocket. "I'm glad to be of help, Mr. Cox. But you're going to have to be real careful from now on."

"Right, right." The heavyset man mopped his brow with his sleeve. He was sweating profusely.

"Another incident like this one, and I won't be able to contain it."

"I understand, Chief, and I really do appreciate it." He reached into a pocket, came up with a sheaf of bills, and began to peel some off.

Tucker threw up a hand. "That's not necessary, sir, I'm just glad to have been able to help." The merchant saw him to the front door, thanking him all the way.

At the station Bartlett dug Patrick's letter of resignation out of the safe. It was full of gratitude and best wishes for the future. "What did you do to Bobby, Chief? I never saw him so worried."

"Oh, I just did him a little favor. Why don't you call him up and tell him I said everything is okay, not to worry about a thing. Tell him I talked to the businessman involved, and he's squared there, too." Tucker began to chuckle. "I'd talk to him myself, but I swear I don't think I could keep a straight face." He went into his office and closed the door.

Bartlett looked puzzled but did as he was told. He dialed the number. Through the closed door he could hear the chief laughing.

12 DURING THE DAYS of mid-December Billy Lee carried with him everywhere a feeling of unease about
the relationship between Skeeter Willis and Tucker
Watts. He had to do something about the sheriff. He thought of
going to Skeeter and warning him off, but the politician in him
shied from such a direct confrontation. Finally, he thought of a
better way.

John Howell, the *Times* Atlanta correspondent, called at his
office on a cold morning and invited him to lunch. "I just want
to chat and get some background for my *Sunday Magazine* piece,
which probably won't happen until the spring," Howell said.
"Where can we get a bite in Delano?"

Billy grinned. "How strong is your stomach?"

"Surely there's a barbecue place, or something?"

"Oh," said Billy, grabbing his coat, "I think we can find you
a more interesting lunch than that."

The two men drove north from Delano toward the center of
the county, Howell asking questions and making notes. Billy was
impressed with how well informed Howell was about his political career. He was surprised when Howell brought up the fact of
Tucker Watts's relationship to Jesse Cole, and thankful that he
was ready for it.

"It's the kind of coincidence which is interesting, but meaningless," he said, "the sort that some people might use to try to make life uncomfortable for Tucker or for me. Well, I'm in no way uncomfortable with it. Tucker told me about it himself, quite voluntarily. The boy, Willie, apparently came to the Watts home in Columbus and left without even spending the night. Tucker didn't even know he had been there until later, after Willie was dead."

"Then you don't mind if I print it?"

Billy grinned. "Would it matter if I did? Print it if you think it interesting. Have you got a camera?"

"I've got a Minox in my brief case. Why?"

"Well, you might want to get a shot or two of this place for the dining-out guide of the *Times*." Billy swung off the main road and onto a dirt one. Shortly they came to a gate with a guardhouse.

"We're having lunch in the county prison camp?" Howell gaped at the barracks beyond.

The guard looked at him nervously. "Yessir, Governor, can I help you?"

Billy never even fully stopped the car. "Just visiting," he called out, and laughed as he saw the guard dive for the telephone. "I like to drop in unexpectedly once in a while," he said to Howell. "It's a custom Hugh Holmes started a long time ago."

Billy headed straight for the mess hall, passing the warden's house on the way. As they drove by, that gentleman appeared at the door, a napkin tucked under his chin, scowling. "I see the captain isn't dining with his charges," Billy said. He parked in front of the mess hall and bounded up the rickety wooden steps, Howell at his heels.

They entered a surprisingly silent hall full of men, the only noise being the dull sound of metal spoons striking plastic trays. Billy grabbed the hand of the nearest guard, an astonished man, and pumped it. "Hey there, glad to see you." It might have been a campaign barbecue. He led Howell to the serving area and picked up a tray. At that moment the breathless warden rushed through the door.

"Good morning, Governor, my name's Hardy, I replaced Jenkins last month." He took Billy by the elbow and attempted to guide him toward the door. "I was just sitting down to some dinner. Why don't you come join me?"

"Tell you what, Captain," said Billy, thrusting a tray into the man's hands, "why don't we all join your men, here? Let me introduce Mr. John Howell of the *New York Times*." He kept up a running patter as he propelled the alarmed warden through the line and to a half-empty table. "Mr. Howell is the restaurant critic for his newspaper, and I was just telling him about how well our county prisoners eat. How's your food, Captain?"

The warden was looking glumly at the mess of dried butter beans and fatback before him. Howell was snapping pictures with his Minox as fast as possible.

"Tell us, Captain, what's your daily allowance per man for food?"

"Uh, two dollars and thirty cents a day, Governor."

"Well," said Billy, poking at his food with a spoon, "the boys must be having T-bone steak tonight, huh? This looks like about fifteen cents' worth to me."

"Well, uh, we missed a delivery this morning. This is just temporary." A prisoner down the table began a coughing fit.

"I sure hope so, Captain. I'd hate for the *New York Times* to think that our prisoners ate this way three times a day. Tell you what, just to give you a hand, why don't I arrange for somebody from the department of corrections to come down here the next day or two and help you do an inventory of the pantry and go over the books and the purchasing orders with you. Would that help you out?"

The warden was sweating now. "Well, sir, I think we can handle it. I was just going to have a talk with the sheriff about improving things. I've only been here a month, and—"

"Oh, yes, I expect you work pretty closely with the sheriff. You know, I wouldn't be a bit surprised if he didn't join us pretty soon. Ah, speak of the devil—"

Billy pointed across the room. Skeeter Willis was coming through the door. Billy stood up to greet him. Skeeter ignored his outstretched hand. "Godammit, Billy, if you want to go snooping around my camp you call me, and—"

"Sheriff, have you met Mr. John Howell of the *New York Times*?"

"*What?*"

"Mr. Howell wanted to have a look at a model camp, and I knew yours would be just the thing. Well, gentlemen, if you'll excuse us, we have to be on our way. No, don't get up, Captain," he put a hand on the man's shoulder and sat him down. "Finish your lunch by all means. I'll see that you get that help down here shortly."

Billy and Howell walked back to the car, followed closely by Skeeter. The sheriff pulled Billy to one side. "Now, look here, Billy, I don't appreciate this."

"Why, Skeeter, all I'm doing is just getting you some publicity. I thought you'd like that. In fact, Mr. Howell was talking about doing a long piece on county government. If you'd like I could steer him to you, let you give him a good look at your operation."

"Now, listen, Billy. There's no call for—"

"I was talking with a fellow in the Justice Department the other day who was expressing just the same kind of interest. Maybe you'd like to talk with him, too?"

Skeeter was nearly purple by now. "Dammit, Billy, you—"

"Tell you what, if you'd really like some attention down here I could speak directly to Bob Kennedy about it. He's taking a keen interest in southern law enforcement these days." Billy walked away from the fuming sheriff and got into the car with Howell. He rolled down the window. "I'd be more than happy to do anything I can in that direction, Skeeter. You just say the word, hear?" He rolled up the window, and, with a wave at the sheriff, drove out of the camp. "You get some nice shots?" he asked Howell.

"Oh, Jesus, that was the funniest thing I ever saw. Did you see the warden trying to eat that slop?"

"Didn't seem to like it much, did he?"

"Do you do this often?"

"Not often enough. Those guys really need watching. I'll get somebody down here in a few days, and it'll be all right for a while, but first chance they get—"

"Yeah, I guess they need a message sent pretty often."

"I think Skeeter got the message," Billy said as he turned back toward Delano.

13   TUCKER turned from Broad into Main Street and moved slowly down the block with the traffic. He caught sight of his new recruit, Gene Legg, fresh from the Marine Corps, walking among the Christmas shoppers. He thought the boy would work out well, after some training and experience.

"I'm a little surprised you didn't hire a black officer," said John Howell, who rode in the passenger seat. The reporter was, as part of his magazine piece, spending a working day with Tucker.

"That might come after a while," Tucker replied. "But I needed a man, and a qualified applicant presented himself, so I hired him. Next time I need a man, if a qualified black applicant turns up, I'll hire him." Tucker knew very well that the next man he hired would be black, even if he had to kidnap him from another police force.

"What do you think about the civil-rights movement, about the changes that are happening?"

"I think the changes are long overdue. As for the movement, it has my sympathy, but I don't regard myself as an active part of it, even though I'm the first black to hold a job formerly held only by white men." Tucker knew he would never have been considered for the job except for the civil-rights movement.

"What will you do if you're required, in the line of duty, to become involved? Locally, I mean."

"I'll do my job, I hope. I tend to divide what happens in the world by what is a police problem and what is not. If something happens in Delano that becomes a police problem, I'll involve myself to the extent necessary to achieve a satisfactory solution."

"You don't see a larger role for yourself, both as a policeman and a black man? You aren't willing to step over the line drawn by your duty in order to influence events?"

"That line is always very fuzzy for a policeman. A cop makes those decisions all the time. Should he make an arrest or just issue a warning? At what point does a domestic argument escalate from a family quarrel to a criminal act? When does a peaceful demonstration become a threat to the community? I hope I've developed a sense of judgment in those areas, and I hope it'll stand me in good stead in the future."

"Do you think your family relationship to Jesse Cole might cause problems for you in Delano?"

Tucker could not hide his surprise. "Did Billy Lee tell you about that?"

"No, I heard about it from . . . another source. I've discussed it with Billy, though, and it doesn't seem to bother him. There certainly seems to be no question of any involvement on your part in helping Willie escape."

Tucker shrugged. "I'm not aware that he was escaping from anything. He certainly had nothing to do with the governor's daddy's death. He just happened to be there, the way I heard it."

"He broke jail."

"Yes, I suppose he did, but you say, yourself, that there's no question of my being involved. He was just my cousin, and I didn't know he had broken jail until he was dead."

"To get back to my question, do you think the relationship will cause you any problems here?"

"Why should it? Are you going to print it?"

"Would you be uncomfortable if I did?"

"I don't know. It all happened so long ago, I don't see what it has to do with what's happening in Delano today."

"Just history, I suppose. Also, I get the impression that certain political opponents would like to find a way to use it to embarrass Governor Lee. It might be better if it were mentioned in passing in my piece than for it to come out under circumstances of those people's choosing."

"If you say so. I don't see how it can hurt him, anyway."

"You still have an aunt here in Delano. Jesse Cole's wife."

"Yes."

"Do you see her often?"

"She comes to Sunday dinner. She's my only living relative, and she and my wife get along well." Tucker felt a trickle of sweat run down the small of his back. "We don't have a lot of friends here. We're kind of neither one thing nor the other. It's nice for my wife to have her to talk to."

"In reading over the announcement of your appointment in the *Delano Messenger*, I noticed there was no mention of your aunt. Small-town newspapers normally bring that in . . . you know, Watts is the nephew of . . . etcetera, etcetera."

"I didn't write the announcement. I suppose they extracted their information from a résumé that covered my career in the army. My aunt isn't a part of my military career. The announcement didn't mention I was black, either, but then I guess that wasn't in the résumé."

Howell grinned and mused over his notes. Tucker fought the urge to change the subject; then Howell did it for him. "Tell me about this guy Sonny Butts, who used to be chief."

"You probably know as much about him as I do."

"He really just disappeared, did he?"

"Apparently so. And with the department's motorcycle."

"Strange."

"Yeah, it was." Tucker paused for a moment. Why not? This guy needed entertaining, and he liked this subject better than the one they had just been talking about. "Come on back to the station, and I'll show you something interesting—something to do with Butts."

As they were entering the station, they brushed past a drunk black man who was being booked in the squad room. Tucker directed Howell to his office and went to the bank of file cabinets. From behind him a voice came, questioningly.

"Willie?"

Tucker froze for just a moment, but prevented himself from turning. He flipped through the files rapidly.

"Willie!"

Tucker extracted a file from the cabinet and turned toward his office.

"Don't you know me?"

Tucker turned to Bartlett. "What's this?"

"This, Chief, is Walter Johnson, a regular customer."

"Willie, it's *Pieback*. You know me, boy." The man leaned drunkenly over the counter and stuck his hand out.

Tucker looked at him in disbelief. He had not laid eyes on Pieback Johnson since they had played at hitching rides in the railroad switching yard when they were, what—thirteen, fourteen? And Pieback, stone drunk, had made him as if it had been yesterday.

"Sorry, Johnson, wrong fellow. You better go take a nap." He joined Howell at the door of his office and ushered him in. Tucker was badly shaken. He busied himself pouring them both a cup of coffee and rattling on about Sonny Butts. Howell looked at him curiously, but said nothing.

"Sonny Butts," Tucker said, tossing the file on his desk, "was a real hell raiser. He or one of his officers shot a black prisoner in the jail while they were allegedly beating him up. There was a local movement against him, but he wasn't even indicted. Then he beat up a man out at the fairgrounds, and the city council voted to fire him because of that, on the same day that the grand jury met and failed to indict him for the killing. Before he heard the results of either meeting he left this station in a hurry on the police motorcycle, and nobody ever saw him again, dead or alive." Tucker sat down and sipped his coffee. "The theory was he thought he would be indicted, so he ran." Tucker took a sip of his coffee. "But it doesn't add up."

"Why not?" Howell asked.

"Because at the last minute, a new witness turned up at the grand jury hearing and cleared him. A witness he would have to have known about."

"So he knew he would be cleared?"

"I think so."

"Maybe he couldn't face being fired by the city council?"

"Maybe. I doubt it. I think he thought he could still save himself."

"Then why did he run?"

Tucker sat back and took another sip of his coffee. "John, this has to be between you and me."

"For how long?"

"Maybe always. Until I can make something of it. But if you

write about this before I say so, I'll never make anything of it."

"Okay, but you have to tell me everything."

"All right." he opened the file on his desk. "I don't think Sonny Butts ran."

Thirty minutes later the two men sat and stared at each other. "This is crazy, you know that, don't you?" Howell laughed.

"Maybe," said Tucker. "Do you have another explanation?" Tucker tapped the last of the missing-persons bulletins in Sonny's file. "Look at the date on this. The boy was last seen less than a week before Sonny disappeared. Considering the time it took to print and mail the bulletins, this might very well have arrived in the mail the morning Sonny vanished—the morning he hopped on his motorcycle and tore out of here."

"Did the disappearances continue after Sonny disappeared?"

"I've had a man going through the files of the years since to see if there are any missing persons that fit this mold."

"And?"

"It's taking him one hell of a long time. The files are all scrambled as a result of a fire here a few years back, and he can only work on it when he has nothing else to do, and that isn't often. So far, he's found nothing between 1946 and 1958; one since '58."

"So the pattern doesn't continue. At least, as far as you know. One doesn't make a pattern."

Tucker shook his head. "No, it doesn't. Something could turn up, though."

"Do you have a suspect?"

"You've seen everything I have. What do you think?"

"Is this guy Funderburke still alive?"

"Very much so."

"But how could he have gotten away with it for so long?"

"He's been lucky. Chief Lee apparently suspected him, but he was killed. There was no reason for him to ever have mentioned his suspicions to anybody else, until Sonny caught on."

"And then when Sonny caught on, Funderburke took him out?"

"You said that, I didn't. At the moment, that's libel, and don't you forget it."

"Right. So what's your next step?"

Tucker leaned back in his chair and grinned. "Ol' Foxy doesn't like colored folks much. Why don't we see how he likes newspaper reporters?"

Tucker walked Howell to his car and gave him directions to Foxy's place.

"What's my excuse for going to see him?" Howell asked.

"You've got a choice of two subject matters: guns or dogs. He's apparently got a big weapons collection, and he raises Labrador retrievers. Take your pick."

"What should I look for?"

"See if you can find a reason to walk around the back of the place. There's a burnt-out kudzu patch back there. If he lets you into the house . . . well, just look at everything you can, see what you can learn about the way he lives. And John—"

"Yeah?"

"Don't let him think for a moment that you just happened by there, that nobody knows where you are." Tucker grinned. "You're not at all unlike the boys in those missing-persons bulletins, you know. Older, but young looking."

"Gee, thanks a lot. That does a lot for my confidence." Howell stopped short, getting into the car. "That's why you want me to go up there, isn't it? You think he'll *like* me, don't you?"

Tucker laughed aloud. "Of course not, John. I'm just calling on your finely honed powers of observation, your reportorial instincts." He pushed the reporter into the car and closed the door after him. "Tell him one of my cops suggested you go see him."

Howell looked at him for a long moment, then started the car. "Right," he said, and put the car into gear.

Tucker watched the reporter drive away; then he walked back into the station, thinking, not about Foxy Funderburke, but about Pieback Johnson. As he entered the squad room Buddy Bartlett was hanging up the phone.

"Hey, Chief, did you hear our former colleague Bobby Patrick is going into politics?"

"What?" Tucker was only half listening.

"Yeah, Sheriff Stimson over in Talbot County, he's been sick for a long time, cancer I think. Well, he resigned, and they're holding a special election next month. Ol' Bobby's running. He just called."

"In Talbot County?"

"Yep, he lives in Woodland, that's over the line, so he's eligible. He figures with his sterling law-enforcement background he's a shoo-in."

"Well, God help Talbot County," Tucker said.

"Chief, you mind if I run out to the house for a few minutes? My TV's broken, and there's nobody to let the repairman in. Shouldn't take more than half an hour."

"Sure, Buddy, go ahead. I'll cover for you."

The policeman departed, and Tucker was left alone in the jail. He stood quietly in the squad room for a moment, thinking. Then he took the cell keys from Buddy Bartlett's desk and walked back to the lockup. Through the bars he could see Pieback on a cell cot and hear him snoring. He was the only prisoner in the jail. He unlocked the outer door and walked back to the cells. Still Pieback snored. He unlocked the cell door and stood next to the bunk. A stench of cheap wine and vomit rose from the sleeping derelict. It would take only a few seconds, Tucker thought. He would never know anything. He just wouldn't wake up. Pieback would be written off as an habitual drunkard in poor health who died in his sleep in a jail cell. Tucker picked up a pillow from the opposite bunk.

14 TUCKER was in the toilet when Buddy Bartlett returned from his errand, sitting on the closed john, his head between his knees, holding a wet paper towel to his face, trying not to be sick.

"Chief?"

The voice jolted him, made him sit upright, take hold of himself. "Yeah," he called back. "I'm in here." He stood up and looked at himself in the mirror. He saw a frightened man looking back at him. He walked quickly from the toilet to his office, calling over his shoulder, "All quiet; the phone didn't even ring." He closed the door behind him and sat down at his desk. Rummaging in a drawer, he found a dozen librium in a bottle and swallowed one quickly, without water. An army doctor had given them to him a year before, at a time when he had been working too hard and getting edgy. He sat back and waited for the tranquilizer to take effect. By the time John Howell returned, more than an hour after his departure, Tucker felt better, more in control.

Howell knocked and stuck his head in. "I've brought a witness." He pushed the door open and held up a puppy. "Isn't she terrific?"

Tucker laughed. "I didn't send you out there to fall in love."

"Well, I guess I did. I picked dogs over guns as my reason for calling, and I got carried away."

"All right, tell me from the beginning, and don't leave anything out."

Howell settled in a chair. "The first thing I noticed was the neatness, the symmetry, just like the doctor said it would be in his report. As I drove up to the house, the flower beds, the shrubs, everything was laid out symmetrically. The house, too, the windows and shutters. I stopped at the corner of the house and started to go to the front door, when he came around from the back and asked me what the hell I wanted."

"In those words?"

"No, but in that tone. I said that Bartlett had told me he raised Labs, and I was interested in them. He asked me my name again—I'd already told him once—and seemed to be making an effort to remember it; then he softened a bit and took me around to the back, where the kennels are."

"You got a good look at the back of the place then."

"Yeah, but I didn't see much of anything. There's a garage and the kennels and the burnt patch, like you said. He told me about the kudzu; he didn't get it all, apparently, in spite of the fire, and he's worried about it coming back next spring. He showed me the dogs, and that's when I got hooked on the puppy. I wasn't expecting puppies, somehow."

"What was his attitude by this time?"

"Softer, like I said, but still . . . wary, I guess. I wanted to get into the house, but I felt a little shaky using the guns as an excuse—I don't know anything about guns—so I just commented on how attractive the place was, said I'd never seen a log cabin before. He said that he'd built most of it himself, so I jumped in and asked if he'd mind if I had a look inside. He said okay, but probably because he couldn't think of an excuse fast enough; so we went inside.

"What's it like? I've never been inside."

"Living room, bedroom, a bath, kitchen. That's it. Rooms are good sized, though. Everything neat as a pin. Not homey, though; almost sterile. Guns all over one wall in the living room. He was just starting to warm up a little, talking about this gun and that, when I mentioned that a guy I once worked on a paper with was a collector, and he brought me up short and asked me if I worked for a newspaper."

"Why would that bother him?"

"I don't know, but he switched off like a light bulb. Couldn't get me out of there fast enough. I don't guess I was there for more than twenty minutes."

"So what do you think?"

Howell shook his head. "Well, Tucker, this is real thin, what you're going on here. I tell you, I *wish* he was the guy; he's perfect casting—the eccentric recluse and all that—it'd make a great story, maybe even a book—but I saw nothing, *nothing* that would make the guy for a string of disappearances, including a motorcycle cop. I don't see how you could even get a search warrant."

"I didn't expect you to find a body on the living room couch, you know. I just wanted your impression. He won't even talk to me, because I'm the wrong color. You're right about the warrant, though. His place is outside the city limits and just over the line in Talbot County, so he isn't even in my jurisdiction. But the thing fascinates me."

"I can see how it would. God knows the atmosphere out there is eerie—it's so neat—that's almost scary by itself. Something else, a feeling I got when I was in the kitchen."

"What kind of feeling?"

"It reminded me of something—I couldn't get it at first, I thought maybe of a hospital—but then I remembered. It was the floor. It's an unusual kitchen floor—glazed tile, and it slants into a drain in the middle of the kitchen, under the table."

"Yeah?"

Howell leaned forward, absently stroking the puppy. "It reminds me of the floor in the morgue in Atlanta, in the room where they do the autopsies. The sort of floor that you can hose down, and it drains by itself. I've never seen a kitchen like that."

Tucker gave an involuntary shudder. "Neither has anybody else," he said.

When Howell had left for Atlanta with his puppy, Tucker sat quietly in his office for a while, thinking. He felt better now, with the Librium calming him. He got up and switched off the lights. As he passed through the squad room, Bartlett was returning from the lockup, tossing keys on his desk, shaking his head.

"Something wrong?" Tucker asked.

"It's ol' Pieback," the policeman said. "I'm sure glad I won't be on tonight when he wakes up. He'll have the DTs, for sure."

"Does that happen often?"

"If he's been on a big enough binge. You saw him this afternoon. He thought he knew you. I tell you, that guy's brain must be pickled by now."

"Is he okay in there, do you think? Does he need a doctor or anything?"

"No, he's snoring like a sawmill, mumbling in his sleep. I'd hate to be in the next cell."

Tucker got into his coat. "I'm calling it a day, I think."

"Right, Chief. See you in the morning. Merry Christmas."

"Merry Christmas," Tucker replied. He walked slowly into the chill dusk and got into his car. He felt reborn in some odd way. He had gone right to the brink and pulled back. But now there was something else he knew he had to do, something he had put off too long, something he had hoped he would never have to do.

She sat at the kitchen table, her coffee gone cold, and stared at him. He could not avoid her gaze.

"So," she said, "what am I supposed to call you now? Willie? Am I Mrs. Cole now?"

"I'm Tucker Watts," he said. "You're Mrs. Tucker Watts. Willie Cole is dead. He was hit by a truck in Alabama in 1932. Nobody even knows where he's buried."

She continued to stare at him.

"I'm the same man you married; the same man I've been since I joined the army."

"I know that," she said finally. "And I love you."

"I love you, too. Nothing's changed. We're the same people. Mama is still Aunt Nellie. It will always be that way."

She cocked her head to one side. "Why did you decide to tell me now, after all these years?"

"Because this afternoon I nearly did something stupid, and it was because you didn't know. Now you know, and I won't ever again have to do anything to hide it from you." He caught a whiff of roast cooking. "I'm hungry," he said.

"Then let's eat, Tucker Watts."

15 TUCKER lived more easily with himself, now that Elizabeth knew everything. Pieback Johnson was an old drunk, anyway, and nobody would pay any attention to him. He lived less easily, though, with his thoughts of Foxy Funderburke. Having no sufficient grounds to visit Foxy's place and search it, he tried another tack—an old police method.

He began to question, almost idly, the people with whom Foxy did business. He spoke to the man who sold him gas for his truck; to the owner of the feed store who sold him dry food for his dogs; to the clerk at McKibbon's who sold him hardware. He learned little, for these people knew little to tell, but eventually Foxy would learn that Tucker was asking questions about him, and it would make him nervous. If Tucker could not find a way to get at Foxy, then he wanted him nervous. Nervous men make mistakes, and although he had no idea what sort of mistake Foxy might make, Tucker was willing to wait to find out.

Then, as he was sitting in his parked car on Main Street one morning in mid-March, someone tapped on the opposite window. Hugh Holmes opened the door. "Morning, Tucker, mind if I sit for a spell?"

"Not at all, Mr. Holmes. I was just making some notes to myself for later in the day."

Holmes settled himself in the passenger seat. "I haven't seen a lot of you lately myself, and I wanted to tell you what a fine impression you seem to be making on the community. The traffic situation on Main Street has improved a hundred percent, and everybody's real pleased about it." Tucker had submitted a proposal to the city council to make Main one-way and to repair all the broken parking meters.

"I'm glad to hear it, sir." Tucker was glad, but he had a feeling Hugh Holmes had something else on his mind.

"The merchants were real glad to see those burglars caught, too. They were losing a lot of merchandise."

"I was glad, myself," Tucker answered, and waited. He was surprised at what came.

"I'm concerned, though, at some things I've been hearing."

"Oh?"

"It's my understanding that you've been conducting some sort of investigation of Foxy Funderburke. Is that the case?"

"I wouldn't call it an investigation. I've just been finding out what I can about him. He's a peculiar fellow."

"You have something in mind? Do you suspect him of something?"

"I don't have any hard evidence that he's done anything wrong."

"But you suspect him of something, is that right?"

"Well—"

"I don't mean to pry into police business, really I don't. There's no need to explain to me what you have in mind."

"I appreciate that, sir."

Holmes gazed off into the middle distance. "Tucker, I know that Delano is a new sort of experience for you, a small town and all."

"Yes, sir, I suppose it is."

"Well, small towns, although they can be rigid in many ways, are tolerant of eccentrics. We've got our share of homosexuals in Delano, I expect, but people leave 'em alone. There are retarded people and crazy people, and people that are just plain hard to get along with, but we make allowances. Now, Foxy, he's been a thorn in the town's flesh for a long time. He's irritated people— me, among them—he's insulted people, and he's behaved oddly, but for the most part he collects his guns and raises his dogs and minds his own business. Oddly enough, considering the sort of person he is, he has some friends in this area, and some of them have been speaking to me."

"I see."

"Don't misunderstand me. If Foxy comes into Delano and runs a stop sign or something, he ought to be ticketed like everybody else. If he sticks up the Bank of Delano, he ought to be sent to prison. You say you have nothing concrete on him."

"No, sir, I don't."

"Well, you've got to remember that, although he does a lot of business in Delano—and that business is appreciated, for Foxy's not a poor man—he lives outside the city limits and in Talbot County. Now, a few weeks ago, for better or for worse, the people of Talbot County elected Bobby Patrick sheriff over there. If you believe Foxy's done something, you have an obligation to take whatever evidence you have to Bobby, hard as that may be for you, and let him pursue it. Foxy's his responsibility, wouldn't you agree?"

Tucker nodded wearily. "Yes, sir, I'd have to agree with that."

"I think you're aware, too, Tucker, that Billy Lee is announcing for governor tomorrow, at the close of the legislature, and that the fact of your presence in Delano is politically a sensitive matter for him."

"Yes, sir, I understand that."

"Now, Billy seems to have got Skeeter Willis off your back—although I wouldn't be a hundred percent confident of that—but if word gets around that you're harassing an innocent citizen—and an eccentric citizen, at that—well, it could get to be an issue around here, and there are people just waiting for you to trip up, so they can embarrass Billy with it."

"I see your point, Mr. Holmes."

"Again, Tucker, if you get something on Foxy, by all means, do something abut it, but go through channels. If you want to make some kind of move yourself, you just be sure you go through channels, first." The two men shook hands, and Holmes got out of the car. "Keep up the good work, Tucker. I'm proud of you." Holmes strolled away toward the bank.

Tucker sat and stared at a display in the drugstore window in front of the car. Holmes was right, of course, and pretty polite about it, too. He was lucky not to get chewed up one side and down the other. He drove slowly back to the station.

In the squad room he asked Bartlett, "What part of those files you reckon you've got through? Back to what year?"

"I'm not doing 'em by year. I've got some of every year done. If I tried to do 'em chronologically it would take me another couple of years, I reckon."

"How much longer will it take you the way you're going?"

Bartlett stared at the filing cabinets and shook his head. "I guess I must be about sixty percent through them. Say, another six months, unless you want me to drop everything and concentrate on that. We'd have to pull another man off the street and back in here, so I could concentrate on it."

Tucker knew they were spread thin enough as it was. He shook his head. "No, we can't do that. Just do the best you can on them. And bring me the missing-persons stuff as you come across it."

"Right."

Tucker went into his office and sat down, cursing himself for his pride. He missed all the attention he had received when he had first taken the job, that was it. He'd had a taste of being a star, and he wanted it again. That was stupid. He was a retired army officer in a petty civil-service job, and if he wanted to keep the top of his head on he'd better get back to traffic patterns and Saturday-night cuttings. That was the job he was here for and that, by God, was the job he would do. He opened his notebook, determined to put Foxy Funderburke out of his mind.

16 THROUGH THE SPRING and summer of 1963, Billy
campaigned a steady five days a week, always spending the weekend at home, partly because he wanted to
be at home and partly because that prevented him from accepting
invitations to preach Sunday-morning sermons at churches
around the state. The thought repelled him, and he rejected
many such invitations, always on the grounds that he would be
at home, attending his own church.

Billy worked the state relentlessly, south and north, urban
and rural. He shook hands until his own was red and sore, and
ate barbecue until bicarbonate was a steady part of his diet. Patricia occasionally joined him, if the event was likely to attract
television coverage, but for the most part she stayed home and
farmed, as she had always done. "If someday you should get to
be president," she told him, "you may have to buy me a farm in
Virginia."

His chief opponent, Jackson Mullins, fought a campaign rid-
dled with code words—"states' rights," "preservation of our
southern traditions," "freedom of social choice," and the like—
while piously declining support from the Klan and other extre-
mist groups. Billy used code words of his own, with references
to "all the people" and such, while avoiding an out-and-out plea
for racial justice. It struck him that he might be running in the

last campaign in which a moderate candidate would have to shroud his appeal to people's best instincts in code words. He hoped so; and once elected, he could speak more forthrightly, a Georgia governor being constitutionally barred from succeeding himself.

On September 3 the Democratic primary was held, and the candidates and their supporters settled into their respective headquarters to drink bourbon whiskey and wait for the results, Billy at a suite in Atlanta's Henry Grady Hotel and Mullins at the Dinkler, down the street. After an evening of still more hand-shaking and confident statements to the press, he gathered in a bedroom with Patricia, Will, Hugh Holmes, and John Howell, who had become, by this time, a friend of the family.

Billy eased himself painfully onto one of the beds and stretched out. "Well, Mr. Holmes, what do you predict?" He had avoided asking the banker until now.

"Well," said Holmes, sprawling his long frame over an armchair, "I think we just might avoid a runoff."

Billy grunted. "By winning a majority or by losing it?"

"That's as far as I'd like to go," said Holmes, and took a tiny sip of his bourbon.

"You think you've got a runoff left in you, Billy?" asked John Howell.

"Jesus, I don't know. I'll tell you the truth, if I won and had to start being governor tomorrow, I'd begin my term with a month's vacation."

"I take it you're not worried about the Republicans?"

Hugh Holmes laughed. "One of the real rewards of being a southerner is you don't have to worry about the Republicans. If Jack Kennedy can take Georgia against Dick Nixon, as he did, then we won't have to worry about Republicans—not for a while, anyway."

"What percentage do you think a Republican could take against Billy in the general election?" asked Howell. "Assuming he wins the primary."

"Twenty percent, tops," said Holmes. "The die-hard segregationists, meaning Mullins's supporters, will stay home before they'll vote for a Republican. There'll be a real low turnout, but Billy'll take eighty percent or better."

"I hope I have the opportunity," Billy chimed in. "I go from feeling absolutely confident to being scared to death. What scares

me is what this state will go through for the next four years if
Mullins wins. We'll have federal marshals and troops in here like
it was Mississippi."

"I wonder what the exact effect of Tucker Watts was on this
campaign," mused Howell.

"My guess," said Holmes, "is that we'd have gotten the black
vote, anyway, because they had no place else to go, but what I
hope is that it will have the effect of turning them out in larger
numbers. I'm encouraged by the registration drives they put
on."

Returns began to trickle, then to pour, in, first from Atlanta
and the cities, then from south Georgia and the rural areas. At
eleven o'clock Billy was leading by ten percentage points; at half
past midnight, by two; and at one o'clock, by slightly more than
a point.

Holmes finished looking at some figures. "That's it, I reckon.
We've got it, and you'd better be glad there's no more county
unit system, or the rural counties would have made Mullins a big
unit-vote winner."

"I can't believe it," said Patricia wearily. "I can never believe
it when it's finally over, even when we've won." The television
reporters were now, finally, giving the primary to Billy. The telephone rang. Billy picked it up and listened. He put his hand over
the receiver and said to John Howell. "Okay, reporter, here's
where you have to decide whether to keep your mouth shut or
leave the room." Howell hesitated, then made a zipping motion
across his lips.

"Good evening, Mr. President, or perhaps I should say good
morning." Everybody in the room snapped to alertness. "It's
kind of you to call at this late hour." Everybody stared at Billy,
as if by watching they could hear both sides of the conversation.
"Thank you, sir. It was close, but we seem to have it. The best
advice I can get is that the Republicans can't pull more than
twenty percent in the general election." Billy laughed at the response. "I agree. Thank you, and please give your family my
best, too. . . . What's that? Well, I don't think they have much to
worry about. . . . Thank you again, and good night." He hung
up the receiver.

"Well," said Patricia excitedly, "what did he say?"

"Oh, about what you'd expect him to. He sent his regards to
you, and then"—Billy cocked his head to one side—"he said, 'I

hear some of Lyndon's staff have already started packing.' "

"You're kidding," said Howell. "Jesus, did I promise to keep my mouth shut?"

"No, no . . . it wasn't like that. He was only kidding. Listen, John, just put that right out of your mind, okay? We can't have any of that kind of talk circulating."

But Howell was pointing at the television set, blinking silently from across the room. "It's Mullins," he said. "He's going to concede." Somebody turned up the volume in time for the ponderous bass tones of Jackson Mullins to fill the room.

"I'll bet you could stick your head out the window and hear him all the way from the Dinkler," Will said. He had been asleep for most of the evening.

"My friends," Mullins was saying, "we have fought a long and hard fight to preserve our way of life in the state of Georgia—"

"Yeah, yeah, Jack, now throw in the towel, and let's get it over with," said Howell.

"—and I want you to know that, as far as I am concerned, the battle is not over."

Billy sat up. "What the hell is he talking about?"

Across the room, Hugh Holmes removed his glasses and began massaging the bridge of his nose. "I knew it," muttered Holmes, almost to himself, "I knew it."

"Knew what?" asked Patricia.

"Shhh," said Billy.

Mullins continued. "I want the word to go out to every supporter, to every contributor, to every working man and woman who voted for me in this primary, that *I will continue*."

"What's happening?" asked Howell, bewildered.

"He's going to try to throw it to the house," said Holmes wearily. "I was afraid he might."

"I want each of you to know that on November fourth my name will be on the ballot as an independent candidate. This battle is far from lost, and with your continued help we can win it!" Mullins folded his notes and walked quickly from the podium. There was pandemonium at the Dinkler.

"What is he doing?" asked Howell, astonished. "He's lost! How can he throw it to the house?"

Holmes slumped in his chair. "In Georgia there is no runoff in the election for governor. A candidate has to win an absolute majority in the general election, or the house elects the governor, one week after the election."

"Are you telling me that—"

"I'm telling you that if the Republicans take twenty percent of the vote and Mullins can pull a fraction more than thirty percent, then Billy will not have an absolute majority in the general election, and one week after that the Georgia House of Representatives will meet and choose between the two leading candidates."

"Can he do that? Can he pull enough votes to throw it into the house?" Howell asked plaintively.

"In my judgment," said Holmes emphatically, "he can."

"Mr. Holmes," Billy said, "in your judgment where would we stand in the house?"

Holmes produced a notebook from a coat pocket and consulted it. "I went through a little theoretical roll call in my head this afternoon," the banker said. "I reckon that if the election were held today in the House we'd be between fifteen and twenty votes short."

There was a stunned silence in the room. Finally, Patricia broke it. "Do you mean that Billy has won the primary, but he'll lose the governorship?"

Holmes nodded. "If he didn't win an absolute majority in the general election, and if the house voted today."

Billy stood up and put on his coat. "Fortunately," he said, with an edge in his voice, "the general election hasn't taken place yet, and the house isn't voting tomorrow." He buttoned his collar and tightened his necktie. "Let's go talk to the press, and then, Trish, let's go home. I want to sleep at home tonight."

The phone rang, and Billy went back to answer it. He spoke briefly while the others stood at the door, then he hung up and joined them, laughing ruefully. "That was Bob Kennedy," he said. "He says Lyndon's people are unpacking."

17 WITH THE EXCEPTIONS of his frustration over the matter of Foxy Funderburke and his fears about Pieback Johnson, Tucker Watts led what he could only consider to be a charmed existence through the first eleven months of his tenure, up until early November. He had improved the personnel, equipment, and operations of the Delano Police Department and had established himself in the community as a reliable man. True, there was a residue of resentment among many people with regard to his color, but he felt he had, at least, reached some sort of truce with that element of the town; that in return for his doing a good job, they would leave him alone. He was wrong.

In looking back on the incident, he would be able to say honestly to himself that he had done the right, indeed the only think possible at each stage of its escalation. But it had still gone terribly wrong. Maybe his temper had been too much of a factor; maybe he had for a moment forgotten how to be a black man in a white world.

He had been home for lunch and was driving back to the station, when he saw the car. They passed each other in front of the school, and the car was doing at least fifty. Although the students were all in class, it particularly offended Tucker that someone would drive more than double the speed limit in a school zone.

He whipped the car into a U-turn and pulled over the offender just inside the city limits. As he walked toward the car, pulling out his ticket pad, the driver opened the door and got out. The man was elderly, but large and strong looking. Tucker thought he looked familiar but did not recognize him until he heard the man's voice.

"What the hell is this all about?" The voice instantly brought back a flood of memories: of chopping wood until his hands bled; of his mother doing laundry until after dark; of his father returning from work nearly hysterical, soaking wet, his face swollen with mosquito bites. It was the first time since his return to Delano that Tucker had laid eyes on Hoss Spence. He snapped back to the present. "May I see your driver's license, please?"

"You're gonna see this stick upside your head if you don't answer me." Spence was carrying a heavy hog cane. "What the hell is this all about?"

"I clocked you doing fifty-two miles an hour in a twenty-mile-an-hour zone—a school zone. That's what it's all about. Now show me your driver's licence." Tucker was prepared for a scene, but not for what came next. He had glanced down at his ticket pad to flip over a page when he saw a blur at the corner of his eye and felt a jarring blow across his left cheek and ear. The sound made his ear ring, and the force of the blow sent him reeling sideways. Suddenly occupied with regaining his balance, he failed to ward off the second blow, which caught him on the neck. When the cane swung the third time, he threw up an arm, and it caught him in the armpit. He was able to clamp down on the cane, get another hand on it, and wrench it from Spence's grasp. He flung it aside and occupied himself with deflecting the man's fists, which were now raining upon him. Finally, he was able to grab his assailant's wrist, spin him around, and trip him to the ground. He pinned Spence with a knee and got one wrist handcuffed, but had more of a struggle before he could cuff the other.

He yanked the old man to his feet, walked him on his toes to the patrol car, opened a rear door, and shoved him inside. He was not gentle, but he was not nearly as rough as he might justifiably have been, he thought. Throughout the scuffle Spence had kept up a stream of invective, most of it racial, and it did not end when he was in the car. Tucker walked back toward Spence's car, retrieved the cane, returned to the police car and picked up the microphone.

"Station, this is mobile one."

"Car one, this is station."

"I've just made an arrest for speeding and assaulting an officer. Send a car and two men out forty-one. Just inside the city limits on the right there'll be a blue, '61 Cadillac four-door. The keys are in it. Bring it back to the station. Roger?"

"Roger. You need any other assistance?"

"Negative, just pick up the car."

Spence continued to rave and mutter all the way to the police station. Tucker said nothing at all. He was trying to separate his childhood feelings about Spence from the current incident. By the time they reached the station, he was satisfied that he had done so.

Bartlett's face registered amazement when he saw Spence, but he managed to keep his mouth shut.

"Put this man in a cell," Tucker said sharply. "If he gives you any trouble, handcuff him to the bars. I'll make out the complaint."

Bartlett returned after a moment. "Jesus, Chief, do you know who that guy is?"

Tucker had spun a blank form into a typewriter and was rattling away on the machine. "I don't much care who he is."

"His name is Spence. They call him Hoss. He's a big-time farmer out near your place, peaches and cows and everything else. He's got a lot of political friends in the county."

"Yeah?" Tucker kept typing.

"Uh, Chief, I let him use the pay phone in the back. He's entitled to a call. I hope that was okay."

"Sure. The man has his rights. I want him to get all his rights before I see him in the county camp."

Bartlett tiptoed away and came back with some ice from the soft-drink cooler. "You'd better put some of this on your face. It's swelling up pretty good."

Tucker ripped the paper out of the machine and took the ice. He had a thought. He went to a cupboard and took out a Polaroid camera which they sometimes used for photographing traffic accidents. "Here," he said, thrusting it at Bartlett. "Take a picture of me." Bartlett obeyed. "If he's got as many friends as you say he has, this might come in handy," Tucker said, watching the image slowly appear on the paper. The phone rang, and Bartlett answered it. He handed it to Tucker.

"This is Chief Watts."

"Tucker, this is Hugh Holmes. I hear you've got Hoss Spence down there. What's the charge?"

"Fifty-two miles an hour in a school zone, resisting arrest, assaulting an officer."

"Did he pull a gun on you?"

"It was a heavy cane, one of those things they use to move pigs with. He could have killed me with the thing."

"Did you provoke him?"

"I asked him for his driver's license."

"That's all?"

"That's all I had a chance to say to him. Then he hit me with the cane."

"All right, Tucker, I'm going to stay out of this. We've got a general election day after tomorrow, and I'm up to my ears in it. Let me give you some advice, though, even though it may be gratuitous."

"I'd be happy to have any advice you'd care to give me, sir." Tucker was cooling off a bit now.

"Be absolutely correct in your procedure with this thing. Were there any witnesses?"

"No, sir."

"That's a pity."

"I've got a real nice photograph of my injuries, though."

"Good. Now, Hoss's lawyer in Greenville has already seen the judge, and you're likely to get a call pretty soon. If I were you, I'd take the call as sufficient to release him. Don't demand a written order. It'll just make things more difficult."

"I understand, sir."

"All right, then. Call me if it gets too sticky, hear?"

"Yes, sir, I will." He hung up. There was the scuffle of feet in the entrance to the squad room.

"I hear you got my daddy in here."

Tucker turned and saw Emmett Spence, not for the first time in recent months. They often passed each other on the highway, being neighbors. Emmett had never so much as acknowledged his presence. "Who are you?" asked Tucker.

"I'm Emmett Spence, godammit, and you've got my daddy in here!"

"Yes, I have got your daddy in here, Mr. Spence. If you want him out, call a lawyer. And watch your language in here."

"I already called a lawyer, you better believe it!"

The telephone rang. Tucker answered it himself.

"Chief, this is Judge Hill in Greenville. I believe you have a Mr. Spence there on a traffic offense?"

"Yes, sir, Judge, for speeding, resisting arrest, and assault."

"Chief, I'm issuing an order releasing Mr. Spence on his own recognizance. I'd take it as a personal favor if you'd go ahead and release him now. I'll see that the order is in today's mail." The judge sounded embarrassed.

"Of course, Your Honor. I'm glad to accommodate you."

"Uh, Chief Watts, I understand there was an altercation of some sort. I think it would be in the best interests of everybody concerned if we could settle this out of court."

"Your Honor, I'd like to be of help, but the man struck me repeatedly with a heavy cane and without provocation. I could have made the charge assault with a deadly weapon."

"Chief, Mr. Spence is an old man, seventy-four, I believe. I hope that in consideration of his age and his standing in the community that we can avoid any further unpleasantness."

"No, sir, I'm afraid I can't do that." It was time for the son of a bitch to pay the piper. "He can plead guilty as charged, if he likes, and of course, the sentence would be up to you."

"Chief, I'm sorry you feel that way. If you'd go ahead and release Mr. Spence, I expect we'll talk about this again."

Tucker hung up. "All right, Bartlett, turn him out."

Spence came into the squad room rubbing his wrists and muttering. "Gimme my cane back," he said to Tucker.

"No, sir, I'm afraid that's evidence. Now, may I see your driver's license, please."

Emmett Spence stepped forward. "Ain't you learned nothing, boy?"

Tucker turned to Emmett. He remembered what a stupid, senselessly cruel child he had been. "I don't believe I said anything to you." He turned back to Hoss Spence. "Mr. Spence, you're going to have to give me your license right now or go back in the cell."

Spence reclutantly produced the license, and Tucker wrote him a traffic ticket. "I would strongly suggest, sir, that in the future you be particularly careful of the way you drive." Spence snatched back the license and the ticket and stalked out of the station.

Emmett lingered for a moment. "Hey, he clipped you a good

one, there didn't he? Well, he ain't through yet, I can tell you
that."

"Emmett!" his father yelled from the door. "Get your ass out
here!"

"Uh, Chief," said Bartlett, anxious to change the subject, "I
came across this while you were at lunch." He handed Tucker a
water-stained manila folder. "I think it might be what you were
looking for."

Tucker opened the folder and quickly leafed through the contents. There were at least two dozen missing-persons bulletins.

"Some of 'em are women," Bartlett said. "You only wanted
males, but they were all in there together."

Tucker started for his office, looking through the bulletins.

"And, Chief?" Bartlett held out a single bulletin. "This came
in the second mail."

Tucker looked at the sheet of paper. Fifteen; disappeared
from Clearwater, Florida, a week before. Suspected runaway.
Tucker walked quickly into his office and shut the door.

Quickly, excitedly, he flipped through the bulletin, weeding
out the females and older males. He then read each of the remaining bulletins, underlining the pertinent information on
where the person had last been seen and elminating those last
seen too far away or seemingly on a route which would not lead
through Delano. He was left with eleven sheets of paper stacked
before him. He faces in the photographs might have been in the
same school class or on the same baseball team. Or, more likely,
in the same drama or glee club. There was a softness about them.

The dates ranged from 1948 through 1960. Tucker turned to
the bulletin which had arrived that morning. That brought
things right up to the present. He took a deep breath and ex-
haled. Now he had enough for a search warrant. He gathered the
bulletins into one file folder, along with the papers of Will Henry
Lee and of Sonny Butts, stuck them in his brief case, and stood
up. He had business in Talbot County.

There were loud voices from the squad room. The door to his
office opened, and Skeeter Willis walked in, pointing a pistol at
him. "Just keep your hands on the desk, boy."

Tucker put his hands on the desk. "What's going on here,
Willis?"

"You're under arrest, that's what's going on here."

"For what?"

Skeeter tossed a paper on the desk. "That's a felony warrant for assault and battery." Skeeter clamped a cuff on one wrist and turned Tucker around roughly, cuffing the other hand. "Now, you just come along real quietlike, and you might not get hurt." Skeeter pushed him out of the office into the squad room. Bartlett was being held at gunpoint by a deputy.

"What's going on, Chief?" The young officer was wide-eyed.

"You know what to do, Bartlett, and for the record, I think there might be an accident on the way to Greenville, or maybe in the jail. You know what to do about that, too."

"Yessir."

"Shut up, both of you," Skeeter yelled. "And you're my witness, Buddy; he had that swollen face when I picked him up, right?"

"Yes, Sheriff, but I think you're making a mistake."

"You let me worry about that, boy." He shoved Tucker toward the door.

"Bartlett," Tucker called back to him, "there's a file—"

"I told you to shut up!" Skeeter shouted, and hurried him out of the building toward a waiting sheriff's car.

18 BILLY HUNG UP the phone. He was sitting in a back room of his Atlanta campaign headquarters, in an empty store building on Peachtree Street. In other parts of the building a dozen volunteers were telephoning voters in Fulton County, asking them to be sure and vote on the coming Tuesday. It was now Friday afternoon.

John Howell, who was sitting across the desk, asked, "What is it? Tucker?"

Billy nodded. "That was Holmes. Tucker is in the Greenville jail on a charge of assaulting a fellow named Spence, who's a big contributer to campaigns of people like Skeeter Willis. Apparently, Tucker stopped Spence for speeding, and there was a scuffle. Tucker arrested the man, and now he's brought charges against Tucker."

"Can he do that? Have a policeman arrested who has just arrested him?"

"Yes, he can. It's not a good system, but any citizen can swear out a warrant against anybody else and have him arrested."

"You can get him out, can't you?"

Billy nodded again. "Yes, but anything could happen to him while Skeeter's got him in that jail." Billy had an idea and explained it to Howell. "Will you do it?"

"Sure." Howell dialed the number. "Sheriff Willis, please."

He waited a moment. "Sheriff? This is John Howell, *New York Times*. I interviewed you a few weeks ago? Right. I understand you have the Delano chief of police in your jail. Is that correct? I see. . . . assaulted an old man . . . Spence, right. Is Mr. Spence a white man, Sheriff? . . . No, I just wondered. Tell me, Sheriff, is Chief Watts in good health at this moment? I mean, was he injured or anything when you arrested him? . . . Did he put up a struggle of any kind or resist in any way? . . . Could I speak to Chief Watts?" Howell covered the phone. "He's stalling. Says he's not sure if they've finished processing Tucker." He listened at the phone again. "I see. Could I speak to him when you've finished?" He shook his head at Billy. "Could I come down there and visit him? . . . Ten to two and two to four? . . . Tomorrow, then? . . . Right, Sheriff, thank you for the information." Howell hung up.

"Well?" Billy asked, anxious.

"Willis says Tucker is just fine. I can't visit him today, visiting hours would be over before I got down there. Tomorrow, he says."

"I've got to get him out of there before tomorrow." Billy said. He picked up the phone, consulted his address book, and dialed. "Hello, Frances? This is Billy Lee, how are you? . . . Just fine, thanks. Can I speak to Judge Hill, please? . . . Where? . . . How long ago? . . . Do you know the name of the people? . . . All right, Frances, thanks very much." He hung up. "Bert Hill, the superior court judge down there, has left for the day. He's on his way up to Lake Lanier to spend the weekend with some friends."

"Is he the only man who can release Tucker?"

"We could go for a federal order, but that would be overkill. Hill is the only person who can do it quickly." Billy had another idea. He consulted the address book again and dialed. "May I speak to Colonel Simpson, please? . . . Jim, this is Billy Lee, how are you? . . . Fine. Listen, Jim, I hate to trouble you, but I urgently need to contact Judge Bert Hill of Meriwether County, and he's on the road somewhere between Greenville and Gainesville, headed for Lake Lanier. I wonder if you could issue some sort of bulletin to your men on that route, ask them to stop him and ask him to call me? It really is urgent. . . . No, it's not state business, exactly, but it's connected with a law-enforcement problem that I can't go into right now. . . . That's great, Jim. . . . I think he drives a green Ford. I don't know the license number, but you

can get that from motor-vehicle registration, can't you? . . .
Thanks again, Jim." Billy gave him his telephone number and
hung up.

"Who was that?" asked Howell.

"Simpson, commander of the Georgia State Patrol. He's going
to put a radio call out to locate the judge. All we can do now is
wait."

Tucker lay on the hard cot, a single dirty army blanket
wrapped around him, and shivered. The cell's only window was
open, and it was too high for him to reach. When he opened his
eyes he could see his breath. Now and then something bit him.
He scratched at himself and swore.

They had taken his watch, but he reckoned it was nearly midnight. They had put him in what was obviously the worst cell in
the county jail. It was thoroughly dirty, and there was no toilet,
just a slop jar. They had taken his uniform and shoes, too, and
he was clad only in a dirty prison bathrobe. They had said that
they had no uniform large enough to fit him.

Tucker was frightened; he had expected someone to have him
released by now. He had told Bartlett months ago what to do. But
nobody had come, and he had heard Skeeter tell the night man
that he would be back around midnight, that there were plans
for Tucker. In the car Skeeter had told him that Judge Hill, the
only man who could release him, was gone until Monday, but
Tucker hadn't believed him. Now he did. It was late Friday
night, and Skeeter had him until Monday morning, it seemed.

He heard a car pull into the parking lot under his window,
and he wished he could see who it was, but the window was too
high. Then he heard Skeeter's voice. "Y'all wait here. I'll go help
him escape." There was answering laughter from more than one
man. Tucker broke into a cold sweat. He got up and looked
around the cell for something to use as a weapon. There was only
the porcelain-covered slop jar and the steel cot, suspended from
the wall by chains. He pulled desperately at the chains, but they
would not budge from the wall. He would have only his hands;
there was nothing else.

He heard the outer door to the lockup scrape open. There
were six cells in this the old wing of the jail, and Tucker was the
only prisoner in the wing. Skeeter came down the corridor, jan-
gling keys, followed by the night man, who had a pistol in his

hand. The night man stuck his weapon through the bars and barked, "Okay, Mr. Chief, up against the wall and spread 'em."

Tucker did as the man ordered. Maybe he would have a better chance out of the cell. The two men came into the cell, and while the night man held the pistol at Tucker's head, Skeeter handcuffed his hands behind him. As they began to move him from the cell, Tucker got a bare toe under the curved edge of the slop jar and flipped it over, splashing against Skeeter's immaculate tans.

"Don't!" Skeeter yelled at the night man, as he drew back to hit Tucker with his pistol. "I don't want a mark on the bastard." Cursing, he wiped his trousers as best he could with Tucker's blanket. "I'm gonna see you pay a little extra for that one, boy," he snarled at Tucker.

They shoved Tucker down the hallway and through the lockup door, the night man prodding him repeatedly in the spine with the pistol. They went down another hallway and through a door into the main office. Skeeter drew his pistol. "All right, I'll take him out," he said to the night man. "You stay here. It's better you don't see no more than you have to."

"Where are you taking me?" demanded Tucker. He felt completely vulnerable, clad in only the thin bathrobe, his hands cuffed behind him.

"Where I should have taken you a long time ago, nigger," Skeeter spat back at him. He spun Tucker around and shoved him toward the outer door. Both men stopped. Billy Lee stood in the doorway; John Howell and two state patrolmen stood behind him.

Billy walked over to Skeeter and handed him a neatly typed document. "That's a release order for Tucker Watts, signed by Judge Hill and notarized. Take the handcuffs off him."

Skeeter stood his ground. "Judge Hill is out of town, Billy. I don't believe that's no proper order. Watts ain't going nowhere."

Billy turned and spoke to one of the patrolmen behind him, "Sergeant"—the man stepped forward—"I've served Sheriff Willis with a signed order for the release of Chief Watts. I'm going to inform him of that fact once more. If he hesitates to obey it, arrest him immmediately for obstruction of justice. I'll take the responsibility."

"Yes, sir," the sergeant said. He turned and looked at Skeeter, waiting.

Billy turned back to Skeeter. "Sheriff Willis, here is an order for the release of that man. Take the handcuffs off him. Now."

Skeeter looked at Billy, then at the patrolman. The patrolman took a step toward him. "All right, all right," he said, and fumbled for his keys.

"You," Billy snapped to the night man. "Get his clothes." The man went to a locker, retrieved Tucker's uniform, and tossed it onto the counter.

Tucker, rubbing his wrists, walked immediately behind a counter, opened a desk drawer, and took out his gunbelt. He placed it on the counter next to his clothes, quickly got dressed, checking to see that the gun was loaded, then buckled it on. "All right, Governor," he said.

"Sergeant," Billy said to the patrolman. "There are four men in a car outside. I want you and the corporal to go out there and turn them inside out. Check for guns and permits; check driver's licences, car registration, everything you can think of. If anybody is in violation of anything, arrest him and jail him at the state patrol station in La Grange."

The two patrolmen left. Billy turned back to the sheriff. "Get him out of here," he said, indicating the night man. Willis jerked his thumb at the man, and he left. "Skeeter," Billy said, looking at the sheriff's soiled trousers, "you don't smell so good." Willis glowered at him but said nothing. "But then, you've smelled bad for a long time. That'll be over soon. You're through. If I win this election I'm going to use every ounce of authority and influence at my disposal to see that you're run out of office. If it's possible, I'll see you in your own country camp, and I don't give a damn about your age. If I don't win, I'll still be not without influence, and I'll pursue you to hell and back." He turned to Tucker. "Let's go."

They walked out of the office, leaving the sheriff struck dumb. "There's probably nothing I can do about him," said Billy, "in spite of my brave talk. I'm sure he's covered his tracks carefully, but it won't hurt him to worry about it." He looked over at the state patrolmen, who had four men spread over their car, searching them. One of the men was Emmett Spence.

"Four pistols, Governor," the sergeant called out. "No permits. There's two shotguns and some rope in the car, too."

"Run 'em in," Billy called back. He turned to Tucker. "I'm sorry we were so long getting you out. We had to find the judge, who was driving north, then we had to get the order dictated and typed and notarized, and this was as quick as we could do it."

"Governor, I can't tell you how glad I am to see you at all," Tucker said. "They were taking me out of the jail, and God knows what they would have done with me. Thank you."

"Don't mention it. Now, listen, Tucker; you're going to have to reduce the charges against Hoss Spence to the traffic violation. I've talked with Judge Hill about this. You'll have to trade for the charge against you, which could be very messy in a jury trial. Spence will still lose his license for a while, and you'll have a good lawsuit against him for having you arrested without cause."

"I'm sorry, but I can't let Spence get away with this, Governor. But I really appreciate your taking the time to come down here."

"I was glad to do it. Now, there's somebody waiting over there for you." He nodded. Elizabeth was waiting for him in the car. She got out, walked over, and embraced him. They got into the car and drove home.

Billy started back to Atlanta. He had a long weekend of campaign work still ahead of him, and he was worried about Tucker's determination to prosecute Hoss Spence.

19 ON SUNDAY MORNING Billy was awakened by a hammering on his Atlanta hotel room door. "Who is it?" he yelled, staying in bed.

"It's John Howell. Open up."

Billy stumbled to the door and unlocked it. "What time is it?" he asked sleepily, as Howell hurried into the room, a stack of newspapers under his arm.

"A little after ten. You're supposed to be at services at eleven. You're going to Ebenezer Street Baptist Church, remember? You're running late, but that's the least of your problems. I've been trying to call you, but the operator refused to ring your room."

"I told her not to put any calls through. I needed the sleep. What's the matter?"

Howell plunked down the Sunday papers on the bed. "Have a look at that."

"BLACK CHIEF ARRESTED, CHARGED WITH BEATING ELDERLY MAN," read a headline which appeared above the newspaper's masthead, and beneath it a subhead, "Mullins Charges Lee Made Improper Use of Lieutenant Governor's Office to Obtain Release of Watts."

"Oh, shit," said Billy sitting down on the edge of the bed and pulling a blanket around his shoulders. He read on.

The Meriwether County Sheriff's Department yesterday arrested Delano Chief of Police Tucker Watts, the South's first black law-enforcement official, and charged him with assault and battery of a prominent Meriwether County farmer, Horace Spence, 74, after Watts stopped Spence's car, allegedly for speeding. Lieutenant Governor William H. Lee, facing a tough general-election battle on Tuesday in the race for governor, apparently used the influence of his office in ordering the commander of the Georgia State Patrol to locate a judge who would sign release papers for Watts. Lee then personally went to the Meriwether County Jail in Greenville, accompanied by two state-patrol bodyguards, where he obtained the release of Chief Watts, and ordered the arrest of four Meriwether County men in the jail's parking lot on charges of carrying unlicensed weapons and of having an expired vehicle-inspection sticker on their car. The men claimed they were returning from a hunting trip and had stopped to drop off one of their party who lived in Greenville. They were ordered released the following morning by a La Grange Superior Court judge from the local state-patrol station.

Sheriff John B. ("Skeeter") Willis said, "This is the second case we've had down here of this so-called policeman harassing elderly white citizens, and we're just not going to put up with it." His remark apparently referred to a Delano citizen, Francis Funderburke, 79, who, when asked about Sheriff Willis's comment said, "We wouldn't be having this problem if this fellow hadn't been forced on the community by Billy Lee, just so he could get the colored vote to help him get elected." Funderburke, a noted dog breeder, declined comment on the specifics of his alleged harassment by Chief Watts.

Jackson Mullins, Lee's independent opponent in the governor's race, contacted at his south Georgia home, said, "This is just one more example of the arrogant misuse of state office by a candidate who will do anything to win the black-bloc vote in this election." Mullins has consistently criticized Lee for using his office improperly in the election.

Lieutenant Governor Lee was said to be sequestered in an Atlanta hotel after the incident and was unavailable for comment.

The telephone rang, and Billy picked it up. "Governor," the operator said, "there's a Mr. Holmes on the line who insists that I put his call through. I know you left instructions not to be disturbed, sir, but—"

"That's all right, put him on. Mr. Holmes? . . . Yes, sir, I've just seen the papers. . . . That's right, I've got to be at Ebenezer Street church in forty-five minutes. . . . I have to go, sir; we've had this scheduled for days. It would look as though I'm backing down if I cancel. In fact, I think a black church might be the best place for me to reply to these charges, especially Dr. King's church. . . . Look, we know that what's going to happen if these charges come to court—Tucker will be vindicated. . . . Yes, it could be too late by then, but I can't change course now; I'm just going to have to ride it out. . . . Thank you, sir, I'd appreciate that. I'm running late, as it is, and I don't really have time to make the call."

He hung up. "Mr. Holmes thinks I ought to cancel at Ebenezer Street, but I can't do that. He's going to see that the telephone volunteers try and get some feel about how this might affect the voting on Tuesday."

"Billy," Howell said, "I think you ought to hold an impromptu press conference on the steps of the church and refute all this in the strongest possible manner. There'll be a lot of press there, anyway. This is on your official schedule."

"You're right," Billy replied.

"My story is in this morning's *Times*, and that gives the whole picture. That'll get picked up by the wire services and should help, too."

"Good. Well, I'd better get a move on." Billy headed for the shower.

Tucker was surprised at how shaken he was by his experience in jail. He woke Saturday morning feeling exhausted, and when the calls from the press began to come in, he checked in briefly at the station and then spent Saturday and Sunday at his mother's house, with instructions to Bartlett that he was to be called only in an emergency.

He scrubbed himself repeatedly with a medicated shampoo to rid himself of the lice and crabs he had picked up in the cell. The feeling of uncleanliness made things even worse for him. He resolved to see that his own jail was fumigated regularly, and he thought he would never again feel the same about locking up someone.

He saw Billy on the Sunday-night news, trying to put things right, but it seemed to him an unsuccessful effort. On Holmes's advice he issued a short written statement, saying that he had

made a proper arrest after having himself been assaulted and that
he believed subsequent court action would prove he acted re-
sponsibly. He hoped it would help.

He spent little time in the station Monday and Tuesday, election day; instead, he drove aimlessly about the town, depressed,
wondering whether he would be able to continue in the job.

Billy had a sense of *déjà vu* on election night, keeping another
campaign vigil he had hoped would be unnecessary. By midnight it was clear he would not have a majority. Mullins did even
better than they had expected. Billy ended up nearly four percentage points short of the majority necessary to keep the election out of the Georgia House of Representatives.

"Where do you think we stand in the house as of this moment?" he asked Holmes.

The banker produced his notebook. "I've been on the phone
all weekend," he said. "We're better off than we were at the time
of the primary, I reckon, but there are still a dozen or so votes
uncommitted. If I had to give you a hard figure right now, I'd say
we were four or five votes short. You've got a lot of telephoning
to do the next week."

"I think we'd better do more than that," Billy said. "I think
we'd better get hold of a light plane and go see some people
around the state."

"Good idea."

"What do you think our chances are, Mr. Holmes? Really."
Billy thought he had never seen the banker look as tired, as old.

Holmes shook his head. "There's so much riding on this for
you, son. I think Kennedy's serious about the vice-presidency
thing, I honestly do. I wish I could tell you we can do it, but I
don't know. I just don't know."

Billy realized, now, that he had been allowing himself to
think not just about the vice-presidency, but about the job as a
stepping stone to the presidency itself. If he lost in the house, it
was all over. He felt a fool for letting himself aim so high.

20 BY WEDNESDAY MORNING Tucker had recovered
himself enough to take hold of his job again. He was
at the station early and went through the mail and
messages that had gathered in his absence. He was relieved to
find there was nothing of importance in the papers piled on his
desk, but when he reached the bottom of the pile his relief vanished. The file on the missing boys was waiting for him. What's
more, there was a Teletype from state-patrol headquarters placing the young man in the most recent of the bulletins in Buena
Vista, forty miles south of Delano. The date was the third, two
days before.

Because he had, as much as possible, emptied his mind of
everything to do with his work, he had banished Foxy Funderburke from his thoughts, as well. But now the file was there; the
boys were staring back at him again. He considered visiting
Foxy, but immediately dismissed the idea. Holmes had warned
him off, and somehow Foxy had become a part of the Hoss
Spence–Skeeter Willis problem, too. His only course was to follow Holmes's advice and go through the established channels,
and that meant Sheriff Bobby Patrick of Talbot County.

Even the appearance of asking Patrick for help repelled him,
and, after his experience in Skeeter's jail, he felt a deep-seated
anxiety about approaching Patrick in his. But there was no other

way to go, and he knew it. He stuck the file in a manila envelope and walked into the squad room. Bartlett was eating a slice of sweet-potato pie and drinking a cup of coffee at his desk.

"Buddy, I'm going down to Talbotton to see Bobby Patrick about something. I'll be back as soon as I can. If you need me call me at the Talbot County Sheriff's Office, and if I'm not there, send a car to the top of the mountain and have me radioed from there. The station antenna would never clear the mountain on line of sight."

"This something to do with that missing-persons stuff, Chief?" Tucker had not shared his theory with Bartlett.

Tucker nodded. "Yeah, and I can't touch it. It's in Patrick's jurisdiction."

Bartlett looked troubled. "Watch yourself, Chief, okay?"

"Sure," Tucker said, and left. As he drove the twenty miles to Talbotton, his apprehension lifted a little. He had finally committed himself to a course of action, and he felt better for it. It occurred to him that he should call John Howell and bring him up to date, as he had promised he would.

He parked in front of the courthouse at a parking meter instead of in one of the official slots, realizing he had unconsciously avoided even that chance of conflict. In the sheriff's department he was received politely, but cooly, by the clerk, who obviously knew who he was. Patrick had somebody in his office, and he would have to wait.

He waited for nearly an hour, growing increasingly restive. He read old copies of *Signposts* and the *Ford Times* and avoided drinking from the water cooler, because he didn't want to have to go to the bathroom, not wanting to create an incident by going to what might be a white facility, and not wanting to ask. Finally, Patrick emerged, shook hands with his departing visitor, and saw Tucker.

Patrick grinned widely. "Well, if it ain't old Tucker. What brings you down here, boy?"

Tucker did not blink at the "boy," knowing that white southerners used it liberally among themselves and that it wasn't necessarily a racial slur, although it might be, coming from Patrick. "I've got some business for you, Bobby."

Patrick waved him into the office and offered him a chair. Tucker noticed that Bobby was wearing every piece of brass available from the police equipment catalogue—badge, collar pins, tie clasp, and a gold eagle on each epaulet of his tan gabardine uniform. A powdery-white Stetson hung on a hat rack in the corner.

"Well, now, Tucker, boy," he practically crowed, "what can I do for you?"

Tucker laid the file before him and opened it. Carefully, he took him through the disappearances, pointed out the geographical distribution of the last sightings, then gave Patrick his conclusions. When he had finished, Patrick said nothing for a moment, simply smiled slightly. He closed the file and handed it back to Tucker.

"Tell you what, Tucker," he said. "Let's go down the hall and see Judge Greene. You tell him all about it. He's the man who'll have to issue a search warrant, anyway. Okay?"

"Fine," Tucker replied, relieved. He had not known quite what to expect, but he had not anticipated such quick cooperation.

They were received immediately and cordially in the judge's chambers. The judge was a grandfatherly man who listened closely to what Tucker had to say, nodding sagely now and then. When Tucker had completed his presentation, the judge looked at Bobby Patrick and chuckled slightly. Patrick chuckled back. Then the judge laughed aloud and Patrick laughed back. Then the two of them laughed until neither could speak. Tucker got up and left the office.

Patrick caught up to him as he started his car. "Hey, listen, Tucker," he grinned, suppressing further laughter. "That's the most fun we've had down here since I took office. You know, Foxy and the judge have been friends for thirty years, hunted together. They're like that." He held up crossed fingers. "Anytime you got something as entertaining as that story, you just come on down here; we want to hear it." Then his face turned cold and hard. "Listen, I know your ass is in a sling with Skeeter Willis, and as far as I'm concerned it couldn't happen to a nicer guy. If you think you can wiggle out of that bind by coming down here with a piece of shit like this, you've got another think coming. I'm not gonna get you off the hook, and you better leave old Foxy alone, too. If I hear about you bothering him again, I'll put your ass *under* the Talbot County jail, you hear me?"

Tucker backed out of the parking place without a word and drove slowly back toward Delano, watching his rearview mirror until he was across the county line, humiliated to the core of him. He checked in briefly at the station, then spent the rest of the day driving listlessly around the town, the file on the seat beside him. He was at a dead end. He had no place else to go.

On Wednesday morning Billy borrowed a single-engine Cessna from a supporter and, with Hugh Holmes, flew out of Franklin D. Roosevelt Memorial Field at Warm Springs for north Georgia. Holmes had identified a dozen legislators not yet firmly committed to either camp, and Billy meant to talk to each of them face to face. Since Georgia was the largest state east of the Mississippi, he needed the plane to do it.

He was worried about Holmes. The banker was looking tired and drawn, and Billy wanted him to stay home and confine himself to telephone calls, but Holmes had insisted on coming along.

"There's a favor owed me here and there," he had said. "It's time I did some collecting. But don't get your hopes up."

At breakfast on Thursday morning Elizabeth put Tucker's eggs on the table and said, "You've got some vacation time coming. I talked with my brother, John, in New York; they want us to come up and visit. Why don't we do that? Maybe even see some shows? You need some time off."

The idea appealed to Tucker. At the end of his rope with his Foxy theory, and in limbo until the business with Hoss Spence was settled, there was nothing important demanding his attention. He had thought, too, that they might not be in Delano much longer, the way things were going. His credibility with the local people had been damaged by the newspaper reports of his arrest, and there was a feeling that the incident had cost Billy the general election. If Billy lost in the house now, the burden on Tucker would be unbearable, even if he were completely vindicated in court. He wasn't sure where they would go, but they had always enjoyed New York on their visits there, and the anonymity of the place appealed to him. He might find some private security work there, and a few days in the city would give him an opportunity to feel out a new situation for them.

"Honey," he said, "if Mr. Holmes and the city manager don't object to my taking some time on short notice, I could get squared away this morning, and we could get a plane from Atlanta tonight."

He went through things with Bartlett at the station and could see no problems. Holmes was out of town, but the city manager had no objections. He booked a flight and began to look forward to the change of scene.

"How about the missing-persons thing, Chief?" asked Bartlett. "Anything come of that?"

"No, nothing," he said wearily. "That one is over."

"I'd like to know what you thought you had."

"When I get back I'll lay it out for you. Maybe someday something will break on it."

The phone rang, and Bartlett answered. "It's for you, Chief. John Howell."

Tucker picked up the phone. "How you doing, John?"

"Not bad. Just wanted to see if anything was new with you. Is there a trial date set for either Spence or you yet?"

"No. I expect it'll get settled after the house vote next week. I'm just about to take a week off. Elizabeth and I are going to visit her brother and his wife in New York. I'm pretty beat, really."

"Yeah, I can imagine. Anything ever come of your detective work on the missing boys?"

"Well, yes and no. Some more stuff turned up, but it's a dead end now. I'll loan you the file if you think you can really get a book out of it. It'll have to be a novel, though."

"I'd like to see it. What time is your flight to New York? Can I buy you a drink at the airport?"

"Sure, why not? Why don't we meet at three o'clock in the upper-level bar. Our plane's at four-thirty, so that'll give us time to talk. I'll bring the file; you can photocopy it and mail it back to me in Delano."

Tucker and Elizabeth drove north, past the Spence place, through Warm Springs. At the Greenville city limits, a sheriff's car pulled behind them and followed closely. Tucker drove very slowly into the town, through the square, and out the other side. The car continued to follow them. Tucker did not recognize the driver, but he could see him using the radio. He said nothing to Elizabeth, who was dozing.

At the Coweta County line the car turned around and was replaced by a sheriff's car from that county. Tucker drove on at a steady forty-five miles an hour, a full ten miles an hour under the speed limit. At the Fayette County line the scene was repeated, and at the border to Clayton County, yet again. By the time they arrived at Atlanta Airport, Tucker's shirt was sticking to him, in spite of the open car window.

John Howell closed the file. "Tucker, you've got to take this to the feds."

Tucker set down his drink. "What are you talking about? This isn't a federal case."

"It might be. There's kidnapping. The Lindbergh Law."

Tucker looked at his watch. They had been late arriving at the airport because of the surveillance, and Elizabeth was downstairs waiting in a ticket line. "I don't know, John. I don't have any experience with that, but I think the FBI won't get involved in kidnapping unless there's a request from local authorities. It's a state crime, as well as a federal one, and I'm not the local authority in this case."

"There's something else," said the reporter. "An old law they've dug up; they're using it in Mississippi and Alabama in the murders of civil-rights workers. When they can't get a local conviction they're bringing a federal case for depriving an individual of his civil rights."

"I've read about that, but do you think the feds would go for a warrant based on that law? It seems kind of far-fetched to me."

"There's one way to find out. I know a senior agent in the Atlanta FBI office. I'll call him right now and get a reading."

"I don't know, John. Maybe when we get back from New York."

The reporter extracted the most recent bulletin from the file. "Tucker, this kid was last seen in Florida, what—less than two weeks ago? He was reported in Buena Vista on Monday. If he was still headed north that would take him through Delano. This is Thursday. If Foxy connected with him, Tucker, he could still be alive." Howell waited. Tucker said nothing. "I'm going to call my guy at the bureau now," Howell said firmly.

"All right," Tucker replied. "I want to see about Elizabeth. I'll be in the Delta check-in area."

Howell ran for the phone, while Tucker took the escalator to the lower level. Elizabeth had nearly reached the counter. Tucker stood with her as they slowly made their way forward. Finally, when they were at the counter, Howell appeared, out of breath.

"We've got an appointment right now. He's waiting for us."

Tucker hesitated. "Come on, Tucker, one more try. If this doesn't work you can at least say to yourself that you did your best."

Tucker turned to Elizabeth. "Listen, honey, I want you to go on without me. I'll call you tonight at your brother's, and I'll try to join you tomorrow. John is right. I have to do this."

Elizabeth nodded. "All right. I'll book you on the same flight tomorrow. Call me tonight and tell me if you'll be on it."

He kissed her, picked up his bag, and walked quickly from the terminal building with Howell.

They sat in the office of the agent in charge of the Atlanta office of the Federal Bureau of Investigation. John Howell's agent friend, Ben Carr, had taken them to his chief after hearing Tucker's story, and Tucker was unwillingly reminded of being taken to the judge by Bobby Patrick. He had the distinct feeling that Carr had simply wanted to have him turned down at the top.

Pope, the AIC, seemed skeptical, but willing to listen. "So you believe this man has murdered and concealed the bodies of, what—sixteen young men, seventeen if the police officer, Butts, was among them? And this has happened over a period of, let's see"—he stared at the ceiling as he figured—"forty-three years?"

"Mr. Pope," Tucker replied, "I'm not saying that all sixteen of these boys are planted around Funderburke's place, but the geographical pattern of the disapperarances makes all of them candidates, I think. Suppose only half a dozen of them are actual victims. Is six murders enough to get the FBI interested?"

"Chief Watts," the agent shot back, "the bureau would be interested if there were only one murder, but apart from the two bodies found in the twenties, there is no hard evidence of any other murder. It's all circumstantial."

"That's an awful lot of circumstance, isn't it?" asked John Howell, pointing at the bulletins spread out over the desk.

The AIC stared for a moment at the bulletins. "There are no blacks among those who disappeared, right?"

"Right," replied Tucker.

"I see what you're getting at, Mr. Pope," Howell injected. "But do you have to be black to get your civil rights violated? And anyway, wouldn't it look better if that law were being enforced more broadly than just in civil-rights cases? Wouldn't that make the government's use of the law more credible?"

"Possibly," Pope admitted. "Listen, I'm going to have to talk to somebody in Washington about this." He looked at his watch. "It's nearly six o'clock, so my chances of reaching anybody in authority today are poor. I'm going to have to get back to you tomorrow."

"You can't ask a federal judge for a search warrant on your own authority?" Tucker asked.

"Frankly, I'd feel better having some support up the line," the AIC answered, "and I should think you'd feel better that way, too, considering the political flap last week, in which Funderburke was an element. In fact, it might help if you could get Lieutenant Governor Lee to make a call or two."

Tucker shook his head. "No, that would be inappropriate. This case has no connection with his office, and I can't ask him to stick his neck out in his present situation."

"I understand. I'll get back to you as soon as I get some word."

"You'd better bunk with me tonight, Tucker," Howell said. "Mr. Pope, here's my card. You can reach the chief at that number."

Billy and Holmes sat in the living room of a small-town lawyer in Toccoa, a north Georgia mountain community. The man, Fred Mitchell, was becoming agitated.

"Billy, I just can't give you an answer. Granted, you won my county in the general election, but Mullins took it in the primary. I've got to think about that. There's this business with your policeman down there; I think you made a big mistake getting that man hired; I'm getting pressure from all sides on this thing, and on top of everything else I've got my sister on my neck. Her boy has run away from home for the third time, and she thinks I'm helping him, hiding him. She's about to drive me crazy. And I've got a case coming up in court tomorrow, and I'm ill prepared for it; so if you'll just let me try to get some time to think about this without pressure, I'll call you when I've decided. I'm sorry I can't give you an answer now, but I just can't."

They stood up and shook hands. Billy and Holmes left for the grass strip where the Cessna was parked. Their next stop was in Athens, and Billy wanted to make it before dark.

21 TUCKER SAT in the hard, wooden chair at noon on Friday and waited for Agent in Charge Pope to finish his telephone conversation. Tucker hurt all over. He had slept on a leather sofa in John Howell's tiny, bachelor apartment, and the sofa had been too short for his frame. He wanted the man to give them the bad news, so he could catch a plane for New York. He had spent a restless night on the uncomfortable sofa worrying about this, and now all he wanted was to be done with it.

Pope hung up the phone. "All right," he said, "We're gong to ask for a warrant."

"Fantastic!" John Howell cried.

Tucker was amazed, but he felt something else was coming.

"But," said Pope, "there is going to have to be an agreement on some limitations."

"What sort of limitations?" Tucker asked.

"First of all," Pope said, counting on his fingers, "there is going to be no team of men going in there and tearing the place apart. Washington doesn't feel that the situation warrants that; they feel—and I can tell you this went all the way to the attorney general's office—they feel that if you think it warrants looking into, and local agencies won't cooperate, it should be looked into. But there is going to be no digging, no prying up floorboards, none of that. I'm going to send Carr and another agent, Sutherland, down there. If they turn up something they feel warrants an all-out search, Carr will report it to me, and I will make the decision, in consultation with Washington, on whether to go further. Clear?"

Tucker nodded. "Yes."

"Second," said Pope, ticking off another finger, "you, Chief Watts, may accompany Carr and Sutherland, in uniform, as an observer. You are not to question or address yourself directly to Funderburke. If you have a question, address it to Carr or Sutherland, and one of them will ask it if he feels it is relevant. Clear?"

"Clear."

"Third," Pope said, pointing a finger at John Howell, "*he* is not to go near the place unless evidence of a crime is discovered. Clear?"

"Now wait a minute," Howell began.

"This is an absolute condition of our application for this warrant. We are not going to be a party to dragging an innocent man through the *New York Times*. If we find evidence on which we can base a prosecution, then you can go in."

"Clear," said Tucker.

Pope looked at his watch. "If you get over to the federal courthouse in a hurry, you can probably catch the judge when he recesses for lunch."

Billy and Holmes were having a late lunch in the Georgian Hotel in Athens, when Holmes was paged for a telephone call. He was gone only a short time.

Holmes sat down heavily. "That was my secretary. A friend of mine at the federal courthouse in Atlanta called. Tucker Watts showed up at Judge Henderson's chambers an hour and a half ago with two FBI agents and got a warrant to search Foxy Funderburke's place."

"*What?*"

"I told you a while back that Tucker had been asking some questions about Foxy. It came out in newspaper stories."

"Yes, but why? I haven't seen Tucker since we got him out of jail, so I never had a chance to ask him about it. What on earth is he looking for at Foxy's?"

"I don't know. I had a talk with him about it, but I didn't ask for details. I just told him that since Foxy lived in Talbot County, he had to go to Bobby Patrick unless Foxy had done something in Delano. I'm sure he'd be reluctant to go to Patrick, maybe that's why he went to the FBI, but for the life of me I can't imagine what he's up to.''

Billy resisted an inclination to bury his face in his hands. "Dear God in heaven, why now? Thanks to that newspaper story, half the people in the state and probably more than half of the legislature thinks that, for political purposes, I've talked Delano into hiring a black police chief who goes around beating up nice old white gentlemen.''

"That certainly seems to be what Mitchell, from yesterday, thinks, and this fellow we talked to this morning, seems to be lining up with him. Mitchell could be the key in north Georgia, you know. He pulls a lot of weight.''

"I think we'd better get home. I've got to find out what the hell's going on.''

"We've still got to stop in Madison and see Wilkinson. He's fence-sitting, and we might swing him.''

Billy checked the time. "All right, but let's make it fast. We have to land at Warm Springs before dark.'' Billy left some money for the check. "Mr. Holmes, do you think Tucker's all right? I mean, do you think he's gone off his rocker? I took him at his word on the thing with Hoss Spence, Hoss is like that, but now—''

Holmes stood up. "I think what I've thought from the beginning, what you thought, too. I think Tucker knows what he's doing. If we were there now, we might interfere with his work, but we're not there, and we're just going to have to trust him, at least for the time being.''

"You're right,'' Billy said, quickening his step, "but I hope he doesn't cost me . . . this election.''

Tucker turned into Foxy Funderburke's private road and stopped. The two FBI agents, Carr and Sutherland, pulled their car up next to his. Tucker had driven his own car from Atlanta, stopping at home to change into a uniform. John Howell had ridden with him.

"Okay, John, I'll ride with them now. Why don't you go back to the station and wait in my office. I'll call you the minute we find something.''

"Oh, no, I'm not budging from here." He pointed. "That's a police radio, isn't it?"

"Yes."

"If you find something, call the station and ask them to radio me."

"All right, if that's the way you want it. We could be some time, you know." Tucker got into the car with the two agents, and they began the drive up the mountain. Tucker looked at his watch. It was almost 3:30. "The road peaks just ahead," Tucker said to Carr, who was driving, "and then it slopes downward slightly to the house. He doesn't seem to use the front door much. Just pull around the end of the house to the back." The agent followed Tucker's instructions. They coasted quietly past the neat flower beds and lawn, now brown, and stopped at the back of the house. The autumn foliage was at its peak.

"Pretty place," said Sutherland.

"Yeah, pretty." Tucker replied.

"His truck's in the garage," Carr said. "So he must be home. Tucker, you stay in the car until he answers the door. If he doesn't like you, I don't want to upset him before I have a chance to show him the warrant." Carr and Sutherland got out of the car, walked to the back door, and knocked. Tucker saw Foxy open the door and Carr hand him the paper. Then he got out and joined the two agents at the back door.

"Mr. Funderburke," Carr was saying, "Chief Watts is accompanying us as an observer and to help us in the search."

"What's this all about?" asked Foxy, indignant. "What are you looking for? I don't want that nigger in my house."

Carr was firm. "Mr. Funderburke, I must warn you that if you resist this search, I will arrest you, and you are liable to be jailed for contempt of court." He continued, more placatingly, "Please understand, sir, that we just want to do our jobs and then leave you in peace. Now please stand aside and let us come into the house."

Foxy hesitated, then stepped back, allowing the two agents to enter, closely followed by Tucker. Tucker had never been inside the house. The first thing he noticed was the kitchen floor. He indicated it to Carr. "That's what Howell was talking about, remember?" Carr nodded.

Foxy said, "Well, Gentlemen, you obviously don't need me. I'll just have a seat in the living room by the fire. I was reading a book when you intruded upon me."

"Thank you, sir," said Carr. "We'll let you know if we have any questions."

After a long, piercing stare at Tucker, Foxy turned, walked into the living room, sat down in a rocker before the fire, and picked up a book. Tucker watched him, and then his gaze traveled to the wall, hung with weapons. "You better keep an eye on him," he said to Carr.

Carr nodded. "Sure, but he seems peaceful enough, considering the unpleasant surprise. He certainly doesn't look as though he has anything to hide. Tucker, why don't you take the kitchen, and we'll start in here."

The three men split up and began a thorough search of each room. Almost immediately, Sutherland found a policeman's uniform in Foxy's bedroom closet. He called Carr, and the two men took it into the living room, while Tucker watched from the doorway.

"Excuse me, Mr. Funderburke," Carr said. "Can you explain why you have a policeman's uniform in your home?"

Foxy looked up from his book. "Gentlemen, some forty years ago I was to be appointed to the job which that nigger"—he pointed at Tucker—"now holds. I bought the uniform in anticipation of that appointment, but I was cheated out of it. I saw no reason to burn the uniform."

"Thank you, sir, I understand," replied Carr, then retreated to the hallway, where he huddled with Sutherland and Tucker.

"Remember the autopsy report on the first murder?" asked Tucker. "The doctor said the injuries looked as though they had been inflicted during a police interrogation."

Carr nodded. "Well, that fits, but alone it means nothing. Let's keep going."

They spent more than an hour in the house, looking into every closet and drawer, in every kitchen cupboard, under, over, and behind every object and piece of furniture in the house. They found nothing. The search moved to the garage and the kennels. Still nothing. Carr called Sutherland and Tucker together.

"Look, this is turning into a dry hole. There's nothing in the kennels or the garage except what you'd expect to find there—the usual tools. There's a well-used pick and shovel in the garage, though. I think our best bet was always if the most recent disappearance was connected with Funderburke. If that's the case, then either the boy would have to be here, or Funderburke would have had to dispose of his body, in which case we could hope for a pretty fresh grave. That's what we have to look for now. It's the only thing we have left." He pointed to the large clearing that was the back yard. "We should check every square foot of bare ground. Even that kudzu couldn't grow over a grave in a few days—not at this time of the year, anyway. Since we can't dig, we may as well forget the area covered by the kudzu. Agreed?"

Tucker agreed, but reluctantly. They began a foot by foot search for fresh earth or a mound. They looked inside each kennel and found only dogs. They searched on every side of the house and found not the slightest indication of recent digging. The shadows grew long, the November light began to fade, and Tucker's hopes with it. He came around a corner of the house to the back and met Carr near the back door. Sutherland was thirty or forty feet away up behind the house, tramping through the kudzu.

Carr shook his head. "Tucker, I know how good this must have looked to you. It looked good to me, what you had. But short of bringing a bunch of men with picks and shovels in here, I don't know what else we can do."

"You're right," Tucker said, "and I appreciate what you guys have done. You went out on a limb, and now it's going to get sawed off." He knew that within the hour the word would go out along Foxy's network of friends, right to Mullins, and by morning the story of the latest assault on decency by the black Delano chief of police would be on the front pages. He didn't know what he would say to Billy. He felt sick inside.

Carr knocked on the back door, and Foxy opened it. "Mr. Funderburke," he said, "we've completed our search. We've found nothing to implicate you in any crime. I want to apologize for this intrusion and thank you for your cooperation. You won't be bothered again."

"That's just fine, mister," Foxy said bitterly. "Now get that nigger off my place."

Tucker and Carr turned away from the back door, and Carr called to Sutherland, "Come on, Mike, we're finished here." Sutherland waved back and began to walk down the hill through the kudzu. Carr turned to Tucker. "Let's go, we'll drop you back at your car. Howell must be wondering what's happened to us."

From up the hill there came a sharp cry, and the two men turned in time to see Sutherland pitch forward on his face and slide a few feet down the hill on the slippery vine. Tucker and Carr walked the few feet across the bare back yard into the kudzu. "You all right, Mike?" Carr called out. "Hang on, we'll give you a hand." By the time they reached him, Sutherland was on his feet. "That was a hard fall," said Carr. "You okay?"

"Yeah," Sutherland replied, brushing himself off. He walked a few steps back up the hill. "I caught my foot on something here." He poked among the vines. "Here it is." Tucker and Carr joined him as he pulled back the big leaves. A bent length of rusty pipe protruded from the ground, capped by a torn black sleeve. A short, curved length of corroded brass was attached to it by a hinge. "Looks like some old plumbing," said Sutherland, "a pipe to or from something."

"I don't know what that is," Carr said, turning away. "And I'm too tired to care much. Let's get out of here." Sutherland turned to follow him.

Tucker stood frozen to the spot, staring. "I know what it is," he said. The two agents stopped and looked back. "It's the handlebar of a motorcycle."

There was a hollow, metallic click from behind them. They turned and found Foxy Funderburke standing at the edge of the kudzu, not ten feet away. He was holding a double-barreled, sawed-off shotgun. Tucker's last thought before the weapon fired was that, from that distance, it would cut all three of them in half.

John Howell was growing restive. He had waited in the car, as patiently as possible, for nearly two hours, kept company only by the crackle of the police radio. Now it was getting really cold, and his patience was gone. Then it occurred to him that the radio had only crackled, had never spoken. He wondered if there was so little police traffic that two hours could pass with nothing broadcast. He got out of the car and looked at his surroundings. The turnoff to Funderburke's place was several hundred yards down the mountain from the pass, down the opposite side of the mountain from Delano. Police radio was VHF, wasn't it? The range depended on the power and on line of sight. Could the police radio broadcast a signal that would reach the opposite side of the mountain?

He got back into the car, picked up the microphone, and pressed the broadcast switch. "Hello, Delano police headquarters, Delano police headquarters, do you read me? Does anybody read me?" He released the switch. Nothing but the crackle came back to him. He tried again, with the same result. "Shit," he said aloud to himself. "I'm damned if I'll wait any longer." He started the car and began to drive slowly up the road. Hell, they might have tried to call him a long time ago. They wouldn't have been this long if they hadn't found something.

He reached the crest of the road and saw the house, a living room light on, looking cozy and snug. He allowed the car to coast down the little hill, then pulled up in front of the house. He got out and looked through the living-room window. There was a fire in the hearth; a reading lamp was on, but the house seemed empty. He noticed that the FBI car was not parked in front and reasoned that everybody must be out back. He started to walk around the building.

He came around the rear corner of the house and stopped. Tucker and the two FBI agents were standing some thirty or forty feet up the hill behind the house, ankle deep in kudzu, staring at something at their feet. Foxy Funderburke was walking quickly, silently, toward them, loading a sawed-off shotgun. Howell heard the click as Foxy snapped the weapon shut. The three men up the hill, hearing the sound, turned. Howell realized what was about to happen. He formed a megaphone with his hands, took a deep breath, and shouted, at the very top of his lungs, "Hey!" Then, without waiting to see what happened, he stepped behind the corner of the house and flattened himself against the logs.

There was an enormous roar, and simultaneously large splinters exploded from the corner of the house. Then came two or three other explosions, so close together he could not be sure of the number. He got quickly down on his hands and knees and stuck his head, close to the ground, around the corner of the house. Tucker, Carr, and Sutherland were all standing in a half crouch, pistols held at arms' length, pointed at Foxy, having all just fired. Foxy was sprawled on his back, twitching, trying to pick up the shotgun. The three men came quickly down the hill, and Tucker kicked the weapon away from him.

Howell got up and ran toward the group. As he reached them, he saw that Foxy was pumping a great deal of blood from his chest into the ground. Foxy seemed to see him for a moment, looked wildly around him, tried to speak, failed, then stopped moving. Carr held fingers at the old man's neck and shook his head. Sutherland took out a penlight and flashed it into the open eyes. "Nothing," he said.

Tucker walked to the house and through the back door. Howell, too dazed to ask questions, followed him. Inside, Tucker found a phone in the living room and dialed a number. "Bartlett? . . . This is the chief. I want you to do some things. First, call Dr. Tom Mudter, and ask him if he can come out to Foxy Funderburke's place right away. . . . No, don't call an ambulance, just ask the doctor to come. Now, how many prisoners have you got in jail? . . . Good, I want you to call the city manager—at home, if he's left the office, and tell him you need all the picks and shovels he's got at the city garage. Call one of the patrol cars in and have the man relieve you, then break out your prisoners, and take them over to the garage, pick up the tools and a truck, and get out to Funderburke's place on the double. Have you got that? . . . Good, and bring all the flashlights you can find—if there's any emergency lighting at the city garage, bring that and some power cable. . . . Never mind, I'll fill you in when you get here. Now move it!" He hung up the phone and looked at Howell. "John," he said, "did I tell you how glad I am to see you?"

22 BILLY LANDED at Roosevelt field with ten minutes to spare before dusk. He resolved, if he were ever elected governor, to find a way to get a beacon and landing lights installed at the little strip.

"Let's go to my house first," he said to Holmes. "We could both use a drink, and we can try and locate Tucker from there. I've got to get a handle on this thing. Your source says he's getting federal search warrants for Foxy's place, and the police station says he's in New York. This whole thing is screwy."

Patricia made them both comfortable and brought them a bourbon. Billy called the police station. Tub Murray answered.

"Tub, this is Billy Lee. Is the chief in New York, or where?"

"Governor, he's out at Foxy Funderburke's, as far as I know," the patrolman answered, sounding confused. "He called here about forty-five minutes ago and told Bartlett to send Dr. Mudter out to Foxy's, and to let all the prisoners out of the jail and bring them out there with a lot of picks and shovels. That's all I know, sir. Maybe you could get hold of him by calling out at Foxy's."

Billy thanked the man and hung up. "This gets crazier by the minute. Tucker's apparently out at Foxy's, and he's asked for Tom Mudter and some picks and shovels." He grabbed the Delano phone book, looked up Foxy's number, and dialed it.

"You know, there was a time when I could have told you

Foxy's number just like that," Holmes said, snapping his fingers. "Even after the dial system went in, I knew a lot of 'em. Funny how you forget things."

Billy looked at him worriedly. The banker had been talking that way all afternoon. He hung up the phone. "Busy." He tried again, with the same result. They sat and quietly sipped their drinks for a few minutes, and Billy tried again. "Still busy. I think we'd better go out there." They stood up. "Mr. Holmes, it's not really necessary for you to go. I can drop you off at home."

"Oh, I wouldn't miss it," Holmes replied. The drink seemed to have revived him. "Let's go."

At the turnoff for Foxy's house, they were stopped by Sgt. Buddy Bartlett. "Oh, I'm sorry, Governor, I didn't recognize you." He slapped his forehead. "Gosh, sir, I forgot to tell the chief you were trying to reach him. I thought he had already left for New York when you called this afternoon."

"Buddy, what's going on up there?" Billy asked.

"I don't really know enough of it to explain it to you, sir. You'd better let the chief do that."

Billy put the car in gear and started up the mountain. As they came to the top of the hill and began their descent, they could see the log house silhouetted against bright lights from behind. They parked in front of the house and walked around to the back. Billy saw Tucker immediately and called to him.

"Good evening, Governor, Mr. Holmes," the chief said.

Billy was baffled by the lights and the digging men. "Tucker, tell me what's going on here, will you?"

"Come over here for a minute, Governor." Tucker led the way up the hill through the kudzu, which was being chopped and raked by a number of men. He stopped before a heap of dirt and metal.

Billy stared at it. "Is that a motorcycle?"

"Yessir, it is," Tucker replied. "We found Sonny Butts."

Billy and Holmes looked at the motorcycle, then at each other.

Tucker pointed them toward the house. "If you'll come inside I'll explain the whole thing to you," he said, and walked them down the hill. As they walked through the kitchen door, John Howell waved at them from the telephone. Dr. Tom Mudter was sitting at the kitchen table, writing.

"Evening, Billy, Mr. Holmes," the doctor said. "Tucker, if

you'll get somebody to move Foxy's truck we can put his body in the garage. We'll need a place for all the remains, anyway. There'll be a lot of cataloguing to do."

"Is Foxy dead?" Billy asked incredulously.

Tucker led them into the living room and sat them down. He opened a file folder and handed it to Billy. "Let me start at the beginning, Governor," he said.

Billy stared down at the sheet of paper before him. Even after so many years, he recognized his father's handwriting immediately.

Billy was still trying to absorb what Tucker had been telling him for the past half hour, when a man in a dirty blue suit came in. Tucker introduced him as Special Agent Carr of the FBI.

"Tucker," said Carr. "We found a fresh grave; you'll never guess where." Tucker raised his eyebrows. "It was in the garage, under Funderburke's truck. If we'd moved it sooner we'd have found it immediately. God only knows why he buried him there. Two to one it'll turn out to be the boy in the latest bulletin."

"How many does that make so far?" Tucker asked.

"Seven, counting the cop. And we've only just begun."

Billy walked out back with Holmes and Tucker. "We need a lot of help, here, Governor," Tucker said. "Do you think you could get us some National Guard assistance?"

Billy nodded. "I'll call the governor right away." He went back into the house.

"Uh, Chief?" Tucker turned. It was Bobby Patrick. "Uh, can I help you out in any way?"

Tucker introduced him to Ben Carr, who looked at him for a moment and said, "Sheriff, you could relieve the chief's man down at the main road. We could use him up here. Just keep anybody from coming up here who doesn't have any business here."

"Right, yeah," said Patrick, backing out of the house, grateful for some official function.

Carr looked at Tucker and laughed. "There's a sheriff who'll probably have a number of candidates opposing him come election time, when word gets out that he and that Talbot County judge didn't want to search this place."

Billy returned from the house. "The governor is calling the National Guard commander at La Grange, who will call you and offer whatever you need." He looked around him. "Mr. Holmes and I are of no use here. I think we'd better go."

"All right, Governor, I'll keep you posted."

"I'd appreciate it if you would. And if there's any kind of assistance I can give you, don't hesitate to call me—at any hour."

"I expect the National Guard can give us all we need," Tucker replied. "Mr. Holmes, we could use three or four more phone lines out here. Do you think you could arrange that?"

"Of course," Holmes replied. "I'll have them out here within the hour."

John Howell joined them. "Billy, I've got a clear beat on this, and I'd appreciate it if you wouldn't tip any other press for another twenty-four hours."

Billy looked around him. "Sure, John. From the looks of this operation it'll be that time before we know the extent of this, and I can't say I want to be the one to announce it. That's up to Tucker and Mr. Carr, I expect." He turned to Hugh Holmes. "Why don't we go home, and leave this to the professionals?"

"I'd like nothing better," replied the banker. Considering all that had happened, Holmes was strangely silent on the way home, Billy thought.

Back at Foxy's, John Howell loaded a camera and began walking slowly about the digging area, photographing everything. He stopped to take a shot of an old black man leaning on his shovel. The man pointed at Tucker across the way.

"That sho' is some chief of poh-leece we got, ain't it?" he said to Howell.

"Yep. He's quite a fellow."

"Always wuz."

"How's that?"

"I'se knowed him since he wuz a boy," the man said. "We used to git in a heap o' mischief when we wuz chillen, Willie an' me."

Howell stopped taking pictures. "You grew up in Columbus, did you?"

"Oh, nossuh. We growed up right here in Delano. Willie's daddy done used to work for Mr. Billy's daddy, when he wuz still farmin'."

Howell looked closely at the man. He seemed perfectly sane and sober. He was one of the prisoners Bartlett had brought out to dig. Howell got out a notebook. "What's your name?" he asked.

"My name's Walter Johnson," he replied, "but folks call me Pieback."

23 BILLY SPENT a quiet Saturday at home, waiting to hear from Tucker. He talked briefly with Holmes, and they agreed it would be better, under the circumstances, to make no more phone calls to legislators.

"This thing at Foxy's is going to overtake us shortly," Holmes had said, "and it will obliterate everything else. Let's don't try to swim against the stream."

Late in the afternoon Tucker Watts and John Howell arrived, both looking exhausted. Patricia pressed some hot soup on them, and Billy mixed them a drink. Soon they were settled in Billy's study before a fire. It had begun to rain outside.

"We're finished out there, for the most part, and it's a good thing, too," Tucker said, glancing out the window. "The FBI has sent a pathologist down, and he and Dr. Mudter are cataloguing the remains, with the help of an anthropologist from the University of Georgia, who's had a lot of experience on archaeological digs."

"How many?" asked Billy, dreading the answer.

Tucker produced a notebook and flipped through several pages, counting. "We think we've found them all now." He paused and took a deep breath. "It comes to forty-three."

Billy had been expecting bad news, but the number struck him like a blow. A moment of nausea came and went.

When Billy didn't respond, Tucker continued. "We've been able to identify seven of them from personal effects buried with the bodies. The rest are being checked against old missing-persons records in Atlanta. Most of them will probably never be identified.

"It's difficult to tell exactly when all this began, but I think it's likely that the one your father dealt with, the boy found by the old Scout hut, was the first victim, and the second body found, the one from Waycross, was the second or third. After those two experiences, Foxy became much more careful, and, as far as we know, no others ever got off the place alive."

Billy was still unable to say anything.

"We found a lot of paraphernalia in a hidden cupboard at the back of a broom closet—handcuffs, rubber hoses, a lot of stuff. We haven't had a psychologist in on this yet, but it seems to me that the whole thing began when Foxy applied for the chief-of-police job and didn't get it. He felt he had been cheated out of it, somehow. Foxy had some sort of police fixation, and he conducted interrogations. None of his victims, of course, would have known the answers to his questions."

"Were these sex crimes?" Billy was finally able to ask.

"Without a doubt," said Tucker. "Only the body found in the new grave in the garage was recent enough for a reliable determination—he had been sodomized—but if we knew the truth about all the victims, I'm sure it would be much the same."

"Have you notified relatives?"

"Batlett's on the phone now. In some cases I suppose we won't be able to find them. The National Guard has provided body bags, and we're moving all the remains to the Atlanta morgue. Those that can't be identified will be interred as quickly as possible, the others will be turned over to families as soon as postmortems are done."

"What other problems can we expect?" Billy asked.

"Funderburke apparently left a sizeable estate—something in the neighborhood of a million dollars, Mr. Holmes reckons—and, as far as we can determine, he had no living relatives. There are likely to be a number of suits against the estate, and I expect most of the proceeds will go to families of the victims."

"That's as it should be," Billy said.

"That's about it, for now, I guess. I'll keep you posted if there are any new developments, but right now I'm going to go home and get some sleep. John's going to use our guest room."

Billy turned to Howell. "When is this going to hit the papers, John?"

"Tomorrow morning. It'll be in the *Times*, of course, and the *Constitution* will pick up our story and photographs. I've already sent a courier to New York with copy and film. The TV people will descend on the town tomorrow, when they hear about it. I'd have a statement ready, if I were you."

"All I can do is express my shock and regret and sympathy for the families and refer everything else to Tucker, I guess."

Billy shook hands with both men and saw them to the door. Then he went back to the study and sat, staring into the fire, immobile.

When they had turned out of Billy's drive and toward Tucker's house, John Howell took a deep breath and spoke. "Tucker, when I was doing the research for the *Sunday Magazine* piece, I went down to Columbus and looked up your birth certificate."

"Oh?" replied Tucker. He gripped the wheel more tightly.

"Naturally, I didn't bother to look for a death certificate. If I went back down there now and looked, what would I find?"

Tucker was too tired to care any more. "You'd find that I died of scarlet fever when I was eight years old," he said.

"The original Tucker was your cousin?"

Tucker nodded. "Uncle Tuck's boy. He still had the birth certificate. That was all I needed to get into the army later. I worked for a sharecropper down in Alabama during that time. My cousin was two years older than me, but I was tall for my age, and there wasn't any problem enlisting. Uncle Tuck wrote out a letter for my mother, saying that I had been hit by a truck in Alabama and killed. She showed it around, and everybody bought it. After that, I was Tucker Watts."

"Who else knows?"

"Elizabeth. I only told her a few months ago."

"Tell me the truth, Tucker, does Billy know?"

Tucker shook his head. "No, but if you're going to print it, I'd better go back out there and tell him right now."

Howell was quiet for a few moments, staring out the window at the passing countryside. "No, I don't think I will. He's been through enough the last couple of months—two elections, and now this house vote on Tuesday. Tomorrow you're going to come out smelling like a rose, and so will Billy, for backing you. If I print this stuff it will muddy the waters, cast doubts on what Billy knew and what he didn't. He has a chance to go all the way, you know."

"What, Washington?"

Howell nodded. "Yep. I have it on good authority that he's at the top of the list if JFK dumps Johnson, and it looks like he's going to."

Tucker grinned. "Wouldn't that be something?"

Howell laughed. "Yeah, maybe you'll get to be head of the FBI."

"John," Tucker said, "I appreciate your not bringing all this out. Billy deserves better than that."

"Yeah." Howell looked out the window at the wet fields. "Boy, I'm some kind of reporter, huh?"

24 BILLY DIDN'T GO to Atlanta for the house vote on Tuesday. John Howell agreed to keep an open line from the capitol to the house outside Delano to report on the voting as it progressed.

Shortly after the house convened, Holmes, at Billy's house to await the vote, received a phone call. He took it in the kitchen, then came back into Billy's study. "That was Fred Mitchell," he said to the little gathering of family and friends, which included Tucker and Elizabeth Watts, "from Toccoa, in north Georgia. Billy and I flew up to see him the other day. The boy that was found in Foxy's garage was Fred's nephew, his sister's boy, from Florida." There was a little gasp from the group. "He asked me to tell Tucker how grateful he is; they might never have known what happened to the boy. He also said to tell you, Billy, that he's voting with you, and he thinks he's got two, maybe three others lined up."

There were two hours of speeches in the house, and at noon the vote was taken. John Howell, on the phone from the capitol, breathed the news to Billy. "Two votes, Governor. You won by two votes."

Billy hung up and reported the news to the gathering. There was cheering and applause. The phone rang again immediately.

Patricia answered it. "It's the White House," she said.

"Ask them to hold on a minute," Billy replied. He turned to the gathering. "Before I tell them how happy I am, I want to tell all of you how happy I am, and how truly grateful I am to each of you. You've given me so much help, and I promise you, I'm not through asking."

He tried to say something else, but couldn't manage it. Instead, he went to the phone and talked for a few minutes. He came back to the group, who were waiting eagerly.

"He says congratulations, and congratulations to Tucker, too. He's going to Texas for a few days later this month, and he wants me to come up to talk with him when he gets back."

Hugh Holmes sat in his study late that night, a brandy in his hand, immensely sad. He had suddenly had the feeling of having finished something, indeed, everything. It had been fifty-four years since he had first set foot on the land that had become Delano, and always since that time his life had been filled with plan and purpose. Now there was no plan, no purpose, in which he could play a meaningful part.

He had done all he could for Billy. He had done all he could for the town. And now Delano, in which he had invested such industry and ingenuity, would become a synonym for perversion and death. No one would ever again speak of the town without reference to what had happened there. He felt a pain in his chest, which quickly spread to his left arm. He knew that pain; he had felt it before, recently. There was a phone at his elbow; help was available—if he wanted it. The pain increased; the brandy glass fell from his fingertips.

He had only to wait. The pain would take him, or it would leave him. He genuinely had no preference.

END

AUTHOR'S NOTE

MORE THAN THIRTY years ago, while rummaging in a closet in my maternal grandmother's home, I found a large chief-of-police badge. It had been torn and pockmarked by buckshot and still bore traces of dried blood. It had belonged to my grandfather, who had died wearing it more than ten years before I was born. The story of his death, as related to me by a great aunt, formed the basis of this book, but so little was I told, and so much have I embroidered upon it, that the event, like everything else in the book, must be regarded as fiction.

Apart from Will Henry, a number of other characters are based on real people, all but one of whom are dead. Except for Delano, all the towns and counties mentioned in the book are real, but none of the people who populate them is. Any living person, but one, who believes himself or herself to be portrayed in this book is mistaken. So careful have I been to avoid such a portrayal, that any resemblance to such a person would be a matter of the wildest coincidence.

ACKNOWLEDGMENTS

I AM INDEBTED to Dr. Thomas J. Holmes, a fine storyteller, who nurtured the seed of this novel with his memories; to the late James S. Peters, who at ninety spoke history and remembrance of a brilliant quality into my tape recorder; to Merrick and Janet Coveney, of County Galway, Ireland, who helped me to find a quiet and beautiful spot in which to begin this book; to Peter and Elizabeth Shepherd, who gave me a similar spot in which to continue it; to my editor, Eric Swenson, for insight, patience, and friendship, and for taking me sailing with him; to Frederick Allen, chief political writer for the *Atlanta Constitution*, for his sage advice on the complexities of Georgia politics; to Dr. Paul Golightly, medical director of the emergency services unit of Grady Memorial Hospital in Atlanta, and to Dr. Sam Gray, both of whom read the medical portions of the manuscript and offered comments; to my mother, for bearing both my person and my personality; to the microfilm department of the University of Georgia Library, which supplied me with copies of old newspapers; to the designers of the microcomputer upon which I wrote, edited, and typed this manuscript, but not to its manufacturers, who were a pain in the ass; and to my dog Fred, without whose entertaining company the solitude necessary for the completion of this book might have been unbearable.

ABOUT THE AUTHOR

STUART WOODS grew up in a small Georgia mill and railroad town and now lives much of the time in Atlanta. He is already at work on a new novel, due in 1982.

**A towering novel of friendship,
betrayal and love**

THE LORDS
OF DISCIPLINE

by Pat Conroy
author of The Great Santini

This powerful and passionate novel is the story of four cadets who become bloodbrothers. Together they will encounter the hell of hazing and the rabid, raunchy and dangerously secretive atmosphere of an arrogant and proud military institute. Together, they will brace themselves for the brutal transition to manhood ... and one will not survive.

Pat Conroy sweeps you dramatically into the turbulent world of these four friends—and draws you deep into the heart of his rebellious hero, Will McLean, an outsider forging his personal code of honor, who falls in love with Annie Kate, a mysterious and whimsical beauty who first appears to him one midnight in sunglasses and raincoat.

(#14716-1 • $3.75)

Read THE LORDS OF DISCIPLINE, on sale January 15, 1982, wherever Bantam Books are sold or order directly from Bantam by including $1.00 for postage and handling and sending a check to Bantam Books, Dept. LD, 414 East Golf Road, Des Plaines, Illinois 60016. Allow 4–6 weeks for delivery. This offer expires 6/82.